Books by Robert J. Sawyer

NOVELS

*Golden Fleece**
*End of an Era**
The Terminal Experiment
Starplex
*Frameshift**
Illegal Alien
*Factoring Humanity**
*Flashforward**
*Calculating God**
*Mindscan**
*Rollback**

The Neanderthal Parallax

*Hominids**
*Humans**
*Hybrids**

The Quintaglio Ascension

Far-Seer
Fossil Hunter
Foreigner

The WWW Trilogy

Wake
Watch
Wonder

COLLECTIONS

Iterations (introduction by James Alan Gardner)
Relativity (introduction by Mike Resnick)
Identity Theft (introduction by Robert Charles Wilson)

*published by Tor Books

For book club discussion guides, visit www.sfwriter.com

Finalist for the Hugo Award for Best Novel of the Year

"A solid sequel to *Hominids*; extremely well done."

—*Publishers Weekly*

"Hi-tech Neanderthals from a parallel continuum, with a social system like none we have ever heard of. Sawyer gives us a rich mix of mind-stretching concepts and personal crises." —F. M. Busby

"The most unusual love story you've ever read. Sawyer, who's among the most creative of today's science fiction writers, excels in creating a parallel Earth where social mores have evolved on an alien plane, and yet, where much of the planet is as it would have been had we not begun destroying its ecology." —*Rocky Mountain News*

"When it comes to stories that showcase hard-edged science and anthropological puzzles in believable settings with appealing characters, nobody does it better than Sawyer." —Paul Levinson

"Tremendous storytelling with a convincing scientific basis, but at its core, it is science fiction as social commentary. Worth reading for the quality of Sawyer's vision and insight, and the depth of his social criticism."

—*Quill & Quire*

"The biggest job of science fiction is to portray the Other. To help us imagine the strange and see the familiar in eerie new ways. Nobody explores this territory more boldly than Robert J. Sawyer."

—David Brin

"Both a love story and an exploration of metaphysics and philosophy; a novel of big ideas. Recommended." —*SFRA Review*

"Sawyer takes on guns, religious assumptions, automobiles, and even the Big Bang in this highly entertaining tale of a (more or less) rational Outsider. The chapter at the Vietnam Wall should be required reading for anyone who wishes to sit in the Oval Office."

—Jack McDevitt

Praise for Robert J. Sawyer

"Sawyer is a writer of boundless confidence and bold scientific extrapolation."
—*The New York Times*

"No reader seeking well-written stories that respect, emphasize, and depend on modern science should be disappointed by the works of Robert J. Sawyer."
—*The Washington Post*

"Can Sawyer write? Yes—with near-Asimovian clarity, with energy and drive, with such grace that his writing becomes invisible as the story comes to life in your mind."
—Orson Scott Card

"Sawyer, an articulate fountain of ideas, is the genre's northern star—in fact, one of the hottest SF writers anywhere. By any reckoning, Sawyer is among the most successful Canadian authors ever."
—*Maclean's*

"Sawyer has undoubtedly cemented his reputation as one of the foremost science fiction writers of our generation."
—*SF Site*

"Sawyer has won himself an international readership by reinvigorating the traditions of hard science fiction, following the path of such writers as Isaac Asimov and Robert A. Heinlein in his bold speculations from pure science."
—*National Post*

"Cracking open a new Robert J. Sawyer book is like getting a gift from a friend who visits all the strange and undiscovered places in the world. You can't wait to see what he's going to amaze you with this time."
—John Scalzi

Humans

Book Two of the Neanderthal Parallax

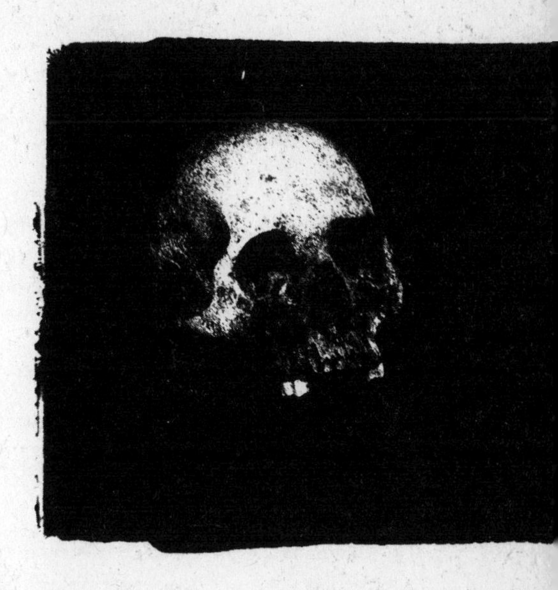

Robert J. Sawyer

A Tom Doherty Associates Book
New York

York University, the Sudbury Neutrino Observatory, and the Creighton Mine all really exist. However, all the characters in this novel are entirely the product of my imagination. They are not meant to bear any resemblance to the actual people who hold or have held positions with these or any other organizations.

HUMANS

Edited by David G. Hartwell

Book design by Angela Arapovic

A Tor Book
Published by Tom Doherty Associates, LLC
175 Fifth Avenue
New York, NY 10010

www.tor-forge.com

The Library of Congress has catalogued the hardcover edition as follows:

Sawyer, Robert J.
Humans / Robert J. Sawyer.—1st ed.
p. cm.
"A Tom Doherty Associates book"
ISBN 978-0-312-87691-3
1. Physicists—Fiction. 2. Neanderthals—Fiction. 3. Prehistoric peoples—Fiction. I. Title.

PR9199.3.S2533 H8 2003
813'.54—dc21 2002075658

ISBN 978-0-7653-2633-1 (trade paperback)

First Edition: February 2003
First Trade Paperback Edition: July 2010

Printed in the United States of America

0 9 8 7 6 5 4 3 2 1

For
Mark Askwith

Master of Multiple Universes

Acknowledgments

For anthropological and paleontological advice, I thank Milford H. Wolpoff, Ph.D., University of Michigan; Ian Tattersall, Ph.D., and Gary J. Sawyer (no relation), both of the American Museum of Natural History; Philip Lieberman, Ph.D., Brown University; Michael K. Brett-Surman, Ph.D., and Rick Potts, Ph.D., both of the National Museum of Natural History, Smithsonian Institution; Robin Ridington, Ph.D., Professor Emeritus, University of British Columbia; and the various experts listed in the Acknowledgments to my previous book, *Hominids.*

Special thanks to Art McDonald, Ph.D., Director, Sudbury Neutrino Observatory Institute, and J. Duncan Hepburn, Ph.D., site manager, Sudbury Neutrino Observatory. Thanks, too, to Sudbury resident Kris Holland, who went over the manuscript with a fine-toothed comb.

Huge thanks to my lovely wife, Carolyn Clink; my editor, David G. Hartwell, and his associate, Moshe Feder; my agent, Ralph Vicinanza, and his associates, Christopher Lotts and Vince Gerardis; Tom Doherty, Linda Quinton, Jennifer Marcus, Jenifer Hunt, and everyone else at Tor Books; Harold and Sylvia Fenn, Robert Howard, Heidi Winter, Melissa Cameron, David Leonard, and everyone else at H. B. Fenn and Company; and my colleagues, Terence M. Green, Andrew Weiner, and Robert Charles Wilson.

Special thanks to Byron R. Tetrick, whose invitation to

contribute to his landmark 2002 anthology, *In the Shadow of the Wall: Vietnam Stories That Might Have Been* (Cumberland House), led to me focusing my thoughts on several key issues; much of Chapter 22, in a different form, first appeared in that anthology.

Beta testers for this novel were the always insightful Ted Bleaney, Michael A. Burstein, David Livingstone Clink, Marcel Gagné, Richard Gotlib, Peter Halasz, Howard Miller, Dr. Ariel Reich, Alan B. Sawyer, and Sally Tomasevic, and I was fortunate enough to be working again with the copyediting team of Bob and Sara Schwager.

Parts of this book were written at John A. Sawyer's vacation home on Canandaigua Lake—thanks, Dad! Thanks, also, to Nicholas A. DiChario, my host on frequent visits to Rochester, New York, where some of this novel is set.

If only there were evil people somewhere insidiously committing evil deeds and it were necessary only to separate them from the rest of us and destroy them. But the line dividing good and evil cuts through the heart of every human being. And who is willing to destroy a piece of his own heart?

—Aleksandr Solzhenitsyn

The Neanderthal World

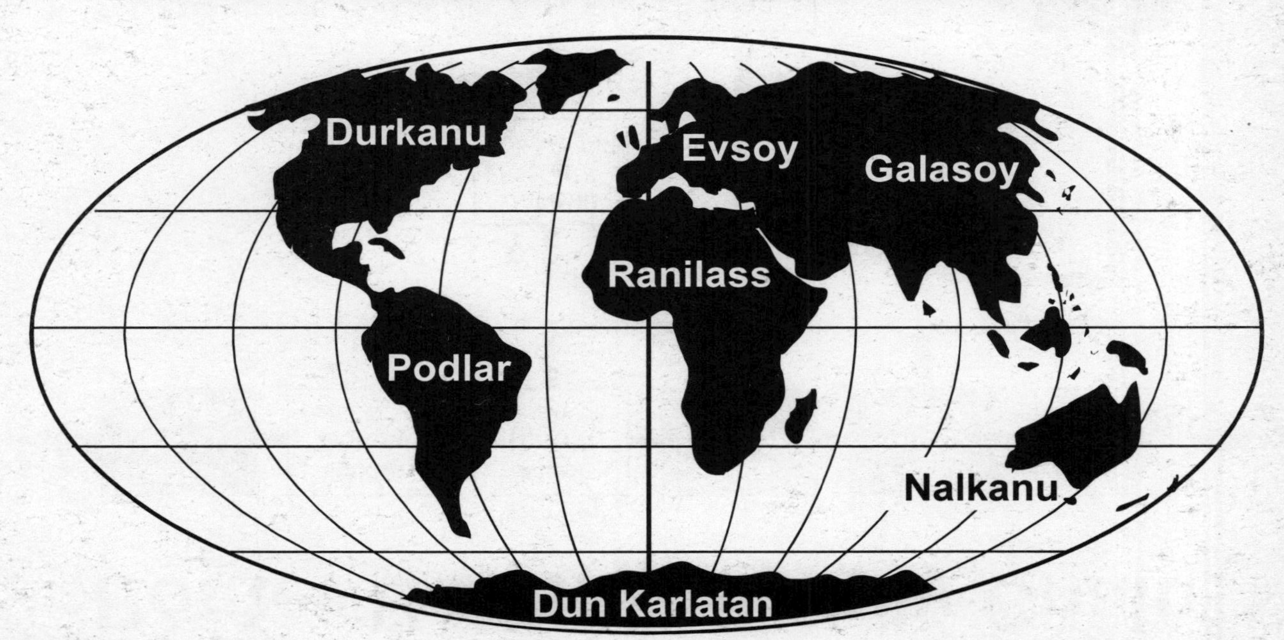

Ponter Boddit's Family Chain

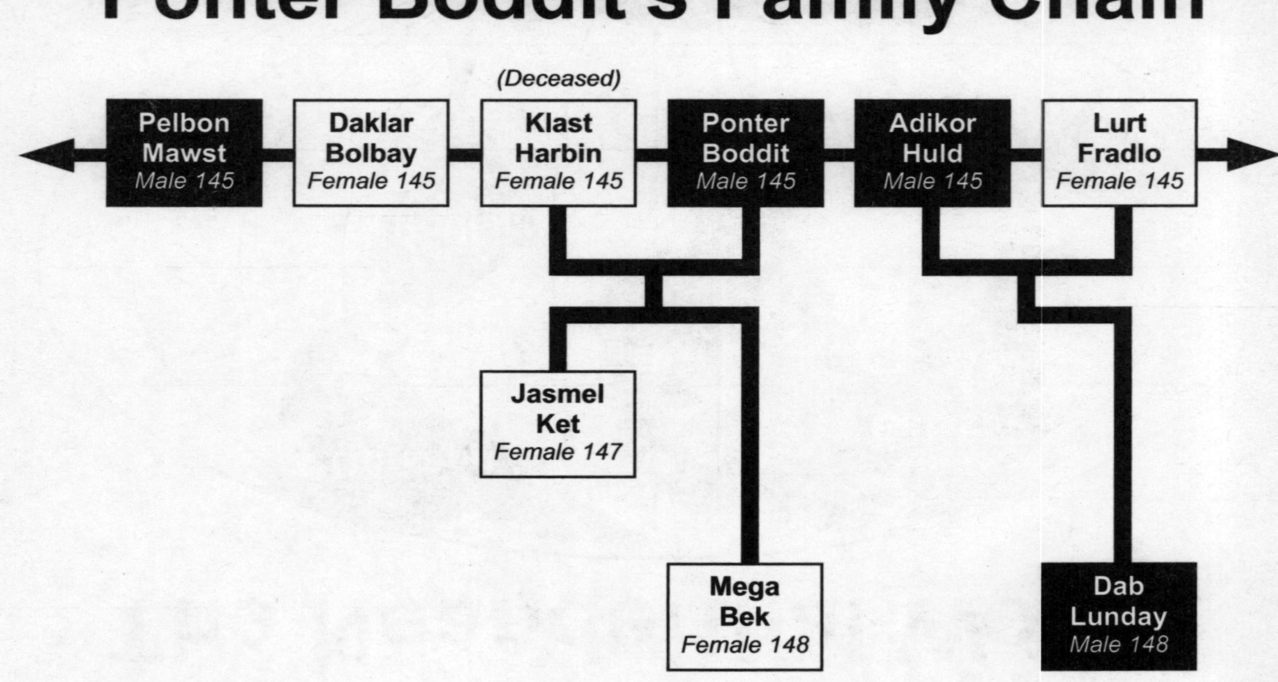

Humans

Prologue

"I've done a terrible thing," said Ponter Boddit, straddling the saddle-seat in Jurard Selgan's office.

Selgan was a member of generation 144, ten years older than Ponter. His hair was a wise gray, and his part had widened into a deep river of scalp, emptying onto the low forehead above his browridge. "Go on."

"I felt I had no choice," said Ponter, looking down, his own browridge shielding him from having to meet Selgan's emerald eyes. "I felt I had *to do it, but . . ."*

"But you regret it now?"

Ponter was silent, staring at the room's moss-covered floor.

"Do *you regret it?"*

"I—I'm not sure."

"Would you do it again, if you had the moment to live over?"

Ponter snorted a laugh.

"What's so funny?" asked Selgan, curiosity, rather than irritation, in his voice.

Ponter looked up. "I thought it was only physicists like me who engaged in thought experiments."

Selgan smiled. "We're not so different, you and I. We each seek to find the truth, to solve mysteries."

"I suppose," said Ponter. He looked at the smooth, gently curving wooden wall of the cylindrical room.

"You haven't answered my question," said Selgan. "Would you do it again, if you could?"

Ponter was silent for a time, and Selgan let him be silent, let him consider his answer. "I don't know," Ponter said at last.

"Don't you? Or is it that you simply do not wish to say?"

Again, Ponter was silent.

"I want to help you," said Selgan, shifting on his own saddle-seat. "That's my only goal. I won't judge you."

Ponter laughed again, but this time it was a rueful laugh. "That's the whole point, isn't it? Nobody *judges us."*

Selgan frowned. "What do you mean?"

"I mean, in that other world—that other Earth—they believe there is a . . . well, we have no word for it, but they call it God. *A supreme, incorporeal being who created the universe."*

Selgan shook his head. "How can the universe have a creator? For something to be created, it has to have a beginning. And the universe didn't. It has always existed."

"You know that," said Ponter. "I know that. But they *don't know that. They think the universe is only—well, they'd say twelve billion years old; a hundred and fifty billion months or so."*

"Then what existed before *that time?"*

Ponter frowned, remembering back to his conversations with the female Gliksin physicist Lou Benoît—how he wished he could pronounce their names properly! "They say there was no *time before then, that time began when the universe was created."*

"What an astonishing notion," said Selgan.

"That it is," agreed Ponter. "But if they accepted that the universe had always existed, there would be no role for this God of theirs."

"Your man-mate is a physicist, isn't he?" asked Selgan.

"Adikor Huld," said Ponter, naming him. "Yes."

"Well, I'm sure you often get to talk about physics with Adikor. Me, I'm more interested in other things. You brought up this—this

'God'—in connection with the concept of judging. Tell me more about that."

Ponter was quiet for a few moments, trying to figure out how to present the concept. "It seems most of them, these other humans, believe in what they call an 'afterlife'—an existence that follows death."

"But that's ridiculous," said Selgan. "It's a contradiction in terms."

"Oh, yes," said Ponter, smiling. "But such things are common in their thinking—so common that they give them a special name, as if by naming them it resolves the paradox. I can't quite say it the way they do; it's something like ox-uh-mor-on."

Selgan smiled. "I would love to treat one of them—learn how such a mind functions." He paused. "This existence that follows death: what do they believe it is like?"

"That's the most interesting thing," said Ponter. "It can take one of two forms, depending on how you comported yourself while living. If you have lived a virtuous life, then you are rewarded with an exceedingly pleasant existence afterward. But if your life—or even a single major action you did during it—has been evil, then the subsequent existence is one of torment."

"And who decides?" said Selgan. "Oh, wait. I get it. This God decides, right?"

"Yes. That's what they believe."

"But why? Why would they believe something so outlandish?"

Ponter lifted his shoulders slightly. "Supposed historical accounts of those who have communicated with this God."

"Historical *accounts?" said Selgan. "Does anyone currently communicate with this God?"*

"Some claim to. But I gather it has not been substantiated."

"And this God, he serves as judge of every individual?"

"Supposedly."

"But there are 185 million people in the world, with many thousands dying every day."

"That's in this *world. In the other world, there are over six billion people."*

"Six billion!" Selgan shook his head. "And each one is assigned, somehow, at death, to one of the two possible further existences you mentioned?"

"Yes. They are judged."

Ponter saw Selgan make a face. The personality sculptor was clearly intrigued by the details of Gliksin belief, but his real interest was in Ponter's thoughts. " 'Judged,' " he repeated, as if the word were a choice piece of meat worth savoring.

"Yes, judged," said Ponter. "Don't you see? They don't have Companion implants. They don't have alibi archives. They don't keep perfect records of every action they take in their lives. They don't have any of that, because they don't believe they need it. They think this God is watching over all, seeing all—even looking out for them, protecting them. And they think that it's impossible to get away—to really, *ultimately—get away with an evil act."*

"But you did something terrible, you said?"

Ponter looked out the window, out at his world. "Yes."

"Over there? In the other world?"

"Yes."

"And you do not accept the existence of this God of theirs?"

Ponter made a derisive sound. "Of course not."

"And so you believe that you will not ever be judged for this bad thing you feel you did?"

"Exactly. I won't say it's the perfect crime. But there is no reason why suspicion will ever fall on me in that world, and no reason why anyone here would ever have cause to demand to see that portion of my alibi archive."

"You called it a crime. Was it a crime by the standards of this other world you were in?"

"Oh, yes."

"And would we *have considered it a crime, had you done it here?"*

Ponter nodded.

"What did you do?"

"I—I am ashamed to say," said Ponter.

"I told you, I will not judge you."

Ponter found himself surging to his feet. "That's the whole point!" he shouted. "No one *will judge me—not here, not there. I have committed a crime. I* enjoyed *committing the crime. And, yes, to indulge in your thought experiment, I would do it again if I had the opportunity to relive the event."*

Selgan said nothing for a time, apparently waiting for Ponter to calm down. "I can help you, Ponter, if you'll let me. But you have to talk to me. You have to tell me what happened. Why did you commit this crime? What led up to it?"

Ponter sat back down, swinging his legs over the saddle-seat. "It began on my first trip to the other Earth," said Ponter. "I met a woman there, named Mare Vaughan . . ."

Chapter One

It was Mary Vaughan's final evening in Sudbury, and she was experiencing decidedly mixed feelings.

She had no doubt that getting out of Toronto had done her good. After what had happened down there—*My God,* she thought, *had it really only been two weeks ago?*—leaving town, getting away from all the things that would have reminded her of that horrible night, was surely the right course. And although it had ended on a melancholy note, she wouldn't have traded her time here with Ponter Boddit for anything.

There was an unreal quality to her recollections; it all seemed so fantastic. And yet there were countless photographs and videos and even some X rays to prove that it had really happened. A modern Neanderthal from a parallel version of Earth had somehow slipped into this universe. Now that he was gone, Mary hardly believed it herself.

But it *had* happened. Ponter had really been here, and she had indeed . . .

Was she overstating it? Magnifying it in her mind?

No. No, it was indeed what had occurred.

She had come to love Ponter, maybe even to be *in* love with him.

If only she'd been whole, complete, unviolated, untraumatized, perhaps things would have been different. Oh, she'd still have fallen for the big guy—of that she was sure—but when he'd reached out and touched her hand that night while they were looking up at the stars, she wouldn't have frozen.

It had been too soon, she'd told him the next day. Too soon after . . .

She hated the word; hated to think it, to say it.

Too soon after the rape.

And tomorrow she had to go back home, back to where that rape had occurred, back to the campus of Toronto's York University, and her old life of teaching genetics.

Her old life of being alone.

She'd miss many things about Sudbury. She'd miss the lack of traffic congestion. She'd miss the friends she'd made here, including Reuben Montego and, yes, even Louise Benoît. She'd miss the relaxed atmosphere of tiny Laurentian University, where she'd done her mitochondrial DNA studies that had proven Ponter Boddit was indeed a Neanderthal.

But, most of all, she realized, as she stood at the side of the country road looking up at the clear night sky, she'd miss *this.* She'd miss seeing stars in a profusion beyond counting. She'd miss seeing the Andromeda galaxy, which Ponter had identified for her. She'd miss seeing the Milky Way, arching overhead.

And—

Yes!

Yes!

She'd especially miss this: the aurora borealis, flickering and weaving across the northern sky, pale green sheets of light, ghostly curtains.

Mary had indeed hoped to catch another glimpse of the aurora tonight. She'd been on her way back from Reuben Montego's place out in Lively (hah!), where she'd had a final barbecue dinner with him and Louise, and she'd pulled over at the side of the road specifically to look up at the night sky.

Humans

The heavens were cooperating. The aurora was breathtaking.

She'd forever associate the northern lights with Ponter. The only other time she'd seen them had been with him. She felt an odd sensation in her chest, the expanding feeling that went with awe battling the contracting sensation that accompanied sadness.

The lights were beautiful.

He was gone.

A cool green glow bathed the landscape as the aurora continued to flicker and dance, aspens and birches silhouetted in front of the spectacle, their branches waving slightly in the gentle August breeze.

Ponter had said he often saw the aurora. Partly that was because his cold-adapted people preferred more northerly latitudes than did the humans of this world.

Partly, too, it was because the phenomenal Neanderthal sense of smell and their ever-vigilant Companion implants made it safe to be out even in the dark; Ponter's hometown of Saldak, located at the same place in his world as Sudbury was in this world, didn't illuminate its streets at night.

And partly it was because the Neanderthals used clean solar power for most of their energy needs, rendering their skies far less polluted than the ones here.

Mary had made it to her current age of thirty-eight before seeing the aurora, and she didn't anticipate any reason to come back to Northern Ontario, so tonight, she knew, might well be the last time she'd ever see the undulating northern lights.

She drank in the view.

Some things were the same on both versions of Earth, Ponter had said: the gross details of the geography, most of the animal and plant species (although the Neanderthals, never having indulged in overkilling, still had mammoths and moas in their world), the broad strokes of the climate. But Mary was a scientist: she understood all about chaos theory, about how the beating of a butterfly's wing was enough to affect weather systems half a world away. Surely just because there was a clear sky here on this Earth didn't mean the same was true on Ponter's world.

But if the weather did happen to coincide, perhaps Ponter was also looking up at the night sky now.

And perhaps he was thinking of Mary.

Ponter would, of course, be seeing precisely the same constellations, even if he gave them different names—nothing terrestrial could possibly have disturbed the distant stars. But would the auroras be the same? Did butterflies or people have any effect on the choreography of the northern lights? Perhaps she and Ponter were looking at the exact same spectacle—a curtain of illumination waving back and forth, the seven bright stars of the Big Dipper (or, as he would call it, the Head of the Mammoth) stretching out above.

Why, he might even right now be seeing the same shimmying to the right, the same shimmying to the left, the same—

Jesus.

Mary felt her jaw drop.

The auroral curtain was splitting down the middle, like aquamarine tissue paper being torn by an invisible hand. The fissure grew longer, wider, starting at the top and moving toward the horizon. Mary had seen nothing like that on the first night she'd looked up at the northern lights.

The sheet finally separated into two halves, parting like the Red Sea before Moses. A few—they looked like sparks, but could they really be that?—arced between the halves, briefly bridging the gap. And then the half on the right seemed to roll up from the bottom, like a window blind being wound onto its dowel, and, as it did so, it changed colors, now green, now blue, now violet, now orange, now turquoise.

And then in a flash—a spectral burst of light—that part of the aurora disappeared.

The remaining sheet of light was swirling now, as if it were being sucked down a drain in the firmament. As it spun more and more rapidly, it flung off gouts of cool green fire, a pinwheel against the night.

Mary watched, transfixed. Even if this was only her second night actually observing the aurora, she'd seen countless pictures of the northern lights over the years in books and magazines. She'd known those still images hadn't done justice to the spectacle; she'd read how the aurora rippled and fluttered.

But nothing had prepared her for this.

The vortex continued to contract, growing brighter as it did so, until finally, with—did she really hear it?—with what sounded like a *pop,* it vanished.

Mary staggered backward, bumping up against the cold metal of her rented Dodge Neon. She was suddenly aware that the forest sounds around her—insects and frogs, owls and bats—had fallen silent, as if every living thing was looking up in wonder.

Mary's heart was pounding, and one thought kept echoing through her head as she climbed into the safety of her car.

I wonder if it's supposed to do that . . .

Chapter Two

Jurard Selgan rose from his saddle-seat and paced around the circumference of his circular office while Ponter Boddit told of his first trip to the Gliksin world.

"So your relationship with Mare Vaughan had ended on an unsatisfactory note?" said Selgan, at last returning to his seat.

Ponter nodded.

"Relationships are often unresolved," said Selgan. "It would be nice if that weren't the case, but surely this can't have been the first time a relationship you were involved in had ended in a disappointing way."

"No, it wasn't," said Ponter, very softly.

"You're thinking of a specific person, aren't you?" said Selgan. "Tell me."

"My woman-mate, Klast Harbin," said Ponter.

"Ah. Your relationship with her ended, did it? Who initiated the split?"

"No one initiated it," snapped Ponter. "Klast died, twenty months ago."

"Oh," said Selgan. "My condolences. Was she—was she an older woman?"

"No. She was a 145, same as me."

Selgan rolled his eyebrow up his browridge. "Was it an accident?"

"It was cancer of the blood."

"Ah," said Selgan. "A tragedy. But . . ."

"Don't say it, Selgan." Ponter's tone was sharp.

"Don't say what?" asked the personality sculptor.

"What you were about to say."

"And you think that was . . . ?"

"That my relationship with Klast was cut off abruptly, just like my relationship with Mare was cut off abruptly."

"Is that the way you feel?" asked Selgan.

"I knew I shouldn't have come here," said Ponter. "You personality sculptors think your insights are so profound. But they're not; they're simplistic. 'Relationship Green ended abruptly, and you are reminded of it by the way Relationship Red ended.' " Ponter snorted dismissively.

Selgan was quiet for several beats, perhaps waiting to see if Ponter would say more of his own volition. When it became clear that he would not, Selgan spoke again. "But you did push for the portal between this world and Mare's world to be reopened." He let the sentence hang in the air between them for a time, and Ponter finally responded.

"And you think that's why I pushed?" Ponter said. "That I didn't care about the consequences, the ramifications, for this world? That all I was worried about was getting to resolve this unfinished relationship?"

"You tell me," said Selgan, gently.

"It wasn't like that. Oh, sure, there's a superficial resemblance between what happened with me and Klast, and what happened with me and Mare. But I'm a scientist." He fixed Selgan with an angry stare of his golden eyes. "A real scientist. I understand when true symmetry exists—it doesn't here—and I understand false analogy."

"But you did push the High Gray Council. I saw it on my Voyeur, along with thousands of others."

"Well, yes, but . . ."

"But what? What were you thinking then? What were you trying to accomplish?"

"Nothing—except what was best for all our people."

"Are you sure of that?" asked Selgan.

"Of course I'm sure!" *snapped Ponter.*

Selgan was quiet, letting Ponter listen to his own words echo off the polished wooden wall.

Ponter Boddit had to admit that nothing he'd ever experienced—indeed, probably nothing that *any* of his people had ever experienced—had been more frightening than being transported bodily from this world to that bizarre other world, arriving in total darkness and almost drowning in a giant water tank.

But, still, of the things that happened in *this* world, this universe, few could compare for sheer terror with addressing the High Gray Council. After all, this wasn't just the local Gray Council; the *High* Gray Council ran the planet, and its members had come here, to Saldak, specifically to see Ponter and Adikor and the quantum computer they'd used twice now to open a portal to another reality.

No one on the High Gray Council was anything younger than a 143, twenty years Ponter's senior. The wisdom, the experience, and, yes, when it struck their mood to be so, the sheer cussed orneriness of people that old was formidable in the extreme.

Ponter could have just let the issue drop. Nobody was pushing for him and Adikor to reopen the portal to the other world. Indeed, except maybe for that female group in Evsoy, there was no one who could gainsay them if Ponter and Adikor simply claimed that the opening of the portal had been an irreproducible fluke.

But the possibility of trade between two kinds of humanity was too significant for Ponter to ignore. Information could certainly be swapped: what Ponter's people knew about superconductivity, say, for what the Gliksins knew about spaceships. But, more than that, *cultures* could be exchanged: the art of this world for the art of that world, a *dibalat* iterative epic, perhaps, for a play by this Shakespeare he'd heard of over there; sculptures by the great Kaydas for the work of a Gliksin painter.

Surely, thought Ponter, these noble thoughts were his sole motivation. Surely he had nothing personally to gain by reopening the portal. Yes, there was Mare. Still, doubtless Mare wasn't really interested in a being so different from herself, a creature who was hairy where males of her kind were smooth, who was stocky when most Gliksins were gracile, a being with a double-crested browridge undulating above his eyes, eyes that were golden instead of Mare's own blue or the dark brown of so many others of her species.

Ponter had no doubt that Mare had really suffered the trauma she'd spoken of, but surely that was only the most prominent of many reasons for her having rebuffed his advance.

But no.

No, that wasn't right.

There *had* been a real, mutual attraction. Across timelines, across species boundaries, it had been real. He was sure of it.

But could things really go better between the two of them if contact were resumed? He cherished his wonderful, beautiful memories of his time with her—and they were *only* memories, for his Companion implant had been unable to transmit anything to his alibi archive from the other side. Mare existed only in his imagination, in his thoughts and dreams; there was no objective reality to compare her to, except a few brief glimpses caught by the robot that Adikor had dangled through the portal to summon Ponter home.

Surely it was better this way. Further contact would spoil what they'd already had.

And yet—

And yet it *did* seem that the portal could be reopened.

Standing in the small anteroom, Ponter looked over at Adikor Huld, his man-mate. Adikor nodded encouragingly. It was time to go into the Council chamber. Ponter picked up the unexpanded Derkers tube he'd brought with him, and the two men walked through the massive doors, ready to face the High Grays.

"The presence here of Scholar Boddit," said Adikor Huld, gesturing now at Ponter, "is direct proof that a person can pass through to the other universe and return unharmed."

Ponter looked at the twenty Grays, ten males and ten females, two from each of the world's ten regional governments. In some forums, males sat on one side of the room and females on the other. But the High Gray Council dealt with matters that affected the entire species, and the males and females who had gathered here from all over the globe alternated in a great circle.

"But," continued Adikor, "except for Ponter's daughter Jasmel, who stuck her head through the portal during our rescue operations, no one else from this world has been to that one. When we first created the portal, it was by accident—an unexpected result of our quantum-computing experiments. But we now know that this universe and that one, the one in which Gliksin people dominate, are *entangled* somehow. The portal from here always opens to that particular one out of the panoply of alternate universes that our physics tells us must exist. And, as far as we can determine from our previous experience, the portal will remain open as long as a solid object is passing through it."

Bedros, an old male from Evsoy, frowned at Adikor. "So

what are you proposing, Scholar Huld? That we shove a stick partway through the portal to keep it open?"

Ponter, standing next to Adikor, turned slightly so that Bedros, at least, would not see his smirk.

Adikor wasn't as fortunate: he was caught in Bedros's gaze, and couldn't look away without seeming disrespectful. "Um, no," he said. "We have something more, ah, versatile in mind. Dern Kord, an engineer of our acquaintance, has proposed that we insert a Derkers tube through the portal."

This was Ponter's cue to unfold the Derkers tube. He got his fingers inside the narrow mouth and pulled. The tube, a latticework of metal, expanded with a ratcheting sound until its diameter was greater than Ponter's height. "These tubes are used to reinforce mining tunnels in emergencies," said Ponter. "Once expanded, they resist being collapsed. Indeed, the only way to get one to return to its original size is by using a defastener to undo the locks at each intersection of the crisscrossing metal segments."

To his credit, Bedros got the idea at once. "And you think one of these will keep the portal open indefinitely, so that people could just walk down it, like a tunnel between the two universes?"

"Exactly," said Ponter.

"What about disease?" asked Jurat, a local female of generation 141. She was seated on the opposite side of the room from Bedros, so Ponter and Adikor had to turn to face her. "I understand you fell ill when you were in the other world."

Ponter nodded. "Yes. I met a Gliksin physicist there who . . ." He paused as one of the High Grays snickered. Ponter had gotten used to the notion, but he understood why it sounded funny; he might as well have referred to "a caveman philosopher." "Anyway," continued Ponter, "she proposed that the timelines split—well, she said forty thousand years ago; that's half a million months. Since then, the Gliksins have lived in crowded conditions, and have bred many animals in large numbers for food. Numerous diseases have likely evolved there to which we have no immunity. And it may be that some diseases have evolved here to which they're not immune, although our lower population density makes that less likely, I'm told. In any event, we will need to provide a decontamination system, and everyone who travels in either direction between the worlds will have to be treated by it."

"But wait," said Jindo, another male, who came from the land south of here on the opposite side of the unoccupied equatorial belt. Fortunately, he was sitting right beside Jurat, so Ponter and Adikor didn't have to turn around again. "This tunnel between worlds has to be located at the bottom of the Debral nickel mine, a thousand armspans beneath the surface, is that right?"

"Yes," said Ponter. "You see, it's our quantum computer that makes accessing the other universe possible, and for it to work at all, it has to be shielded from solar radiation. The huge amount of rock overhead provides that shielding."

Bedros nodded, and Adikor turned to face him. "So it's not as though people could travel in great numbers between the two worlds."

"Meaning," said Jurat, picking up Bedros's point, "that we don't have to worry about an invasion." Adikor turned to face her, but Ponter continued to look at Bedros. "Not only will individuals have to come through this narrow tunnel, but they will have to make it all the way up to the surface before they can get out into our world."

Ponter nodded. "Exactly. You've reached the marrow."

"I appreciate your enthusiasm for your work," said Pandaro, the president of the Council, a Galasoyan 140 female, who, to this point, had been silent. She was sitting halfway between Bedros and Jurat, so Ponter turned left and Adikor turned right until they were both facing her. "But let me see if I understand you correctly. There is no way the Gliksins can open a portal to this world, right?"

"That's right, President," said Ponter. "Although I certainly didn't learn everything about their computing technology, they are a long way away from building a quantum computer anything like the one Adikor and I created."

"How far away are they?" asked Pandaro. "How many months?"

Ponter looked at Adikor briefly; Adikor, after all, was the hardware expert. But Adikor conveyed with an expression that Ponter should go ahead and answer. "At least three hundred, I'd say, and possibly many more."

Pandaro spread her arms, as if the answer were obvious. "Well, then, there is no rush to deal with this matter. We can take the time to study the issue, and—"

"No!" exclaimed Ponter. Every eye in the chamber fell on him.

"I beg your pardon?" said the president, her tone cool.

"I mean," said Ponter, "it's just that—that we don't know how reproducible this phenomenon is over the long term. Any number of conditions might change, and—"

"I understand your desire to continue your work, Scholar Boddit," said the president, "but there is the question of disease transfer, of contamination, and—"

"We already have the technology to shield against that," said Ponter.

"In theory," said another Councilor, also a female. "But in practice, the Kajak technique has never been used in such a way. We can't be sure—"

"You are so *timid,*" snapped Ponter. Adikor was looking at

him with shock, but Ponter ignored his partner. "*They* would not be so frightened. They've climbed their world's highest mountains! They've gone far beneath the oceans! They've orbited the Earth! They've gone to the moon! It wasn't the cowardice of old men and women that—"

"*Scholar Boddit!*" The president's tone thundered through the Council chamber.

Ponter stopped himself. "I—I'm sorry, President. I didn't mean—"

"I think it's abundantly clear what you meant," said Pandaro. "But our role is to be cautious. We have the welfare of the entire world on our shoulders."

"I know," said Ponter, trying to keep his voice calm. "I know, but there's so much at stake here! We can't wait for endless months. We have to act now. *You* have to act now."

Ponter felt Adikor's hand land gently on his upper arm. "Ponter . . ." he said softly.

But Ponter twisted free. "We haven't gone to the moon. We'll probably never go to the moon—and that means we'll never go to Mars, or the stars. This parallel Earth is the only other world our people will ever have access to. We can't let the opportunity slip away!"

It might be apocryphal, but Mary Vaughan had heard the story so often she suspected it was probably true. They said that when Toronto decided to build a second university in the 1960s, the plans for the campus had been bought from an extant university in the southern U.S. It had seemed like an expedient thing to do, but no one had taken into account the climatic differences.

That used to create problems, at least in winter. The campus had originally had lots of spaces between buildings, but those had been filled in over the years with new construction. Now the campus was cluttered: crowded with glass and steel, with brick and concrete.

Still, there *were* things about the campus that appealed to Mary. Most notable was the name of the business school, which she was now passing: "The Schulich School of Business"—and, yes, Schulich was pronounced "shoe lick."

It was still a week before classes would begin, and the campus was mostly deserted. Although it was broad daylight, Mary still found herself feeling apprehensive as she walked along, going around corners, passing walls, squeezing through passageways.

This was where it had happened, after all. This was where she'd been raped.

Like most North American universities, York actually had more female undergraduates than males these days. Still, with over forty thousand full-time students, there were perhaps twenty thousand males who could have been responsible—assuming that the animal had been a York student.

But no, no, that wasn't right. York was in Toronto, and a more cosmopolitan city would be hard to find. The man who'd raped her had white skin and blue eyes. A large chunk of York's population didn't fit that description.

And he'd been a smoker; Mary vividly remembered the reek of tobacco on his breath. Although it pained her every time she saw a student lighting up—these kids, after all, had been born in the 1980s, two decades after U.S. Surgeon General Luther Terry had announced that smoking was deadly—it was true that a minority of women, and even fewer men, smoked.

So the person who had attacked her wasn't just anyone; he'd been part of a subset of a subset of a subset: males, with blue eyes and white skin, who smoked.

If Mary could ever find him, she could prove his guilt. There weren't many occasions when being a geneticist turned out to have practical applications in one's own life, but it *had* come in handy that horrible night. Mary knew how to preserve samples of the man's semen, which would contain DNA that could conclusively identify him.

Mary continued to walk across the campus. There were no crowds to fight through yet. But, actually, she'd probably feel safer then. After all, the rape had occurred during the summer holidays, when fewer people were around. Crowds meant safety—whether on the African savannah or here in Toronto.

And now, as she walked along, Mary realized a man was coming toward her. Her pulse accelerated, but she stayed her course; she couldn't spend the rest of her life veering out of the way every time she was getting near a male. Still . . .

Still, it was a white man—that much was obvious.

His hair was blondish. She'd not seen her assailant's hair; he'd worn a ski mask. But blue eyes often went with light hair.

Mary closed her eyes for a second, shutting out the bright sunlight, shutting out her world. Maybe she *should* have followed Ponter through the gateway to the Neanderthal universe. Certainly that thought had crossed her mind as she'd run across the Laurentian campus, searching for Ponter, rushing to get him down to the bottom of the Creighton Mine before the reopened portal to his reality slammed shut again. After all, at least there she'd have known for sure that her attacker was nowhere around.

The approaching man was now less than a dozen meters away. He was young—probably a summer student—and wearing blue jeans and a T-shirt.

And he was wearing sunglasses. It was a bright summer's day; Mary herself was wearing her FosterGrants. There was no way to tell what color his eyes were, although they couldn't be the golden of Ponter's—she'd never seen any other human with eyes like that.

Mary tensed as the man came closer, and closer still.

Even if he hadn't been wearing sunglasses, though, Mary wouldn't have known what color his eyes were. As the man passed by her, she found herself averting her gaze, unable to look at him.

Damn, she thought. *God damn.*

Chapter Three

"So," said Jurard Selgan, "despite your . . . your . . ."

Ponter shrugged. "My bullying," he said. "We're not supposed to be afraid of facing things head on here, are we?"

Selgan tipped his head, accepting Ponter's assessment. "Very well, then. Despite your bullying, the High Gray Council did not immediately make a decision, did it?"

"No," said Ponter. "No, and I suppose it was correct in taking at least a little time to think things through. Two were just about to become One, and so the Council adjourned, reserving its decision until after that was over . . ."

Two becoming One: so simple a phrase, and yet so fraught with meaning and complexity for Ponter and his people.

Two becoming One: the monthly four-day holiday around which all life was structured.

Two becoming One: the period during which adult males, who normally lived at the city's Rim, came into the Center to spend time with their women-mates and children.

It was more than just a break from work, more than simply a variation in routine. It was the fire that sustained culture; it was the gut ties that bound families.

A hover-bus settled out front of Ponter and Adikor's house. The two men entered through the door at the back and found a pair of adjacent saddle-seats upon which to sit. The driver activated the fans, and the bus rose above the ground and started moving on to the next house, off in the distance.

Usually, Ponter gave no thought to something as mundane as a hover-bus, but today he couldn't help pondering how elegant a solution it was compared to what they'd done about transportation in the Gliksin world. There, vehicles of all sizes rolled on wheels. Everywhere he'd gone on the Gliksin world (admittedly only a few places), he'd seen wide, flattened trails covered with artificial stone to make it easy for those wheels to roll.

And as if that weren't bad enough, the Gliksins used a chemical reaction to propel their wheeled vehicles—a reaction that gave off a noxious smell. Apparently it wasn't as irritating to the Gliksins as it had been to Ponter; not surprising, he supposed, given their minuscule noses.

What a wonderful quirk of nature that had been! Ponter knew that his kind had developed their large noses—much bigger than those of any other primate—during the last glacial epoch. According to Doctor Singh, the Gliksin who had looked after him at their hospital, Neanderthals had six times the nasal capacity of Gliksins. The original reason had been to humidify cold air before it was drawn into the sensitive tissues of the lungs. But when the great ice sheets had eventually retreated, the large noses had been retained because they'd provided the beneficial side effect of an excellent sense of smell.

If it hadn't been for that, maybe Ponter's kind would have used the same petrochemicals, resulting in the same level of atmospheric pollution. The irony did not escape Ponter: the kind of humans he'd hitherto only known as fossils were poisoning their skies with what they themselves called fossil fuels.

And worse than that: *every* adult Gliksin seemed to have his or her own personal vehicle. What an unspeakable waste of resources! Most of these cars spent the bulk of each day just sitting. Ponter's own city of Saldak had some three thousand travel cubes for a population of twenty-five thousand—and Ponter often thought *that* was too many.

The hover-bus came to rest at the next house. Ponter and Adikor's neighbors, Torba and Gaddak, as well as Gaddak's twin sons, came on board. Males left their mothers and moved in with their fathers at the age of ten years. Adikor had only one child, an eight-year-old boy named Dab, who would come live with him and Ponter the year after next. Ponter had two children, but both were girls: Megameg Bek, a 148, also eight years old, and Jasmel Ket, a 147, now eighteen.

Ponter himself, as well as his man-mate Adikor, were members of generation 145, making them both thirty-eight years old. That had been another bizarre thing about the Gliksin world: instead of controlling their breeding cycles, so that children were born only every tenth year, they gave birth constantly, every year. Rather than nice, neat, discrete generations, their world had a smooth continuum of ages. Ponter hadn't spent enough time there to figure out how they managed the economics of that. Without manufacturers shifting their focus from baby-wear to toddler clothes to young adult garb, in step with the growing of a generation, the Gliksins simultaneously had to produce clothes for people of any age. And they had this ridiculous concept of "fashion," or so Lou Benoît had told him: perfectly good clothes were discarded for reasons of capricious esthetics.

The hover-bus took off again. Torba and Gaddak's house had been the last stop on the Rim; Ponter settled back for the long drive through the countryside into the Center.

As usual, the women had put up decorations: great pastel streamers stretching from tree to tree, circular bands of color around birch and cedar trunks, banners waving from the roofs of buildings, golden frames surrounding the solar collectors, silver ones adorning the composting units.

Ponter used to harbor a suspicion that the women left the decorations up all the time, but Adikor had said there'd been no sign of them when he'd come into the Center during Last Five, looking for someone to defend him against Daklar Bolbay's spurious charge.

The hover-bus settled to the ground. It wasn't yet the time of falling leaves, although next month's Two becoming One would be during the start of that, and the fans would then send brown and red and yellow and orange foliage whirling about. Ponter would be glad when the cold weather returned.

The computer scientist in Ponter couldn't help noticing that Torba, Gaddak, and Gaddak's twin boys were the first to disembark: the hover-bus operated on a last-in/first-out system. Ponter and Adikor were the next to step out. Lurt, Adikor's woman-mate, hurried over to him, accompanied by little Dab. Adikor swept his son up in his arms and lifted him high over his head. Dab laughed, and Adikor was smiling widely. He set Dab down and gathered Lurt into a hug. It hadn't been a full month since he'd seen them—they'd both been on hand during Adikor's *dooslarm basadlarm,* the preliminary hearing into whether Adikor had murdered Ponter, a charge raised by Daklar Bolbay over Ponter's disappearance when he'd slipped into the other universe. Still, Adikor was clearly delighted to see his woman and his child.

Ponter's woman-mate Klast was dead, but he'd expected his two daughters to come greet him. Granted, he'd seen them recently, too; indeed, Jasmel had been instrumental in recovering Ponter from the Gliksin world.

Adikor looked at Ponter apologetically. Ponter knew that Adikor loved him deeply—and he showed that love twenty-five days out of each month. But this was the time for him to be with Lurt and Dab, and, well, he wanted to savor every beat of it. Ponter nodded, letting Adikor go, and Adikor headed off, one arm around Lurt's waist, the other holding little Dab's left hand.

Other men were joining up with their women, and boys were going off with girls from the same generation. Yes, there'd certainly be much sex over the next four days, but there'd also be a lot of playing and fun and family outings and feasting.

Ponter looked around. The crowd was dissipating. It was an unpleasantly warm day, and he sighed—but not just because of that.

"I can call Jasmel, if you wish," said Hak. Hak was Ponter's Companion implant, embedded in the inside of his left forearm, just above the wrist. Like most Companions, it consisted of a high-contrast, matte-finish rectangular display screen about as long and wide as a finger, with six small control buds set beneath it, and a lens at one end. But unlike most Companions, which were pretty stupid, Hak was a sophisticated artificial intelligence, a product of Ponter's colleague Kobast Gant.

Hak hadn't spoken aloud, although she could; Ponter thought of it as a she, since Kobast had programmed the device with the voice of Ponter's late woman-mate. On days like today, though, that seemed a terrible mistake: it reminded him of how much he missed Klast. He'd have to speak to Kobast about getting a different voice.

"No," said Ponter, softly. "No, don't call anyone. Jasmel has a young man, you know. He probably came in on an earlier hover-bus, and she's off with him."

"You're the boss," said Hak.

Ponter looked around. The buildings here in the Center

were much like those out at the Rim. Most had main structures grown through arboriculture, tree trunks shaped around building forms that had subsequently been removed. Many had brick or wooden additions tacked on. All had solar-collecting arrays, either on their roofs or propped up on the ground adjacent to them. In some hostile climates, buildings had to be entirely manufactured, but Ponter always thought such structures were ugly. And yet the Gliksins seemed to make *all* their buildings that way, and to cram them together like herds of herbivorous animals.

Speaking of animals, there would be a mammoth hunt this afternoon, providing fresh meat for tomorrow's feast. Perhaps Ponter would join the hunting party. It had been a long time since he'd taken spear in hand and brought down prey in the old-fashioned way. At least it would give him—him, and the other men who had no one to spend time with—something to do.

"Daddy!"

Ponter turned around. Jasmel was running toward him, accompanied by her boyfriend, Tryon. Ponter felt a grin splitting his features. "Healthy day, sweetheart," he said, as they came up to him. "Healthy day, Tryon."

Jasmel hugged her father. Tryon stood awkwardly at one side. When Jasmel released Ponter, Tryon said, "It's good to see you, sir. I understand you've had quite an adventure."

"That I have," said Ponter. He supposed he possessed the same ambivalence toward this young man that any father of a young woman had. Yes, Jasmel had said nothing but good about Tryon—he listened to her when she spoke, he was kind during sex, he was studying to be a leather worker and so was going to make a valuable contribution to society. Still, Jasmel was his daughter, and he wanted nothing but the best for her.

"Sorry we were late," said Jasmel.

"That's all right," replied Ponter. "Where is Megameg?"

"She's decided she doesn't really like being called that anymore," said Jasmel. "She wants to be just Mega."

Mega was her real name; Megameg was a diminutive form. Ponter felt a wave of sadness washing over him. His big girl was all grown-up, and his little girl was growing up fast. "Ah," he said. "Where's Mega, then?"

"Playing with friends," said Jasmel. "You'll see her later."

Ponter nodded. "And what have you two got in mind for this morning?"

"We thought we'd all play a game of *ladatsa,*" offered Tryon.

Ponter looked at the young man. He was handsome, Ponter supposed, with wide shoulders, a wonderfully prominent browridge, a sharply defined nose, and deep purple eyes. But he'd adopted some of the affectations of youth. Instead of letting his reddish blond hair part naturally down the center, he was forcing it all to his left side, presumably holding it in place with some sort of goop.

Ponter was about to say yes to the offer of *ladatsa*—it had been many tenmonths since he'd kicked a ball—but he thought back to himself at this age, twenty years ago, when he'd been courting Klast. The last thing he'd have wanted was Klast's father hanging around.

"No," he said. "You two run along. I'll see you this evening for dinner."

Jasmel looked at her father, and he could see that she knew it wasn't what he really wanted. But Tryon was no fool; he immediately thanked Ponter, took Jasmel's hand, and started her walking away.

Ponter watched them go. Jasmel would presumably give birth to her first the year after next, when generation 149 was scheduled to be born. Things would change then, Ponter thought. He'd at least have a grandchild to look after when Two became One.

The hover-bus had long since departed, going back to the Rim to fetch another load of men. Ponter turned and started heading into town. Perhaps he'd get a bite to eat, and—

His heart jumped. This was the last person he'd expected to see, but—

But there she stood, as if waiting for him.

Daklar Bolbay.

"Healthy day, Ponter," she said.

He'd known Daklar for a long time, of course. She had been Klast's woman-mate. Indeed, if anyone could understand what the loss of Klast had meant to Ponter, it was Daklar. But . . .

But she'd made things miserable for Adikor in Ponter's absence. Accusing him of murder! Why, Adikor could no more have killed Ponter—or anyone, for that matter—than Ponter himself could have.

"Daklar," said Ponter, forgoing the usual pleasantry.

Daklar nodded, understanding. "I can't blame you for being displeased with me," she said. "I know I hurt Adikor, and to hurt one's mate is to hurt oneself." She locked her eyes onto Ponter's own. "I apologize, Ponter, fully and completely. I'd hoped to get here in time to say the same thing to Adikor, but I see he's already gone."

"You say you're sorry," said Ponter. "But what you did—"

"What I did was horrible," interjected Daklar, looking down at her feet, encased in the fabric pouches at the ends of her black pant. "But I'm seeing a personality sculptor, and I'm taking medication. The treatment has only just begun, but I already feel less . . . angry."

Ponter had some inkling of what Daklar had gone through.

Not only had she lost the woman they had shared, dear Klast, but before that she'd lost her man-mate, Pelbon, who'd been whisked away one morning by enforcers. Oh, he'd been returned, but not whole. He had been castrated, and their relationship had crumbled.

Ponter had been enormously sad when Klast had died, but at least he'd had Adikor and Jasmel and Megameg to help him get through it. How much worse it must have been for Daklar, who had no man-mate and, because of what had been done to Pelbon, no children.

"I'm glad you're feeling better," said Ponter.

"I am," confirmed Daklar, nodding again. "I know I've got a long way to go, but, yes, I am feeling better, and . . ."

Ponter waited for her to go on. Finally, he prodded her. "Yes?"

"Well," she said, now avoiding his eyes, "it's just that I'm by myself, and . . ." She paused again, but this time continued of her own volition. "And you're by yourself, too. And, well, Two becoming One can be so very lonely when you have no one to spend the time with." She briefly glanced at his face, but then looked away, perhaps afraid of what she might see there.

Ponter was startled. But . . .

But Daklar was intelligent, and that *did* appeal to Ponter. And her hair was showing wonderful streaks of gray mixed in with the brown. And—

But no. No. It was madness. After what she'd done to Adikor . . .

Ponter's jaw twinged. It did that occasionally, but usually only on cold mornings. He brought up a hand to rub it through his beard.

His jaw had been broken, some 229 moons ago, by Adikor,

during a stupid fight. Had Ponter not lifted his head in time, Adikor's blow would have killed him.

But Ponter *had* lifted his head quickly enough, and, although almost half his mandible and seven teeth had needed to be replaced with synthetic duplicates, he had lived.

And he'd forgiven Adikor. Ponter had made no accusation; Adikor had been spared from the enforcers' scalpel. Adikor had undergone treatment for anger management, and in all the months since, he'd never so much as threatened to hit Ponter or anyone else.

Forgiveness.

He'd talked a lot with Mare, over in the other world, about her belief in God, and about the putative human son of God, who had tried to inculcate forgiveness in Mare's people. Mare had been an adherent of that man's teachings.

And, after all, Ponter *was* alone. There was no telling what the High Gray Council would decide about reopening the portal to Mare's world, and, even if they did choose to allow it, Ponter wasn't absolutely sure that the gateway could be reestablished.

Forgiveness.

It was what he'd given Adikor half a lifetime ago.

It was what Mare's belief system held as the highest virtue.

It was what Daklar seemed to need from him now.

Forgiveness.

"All right," said Ponter. "You must make your peace with Adikor, but contingent on that, I dispel any animosity between us over recent events."

Daklar smiled. "Thank you." She paused, though, and the smile faded. "Do you wish my company—until your children are free, that is? I may be Mega's *tabant,* and she and I and Jasmel still share a house, but I know you need time alone with them, and I will not interfere with that. But until then . . ."

She trailed off, and her eyes briefly met Ponter's again, clearly inviting him to fill the void.

"Until then," said Ponter, making his decision, "yes, I would be glad of your company."

Chapter Four

Mary Vaughan's lab at York University was much as she had left it—not surprisingly, since, despite all the things that had happened to her, it had only been twenty-three days since she'd last been here.

Daria Klein—one of Mary's grad students—had clearly been in repeatedly during Mary's absence, though. Her work area had been rearranged, and the chart on the wall showing her sequencing of the ancient Egyptian Y chromosome she was working on had many more spaces filled in.

Arne Eggebrecht of the Pelizaeus Museum in Hildesheim, Germany, had recently suggested that an Egyptian body purchased from an old Niagara Falls tourist attraction might in fact have been Ramses I, founder of the line that contained Seti I, Ramses II (the one portrayed by Yul Brynner in *The Ten Commandments*), Ramses III, and Queen Nefertari. The specimen was now housed in Atlanta's Emory University, but DNA samples had been sent to Toronto for analysis; Mary's lab was world-renowned for its success in recovering ancient DNA, a fact that had led directly to her involvement with Ponter Boddit. Daria had made considerable progress on the putative Ramses in Mary's absence, and Mary nodded approvingly.

"Professor Vaughan."

Mary's heart jumped. She turned around. A tall, thin man in his midsixties was standing in the lab's doorway. His voice was deep and rough, and he had a Ronald Reagan pompadour.

"Yes?" said Mary. She felt her stomach knotting; the man was blocking the only way out of the room. He was wearing a dark gray business suit, with a gray silk tie, its knot loosened. After a moment, he stepped forward, pulled out a thin silver business-card case, and proffered a card to Mary.

She took it, embarrassed to see that her hand was shaking as she did so. It said:

SYNERGY GROUP
J. K. (Jock) Krieger, Ph.D.
Director

There was a logo: a picture of the Earth, divided neatly in half. On the left half, the oceans were black and the landmasses white, and on the right half the opposite color scheme was used. The street address given was in Rochester, New York, and the e-mail address ended in ".gov," signifying a U.S.-government operation.

"What can I do for you, Dr. Krieger?" asked Mary.

"I'm the director of the Synergy Group," he said.

"So I see. I've never heard of it."

"No one has yet, and few will, ever. Synergy is a U.S.-government think tank that I've been putting together over the last couple of weeks. We're modeled more or less on the RAND Corporation, although on a much smaller scale—at least at this stage."

Mary had heard of RAND, but really didn't know anything about it. Still, she nodded.

"One of our principal sources of funding is the INS," said Krieger. Mary lifted her eyebrows, and Krieger explained: "The U.S. Immigration and Naturalization Service."

"Ah," said Mary.

"As you know, the Neanderthal incident caught us—caught *everybody*—with their pants down. The whole thing was over practically before it had even begun, and for the first few days we'd just dismissed it as another crazy tabloid story—like finding Mother Teresa's face in a prune Danish, or a Bigfoot sighting."

Mary nodded. She hadn't believed it herself at the outset.

"Of course," continued Krieger, "it may be that the portal between our universe and the Neanderthal one might never reopen. But, in case it ever does, we want to be ready."

"We?"

"The United States government."

Mary felt her back stiffen slightly. "The portal opened on Canadian soil, and—"

"Actually, ma'am, it opened a mile and a quarter *beneath* Canadian soil, at the Sudbury Neutrino Observatory, which is a joint project of Canadian, British, and American institutions, including the University of Pennsylvania, the University of Washington, and the Los Alamos, Lawrence Berkeley, and Brookhaven National Laboratories."

"Oh," said Mary. She hadn't known that. "But the Creighton Mine, where SNO is located, belongs to Canada."

"More precisely, it belongs to a Canadian publicly traded corporation, Inco. But, look, I'm not here to argue sovereignty issues with you. I just want you to understand that the United States has a legitimate interest in this matter."

Mary's tone was frosty. "All right."

Krieger paused; he clearly felt he'd gotten off on the wrong foot. "If the portal between our world and the Neanderthal world ever reopens, we want to be ready. Defending the portal doesn't seem too difficult. As you may know, the Twenty-second Wing Command of the Canadian Forces, based at North Bay, has been charged with securing the portal against invasion or terrorist attacks."

"You're kidding," said Mary, although she suspected he wasn't.

"No, I'm not, Professor Vaughan. Both your government and mine are taking all this very seriously."

"Well, what's this got to do with me?" asked Mary.

"You were able to identify Ponter Boddit as a Neanderthal based on his DNA, correct?"

"That's right."

"Would the test you did be able to identify every Neanderthal? Could it reliably tell if any given person was a Neanderthal or a human?"

"Neanderthals *are* human," said Mary. "We're congeners; we all belong to the genus *Homo. Homo habilis, Homo erectus, Homo antecessor*—if you believe that's a legitimate species—*Homo heidelbergensis, Homo neanderthalensis, Homo sapiens.* We're all humans."

"I concede the point," said Krieger, with a nod. "What should we call ourselves to distinguish us from them?"

"Homo sapiens sapiens," said Mary.

"Not very catchy, is it?" replied Krieger. "Didn't I hear someone call us Cro-Magnons? That's got a pleasant ring to it."

"Technically, that term refers to a specific population of anatomically modern humans from the Upper Paleolithic of southern France."

"Then I ask again: what should we call ourselves to distinguish us from the Neanderthals?"

"Well, Ponter's people had a term for fossil humans from their world that looked like us. They called them *Gliksins.* It would be an appropriate parity: we call them by a name that really refers to their fossil ancestors, and they call us by a name that really refers to our fossil ancestors."

"Gliksins? Is that what you said?" Krieger frowned. "All right, I guess that will do. Can your DNA technique reliably distinguish between *any* Neanderthal and *any* Gliksin?"

Mary frowned. "I doubt it. There's a lot of variation within species, and—"

"But if Neanderthals and we Gliksins are different species, surely there are genes that only they have, or only we have. The genes that give them those browridges, for instance."

"Oh, lots of us Gliksins have browridges. They're very common among males from Eastern Europe, for instance. Of course, the doubly arched Neanderthal one is quite distinctive, but . . ."

"Well, what about those triangular projections into their nasal cavities?" asked Krieger. "I've heard that they are truly diagnostic of a Neanderthal."

"Yes, that's right," said Mary. "I suppose if you wanted to look up each person's nose . . ."

Krieger did not sound amused. "I was thinking you might be able to find the gene responsible for that."

"Oh, possibly, although they themselves may already know. Ponter implied that they long ago undertook the equivalent of our Human Genome Project. But, sure, I suppose I could search for a diagnostic marker."

"Can you do it? How fast can you do it?"

"Take it easy," said Mary. "We only have DNA from four prehistoric Neanderthals and one contemporary one. I'd really rather have a much larger sample base."

"But can you do it?"

"Possibly, but why?"

"How long would it take?"

"With my current facilities? And if I did nothing else? A few months, perhaps."

"What if we gave you all the equipment and all the support

staff you could possibly need? What then? Money is no object, Professor Vaughan."

Mary felt her heart pounding. As a Canadian academic, she had *never* heard those words before. She'd had friends at university who had gone on to do postgraduate work in the States; they'd often reported back about big five- and six-figure research grants and state-of-the-art equipment. Mary's own first research grant had been for a paltry $3,200—and Canadian dollars, at that.

"Well, with, ah, with unlimited resources, I suppose I could do it fairly quickly. A matter of weeks, if we're lucky."

"Good. Good. Do so."

"Umm, with all due respect, Dr. Krieger, I'm a Canadian citizen; you can't tell me what to do."

Krieger was immediately contrite. "Of course not, Professor Vaughan. My apologies. My enthusiasm for the project got the better of me. What I meant to say was, would you please undertake this project? As I said, we will provide whatever equipment and staff you need, and a sizable consultancy fee."

Mary's head was swimming. "But why? Why is this so important?"

"If the gateway between the two worlds ever opens again," Krieger said, "we may have many Neanderthals coming into our world."

Mary narrowed her eyes. "And you want to be able to discriminate against them?"

Krieger shook his head. "Nothing like that, I assure you. But we'll need to know for immigration reasons, for providing appropriate health care, and so on. You don't want an unconscious person being given the wrong medicine because doctors couldn't tell if he was Neanderthal or Gliksin."

"Surely you can simply look to see if he has a Companion implant. Ponter says all his people have them."

"Without disparaging your friend in the least, Professor Vaughan, we have only his word for that. For all we know, he was in fact a parolee in his universe, and that thingamajig was some sort of tracking device worn only by him and other criminals."

"Ponter is not a criminal," said Mary.

"Nonetheless, you can surely appreciate that we prefer to have our own methods for determining which species a person belongs to, rather than having to rely on something we've heard anecdotally."

Mary nodded slowly. It did, sort of, make sense. And, after all, there was benign precedent: the Canadian government already put a lot of work into defining who is and who isn't a Status Indian, so that social programs and entitlements could properly be administered. Still . . . "There's no reason to think the portal might open again, is there? I mean, there haven't been any signs, have there?" She'd love to see Ponter again, but . . .

Krieger shook his head. "No. But we believe in being prepared. And I'll be honest: I grant that your Mr. Boddit looked, shall we say, distinctive. But it's possible that another Neanderthal might have less pronounced features, and be able to slip into a population of our kind of humans."

Mary smiled. "You've been talking to Milford Wolpoff."

"Indeed. As well as Ian Tattersall and just about every other Neanderthal expert you can name. There seems to be no consensus among them about how much Neanderthals differed from us."

Mary nodded; that much was certainly true. Some, like Wolpoff, held that Neanderthals were just another variety of *Homo sapiens*—at best a race, if that term had any validity, and certainly members of the same species as modern humans. Others, including Tattersall, felt the opposite: that Neanderthals were a species in their own right, *Homo neanderthalensis.* To date, all DNA studies seemed to support the latter view—but Wolpoff and company felt the few Neanderthal DNA samples available, including the 379 nucleotides of mitochondrial DNA that Mary herself had extracted from the Neanderthal type specimen at the *Rheinisches Landesmuseum,* were either aberrant or misinterpreted. It wasn't too much to say that this was the most hotly contested issue in all of paleoanthropology.

"We still only have complete genetic material from one Neanderthal," said Mary, "namely Ponter Boddit. It might be impossible to find anything diagnostic in that one sample."

"I understand that. But we won't know for sure until you try."

Mary looked around the lab. "I have duties here, at York. Classes to teach. Grad students."

"I understand that, too," said Krieger. "But I'm sure arrangements can be made to cover your responsibilities. I've already had a word with the university's president."

"You're talking about a full-time research project?"

"We'll certainly compensate you for the entire academic year, yes."

"Where would I work? Here?"

Krieger shook his head. "No, we'd want you to come to our secure facility."

"In Rochester, right?"

"Rochester, New York, yes."

"That's not that far from here, is it?"

"I flew in today," said Krieger, "and that takes no time at all. I understand it's about three and a half hours by car."

Mary considered. She would still be able to come up and see her mother and friends. And she had to admit that nothing interested her more right now than studying Ponter's DNA; her class load would just be an inconvenience.

"What, ah, terms did you have in mind?"

"I can offer you a one-year consulting contract at $150,000 U.S., starting immediately, with full medical benefits." He smiled. "I know that's a key point with you Canadians."

Mary frowned. She'd more or less prepared herself for returning to York University, to the site of the rape, but . . .

But no. No, that wasn't true. She'd hoped she could stand being here, but, if this morning had been any indication, she was still jumpy as hell.

"I have an apartment here," said Mary. "A condo."

"We'll take care of the mortgage payments, taxes, and maintenance fees for you while you're away; your home will be waiting for you when this job is done."

"Really?"

Krieger nodded. "Yes. This is the biggest thing that's happened to this planet since—well, *ever.* What we're looking at here, Professor Vaughan, is the end of the Cenozoic, and the beginning of the next era. There haven't been two versions of humanity on this planet for thirty-five thousand years or so—but, if that portal reopens, there *are* going to be two versions again, and we want to make sure it goes right this time."

"You make it sound very tempting, Dr. Krieger."

"Jock. Call me Jock." A pause. "Look, I used to be with the RAND Corporation. I'm a mathematician; back when I graduated from Princeton, seventy percent of all math grads from major universities applied for jobs at RAND. That was where you got the money and resources to do pure research. In fact, the joke was that RAND actually stood for 'Research And No Development'—it's a think tank in the purest sense."

"What *does* it stand for?"

"Just 'Research and Development,' supposedly. But the fact is its funding came from the U.S. Air Force, and it existed for a fundamentally unpleasant reason: to study nuclear conflict.

I'm a game theorist; that's my specialty, and that's why I was there—doing simulations of nuclear brinksmanship." He paused. "You ever see *Dr. Strangelove*?"

Mary nodded. "Years ago."

"Old George C. Scott, he's clutching a 'BLAND' corporation study there in the War Room. Freeze-frame it next time you're watching the DVD. The study is labeled *World Targets in Megadeaths.* That's about right for what we had to do. But the Cold War is over, Professor Vaughan, and now we're looking at something incredibly positive." He paused. "You know, despite its military roots, RAND did lots of far-out thinking. One of our studies was called *Habitable Planets for Man,* and it was all about the likelihood of finding earthlike planets elsewhere in the galaxy. Stephen Dole put that one together in 1964, just when I started at RAND. But, even then, back in the glory days of the space program, very few of us seriously thought we'd have access to another earthlike world in our lifetime. But if that portal reopens, we will. And we want contact to go as positively as possible. When the first Neanderthal embassy opens up—"

"A Neanderthal embassy!" exclaimed Mary.

"We're thinking ahead, Professor Vaughan. That's what Synergy is all about—not just the best of both worlds, but making something that's *more* than the sum of its parts. It's going to be *wild.* And we want you along for the ride."

Chapter Five

Ponter and Daklar walked through the square, chatting. Lots of children were about, playing games, chasing each other, having fun.

"I've always wanted to ask a man," said Daklar. "Do you miss your children when Two are separate?"

A little boy—a 148—ran right in front of them, catching a flying triangle. Ponter never regretted having two daughters, but sometimes he did wish he had a son, as well. "Of course," he said. "I think about them constantly."

"They're such wonderful girls, Jasmel and Mega," said Daklar.

"I thought you and Jasmel crossed spears while I was away," said Ponter.

Daklar laughed ruefully. "Oh, yes, indeed. She spoke on behalf of Adikor at the *dooslarm basadlarm,* and I was the one accusing him. But I'm no fool, Ponter. Obviously I was wrong, and she was right."

"So things are pleasant between the two of you now?"

"It'll take some time," said Daklar. "You know how Jasmel is. Stubborn as a stalactite—hanging on despite everything trying to pull her down."

Ponter laughed. He did indeed know Jasmel—and, it seemed, Daklar knew her, too. "She *can* be difficult," Ponter said.

"She's just turned 225 months old," said Daklar. "Of course she's difficult. So was I, at her age." She paused. "There's a lot of pressure on young ladies, you know. She's expected to take two mates before winter. I know Tryon is likely to become her man-mate, but she's still searching for a woman-mate."

"She'll have no trouble," said Ponter. "She's quite a find."

Daklar smiled. "That she is. She's got all of Klast's best qualities and . . ." She paused again, perhaps wondering if she were being too forward. "And all of yours, as well."

But Ponter was pleased by the remark. "Thank you," he said.

Daklar looked down. "When Klast died, Jasmel and Mega were very sad. Megameg was too young to really understand, but Jasmel . . . It's hard for a girl, not having a mother." She fell silent, and Ponter wondered if she was gathering for him to volunteer that Jasmel had had an excellent substitute. Ponter was beginning to think that was probably true, but he didn't know what to say. "I've tried to be a good *tabant*," continued Daklar, "but it's not the same as having their mother look after them."

Again, Ponter wasn't sure what the politic answer was. "No," he said at last. "I imagine it's not."

"I know there was no way they could have gone to live with you and Adikor," said Daklar. "Two girls, out at the Rim . . ."

"No," agreed Ponter. "That would have been impossible."

"Did you . . ." Daklar trailed off, looking again at the closely cropped grass covering the square. "Did you resent the fact that I ended up looking after them?"

Ponter shrugged a little. "You were Klast's woman-mate. You were the logical one for her to name as *tabant*."

Daklar tipped her head slightly. Her voice was soft. "That wasn't what I asked."

Ponter closed his eyes and exhaled. "No, it wasn't. Yes, I

suppose I resented it—forgive me for saying so. I mean, I am their *father;* their genetic relative. You . . ."

Daklar waited for him to go on, but when it became clear that he wasn't inclined to, she finished his thought for him. "I wasn't a blood relation," she said. "They weren't my children, and yet I ended up taking care of them."

Ponter said nothing; there was no polite response.

"It's all right," said Daklar, touching Ponter's arm for a beat. "It's all right for you to feel that way. It's natural."

Several geese flew by overhead, and some thrushes that had been sitting on the grass took wing as the two of them drew nearer. "I love my children very much," Ponter said.

"I love them, too," said Daklar. "I know they're not mine, but I've lived with them their whole lives, and, well, I love them as if they were."

Ponter stopped walking and looked at Daklar. He'd never really delved into this type of relationship before; he'd always sort of assumed that another person's children were a bit of a nuisance—certainly Adikor's Dab was a mischievous sort. In a normal family, Daklar would have had children of her own. A daughter or a son of generation 148 would still be living with her mother and her mother's woman-mate, and a daughter of generation 147 would also still be at home, although she'd be pairing off with a man-mate and a woman-mate of her own in the next several months.

"You look surprised," said Daklar. "I *do* love Jasmel and Mega."

"Well, I—I guess I never thought about it."

Daklar smiled. "So you see, we have a lot in common. We both loved the same woman. And we both love the same children."

Ponter and Daklar decided to start by watching a play performed in an outdoor amphitheater. Ponter had always liked live theater, and this was one of his favorites: *Wamlar and Kolapa,* a historical piece about a male hunter and a female gatherer. This kind of drama could only be performed when Two became One and both male and female actors could work together. The plot depended on all sorts of twists and turns that would be impossible in the modern Companion era: people going missing, others failing to communicate over distances, still others being unable to prove that they'd been at a specific place at a specific time, and conflicting accounts of events.

Ponter found his knee pressing against Daklar's as they sat cross-legged side by side in the amphitheater.

It really *was* a good play.

After the play, Ponter and Daklar went to visit little Megameg, who was playing with friends. She seemed delighted to see her father and ran toward him from across the yard.

"Hey, sweetie," Ponter said, lifting her up.

"Hi, Daddy!" She looked over at Daklar and said, in a tone that Ponter realized was equally warm, "Hi, Daklar!"

He felt a brief twinge, wishing that there was some obvious preference for him over her, for her biological father over her legal guardian. But it quickly passed. His young daughter, he knew, had plenty of love to go around. He squeezed her again, then put her down.

"Watch me do a trick!" she said. She ran a few paces away from them and did a back flip.

"Wow!" said Ponter, beaming with pride.

"Wonderful!" said Daklar, clapping her hands together. Ponter looked at Daklar and smiled. Daklar smiled back at him.

Megameg evidently wanted to do another trick, but Ponter

and Daklar weren't looking at her. "Daddy! Mommy! Watch!" she shouted.

Ponter's breath caught in his throat. Megameg looked embarrassed. "Oops!" she said in her little voice. "I mean, Daddy, Daklar—watch!"

By midafternoon, Ponter was growing increasingly nervous. After all, this *was* Two becoming One, and he wasn't an idiot. But he hadn't had sex with a woman—well, his first thought was he hadn't done it since Klast had died, two tenmonths ago. But it had been longer than that. Oh, he had loved Klast until the day she died, but the cancer had had its effects before then. It had been . . . actually, he wasn't sure. Ponter had never allowed himself to think that *this* was the last time he'd make love to Klast, that this was the final time he would slip into her, but . . .

But there *had* been a final time, an ultimate coupling before she was too weak to be able to do it again. That must have been a full tenmonth prior to her death.

So. At least thirty months. Yes, he'd been satisfied by Adikor during that span, but . . .

But it wasn't the same. Physical relations between two men—or two women, for that matter—although equally signs of love, were entertainment, fun. But *sex* was the act of potential procreation.

There was no way Daklar, or any woman, could become pregnant during this Two becoming One. All the women, living together, inhaling each other's pheromones, had their menstrual cycles synchronized. It wouldn't be possible for any of them to get pregnant at this time of month. Yes, next year, when generation 149 was to be conceived, the High Gray Council would change the dates of Two becoming One so that they coincided with the time of maximum fertility.

Still, even if there was no chance of Daklar conceiving, it *had* been a long while since . . .

"Let's take the kids over to Darson Square and get something to eat," said Daklar.

Ponter felt his eyebrow rolling up his browridge. *The kids.* No question as to which kids. His kids.

Her kids.

Their kids.

She certainly knew the way to endear herself. A sexual overture would have left him flustered, unsure. But an outing with the kids . . .

It was just what he needed.

"Sure," he said. "Sure thing."

Ponter beckoned Megameg over to them, and they went off to find Jasmel—which was easy enough, since her Companion and Hak could communicate with each other. Lots of children were still out playing, but many adults had adjourned into homes for lovemaking. A few adults—men and women both—remained outdoors.

Ponter hadn't really seen much in the way of children over in the Gliksin world, but he'd gathered that they weren't left alone like this. Gliksin society was doubly wounded. First, they'd never had a purging of their gene pool, eliminating the most undesirable psychological traits. And, second, no Lonwis Trob had ever appeared to liberate them: without Companion implants and alibi recorders, Gliksins were still subject to personal assault, and, based on what little he'd seen on the Gliksin video system, children were common targets.

But here, in this world, children could roam freely day and night. Ponter wondered how parents stayed sane in the Gliksin universe.

"There she is!" said Daklar, spotting Ponter's daughter before he himself did. Jasmel and Tryon were looking at a display of flensing implements set up in an outdoor booth.

"Jasmel!" called Ponter, waving. His daughter looked up, and he was delighted to see an instant smile, not a look of disappointment that her time with Tryon was being interrupted.

Ponter and Daklar closed the distance. "We were thinking of going to Darson Square, maybe get some buffalo to eat."

"I should really spend a little time with my own parents," said Tryon, whether picking up a hint from Ponter's posture or actually wanting to do what he said, Ponter couldn't say. Tryon leaned over and licked Jasmel's face. "See you tonight," he said.

"Let's go," said Megameg, reaching up and taking Ponter's hand with her left one and Daklar's hand with her right one. Jasmel fell in next to Ponter, and he put an arm around her shoulders, and the four of them headed off together.

Chapter Six

Although Mary would have preferred a chance to sleep on it, Jock Krieger's offer was really a no-brainer for her: it was simply too good to pass up.

And today was the only departmental meeting before the beginning of the academic year. Not everybody would be in attendance—some faculty members would still be at their cottages, or simply steadfastly refusing to come to the university prior to the first Tuesday in September. But most of her colleagues would be there, and this would be the best opportunity to arrange for them to cover her classes. Mary knew she was lucky: she'd been a woman at the right time, when York and many other universities were correcting historical imbalances in hiring practices, especially in the sciences. She'd had no trouble getting first a tenure-track position, and ultimately actual tenure, while many males of her age were still eking out an existence with sessional teaching assignments.

"Welcome back, everyone," said Qaiser Remtulla. "I hope you all had great summers?"

There were nods from the dozen people sitting around the conference table. "That's good," said Qaiser. She was a Pakistani woman of fifty, dressed in a smart beige blouse and matching slacks. "Of course," she said, grinning now, "I'm sure no one had quite so exciting a holiday as our Mary."

Mary felt herself blushing, and Cornelius Ruskin and a couple of the others applauded briefly. "Thanks," she said.

"But," continued Qaiser, "if we can work it out, Mary would like to take a leave of absence."

Across the table from her, Cornelius sat up straight. Mary smiled; he knew what was coming, and was ready to leap at his opportunity.

"Mary's set to teach the 2000-level Genetics course; the third-year Regulation of Gene Expression course; and the fourth-year Eukaryotic Genetics course," said Qaiser. "Plus she's got two Ph.D. students she's been supervising: Daria Klein, who's doing work on ancient human DNA, and Graham Smythe, who is—what's he doing again, Mary?"

"A reevaluation of songbird taxonomy, based on mitochondrial DNA studies."

"Right," said Qaiser, nodding. She looked out over her half glasses. "If anyone is interested in picking up any extra course work . . ."

By the first syllable of "anyone," Cornelius Ruskin's hand was in the air. Mary felt sorry for poor Cornelius. He was thirty-five or thirty-six, and had had his Ph.D. in genetics for eight years. But there were no full-time jobs for white males in the department. Ten years ago, he'd have been well on his way to tenure; today, he was picking up $6,000 per half course and $12,000 per full course, and living in a dump of an apartment building in Driftwood, a nearby neighborhood even students avoided—his "penthouse in the slums," Cornelius called it.

"I'll take Regulation," Cornelius said. "And Eukaryotic Genetics."

"You can have Eukaryotics and the 2000-level introductory course," said Qaiser. "Can't give all the plums to the same person."

Cornelius nodded philosophically. "Deal," he said.

"Well, in that case," said Devon Greene, another white

male, another sessional instructor, "can I have the Regulation of Gene Expression course?"

Qaiser nodded. "It's all yours." She looked at Karen Clee, a black woman the same age as Mary. "Can you take—let's see—how 'bout Ms. Klein?"

The sessional instructors couldn't supervise Ph.D. students; those duties had to go to full-time faculty. "I'd rather have the bird guy," said Karen.

"Okay," said Qaiser. "Who wants Ms. Klein?"

No response.

"Let me put it this way," said Qaiser. "Who wants Ms. Klein and Mary's old office?"

Mary smiled. She *did* have prime office space, with a nice view overlooking the greenhouse.

"Sold!" said Helen Wright.

"There it is," said Qaiser. She turned to Mary and smiled. "It looks like we'll be able to muddle through without you this year."

After the departmental meeting, Mary returned to her lab. She wished that Daria and Graham, her grad students, were in today; she really owed them personal explanations.

And yet what explanation could she give? The obvious one—a great job offer in the United States—was only part of the story. Mary had had overtures from U.S. universities in the past; it wasn't as though she had never been courted before. But she'd always turned them down, telling herself that she preferred Toronto, that she found its climate "invigorating," that she'd miss the CBC and the wonderful live theater and Caribbana and Sleuth of Baker Street and Yorkville and Le Sélect Bistro and the ROM and smoke-free restaurants and the

Blue Jays and *The Globe and Mail* and socialized medicine and the Harbourfront Reading Series.

Of course, she could tell them about the job's perks—but the main reason she was leaving was the rape. She knew rapes happened everywhere; she'd be no safer in another city. But just as getting away from the reminders of it had helped spur her on to Sudbury to investigate the crazy story of a live Neanderthal found there, so, it seemed, the same thing would drive her now to leave Toronto again. Perhaps, had Daria been in, she could have told her about it—but there was no way she could discuss it with Graham Smythe . . . or any other man, at least in this world.

Mary set about packing her personal effects from the lab, putting them in an old plastic milk crate that had been kicking around the department for years. She had a wall calendar with pictures of covered bridges; she also had a framed snapshot of her two nephews, and a coffee mug with the *Canada AM* logo on it—she'd been on that show almost a decade ago, after she'd recovered DNA from a thirty-thousand-year-old bear that had been found frozen in Yukon permafrost. Most of the books on the lab's shelves belonged to the university, but she retrieved a half dozen volumes that were her own, including a recent edition of the *CRC Handbook.*

Mary looked around the lab, hands on hips. Somebody else could take over trying to sequence DNA from a passenger pigeon—that had been what she'd been working on before she'd left for Sudbury. And although Mary herself had bought most of the plants in the lab, she knew she could count on Daria to water them.

So: everything was set. She picked up the milk crate, which was quite heavy now, and headed for the door, and—

No. No, there was something else.

She *could* leave them here, she supposed. No one would throw them out in her absence, after all. Hell, there were specimens in there that belonged to old Daniel Colby, and he'd been dead for two years.

Mary set down her crate and crossed over to the refrigerator used to store biological specimens. She opened the door and let a blast of cold air wash over her.

There they were: two opaque specimen containers, both labeled "Vaughan 666."

One contained her panties from that night, and the other—

The other contained the filth he'd left inside her.

But no. No, she wouldn't take them with her. They'd be fine here, and, besides, she didn't even want to touch them. She closed the refrigerator door and turned around.

Just then, Cornelius Ruskin stuck his head in the lab's door. "Hey, Mary," he said.

"Hi, Cornelius."

"Just wanted to say we're going to miss you around here, and—well, I wanted to thank you for the extra course work."

"No problem," said Mary. "I can't think of anyone better qualified to do it." She wasn't just being polite; she knew it was true. Cornelius had been quite the wunderkind; his undergrad had been at U of T, but his Ph.D. was from Oxford, where he'd studied at the Ancient Biomolecules Centre.

Mary started toward the milk crate. "Let me get that," said Cornelius. "You taking it out to your car?"

She nodded. Cornelius bent from his knees, just like you're supposed to, and lifted the crate. They headed out into the corridor. Coming the other way was Jeremy Banyon, a grad student, but not one of Mary's. "Hello, Professor Vaughan," he said. "Hello, Doctor Ruskin."

Mary saw Cornelius manage a tight little smile. Mary and

the other full-time faculty were always called "Professor," but Cornelius wasn't entitled to that honorific. It was only in the halls of academe that being referred to as "Doctor" was the consolation prize, and she could see in his expression how much Cornelius coveted the P-word.

Mary and Cornelius went down the stairs and out into the sultry August heat. They made their way over to the parking lot by York Lanes, and he helped her put her things in the trunk of her Honda. She bade him farewell, got in, started the engine, and drove off to her new life.

Chapter Seven

"Interesting that you started another relationship so quickly," said Selgan, his tone neutral.

"I wasn't starting *a relationship," snapped Ponter. "I had known Daklar Bolbay for over 200 months by this point."*

"Oh, yes," said Selgan. "After all, she had been your woman-mate's woman-mate."

Ponter folded his arms across his chest. "Exactly."

"So naturally you had known her," agreed Selgan, nodding.

"That's right." Ponter had a defensive tone in his voice.

"And, in all that time that you had known Daklar, did you ever fantasize about her?"

"What?" said Ponter. "You mean sexually?"

"Yes, sexually."

"Of course not."

Selgan shrugged slightly. "It's not that unusual. Lots of men fantasize about the females their women-mates are bonded to."

Ponter was quiet for a few beats, then, softly, he allowed, "Well, there's a difference between idle thoughts and fantasizing . . ."

"Of course," said Selgan. "Of course. Had you often had idle thoughts about Daklar?"

"No," snapped Ponter. He fell silent yet again, then: "Well, 'often' is a subjective term. I mean, sure, now and then, I suppose, but . . ."

Selgan smiled. "As I said, there's nothing unusual about it. A lot of pornography exists devoted to that very theme. Have you ever partaken of—"

"No," *said Ponter.*

"If you say so," said Selgan. "But I detect an undercurrent of discomfort. Something about this change in your relationship with Daklar disturbed you. What was it?"

Ponter fell silent again.

"Was it," asked Selgan, "that you somehow felt it was wrong, because Klast had died so recently?"

Ponter shook his head. "That wasn't it. Klast was dead; gone. In fact, being with Daklar helped me to recall *Klast. After all, Daklar was the only person in the world who knew Klast as intimately as I did."*

"All right, then," said Selgan. "Let me ask you another question."

"I doubt I could prevent you from doing so," said Ponter.

"That much is true," replied Selgan, smiling. "At this point, you did not know what decision the High Gray Council was going to make with respect to reopening contact with the Gliksin world. Was your discomfort related to a feeling that you were being unfaithful to Mare by spending time with Daklar?"

Ponter laughed derisively. "You see? I told you, you personality sculptors always look for simple, pat answers. I was not bonded to Mare Vaughan. I was not committed to her in any way. My discomfort—"

Ponter had cut himself off, and Selgan waited for a time, presumably to see if he would go on. But he didn't. "You stopped yourself," said Selgan. "A thought was complete in your brain, but you decided not to give it voice. What was that thought?"

Ponter took a deep breath, no doubt sucking in Selgan's pheromones, trying to perceive the nature of the trap that was being set for him. But Selgan had an inordinate ability to control his own bodily scents; that's what made him an effective therapist. He waited patiently, and finally Ponter spoke again. "It wasn't Mare *I was being disloyal to. It was Adikor."*

"Your man-mate," said Selgan, as if trying to place the name.

"Yes," said Ponter.

"Your man-mate who had whisked you back from that other world, from Mare Vaughan . . ."

"Yes. No. I mean, he—"

"He did what he had to do, no doubt," said Selgan. "But, still, down deep, there was a part of you that . . . well, what?"

Ponter closed his eyes. "That resented him."

"For bringing you home."

Ponter nodded.

"For taking you away from Mare."

Another nod.

"For taking you away from a potential replacement for Klast."

"No one *can replace Klast," snapped Ponter. "No one."*

"Of course not," said Selgan quickly, lifting his hands, palms out. "Forgive me. But, still, it appealed to you—to some part of you—to flirt with Daklar, the woman who had almost had Adikor castrated in your absence. Your subconscious wanted to punish him, no? To make him pay for having torn you back from that other world?"

"You're wrong," said Ponter.

"Ah," said Selgan lightly. "Well, I often am, of course . . ."

Two had finally ceased being One, and Ponter and Adikor had returned with the other males to the Rim. Ponter hadn't said anything about his time with Daklar while they were commuting back home on the hover-bus. Not that Adikor would have been upset that Ponter was spending time with a woman; to be jealous of your man-mate's involvements with those of the opposite sex was the height of gaucherie.

But Daklar wasn't just any woman.

No sooner had Ponter and Adikor gotten off the hover-bus outside their house than Pabo, Ponter's large reddish brown dog, came rushing out the front door to greet them. Sometimes Pabo came into the Center with Ponter and Adikor, but this time they'd left the old girl at home; she had no trouble hunting her own food while Ponter and Adikor were away.

They all entered the house, and Ponter took a seat in the living area. It was normally his job to prepare the evening meal, and he usually got to that as soon as they came home, but today he wanted to talk to Adikor first.

Adikor made a trip to the bathroom, and Ponter waited, fidgeting. At last he heard the sound of the plumbing jets. Adikor emerged and noted Ponter on one of the couches; he raised his eyebrow at Ponter.

"Sit down," said Ponter.

Adikor did so, mounting a saddle-seat facing Ponter.

"I wanted you to hear it from me before you heard it from anyone else," Ponter said.

Adikor could have prodded him to go on, Ponter thought, but instead he just looked at him expectantly.

"I spent most of Two becoming One with Daklar."

Adikor visibly sagged in the saddle-seat, his splayed legs hanging loosely at his sides. "Daklar?" he repeated, then, as if there could be another: "Daklar *Bolbay?*"

Ponter nodded.

"After what she did to me?"

"She wants forgiveness," said Ponter. "From you, and from me."

"She tried to have me castrated!"

"I know," said Ponter, softly. "I know. But she didn't succeed."

"No blade, no injury," snapped Adikor. "Is that it?"

Ponter was quiet for a long time, composing his thoughts.

He'd rehearsed this all in his head during the hover-bus ride back from the Center, but, as was always the case in such matters, reality had already diverged widely from the planned script. "Look, there are my children to think of. It won't do for their father and the woman they live with to be at odds."

"I *do* care about Megameg and Jasmel," said Adikor. "But it was not me who created this conflict."

Ponter nodded slowly. "Granted. But, still . . . they have been through so much in the last two tenmonths."

"I know," said Adikor. "I am so very sorry that Klast died, but, again, it was not me who created the conflict here. It was Daklar Bolbay."

"I understand that," said Ponter. "But . . . but forgiveness isn't only of benefit to the person who is being forgiven. It's also of benefit to the person *doing* the forgiving. To carry hate and anger around inside you . . ." Ponter shook his head. "It's far better to let it go, totally and completely."

Adikor seemed to consider this, and, after a few moments, he said, "Two-hundred-odd months ago, I did you an injury."

Ponter felt his mouth go tight. They never spoke of this—*never.* That was part of what had made it possible to go on.

"And," continued Adikor, "you forgave me."

Ponter was impassive.

"You've never asked me for anything in return," said Adikor, "and I know that is not what you are doing now, but . . ."

Pabo, evidently disturbed by the break from routine—it was time to make dinner!—came into the living area and nuzzled Ponter's legs. He reached down and scratched the top of the dog's head.

"Daklar does want forgiveness," said Ponter.

Adikor looked at the moss-covered floor. Ponter knew what he was thinking. Emasculation was the highest degree of punishment allowed under law, and Daklar had sought it when no crime had existed. Her own unfortunate circumstances provided the motive, if not the excuse, for her behavior.

"Are you going to bond with her?" asked Adikor, without looking up. As it happened, Ponter himself quite liked Adikor's woman-mate, the chemist Lurt, but there was certainly no law that said you had to get along with your mate's other mate.

"It's premature to even think about that," said Ponter. "But I did spend four enjoyable days with her."

"Did you have sex?"

Ponter wasn't offended by the question; it was normal enough for two mated men to discuss their intimate encounters with women—indeed, it was a common way of dealing with the difficult-to-express notions of what each man found pleasing.

"No," said Ponter. He shrugged. "I might have, if a real opportunity had presented itself, but we spent most of our time with Jasmel and Megameg."

Adikor nodded, as if Ponter were revealing a vast conspiracy. "The way to win a man's love is by paying attention to his children."

"She is their *tabant,* you know. They are her children in a way, too."

Adikor made no reply.

"So," said Ponter, at last, "will you forgive her?"

Adikor looked up at the painting on the room's ceiling for a time, then: "Ironic, isn't it? This issue between you and me now exists only because of your kindness to me all those tenmonths ago. If you had made a public accusation after what I did to you, I would have been castrated back then. Had that been done, I would have had no testicles for Daklar to come after in your absence." He lifted his shoulders. "I have no choice but to forgive her, since you wish it."

"You have a choice," said Ponter.

"As did you, all those months ago." Adikor nodded. "I will forgive her."

"You are a good man," said Ponter.

Adikor frowned, as if contemplating the platitude. "No," he said. "No, I am an *adequate* man. But you, my friend . . ."

Ponter smiled and rose to his feet. "It's time I got to work on dinner."

Even though Two had just ceased being One, Ponter and Adikor headed back In, back to the Council chamber. The High Grays had announced that they were ready to make a decision about reopening the portal.

The Council chamber was packed with spectators of both sexes. Adikor looked rather uneasy, and it took Ponter a moment to figure out why. The last time Adikor had seen this chamber when it had been crowded like this, it was being used for the *dooslarm basadlarm.* But Adikor said nothing about his discomfort—after all, to do so would be to again bring up the matter of his unfortunate history with Daklar—and Ponter loved him all the more for that.

There were eleven Exhibitionists in the audience, dressed in silver. Ponter had never quite gotten used to the Gliksin idea of "news:" a constant reporting—some channels devoted ten tenths a day to it—of bad things happening all over the world. The Companion implants, which had ensured the safety of citizens here for almost a thousand months now, had all but put an end to theft and murder and assault. Still, humans here were equally hungry for information—Ponter had read that gossiping served the same purpose in people as grooming pelts for insects did in other primates, binding them together. And so some citizens made their contribution by allowing the transmissions from their implants to be publicly received by anyone who wished; people tuned their Voyeurs to whichever Exhibitionist they preferred to watch.

A couple of Exhibitionists always sat in on Council sessions, but the item to be announced today was of wide interest, and even Exhibitionists who normally only attended sporting events or poetry readings were in attendance.

High Council president Pandaro rose to address the assembled group. She used a carved wooden cane to help support herself as she did so. "We have studied the issues Scholar Huld and Scholar Boddit have put before us," she said. "And we have pored over Scholar Boddit's lengthy narrative of his trip to the Gliksin world, and the limited physical evidence we have from it."

Ponter fingered the small gold object he sometimes wore around his neck. He'd hated giving it up for analysis, and was delighted to have it back. Mare had handed it to him just before he'd left her world, a pair of overlapping mutually perpendicular gold strips, one longer than the other.

"And, after this deliberation," Pandaro continued, "we believe the potential value in gaining access to another version of Earth, and another kind of humanity, with scientific expertise and goods to trade, is too great to ignore."

"It's a mistake!" shouted a man's voice from the opposite seating gallery. "Don't do it!"

Councilor Bedros, next to President Pandaro, fixed a steady gaze on the person who had shouted out. "Your opinion was noted if you bothered to vote in the poll on this matter. Regardless, it is the job of this Council to make decisions, and you will do us the courtesy of waiting until you hear ours."

Pandaro continued. "The High Gray Council," she said, "by a fourteen-to-six margin, recommends that Scholars Huld and Boddit attempt to reopen the portal to the parallel universe, with reports to be made to this Council every ten days, and with the decision to continue this work subject to review every three months."

Ponter rose, and made a little bow. "Thank you, President." Adikor was on his feet, too, now, and the two men embraced.

"Save that for later," said Pandaro. "Let's get down to the marrow of the security and health issues . . ."

Chapter Eight

"Welcome to the Synergy Group, Professor Vaughan."

Mary smiled at Jock Krieger. She hadn't really known what to expect by way of facilities. The Synergy Group, it turned out, was housed in—well, a house: an old-money mansion in the Seabreeze section of Rochester, right on the shore of Lake Ontario. Ponter would have liked this place: Mary had seen a heron walking along the sandy beach, and ducks, geese, and swans in the harbor, which was lined with pleasure craft.

"Let me show you around," continued Krieger, ushering Mary farther into the old house.

"Thanks," said Mary.

"We've got twenty-four people on staff currently," said Krieger, "and we're still growing."

Mary was stunned. "Twenty-four people all working on Neanderthal immigration issues?"

"No, no, no. Synergy is involved in a lot more than just that. The DNA project is a particularly high priority, because it's something we may need right away if the portal ever opens again. But here at Synergy we're studying all aspects of the Neanderthal situation. The U.S. government is particularly interested in the Companion implants, and—"

"Big Brother is watching," said Mary.

But Krieger shook his head. "No, my dear, nothing like that. It's simply that, if we believe what Ponter said, the Companion implants can make a 360-degree detailed recording of everything that's going on around an individual. Now, yes, we do have four sociologists here evaluating whether the particular uses the Neanderthals put that kind of monitoring to might ever have any applicability in this world—although frankly, I doubt it; we value privacy too much. But, again, if the portal reopens, we want to be on an even footing. If their emissaries can effortlessly record everything they see and hear at all times, obviously we'd like our emissaries to their world to have the same advantage. It's all about trade, after all—fair trade."

"Ah," said Mary. "But Ponter said his Companion wasn't able to transmit anything to the alibi archives from here; none of the images from his visit were recorded."

"Yes, yes, a minor technological problem, I'm sure. A recorder could be built on this side."

They had been walking down a long corridor and had now reached its end. Krieger opened a door. Inside were three people—a black man, a white man, and a white woman. The black man was leaning way back in a chair, tossing crumpled-up pieces of paper at a wastebasket. The white guy was staring out at the beach and Lake Ontario beyond. And the woman was pacing back and forth in front of a whiteboard, a felt-tipped marker in hand.

"Frank, Kevin, Lilly, I'd like you to meet Mary Vaughan," said Krieger.

"Hi," said Mary.

"Are you in imaging?" asked the one who must be Lilly.

"Sorry?"

"Imaging," said Frank, and "Imaging," repeated Kevin—or perhaps it was the other way around. "You know," added the black man, helpfully, "photography and all that."

Krieger explained. "There's a reason we're in Rochester," he said. "Kodak, Xerox, and Bausch & Lomb all have their headquarters here. As I said, replicating the Companion technology is a priority; there's no city in the world that has more experts on imaging and optics."

"Ah," said Mary. She looked at the three occupants of the room. "No, I'm a geneticist."

"Oh, I know you!" declared the black man. He got up out of his chair, the chair's back making a relieved sound as it resumed a normal position. "You're the woman who spent all that time with NP."

"NP?"

"Neanderthal Prime," said Krieger.

"His name is Ponter," said Mary, somewhat miffed.

"Sorry," said the black man. He extended his hand. "I'm Kevin Bilodeau, formerly with the skunkworks at Kodak. Listen, we'd love to pick your brain about the Companion implant. You saw it up close. What sort of arrangement of lenses did it have?"

"There was only one," said Mary.

"You see!" crowed Lilly, looking accusingly at the man who, by process of elimination, must be Frank.

"Ponter said it used sensor fields to record images," said Mary.

"Did he say what sort of sensors?" "Did he mention charge-coupled devices?" "Holography—did he say anything about holography?" "What sort of resolution did the sensors have?" "Did he mention a pixel count?" "Can you describe—"

"People!" said Jock loudly. "People! Mary's going to be with us for a good, long time. You'll have plenty of opportunity to chat with her. She's still getting the orientation tour."

The three apologized, and they all made small talk for a few moments, then Krieger led Mary out of the room. "They're certainly enthusiastic," she said, once the door was closed.

Krieger nodded. "Everyone here is."

"But I don't see how they can accomplish what you've asked. I mean, I've heard of reverse engineering, but without a sample of a Companion implant, how can they hope to duplicate it?"

"Just knowing that it's possible may be enough to get them going in the right direction." Krieger opened the door on the opposite side of the hall, and Mary felt her eyes going wide.

"Louise!" she exclaimed.

Sitting at a worktable, a notebook computer open in front of her, was Louise Benoît, the physics postdoc who had saved Ponter's life when he'd first appeared inside the heavy-water tank at the heart of the Sudbury Neutrino Observatory.

"Hello, Mary," said Louise, speaking with the French accent Mary had come to know so well. She rose, and her thick brown hair tumbled halfway down her back. Mary was 38 and she knew Louise was 28—but Mary also knew that she herself hadn't looked that good even when she was 18. Louise was busty, leggy, and had a model's face; Mary had instinctively disliked her the first time they'd met.

"I'd forgotten that you knew Dr. Benoît," said Krieger.

Mary shook her head in amazement. "You're a one-man brain drain, Jock." She looked again at Louise, wondering how anyone could be so radiant without makeup. "It's good to see you, Louise." And then, the cat in her coming to the fore, "How's Reuben?"

Reuben Montego was the on-site physician at the Creighton Mine. Louise had had quite a torrid little affair with him while Mary, Ponter, Reuben, and she were all quarantined in Sudbury. Mary had assumed they were simply passing time, so she was surprised by Louise's response. "He's fine," she said. "He helped me move my stuff down here, and I'm going up to see him again next weekend."

"Ah," said Mary, realizing she'd been put in her place. "And what's your job here?"

"Dr. Benoît is heading our Portal Group," said Krieger.

"That's right," said Louise. "We're trying to work out the technology to open a portal from our side into the other universe."

Mary nodded. Louise hadn't spent all her time making love with Reuben; she'd also had many long late-night conversations of her own with Ponter Boddit, and doubtless knew more about the Neanderthal view of physics than anyone else on this version of Earth. Mary was ashamed of herself; Louise had never done anything to her—her only crime was being beautiful. "It'll be nice to spend some time with you again," said Mary.

"Say," said Louise, "I could use a roommate down here. What do you think? We seemed to get along well when we were quarantined at Reuben's."

"Umm, no," said Mary. "No thanks. I, ah, I like my privacy."

"Well, you'll have no trouble finding a place here in Rochester," said Louise.

Krieger nodded. "Both Xerox and Kodak have had a lot of layoffs in the last few years, and they're the city's principal employers. You can buy houses for a song, and you'll have your pick of hundreds of apartments."

"Good to know," said Mary.

"Try Bristol Harbour Village," said Louise. "It's an hour from here, but it's right on one of the Finger Lakes. Gorgeous. Lots of deer, and you can see the stars at night."

"Speaking of night skies," said Mary, realizing Louise might be the one to ask about this, "on my last night in Sudbury, I saw the aurora borealis go nuts. What would cause that?"

Louise looked at Mary for a few seconds, as if she couldn't believe the question. "Haven't you seen the newspapers?"

Mary shook her head. "I've been busy getting ready to move here."

"Earth's magnetic field is behaving erratically," said Louise. "Readings from all over the globe confirm that. The geodynamo strength is fluctuating substantially."

"What could cause that?"

Louise shrugged. "No one knows."

"Is it dangerous?"

"Probably not."

"Probably?" said Mary.

"Well," said Louise, "nothing quite like this has ever been recorded. There are a number of experts who think that Earth's magnetic field is collapsing, as a prelude to a pole reversal."

Mary had heard vaguely of these, but she was pleased that Krieger was the one who said, "Which is?"

"Earth's magnetic field switches polarity from time to time—you know, the north pole becomes the south pole, and vice versa," said Louise. "It's happened over three hundred times in the geological record, but never in historical times, so we really don't know much about the process. But it's always been assumed that the reversals occur by the field collapsing, then growing back up again."

"And you say there's nothing to worry about," said Krieger. "It's not associated with mass extinctions, is it?"

Louise shook her head. "No. The field was actually reversed from its present orientation at the time the dinosaurs died out, but it had been in that state for over a million years before the end of the Cretaceous." She smiled that megawatt smile. "The worst thing we'll have to do is repaint our compasses."

"That's a relief," said Mary.

Louise nodded. "And even that may not be necessary," she said. "As far as we can tell, which pole ends up being north and which one ends up being south is determined quantum mechanically, meaning it's entirely random—and that means there's only a fifty-fifty chance of the field reemerging with its polarity reversed."

Krieger raised his eyebrows. "But if that's true, then if there'd been a magnetic-field collapse when the dinosaurs died out, we wouldn't know about it if the field had come up with the same polarity it had had before."

"You're worrying for nothing, Jock," said Louise. "The magnetic-field collapses that we *do* know about aren't associated with extinctions. So it doesn't make any sense to assume that the ones that we missed, because the field happened to come up with the same polarity it had before it collapsed, had any biological effects." She smiled at Krieger, who, Mary noted, still seemed lost in his own thoughts. "Don't worry," Louise said, "I'm sure we'll all come through this one just fine."

Chapter Nine

"You told me earlier," said Jurard Selgan, "that your sole interest in seeing the portal reopened was in bringing benefits to the people of our world."

Ponter nodded curtly. "That's right."

"And since the ability to be in contact with that other world depended on the quantum computer that you had developed with Adikor Huld, naturally you would stay here, on this Earth, helping to oversee the quantum-computing facility."

"Well . . ." began Ponter, but then he trailed off.

"You did say you had no personal interest in this issue, didn't you?"

"Yes, but—"

"But you fought the High Gray Council yet again, didn't you? You insisted *that you personally be allowed to return to the other Earth."*

"It was the only thing that made sense," said Ponter. "No one else from our world had ever been there. I knew some of the people, and had learned a great deal about their world."

"And you refused to transfer the Gliksin linguistic database your Companion implant had gathered to anyone else unless you were guaranteed the right to be part of the next group traveling to the other world."

"It wasn't like that," said Ponter. "I merely suggested that my presence would be useful."

Selgan's tone was gentle. "You did more than just 'merely suggest,'" he said. "Like most of the world, I saw much of this on my Voyeur. If your own memory of the events has faded, we can easily access your alibi archives from that day. That's why my therapy center was built here, close to the Alibi Archive Pavilion. Shall we go over there and—"

"No," *said Ponter. "No, that won't be necessary."*

"So you did use—is 'coercion' too strong a word?—to get yourself back into the other world?"

"I wanted to make the greatest possible contribution I could. The Code of Civilization requires that of each of us."

"Yes, it does," agreed Selgan. "And if that contribution—if the greater good—could best be served by committing a crime, well, then . . ."

"You're wrong," said Ponter. "I hadn't even contemplated my crime yet. My only goal . . ." He paused, then continued. "My only goals *were to help with continued contact, and, yes, to see my friend Mare Vaughan. I never would have gone over there if I'd known what I was going to end up doing . . ."*

"That's not entirely true, is it?" said Selgan. "You said even if you had the opportunity to relive the moment of your crime, you still would have committed it."

"Yes, but . . ."

"But what?"

Ponter sighed. "But nothing."

The High Gray Council had finally acquiesced to Ponter's demand that he be allowed to leave the quantum computer in Adikor's care, so that he could return to the Gliksin world. He'd expected a reluctant agreement—and he was sure that was what it was—but he hadn't expected to have the title of "Envoy" bestowed upon him.

As much as he wanted to return, to see Mare again, he did have mixed feelings. His last visit had been an accident, and he'd been terrified that he would never get home. Although he and Adikor *did* believe that the portal could be reopened, and kept open indefinitely, no one really knew for sure. Ponter had almost lost Adikor, Jasmel, and Megameg once before; he wasn't sure he could stand the possibility of losing them again.

But no. He would go. Despite his concerns, Ponter *wanted* to go. Yes, he was interested in finding out how things would develop with Daklar Bolbay. But it would be most of another month until Two became One again—his next opportunity to see her—and, if all went well, he would be back in this world long before then.

Besides, this time Ponter would not be traveling alone. He'd be accompanied by Tukana Prat, a female of generation 144, ten years his senior.

The first time the portal opened had been an unforeseen event. The second time, it was a desperate rescue attempt. This time it would be a planned, orderly operation.

There was always a chance that things would go wrong; that the portal would open to some other world, or that Ponter had misconstrued the Gliksins, and that they were actually waiting for an opportunity to swarm through from the other side. To that end, Bedros, one of the elder members of the Council, would hold a detonator in his hand. Mining explosives had been placed all around the rooms of the subterranean quantum-computing facility. If things turned bad, Bedros would detonate the explosives, bringing thousands of *pertavs* of rock collapsing down, filling in the chamber. And although the transmissions from Bedros's Companion implant couldn't reach the surface from here, they *could* reach the explosives; if Bedros should die—if Gliksins or other creatures swarmed through with weapons firing—his Companion would set off the explosives.

Adikor, meanwhile, would hold a less-stringent panic button. If something went wrong, he could shut off all power to the quantum computer, which might sever the link. And if he died, his Companion could do the same thing. Up on the surface, the entrance to the Debral nickel mine had likewise been rigged with explosives, and enforcers stood watch there, ready to act in case of emergency.

Of course, Ponter and Tukana weren't going to just burst through to the other side. A probe was to be sent through first, with cameras, microphones, devices for sampling air, and more. The probe had been painted bright orange and had a ring of lights encircling it. They wanted there to be no possibility of the Gliksins misconstruing it as a stealthful attempt to eavesdrop—Ponter had explained the strange Gliksin obsession with privacy to the others.

Like the robot that had been sent through before to help rescue Ponter, the probe would feed its data back to this side through fiber-optic cabling. But unlike that hapless robot, it would also be anchored by a strong synthetic-fiber rope.

Although the probe was high-tech, and the Derkers tube that would be used to force the portal to stay open was a reasonably sophisticated piece of mechanical engineering, the actual insertion of the tube was to be a decidedly low-tech operation.

Ponter and Adikor's quantum computer had been built to factor truly huge numbers. When so doing, it accessed parallel universes in which other versions of itself already existed, and each of those other versions tried a single potential factor. By combining the results from all the universes, millions of potential factors could be checked simultaneously.

But if the number being factored was so gargantuan that it had more candidate factors than there were parallel universes in which this quantum-computing facility already existed, the quantum computer would be forced to try accessing universes in which versions of itself did *not* exist. But as soon as it did connect with one of those universes, the factoring process would crash, creating the gateway.

The quantum-computing facility had originally consisted of just four rooms: a dry toilet, an eating room, the control room, and the massive computing chamber itself. But three more rooms had just been added: a small infirmary, a sleeping room, and a large decontamination facility. People would have to pass through decontamination going in either direction, to reduce the chance of taking something inimical from here to the other world, and to cleanse them of any pathogens they might have brought back. The Gliksins had limited decontamination technology; either having almost no body hair made it easy for Gliksins to keep clean, or having tiny noses made them blissfully ignorant of their own filthiness. But tuned-laser bodily decontaminators—to which the specific protein structures of human skin, flesh, organs, and hair were transparent, but which vaporized germs and viruses—had long been in use in this world.

There had never been so many people in the quantum-computing facility before. Ponter and Adikor were there. So was Ambassador Prat, and three members of the High Gray Council, including both of the local representatives. Dern, the roboticist, was on hand, too, to operate the probe. And two Exhibitionists were there with recording units, taking pictures they would relay once they got back up to the surface.

And now, it was time.

Adikor stood at his control console on one side of the room, and Ponter stood at his on the other. Dern had a separate console, perched on a tabletop.

"Got everything you need for the trip?" asked Adikor.

Ponter did a final check. Hak, of course, was always there—

and had been upgraded with a full medical/surgical database, in case anything happened to Ponter or Tukana in the Gliksin world.

A wide leather band covered with pouches encircled Ponter's waist. He'd already done the inventory: antibiotics, antivirals, immune-system boosters, sterilized bandages, a cauterizing laser scalpel, surgical scissors, and a selection of drugs including decongestants, analgesics, and soporifics. Tukana wore a similar belt. They also both had suitcases containing several changes of clothes. "All set," said Ponter, and "All set," repeated Tukana.

Adikor looked at Dern. "What about you?"

The fat man nodded. "Ready."

"Whenever you want to proceed, then," said Adikor to Ponter.

Ponter gave Adikor a splayed-fingers gesture. "Let's find our cousins."

"All right," said Adikor. "Ten!"

One Exhibitionist was standing next to Adikor; the other, next to Ponter.

"Nine!"

The three members of the High Gray Council looked at each other; more had wanted to attend, but it was decided that three was the maximum that could be risked.

"Eight!"

Dern pulled out some control buds on his console.

"Seven!"

Ponter looked over at Ambassador Prat; if she was the least bit nervous, she was hiding it well.

"Six!"

He then looked over his shoulder at Adikor's broad back. They had deliberately not said any elaborate goodbyes last night; neither wanted to admit that if something went wrong, there was a chance that Ponter would never come home again.

"Five!"

And it wasn't just Adikor he stood to lose. The thought of his children ending up with no parents so early in life had been Ponter's biggest worry about repeating his journey.

"Four!"

A lesser—but still significant—worry was that Ponter would fall ill again in the Gliksin world, although doctors here had boosted his immune system, and Hak had been modified to constantly monitor his blood for foreign bodies.

"Three!"

There was also concern that either Ponter or Tukana might develop allergies to things on the other side.

"Two!"

And Ponter had some misgivings about the long-term stability of the gateway, which was, after all, based on quantum processes that were by their very nature inherently unpredictable. Still . . .

"One!"

Still, with all the potential problems, with all the potential negatives, there was one very positive aspect about returning to the Gliksin world . . .

"Zero!"

Ponter and Adikor simultaneously pulled buds on their control panels.

Suddenly, a great roar came from the computing chamber, which was visible through a window in the control room. Ponter knew what was happening, although he'd never been a spectator to it before. Everything that wasn't bolted down in the computing chamber was being shunted to the other universe. The glass-and-steel register cylinders—even the wonky one, number 69—stayed put, but all the air in the chamber was being swapped for a comparable mass in the other universe.

When Ponter had been accidentally transferred over, the corresponding space on the other side had contained a giant acrylic sphere full of heavy water—the heart of a Gliksin neutrino detector.

But this time, no heavy water came gushing through. The chamber had been drained before Ponter had returned, so that the damage his arrival had done to the acrylic sphere could be repaired.

Right on cue, the gaudy probe—cylindrical, about an armspan long—tumbled through the blue fire that marked the portal, the light hugging the probe's contours in profile as it did so. All that was visible now were the anchoring and telecommunications cables attached to the probe, pulled taut, disappearing into midair at about waist height. Ponter swung his attention to the large, wall-mounted monitor that had been added to the control room to display what the probe was seeing.

And what it was seeing was—

"Gliksins!" exclaimed Ambassador Prat.

"I'd only half believed it," said Councilor Bedros.

Adikor turned to look at Ponter, grinning. "Anyone you know?"

Ponter squinted at the scene. As before, the portal had appeared several body-heights above ground; the quantum-computing facility seemed to be slightly higher up and slightly to the north of the center of the neutrino-detector chamber. A dozen or more Gliksins were working inside the still-dry chamber. They were all clad in coveralls, and they all had those yellow plastic turtle shells on their heads. Most of the Gliksins had the same pale skin that Ponter's people had, but two had dark brown skin. Ponter got the impression that almost all the workers were males, but it was so hard to tell with Gliksins. Of course, the one face he'd hoped to see was female, but there was no reason she should be doing repair work down at the bottom of a mineshaft.

All the faces were looking directly at the probe, and several of the individuals were pointing with their scrawny arms.

"No," said Ponter. "Nobody I know."

The probe's microphones were picking up sounds, all echoing weirdly in the cavernous chamber. Ponter couldn't understand much of what was being said, but he did pick out his own name at one point. "Hak," said Ponter, speaking to his Companion, "what are they saying?"

Hak had a new voice now; while getting upgrade work done on his Companion, Ponter had had Kobast Gant program in a pleasant male voice that wasn't based on anyone Ponter knew.

Hak spoke through his external speaker, so that the entire assembled group could hear. "The male at the right side of the screen just invoked that thing they call God—apparently in this context, it's an exclamation of surprise. The male next to him referred to the putative son of the God thing. And the woman next to him said, 'Wholly feces.' "

"Very strange," said Tukana.

"The male at the right," continued Hak, "has now yelled for somebody out of our view to get Doctor Mah on the telecommunications link."

As Hak spoke, several of the humans came close to the probe. Ponter enjoyed hearing the gasps from the three High Gray Council members and Ambassador Prat as they got their first close-up views of the strange, pinched Gliksin faces, with their preposterously small noses.

"Well," said Dern, the roboticist, "it looks like we've reestablished contact, and it seems conditions on the other side are suitable."

The three High Gray Council members conferred for a few beats, then Bedros nodded. "Let's do it," he said.

Ponter and Dern each took an end of the unexpanded Derkers tube. Adikor opened the door leading out to the computing floor. There was no equalizing hiss, no popping of ears; although the air in the computing chamber now presumably was mostly from the Gliksin world, comparable volumes had been exchanged. The Gliksins carefully filtered the air in the neutrino-detector facility, and the air Ponter was breathing now had no smell at all.

The point of entry to the other universe was clearly marked by the two cables disappearing into a blue-limned hole in space. Dern, who had been on hand when Ponter was recovered the first time, maneuvered the tip of the collapsed Derkers tube so that it was in contact with the probe's anchor cable. Ponter swung the length of the tube—a good eight armspans—and lined it up parallel to the anchor cable.

"Ready?" asked Dern, looking over his shoulder at Ponter.

Ponter nodded. "Ready."

"All right," said Dern. "Gently now."

Dern began feeding the collapsed tube through the portal, which widened just enough to accommodate its narrow diameter. Ponter pushed gently from the rear. Adikor had brought a portable monitor with him, which was repeating the view from the probe. He angled the device so that Dern and Ponter could see what was happening on the other side. Although the probe had been lowered to the bottom of the neutrino-detector chamber, so that the two cables attached to it took a downward turn as soon as they went through the portal, the Derkers tube was protruding parallel to the floor far below. The Gliksins couldn't reach it; it was too far above their heads. But they were pointing at it, and shouting among themselves.

"That's far enough," said Dern, noting that the tube was halfway through—he'd put a little reference mark at the appropriate spot along the tube's length. Ponter stopped feeding more through. Dern came down to the tube's end to help Ponter pull it open.

At first, Ponter and Dern could each barely fit a hand into the narrow mouth of the tube. But the tube yielded as they pulled in opposite directions, expanding its diameter more and more, its ratcheting mechanisms making loud clickings as it did so.

Ponter got his other hand into the widened mouth, and Dern got his left hand in, too, and they continued to pull the mouth open. Soon, the tube was a good armspan in diameter—but that was only a third of its maximum extent, and they went on opening it wider and wider.

Ambassador Prat and the three High Gray Councilors had come out onto the computing floor now. One of the Exhibitionists was with them; the other was standing at the topmost step leading up to the control room—he clearly wanted to be able to get away if something went wrong.

Old Bedros looked like he wished to lend a hand—history was being made here, after all. Ponter nodded for him to go ahead. Soon, six hands were pulling at the tube's widening mouth. On the portable monitor, Ponter could see the Gliksins' strange pointed jaws dropping in astonishment.

Finally, it was done: the tube had reached its maximum diameter, and its bottom was resting on the granite floor of the computing chamber. Ponter looked at Tukana, and gestured for her to go ahead. "You're the ambassador," he said.

The gray-haired woman shook her head. "But they know you—a recognizable, friendly face."

Ponter nodded. "As you wish." Adikor gave Ponter a great hug. Then Ponter moved back to the mouth of the tube, took a deep breath—despite what he'd seen through the probe's eyes, he couldn't help remembering what had happened to him the last time he'd gone through to the Gliksin world. He began to walk down the tube's length. From the interior, the only sign of the portal was a faint blue ring of light visible through the translucent membrane spread between the criss-crossing metal components of the tube—it seemed that by forcing the portal wide open like this, they wouldn't have to bear the disquieting sight of seeing cross sections of themselves as they passed through it.

Ponter walked toward the blue ring, and then, with one giant step, moved across the threshold into Gliksin world. Through the tunnel's opening, he could see the far wall of the neutrino-detector chamber, quite some distance away. It only took a few beats for him to make it to the very end of the tunnel, which, since Adikor and Dern were holding it steady at the other end, wasn't dipping down much under Ponter's weight.

Ponter stuck his head out the end of the tube and looked down at the Gliksins far below, with what, he knew, must be a massive grin on his face. He spoke a few words, and Hak provided the translation in the loudest volume its external speaker could muster. "Would one of you be kind enough to fetch a ladder?"

Chapter Ten

There actually was a suitable ladder on Ponter's side of the portal—but it would be very awkward to get it through the narrow confines of the computing center. So he waited while the Gliksins got one from the far side of the neutrino-detector chamber. It looked like the same ladder Ponter had climbed up when he'd come back home.

It took a few tries, but finally the ladder was propped up against the open end of the Derkers tube protruding out of what Ponter knew must look to the Gliksins like thin air.

Behind him, Ponter could see Dern and Adikor using power tools to affix their end of the Derkers tube to the granite floor of the quantum-computing chamber.

Once the ladder was in place, Ponter retreated down the tube and let Adikor and Dern come along to where Ponter had been. They took a moment to stare out at the fascinating spectacle of the neutrino-detector chamber and the alien beings below, then got to work, struggling with ropes, lashing the ladder's top to the mouth of the Derkers tube. Ponter could hear Adikor muttering, "Incredible, incredible," over and over again as he worked.

Adikor and Dern then returned to their side of the tube, and Ponter and Ambassador Prat walked its length. Ponter turned around and backed down the ladder, descending carefully to the neutrino-detector chamber's floor. As he got close to the bottom, he felt Gliksin hands on his arms, helping him down. He got one foot then another onto the chamber's floor, and turned around.

"Welcome back!" said one of the Gliksins, his words translated into Ponter's cochlear implants by Hak.

"Thank you," said Ponter. He looked at the faces surrounding him, but didn't recognize anyone. That wasn't surprising; even if they'd called someone he knew the moment they'd seen the probe, that person would still be in transit from the surface.

Ponter moved away from the ladder and tipped his head up to look at the mouth of the tube. He waved at Ambassador Prat and shouted out, "Come on down!"

The ambassador turned around and made her way down the ladder.

"Hey, look!" said one of the Gliksins. "It's a lady Neanderthal!"

"She is Tukana Prat," said Ponter. "Our ambassador to your world."

Tukana reached the ground and turned around. She slapped her hands together, removing the dust that had transferred to her palms from the ladder. A Gliksin—one of the two dark-skinned men—stepped forward. He looked rather at a loss for what to do, then, after a moment, he bowed at Tukana and said, "Welcome to Canada, ma'am."

The problem with relying on Hak for translations was that everything had to be filtered through its sense of humor. "We had planned to ask you to take us to your ladder," said Hak, through his external speaker, "but I see you have already done that."

Ponter could follow enough of the Gliksin language to realize what was going on. He slapped his left forearm. "Ouch!" said Hak into Ponter's cochlear implants. Then, through his speaker, he said, "Sorry. I mean, 'Take us to your leader.' "

The dark-skinned man who had stepped forward said, "Well, I'm Gus Hornby; I'm the head engineer here. And we've already called Doctor Mah in Ottawa—she's SNO's director. She could be here later today, if need be."

"Is Mare Vaughan around?" asked Ponter.

"Mare? Oh—Mary. Professor Vaughan. No, she's gone."

"Lou Benoît?"

"You mean Louise? She's gone, too."

"Reuben Montego, then."

"The doctor? Sure, we can get him down here."

"Actually," said Ponter, with Hak translating, "we would prefer to go up to see him."

"Um, sure," said Hornby. He looked up at the tunnel protruding from midair. "You're assuming that will stay open?"

Ponter nodded. "It is our hope."

"So you can just walk through to—to, um, to your side?" said one of the other Gliksins.

"Yes."

"Can I go have a look?" asked the same Gliksin, who had light skin, orange hair, and sky-colored eyes.

Ponter looked at Tukana, who looked back at him. Finally, Tukana said, "My government wishes to meet someone who can speak on behalf of your people."

"Oh," said the orange-haired one. "Well, I can't, really . . ."

Ponter and Tukana walked across the bottom of the vast chamber, accompanied by the crowd of Gliksins. Pieces of the acrylic sphere that had once been in the center of this space were stacked against its circular walls, and countless sunflower-like photomultiplier assemblies were likewise gathered up.

When they came to the far side of the chamber, there was another ladder, even taller than the one now reaching up to the Derkers tube. This ladder was used to access the entrance hatch for the neutrino-detector chamber, the same square hatch that had blown open when Ponter and all the air from the quantum-computing chamber had last transferred over. Hornby headed up the ladder first, then passed through the hatch. Tukana began her ascent.

Ponter looked back at the tunnel that led to his world, and his heart jumped when he saw Adikor standing just inside its mouth looking down at him. Ponter thought about waving at him, but to do so would be too much like saying goodbye, and so he just smiled, although there was no way Adikor could see his expression over such a distance. That was probably all to the good, since the smile, Ponter knew, was forced. He took hold of the ladder's sides and began climbing up, hoping that this would not be the last time he'd ever see his beloved man-mate.

Ponter shouldered his way through the opening, hauling himself to his feet. Suddenly, five Gliksins wearing identical green clothes moved toward him, each one carrying a large projectile-firing weapon.

Ponter had read his share of speculative literature; he knew stories about parallel worlds, in which evil versions of people from the familiar universe existed. His first thought was that, somehow, he'd transferred to a different universe.

"Mr. Boddit," said one of the—*soldiers,* that was the word, wasn't it? "My name is Lieutenant Donaldson, of the Canadian Forces. Please step away from the hatch."

Ponter did so, and Ambassador Prat emerged through the hatch, hoisting herself up onto the metal deck. The walls surrounding the deck were covered with dark green plastic sheeting, and conduits and plastic pipes hung from the ceiling. What looked like some form of computing equipment lined some of the walls.

"Ma'am?" said Donaldson, looking at Tukana.

Ponter spoke, and Hak translated. "This is Tukana Prat, our ambassador to your world."

"Ambassador, Mr. Boddit, I'll have to ask both of you to come with me."

Ponter didn't move. "Are we unwelcome here?"

"Not at all," said Donaldson. "Indeed, I'm sure our government will be happy to recognize the Ambassador, and grant you both full diplomatic courtesy. But for now, you must come with me."

Ponter frowned. "Where are you taking us?"

Donaldson gestured toward the door leading out from the deck. It was currently closed. Ponter shrugged, and he and Tukana walked toward it. One of the other soldiers moved ahead and opened the door. They entered a cramped, narrow control room. "Keep moving ahead quickly, please," said Donaldson.

Ponter and Tukana did so. "As you may remember, Mr. Boddit," said Donaldson, walking behind them, "the Sudbury Neutrino Observatory is located sixty-eight hundred feet below the ground, and is maintained in clean-room conditions, to prevent the introduction of any dust or other contaminants that might affect the detector equipment."

Ponter looked back briefly at Donaldson but continued to walk.

"Well," continued Donaldson, "we have beefed up the facilities even more, on the chance that you or others of your kind might return. I'm afraid you're going to have to be quarantined here until we're sure it's safe to let you up to the surface."

"Not again!" said Ponter. "We can prove that we are free of contamination."

"That's not my judgment call to make, sir," said Donaldson. "But the people who *can* make it are on their way here even as we speak."

Chapter Eleven

Mary Vaughan was bent over a microscope when the door to her lab at the Synergy Group burst open. "Mary!"

She looked up, and saw Louise Benoît standing in the doorway. "Yes?"

"Ponter is back!"

Mary's heart started pounding. "Really?"

"Yes! I just heard it on the radio. The portal between the universes has reopened at SNO, and Ponter and another Neanderthal have come over to our side."

Mary got up and looked at Louise. "Fancy a drive to Sudbury?"

Louise smiled, as if she'd expected such an offer. "There's no point. The Neanderthals are being quarantined down in the SNO facility; there's no way we could get down to see them."

"Oh," said Mary. She tried not to sound disappointed.

"But they're coming to New York City to speak at the UN once they're released."

"Really? How far is that from here?"

"I don't know. Five or six hundred kilometers, I suppose. Closer than it is from here to Sudbury, anyway."

"I've been meaning to try to get down to see *The Producers* . . ." said Mary, with a grin. But the grin soon faded. "Still, I probably won't be able to get to see Ponter there, either. He'll be tied up with all sorts of diplomatic stuff."

But Louise's tone was upbeat. "You're forgetting who you're working for, Mary. Our man Jock seems to have keys to open just about any door. Tell him you need to go down and collect some DNA samples from the Neanderthal accompanying Ponter."

Mary's smile returned. At that moment, she liked Louise very much indeed.

"Ponter Boddit, my man!"

Reuben Montego entered the two-room quarantine chamber, and held out a clenched fist. Ponter touched his own knuckles against Reuben's. "Reuben!" he declared, saying the name for himself. Then, Hak picking up on his behalf: "It is so good to see you again, my friend."

Ponter turned to Tukana and spoke quickly in the Neanderthal tongue. "Reuben's the physician here at the Creighton Mine. He's the one who first treated me when I almost drowned upon arriving here, and it was at his house that Mare Vaughan, Lou Benoît, and I were originally quarantined." Then, turning to Reuben, and with Hak once again translating: "Friend Reuben, this is Ambassador Tukana Prat."

Reuben smiled broadly—for a Gliksin—and executed a gallant bow. "Madam Ambassador," he said. "Welcome!"

"Thank you," said Tukana, via her own Companion implant, which had been upgraded to match Hak's capabilities. "I am delighted to be in this world." She looked around the small, austere room. "Although I *was* hoping to see more of it."

Reuben nodded. "We're working on that. We've got experts on the way from the Laboratory Centre for Disease Control in

Ottawa, and the Centers for Disease Control and Prevention in Atlanta. I understand you used some kind of laser-sterilization device. That's a new one on us, and our experts will have to be satisfied that it really works."

"Of course," said Ambassador Prat. "Although we look forward to establishing equitable trade with your world, we understand that this technology is one we must freely reveal. Your experts are welcome to travel over to our side of the portal and examine the equipment. The equipment's designer, Dapbur Kajak, is on hand, and she will gladly explain its principles and subject it to any tests you require."

"Excellent," said Reuben. "Then we should get this all straightened away quite quickly."

Ponter waited until he was sure Reuben had finished with this topic, then he said, speaking for himself, "Where is Mare?"

Reuben smiled as if he'd anticipated the question. "She got hired up by some U.S. think tank. She's in Rochester, New York, now."

Ponter frowned. He'd hoped Mare would be here in Sudbury, but there was no reason for her to dally after Ponter had left. Her home, after all, hadn't been in this city. "How have you been, Reuben?" asked Ponter. It was a Gliksin peculiarity to constantly inquire after another's health, but Ponter knew it was the expected pleasantry.

"Me?" said Reuben. "I've been fine. I've had my fifteen minutes of fame, and frankly am glad it's over."

"Fifteen minutes?" repeated Tukana.

Reuben laughed. "An artist here once said that in the future, everyone will be famous for fifteen minutes."

"Ah," said Ponter. "What sort of artist?"

Reuben was clearly trying to suppress a grin. "Um, well, he was best known for painting pictures of soup cans."

"It sounds," said Ponter, "as though fifteen minutes might have been more than his fair share."

Reuben laughed again. "I've missed you, my friend."

A team from the LCDC arrived, followed shortly by one from the CDC. One woman from each organization became the first members of *Homo sapiens sapiens* to travel to the Neanderthal universe. Periodically, one or the other would stick her head through the end of the tunnel and ask for some equipment to be passed through to the other side.

Ponter tried to wait patiently, but it was frustrating. A whole alien world awaited them! Both he and Tukana had already given multiple samples of blood and tissues, as well as undergoing complete physical examinations by Reuben.

Despite the quarantine, Ponter and Tukana were not without visitors. The first nonmedical one was a pale Gliksin woman with short brown hair and small round glasses. "Hello," she said, with what Ponter recognized from his time with Lou Benoît as a French-Canadian accent, "My name is Hélène Gagné. I'm with Canada's Department of Foreign Affairs and International Trade."

Tukana stepped forward. "Ambassador Tukana Prat, representing the High Gray Council of—well, of Earth." She nodded at Ponter. "My associate, Scholar—and Envoy—Ponter Boddit."

"Greetings," said Hélène. "Delighted to meet you both. Envoy Boddit, we promise things will go a little more smoothly than on your last visit."

Ponter smiled. "Thank you."

"Before we proceed further, Madam Ambassador, I'd like to ask you a question. I understand the geography of your world and this one are the same, correct?"

Tukana Prat nodded.

"All right," said Hélène. She was carrying a small briefcase. She opened it, and removed a simple world map that showed only landforms but no borders. "Can you show me where you were born?"

Tukana Prat took the map, glanced at it, and pointed at a spot on the west coast of North America. Hélène handed her a felt-tipped marker, its cap removed. "Can you mark the spot—as precisely as possible, please?"

Tukana looked surprised at the request, but did so, putting a red dot on the northern tip of Vancouver Island. "Thank you," said Hélène. "Now, will you sign next to that spot?"

"Sign?"

"Umm, you know, write out your name."

Tukana Prat did so, drawing a series of angular symbols.

Hélène removed a notary's seal from the briefcase and embossed the map, then added her own signature and date. "All right, that's what we were hoping would be the case. You were born in Canada."

"I was born in Podnilak," said Tukana.

"Yes, yes, but that's in what corresponds to Canada—to Vancouver Island, British Columbia, to be precise—on this world. That makes you, by all established law, a Canadian. And we already know that Envoy Boddit was born near Sudbury, Ontario. So, if you and Envoy Boddit don't object, the first thing we're going to do after you leave quarantine is bestow Canadian citizenship on the two of you."

"Why?" asked Tukana Prat.

But before Hélène could answer, Ponter spoke up. "This matter was raised during my first trip. One requires documents to travel between nations on this version of Earth. The most important one"—he paused, while Hak reminded him of the name—"is a passport, and you cannot have a passport without a citizenship."

"That's right," said Hélène. "We took a fair bit of heat from other governments, particularly the U.S., when you were last here because you were kept entirely in Canada. Well, once you're released from here, we'll take you to Ottawa—that's Canada's capital—where you will be made citizens under Section 5, Paragraph 4, of the Canadian Citizenship Act, which lets the minister grant citizenship to anyone in extraordinary circumstances. Don't worry: it won't affect your ability to remain citizens of whatever jurisdiction is appropriate in your world; Canada has always recognized dual citizenship. But when you travel outside of Canada, you will be registered as Canadian diplomats, and therefore afforded full diplomatic immunity and courtesy. That will let us cut through all sorts of red tape until formal relations are opened between each of our nations and your world."

"Each of your nations?" said Tukana. "We have a unified worldwide government now. Do you not have the same thing?"

Hélène shook her head. "No. We have something called the 'United Nations'—we'll be taking you to the UN headquarters right after you have a state dinner with our prime minister in Ottawa. But it isn't a world government; it's just a forum in which individual national governments can discuss matters of mutual concern. As time goes on, your government will have to be formally recognized by each of the nations that compose the UN."

"And how many of those are there?" asked Tukana.

Ponter smiled. "You are not going to believe this," he said.

"There are currently a hundred and ninety-one member states," said Hélène. "So you see, it will take years for your government to negotiate treaties and so forth with each of those nations. But Canada, of course, already has treaties with all of them, so by becoming Canadian diplomats, at least in name, you can travel to any of these countries and speak with their government leaders."

Tukana looked baffled. "I am sure that is all as it should be."

"It is."

"Great," said Ponter. "When do we get out of here?"

"Soon, I hope," said Hélène. "I can't leave the SNO chamber myself now, until the two of you are cleared. But the doctors seem impressed by what they've seen of your decontamination technology."

That news delighted Ponter, since it sounded like they'd be released shortly—he'd spent almost all of his last trip to Canada quarantined, after all, and didn't look forward to more of the same, especially deep underground.

That afternoon, Tukana retired to the second of the two rooms in the quarantine suite. Like many people of her generation, she seemed to enjoy a nap. Ponter busied himself practicing his English with Hak's help until Reuben Montego returned, accompanied by a short, hairy, beige male Gliksin, his appearance quite a contrast to Reuben's dark skin and completely shaved head. "Hey, Ponter," said Reuben. "This is Arnold Moore, a geologist."

"Hello," said Ponter.

Arnold extended his hand, which Ponter took. "Dr. Boddit," he said, "it's a real pleasure to meet you. A real pleasure!"

Boredom had taken its toll; Ponter could not resist a little sarcasm. "Are you sure it is safe to touch me?"

But the comment was lost on Arnold. "Oh, I've been wanting to come down from the first moment I heard you were here! This is an absolute treat. An absolute treat!"

iled wanly. “Thank you,” he said.

,” said Arnold, indicating the chair Ponter had risen

lease sit down.”

onter did so, and Arnold turned around another chair d straddled it, with his arms crossed on top of the chair’s upright part, which was now in front of him. Ponter felt his eyebrow going up; that looked like a more comfortable way to sit. He got up again and rotated his own chair, sitting on it in a similar fashion. It wasn’t as nice as a proper saddle-seat, but this posture certainly was an improvement.

Reuben excused himself and headed off to confer with the immunologists who were crawling all over the facility.

“I have a question to ask you,” said Arnold.

Ponter nodded for him to continue.

“We’ve noted something unusual happening to this version of Earth,” said the geologist, “and I was wondering if you could tell me if the same thing is happening on your version?”

“What?”

“Well, the aurora borealis—and the aurora australis, too—have been acting up.”

Ponter was quite surprised. “No, nothing like that is currently occurring. In fact, I saw the night lights last evening; they were perfectly normal.”

Arnold looked disappointed. “We were hoping you guys would have some insight. Our best guess is that Earth’s magnetic field is collapsing, and the poles are perhaps going to reverse.”

Ponter raised his eyebrow again, rolling it up his browridge. “When was the last time something like that happened here?”

“I’m not sure off the top of my head. Many thousands of years ago.”

“There have been no field collapses since?”

"No."

"Fascinating. We had one—Hak?"

"Six years ago," said Hak, through his external speaker.

"You mean it *ended* six years ago?"

"Yes."

"But it must have started centuries earlier."

Ponter shook his head. "It started twenty-five years ago."

"Let me get this straight," said Arnold, eyes wide. "Your entire field collapse took just—what?—nineteen years?"

"That is correct," said Ponter. "Up until twenty-five years ago, the magnetic field was at its normal strength. Then it collapsed; the planet did not have any appreciable magnetic field for the next nineteen years. And then, six years ago, the field popped back up."

" 'Popped up'?" repeated Arnold, astonished. "No, you must be joking."

"When I joke," said Ponter, "I strive to be much funnier."

"But . . . but . . . we've always believed the magnetic field would take hundreds, and probably thousands, of years to collapse."

"Why?"

"Well, you know, because of the size of the Earth."

"The sun's magnetic field reverses every hundred and forty months or so—every eleven years—and the sun is about a million times the size of Earth."

"Yes, but . . ."

"I do not mean to sound grayer than you," said Ponter. "We knew very little about field collapses, too, until we actually experienced one happening. Some of our geologists were astonished by the rapidity, as well."

"Geomagnetic collapse and reestablishment in less than two decades," said Arnold. "Incredible."

"It was an interesting time to do physics," said Ponter. "Our people learned a great deal about the—the process by which the field . . . you must have a word for it?"

Arnold nodded. "The geodynamo."

Ponter frowned; another *ee* phoneme. But he let Hak take care of supplying it as needed; it was only proper names that Ponter had his Companion repeat exactly as he spoke them. "Yes. We learned much about the geodynamo."

"We'd love to hear what you know," said Arnold.

Ponter was glad that Tukana was asleep; he'd probably given away too much information already. But this concept of trading data—it upset the scientist in him. All data should be freely exchanged. Still, he decided to shift the topic slightly. "Is Inco worried that the demand for nickel will abate during the period of collapse?" Nickel was widely used in compasses on both versions of Earth—and the deposit here in Sudbury was one of the world's largest.

"What? Hmm, I hadn't even thought about that," said Arnold.

Ponter was confused. "Reuben said you were a geologist . . . ?"

"Yes, I am," said Arnold, "but I don't work for Inco. I'm with Environment Canada. I flew here from Ottawa as soon as word came that contact with your world had been reestablished."

"Ah," said Ponter, still not understanding.

"My job is protecting the environment," said Arnold.

"Is that not *everyone's* job?" asked Ponter, being, he knew, a bit disingenuous.

But again the subtlety was lost on Arnold. "Yes, indeed," he said. "Yes, indeed. But I wanted to find out what your people might know about environmental effects associated with magnetic-field collapses. I was hoping you might have some data from the fossil record—but to have complete studies of a recent collapse! That's fabulous."

"There were no appreciable environmental effects," said Ponter. "Some migratory birds were confused, but that was about it."

"I suppose they would be, at that," said Arnold. "How did they adapt?"

"The affected birds have a powerfully magnetic substance in their brains . . ."

"Magnetite," supplied Arnold. "Lodestone. Three iron atoms and four oxygens."

"Yes," said Ponter. "Other kinds of birds navigate by the stars, and some individuals of the species that use brain magnetite for determining direction turned out to be able to use the stars, too. It is ever the way in nature: variation within a population provides vigor when the environment changes, and most crucial capabilities have a backup system."

"Fascinating," said Arnold. "Fascinating. Tell me, though: how did you originally determine that Earth's magnetic field does, in fact, periodically reverse? That's a fairly new insight for us."

"The alternation of the planet's magnetic-field polarity is recorded at meteor-impact sites."

"It is?" said Arnold, his one long eyebrow—how refreshing to see someone who looked normal, at least in that regard!—rising up his forehead.

"Yes," said Ponter. "When an iron-nickel meteor slams into the Earth, the impact aligns the meteor's magnetic field."

Arnold frowned. "I suppose it would, at that. Just like hitting an iron bar with a hammer and turning it into a magnet."

"Exactly," said Ponter. "But if you did not learn of this from meteorites, how did your people come to know that Earth's magnetic field periodically reverses?"

"Sea-floor spreading," replied Arnold.

"What?" said Ponter

"Do you know about plate tectonics?" asked Arnold. "You know, continental drift?"

"The continents drift?" said Ponter, making his face agog. But then he held up a hand. "No, that time I *was* making a joke. Yes, my people know this. After all, the coastlines of Ranilass and Podlar clearly once were attached to each other."

"You must mean South America and Africa," said Arnold, nodding. He smiled ruefully. "Yes, you'd think it would be blindingly obvious to everyone, but it took decades for our people to accept the notion."

"Why?"

Arnold spread his arms. "You're a scientist; surely you understand. The old guard thought they knew how the world worked, and they weren't about to give up their theories. As with so many paradigm shifts, it wasn't really a case of convincing anyone to change their minds. Rather, it was waiting for the previous generation to pass on."

Ponter tried to conceal his astonishment. What an extraordinary approach to science these Gliksins had!

"In any event," continued Arnold, "we ultimately found proof for continental drift. At the middle of the oceans there are places where magma wells up from the mantle, forming new rock."

"We surmised such things must exist," said Ponter. "After all, since there are places where old rock is pushed down—"

"Subduction zones," supplied Arnold.

"As you say," said Ponter. "If there are places where old rocks go down, we knew there must be places where new rock comes up, although, of course, we have never seen them."

"We've taken core samples from them," said Arnold.

Ponter's face went honestly agog this time. "In the middle of the oceans?"

"Yes, indeed," said Arnold, clearly glad for once that his side was coming out ahead. "And if you look at rocks on both sides of the rifts from which magma is welling up, you see symmetrical patterns of magnetism—normal on either side of the rift, reversed equal distances to the left and right of the rift, normal again on either side but farther out, and so on."

"Impressive," said Ponter.

"We have our moments," said Arnold. He grinned, and was clearly inviting Ponter to do the same.

"Sorry?" said Ponter.

"It's a pun; a play on words. You know: 'magnetic moment'—the product of the distance between a magnet's poles and the strength of either pole."

"Ah," said Ponter. This Gliksin obsession with word play . . . he would never understand it.

Arnold looked disappointed. "Anyway," he said, "I'm surprised that your magnetic field collapsed before ours did. I mean, I understand the Benoît model: that this universe split from your universe forty thousand years ago, at the dawn of consciousness. Fine. But I can't see how anything your people or mine might have done in the last four hundred centuries could have possibly affected the geodynamo."

"It *is* puzzling," agreed Ponter.

Arnold clambered off his chair and rose to his feet. "Still, because of it, you've been able to satisfy my particular concern better than I would have thought possible."

Ponter nodded. "I am glad. You should indeed—how would you phrase it?—you should sail effortlessly through the period of magnetic-field collapse." He blinked. "After all, we certainly did."

Chapter Twelve

Mary tried to concentrate on her work, but her thoughts kept turning to Ponter—not surprisingly, she supposed, since Ponter's DNA was precisely what she was working on.

Mary cringed every time she read a popular article that tried to explain why mitochondrial DNA is only inherited from the maternal line. The explanation usually given was that only the heads of sperm penetrate eggs, and only the midsections and tails of sperm contain mitochondria. But although it was true that mitochondria were indeed deployed that way in sperm, it wasn't true that only the head made it into the ovum. Microscopy and DNA analyses both proved that mtDNA from the sperm's midsection does end up in fertilized mammalian eggs. The truth was no one knew why the paternal mitochondrial DNA isn't incorporated into the zygote the way maternal mitochondrial DNA is; for some reason it just disappears, and the explanation that it had never gotten in there in the first place was nice and pat, but absolutely not true.

Still, since there were thousands of mitochondria in each cell, and only one nucleus, it was much easier to recover mitochondrial rather than nuclear DNA from ancient specimens. No nuclear DNA had ever been extracted from any of the Neanderthal fossils known from Mary's Earth, and so Mary had been concentrating on studying Ponter's mitochondrial DNA, comparing and contrasting it with Gliksin mtDNA. But there didn't seem to be any one sequence she could point to that was present in Ponter and the known fossil Neanderthal mitochondrial DNA, but in none of the Gliksins, or vice versa.

And so Mary at last turned her attention to Ponter's nuclear DNA. She'd thought it would be even more difficult to find a difference there, and indeed, despite much searching, she hadn't found any sequence of nucleotides that was reliably different between Neanderthals and *Homo sapiens sapiens;* all her primers matched strings on DNA from both kinds of humans.

Bored and frustrated, waiting for Ponter to be released from quarantine, waiting to renew their friendship, Mary decided to make a karyotype of Neanderthal DNA. That meant culturing some of Ponter's cells to the point where they were about to divide (since that's the only time that chromosomes become visible), then exposing them to colchicine to immobilize the chromosomes at that stage. Once that was done, Mary stained the cells—the word "chromosomes," after all, meant "colored bodies," referring to their tendency to easily pick up dye. She then sorted the chromosomes in descending order of size, which was the usual sequence for numbering them. Ponter was male, and so had both an X and a Y chromosome, and, just as in a male of Mary's kind, the Y was only about one-third the size of the X.

Mary arrayed all the pairs, photographed them, and printed out the photo on an Epson inkjet printer. She then started labeling the pairs, beginning with the longest, and working her way to the shortest: 1, 2, 3 . . .

It was straightforward work, the kind of exercise she'd put her cytogenetics students through each year. Her mind wandered a bit while she was doing it: she found herself thinking about Ponter and Adikor and mammoths and a world without agriculture and . . .

Damn!

She'd obviously screwed up somehow, since Ponter's X and Y chromosomes were the twenty-fourth pair, not the twenty-third.

Unless . . .

My God, unless he actually had *three* chromosome 21s—in which case he, and presumably all his people, had what in her kind produced Down's syndrome. That made some sense; those with Down's had an array of facial morphologies that differed from other humans, and—

Good grief, thought Mary, *could it be so simple?* Down's sufferers did have an increased incidence of leukemia . . . and wasn't that what Ponter said had killed his wife? Also, Down's syndrome was associated with abnormal levels of thyroid hormones, and those were well-known to affect morphology—especially facial morphology. Could it be that Ponter's people all had trisomy 21—one small change, manifesting itself slightly differently in them than it did in *Homo sapiens sapiens,* accounting for all the differences between the two kinds of humans?

But no. No, that didn't make sense. Principal among Down's effects, at least in *Homo sapiens sapiens,* was an *under*-development of muscle tone; Ponter's people had exactly the opposite condition.

And, besides, Mary had spread out an even number of chromosomes in front of her; Down's syndrome resulted from an odd number. Unless she'd accidentally brought some chromosomes in from another cell, it appeared that Ponter did indeed have twenty-four pairs, and . . .

Oh, my God, thought Mary. *Oh, my God.*

It was even *more* simple than she'd thought.

Yes, yes, *yes!*

She had it!

She had the answer.

Homo sapiens sapiens had twenty-three pairs of chromosomes. But their nearest relatives, at least on this Earth, were the two species of chimpanzees, and—

And both species of chimps had *twenty-four* pairs of chromosomes.

Genus *Pan* (the chimps) and Genus *Homo* (humans of all types, past and present) shared a common ancestor. Despite the popular fallacy that humans had evolved from apes, in fact, apes and humans were *cousins.* The common ancestor—the elusive missing link, not yet conclusively identified in the fossil record—had existed, according to studies of the genetic divergence between humans and apes, something like five million years ago in Africa.

Since chimps had twenty-four pairs of chromosomes and humans had twenty-three, it was anyone's guess as to what number the common ancestor had possessed. If it had had twenty-three, well, then, sometime after the ape-human split, one chromosome must have become two in the chimp line. If, on the other hand, it had had twenty-four, then two chromosomes must have fused together somewhere along the *Homo* line.

Until today—until right now, until this very second—no one on Mary's Earth had known for sure which scenario was correct. But now it was crystal clear: common chimps had twenty-four pairs of chromosomes; bonobos—the other kind of chimp—had twenty-four as well. And now Mary knew that Neanderthals also had an even two dozen. The consolidation of two chromosomes into one had happened long after the ape-human split; indeed, it had happened sometime after the *Homo* branch had bifurcated into the two lines she was now studying, only a couple of hundred thousand years ago.

That was why Ponter's people still had the huge strength of apes, rather than the puniness of humans. That was why they had ape physiognomy, with browridges and no chins. Genetically, they *were* apelike, at least in chromosome count. And something about the fusing of two chromosomes—it was numbers two and three, Mary knew, from studies of primate genetics she'd read years before—had caused the morphological differences that gave rise to the adult human form.

Indeed, the particular cause of the differences was easy enough to identify: it was neoteny, the retention into adulthood of childhood characteristics. Baby apes, baby Neanderthals, and baby Gliksins all had similar skulls, with vertical, ridgeless foreheads, and no particular protrusion of the lower face. As the other kinds grew, their skull shapes changed. But Mary's kind alone retained their childlike crania into adulthood.

But Ponter's people *did* mature cranially. And the differing chromosome count might be the cause.

Mary pressed her two hands together in front of her face. She had done it! She had found what Jock Krieger wanted, and—

And . . . *my God.*

If the chromosome counts differed, then Neanderthals and her flavor of *Homo sapiens* weren't just different races, or even just subspecies of the same species. They were fully separate species. No need to double up the "wisdom" part in *Homo sapiens sapiens* to distinguish Mary's kind from Ponter's, for Ponter's people couldn't possibly be *Homo sapiens neanderthalensis.* Rather, they were clearly their own specific taxon, *Homo neanderthalensis.* Mary could think of some paleoanthropologists who would be thrilled by this news—and others who would be extremely pissed off.

But . . .

But . . .

But Ponter belonged to another species! Mary had seen *Showboat* when it was on stage in Toronto; Cloris Leachman had played Parthy. She knew that miscegenation was once a big issue, but . . .

But miscegenation wasn't the appropriate term for a human mating with something from outside her own species—not that Ponter and Mary had done that, of course.

No, the appropriate term was . . .

My God, thought Mary.

Was bestiality.

But . . .

No, no.

Ponter wasn't a beast. The man who had raped her—Mary's conspecific, a member of *Homo sapiens*—had been a beast. But Ponter was no animal.

He was a gentleman.

A gentle man.

And, regardless of chromosome count, he was a human being—a human being she was very much looking forward to seeing again.

Chapter Thirteen

Finally, after three days, the specialists from the Laboratory Centre for Disease Control and the Centers for Disease Control and Prevention—the comparable U.S. agency—agreed that Ambassador Tukana Prat and Envoy Ponter Boddit were free of infection and could leave quarantine.

Ponter and Tukana, accompanied by five soldiers and Dr. Montego, trudged down the mining tunnel to the metal-cage elevator, and made the long ride to the surface. Apparently, word had preceded them that they were on the way up; a large number of miners and other Inco workers had assembled in the huge room up top that contained the elevator station.

"There is a crowd of reporters waiting in the parking lot," said Hélène Gagné. "Ambassador Prat, you'll need to make a brief statement, of course."

Tukana lifted her eyebrow. "What sort of statement?"

"A greeting. You know, the usual diplomatic thing."

Ponter had no idea what that meant, but, then again, it wasn't his job. Hélène led Tukana and him out of the large room and through the doors into the Sudbury autumn. It was at least two degrees hotter than the world Ponter had left behind, maybe more, but, of course, three days had passed while they were underground; the difference in temperature didn't necessarily mean anything.

Still, Ponter shook his head in amazement. He'd never exited this place while conscious before; the only previous time he'd come up from the mine, he'd been knocked out with a head wound. But now he had a chance to really see the giant mining site, the great tear in the ground these humans had made; the huge stretches of land from which all trees had been cleared; the vast—"parking lot," they called it, covered with hundreds of personal vehicles.

And the smell! He reeled at the overpowering stench of this world, the nauseating reek. Adikor's woman, Lurt, had explained the likely sources of the odors, based on Ponter's descriptions of them: nitrogen dioxide, sulfur dioxide, and other poisons given off by the burning of petrochemicals.

Ponter had warned Tukana about what to expect, and she was discreetly trying to cover her nose with her hand. Still, as much as he fondly remembered the people here, Ponter had forgotten—or suppressed—his memories of what a truly awful job they had done of looking after their version of the planet.

Jock Krieger sat at his desk, surfing the two Webs—the public one, and the vast array of classified government sites, available over dedicated fiber-optic lines, that only those with appropriate security clearance could access.

Jock had never liked it when something came up that he didn't understand; the only thing that made him feel a lack of control was ignorance. And so he was trying to rectify that by searching for information about geomagnetic collapses, especially with the word from Sudbury that apparently such things happened very quickly.

Jock had expected there to be thousands of Web pages devoted to this topic, and although all the news sites had cobbled together something in the last week, mostly regurgitating the same three or four "expert" opinions, there were really very few concrete studies of this phenomenon. Indeed, about half the hits he found on the World Wide Web were so-called creation scientists trying to explain away the evidence for prehistoric geomagnetic reversals, apparently because the sheer number of them would have taken up too much time if the Earth was only a few thousand years old.

But a citation for one real paper caught Jock's eye, a 1989 piece from *Earth and Planetary Science Letters* called "Evidence Suggesting Extremely Rapid Field Variation During a Geomagnetic Reversal." The authors were listed as Robert S. Coe and Michel Prévot, the former from the University of California at Santa Cruz, and the latter from the *Université des Sciences et Techniques* at Montpellier—the one in France, Jock presumed, rather than the one in Vermont. UCSC was definitely a legit institution, and the other one—a few clicks of the mouse—yes, it was on the up-and-up, too. But the damn article wasn't online; like so much of the world's wisdom pre-1990, apparently no one had bothered to computerize it. Jock sighed. He'd have to go to an actual library to get a copy.

Mary went down the corridor, then down the staircase, to Jock Krieger's office on the first floor. She knocked, waited for him to call out "Come in," and then did just as he had said.

"I've got it," said Mary.

"Well, then, keep your distance," said Jock, closing his Web-browser window.

Mary was too excited even to get the joke then, although it came to her later that day. "I've figured out how to distinguish Gliksins from Neanderthals."

Jock rose from his Aeron chair. "Are you sure?"

"Yes," said Mary. "It's a piece of cake. Neanderthals have twenty-four pairs of chromosomes, whereas we have only twenty-three. It's a glaring difference, as big on the genetic level as the difference between male and female."

Jock's gray eyebrows arched up toward his pompadour. "If it was that obvious, what took so long?"

Mary explained her misguided preoccupation with mitochondrial DNA.

"Ah," said Jock, nodding. "Good work. Very good work."

Mary smiled, but her smile soon faded. "The Paleoanthropology Society is having its annual meeting in a couple of weeks," she said. "I'd like to present my Neanderthal karyotype there. Someone else is bound to make one sooner or later, but I'd like to get priority."

Krieger frowned. "I'm sorry, Mary, but you're under a nondisclosure agreement here."

Mary was gearing up for a fight. "Yes, but—"

Jock raised a hand. "No, you're right. Sorry. It's hard to get out of the RAND mode. Yes, of course, you can present your discovery. The world has a right to know."

Hélène Gagné looked out at the hundreds of journalists who had gathered in the Creighton Mine parking lot. "Ladies and gentlemen," she said, speaking into a microphone on a telescoping stand, "thank you for coming. On behalf of the people of Ontario, the people of Canada, and the people of the world, it's my pleasure to welcome the two emissaries from the parallel version of Earth. I know some of you in the media already are acquainted with Dr. Ponter Boddit, who now has the title of 'Envoy.' " She made a gesture at Ponter, and, after a moment, Ponter realized he should probably acknowledge it somehow. He lifted his right hand and waved enthusiastically which, for some reason, prompted amusement amongst the Gliksin journalists.

"And this," continued Hélène, "is the ambassador, Ms. Tukana Prat. I'm sure she has a few words for us." Hélène looked expectantly at Tukana, who, after some additional gesturing by Hélène, moved to the microphone.

"We are glad to be here," said Tukana. She then politely backed away from the mike.

Hélène looked mortified, and quickly took Tukana's place. "What Ambassador Prat means," she said, "is that on behalf of her people, she is pleased to open formal contact with our people, and looks forward to a productive and mutually beneficial dialogue on matters of common concern." She turned to Tukana, beseeching approval for these comments. Tukana nodded. Hélène went on. "And she hopes that her people and ours can find numerous opportunities for trade and cultural exchange." She again looked at Tukana; the female Neanderthal at least didn't seem inclined to object. "And she'd like to thank Inco, the Sudbury Neutrino Observatory, the mayor and council of the city of Sudbury, the government of Canada, and the United Nations, where she will be speaking tomorrow, for their hospitality." She looked once more at Tukana, gesturing at the mike. "Isn't that right?"

Tukana hesitated for a moment, then moved back to the microphone stand. "Um, yes. What she said."

The journalists howled.

Hélène leaned close to Tukana and put a hand over the mike, but Ponter could hear her anyway. "We have got a *lot* of work to do before tomorrow," she said.

After Mary left his office, Jock Krieger looked out his window. He'd had his pick of office space, of course. Most would have opted for the lake view, but that meant looking north, away from the United States. Jock's window faced south, but since the mansion housing the Synergy Group was on a spit of land, Jock's view did include a lovely marina. He steepled his fingers in front of his face, stared out at his world, and thought.

Tukana and Ponter were both astonished by the Canadian Forces jet that took them to Ottawa. Although their people had developed helicopters, jet planes were unknown on the Neanderthal world.

After Tukana got over the shock of being airborne, she turned to Hélène. "I am sorry," said the ambassador. "I believe I did not live up to your requirements earlier today."

Hélène frowned. "Well, let's just say that humans here expect a little more pomp and circumstance."

Tukana's translator bleeped twice.

"You know," said Hélène, "a little more ceremony, some more kind words."

"But you said nothing of substance," said Tukana.

Hélène smiled. "Exactly. The prime minister is quite easygoing; you won't have any trouble with him tonight. But tomorrow you'll face the General Assembly of the United Nations, and they'll expect you to speak at some length." She paused. "Forgive me, but I thought you were a career diplomat?"

"I am," said Tukana, defensively. "I have spent time in Evsoy and Ranilass and Nalkanu, representing the interests of Saldak. But we try to get to the point as quickly as possible in such discussions."

"Don't you worry about offending people by being brusque?"

"That is why ambassadors travel to these places instead of doing negotiations by telecommunications. It allows us to smell the pheromones of those we are talking with, and them to smell ours."

"Does that work when you're addressing a large group?"

"Oh, yes. I have had negotiations that have involved ten people or even eleven."

Hélène felt her jaw dropping. "You will be speaking before eighteen hundred people tomorrow. Will you be able to detect whether you are giving offense to anyone in a group that large?"

"Not unless the offended individual happens to be one of those closest to me."

"Then, if you don't mind, I'd like to give you a few pointers."

Tukana nodded. "As I believe you would say, I am all ears."

Chapter Fourteen

Mary had returned to her second-floor lab, and was now sitting in a black leather swivel chair, the kind of lush executive furnishings never found in a professor's university office. She had swung around, away from her desk, and was looking out the large north-facing window at Lake Ontario. She knew Toronto was opposite Rochester, but even on a clear day she couldn't see it from here; the far shore was beyond the horizon. The world's tallest freestanding structure, the CN Tower, was right on Toronto's lakeshore. She'd half hoped it, at least, would stick up over the curve of the Earth's surface, but . . .

But she remembered Ponter saying that it had been a mistake to have his Companion implant, Hak, programmed with his dead wife's voice. Instead of giving comfort, it had been a painful reminder of things lost. Perhaps it was just as well that Mary couldn't see any part of Toronto through her window.

Seabreeze had been a delightful place in the summer, she'd been told, but now that fall was beginning, it was getting fairly grim. Mary had become partial to the news on WROC, the local CBS affiliate, but every weather forecast she had heard used the term "lake effect"—something she'd never encountered when she'd lived on the north side of the same lake. Toronto was reasonably snow-free in winter, but apparently Rochester got hammered with the white stuff, thanks to cool air moving down from Canada picking up moisture as it traveled over Lake Ontario.

Mary got a coffee mug, filled it with her favorite potion of Maxwell House laced with chocolate milk, and took a sip. She'd become quite taken with Upstate Dairy's Extreme Chocolate Milk, which, like the fabulous Heluva Good French Onion Dip, wasn't available in Toronto. There were, she supposed, a few compensations for being away from home . . .

Mary's reverie was broken by the phone on her desk ringing. She put down her coffee mug. There were very few people who had her number here—and it wasn't an internal Synergy Group call; those were heralded by a different ring.

She picked up the black handset. "Hello?"

"Professor Vaughan?" said a woman's voice.

"Yes?"

"It's Daria."

Mary felt her spirits lifting. Daria Klein—her grad student, back at York University. Of course, Mary had given her new phone number to her old department; after leaving them in the lurch just before the beginning of classes, it had been the least she could do.

"Daria!" exclaimed Mary. "How good to hear from you!" Mary pictured the slim brown-haired girl's angular, smiling face.

"It's nice to hear your voice, too," said Daria. "I hope you don't mind me phoning. I didn't just want to send an e-mail about this." She could practically hear Daria jumping up and down.

"About what?"

"About Ramses!"

Mary's first thought was to quip, "You know, they're only ninety-seven percent effective," but she didn't. Daria was obviously referring to the ancient Egyptian body whose DNA she'd been working on. "I take it the results are in," said Mary.

"Yes, yes! It is indeed a member of the Ramses line—presumably Ramses the First! Chalk up another success for the Vaughan Technique!"

Mary probably blushed a bit. "That's great," she said. But it was Daria who had done the painstaking sequencing. "Congratulations."

"Thanks," said Daria. "The people at Emory are delighted."

"Wonderful," said Mary. "Great work. I'm really proud of you."

"Thanks," said Daria again.

"So," said Mary, "how are things at York?"

"Same old same old," said Daria. "The teaching assistants are talking about going on strike, the Yeomen are getting slaughtered, and the provincial government has announced more cutbacks."

Mary gave a rueful laugh. "Sorry to hear that."

"Yeah, well," said Daria, "you know." She paused. "The real scary news is that a woman was raped on campus earlier this week. It was written up in the *Excalibur*."

Mary's heart stopped for a second. "My God," she said. She swiveled her chair back to look out the window again, visualizing York.

"Yeah," said Daria. "It happened near here, too—near Farquharson."

"Did they say who the victim was?"

"No. No details were given."

"Did they catch the rapist?"

"Not yet."

Mary took a deep breath. "Be careful, Daria. Be very careful."

"I will," said Daria. "Josh is meeting me here after work every day." Josh—Mary never could remember his last name—

was Daria's boyfriend, a law student at Osgoode Hall.

"Good," said Mary. "That's good."

"Anyway," said Daria, her tone one of determination to move things back to a lighter note, "I just wanted to let you know about Ramses. I'm sure there's going to be a fair bit of press coverage for it. Someone's coming by the lab tomorrow from the CBC."

"That's great," said Mary, her mind racing.

"I'm really pumped," agreed Daria. "This is *so* cool."

Mary smiled. It was indeed.

"Anyway, I'll let you go," said Daria. "I just wanted to bring you up to date. Talk to you again!"

" 'Bye," said Mary.

" 'Bye," repeated Daria, and the phone went dead.

Mary tried to put down the handset, but her hand was shaking, and she missed the cradle.

Another rape.

But did that mean another rapist?

Or . . . or . . . or . . .

Or was the monster, the animal, the one she had failed to report, striking again?

Mary felt her stomach turning over, as though she were in an airplane locked in a nosedive.

Damn it. God damn it.

If she had reported the rape—if she'd alerted the police, the campus newspaper . . .

Yes, it had been weeks since she herself had been attacked. There was no reason to think it was the same rapist. But, on the other hand, how long does the thrill, the high, of violating someone last? How long does it take to muster the courage—the awful, soul-destroying courage—to commit such a crime again?

Mary had warned Daria. Not just now, but early on, via

e-mail from Sudbury, Ontario. But Daria was only one of thousands of women at York, one of . . .

Mary had co-taught with the Women's Studies Department; she knew the correct feminist phraseology was that all adult females were *women.* But Mary was thirty-nine now—her birthday had come and gone, unremarked by anyone—and frosh at York were as young as eighteen. Oh, they were indeed women . . . but they were also girls, at least in comparison to Mary, many away from home for the first time, just beginning to find their way in life.

And a beast was preying on them. A beast that, perhaps, she had let get away.

Mary looked out the window again, but this time she was glad she couldn't see Toronto.

A while later—Mary had no real idea how long—the door to her lab opened, and Louise Benoît stuck her head through. "Hey, Mary, how 'bout some dinner?"

Mary swiveled her leather chair to look at Louise.

"Mon dieu," exclaimed Louise. *"Qu'est-ce qu'il y a de mal?"*

Mary knew enough French to understand the question. "Nothing. Why do you ask?"

Louise, switching to English, sounded as though she couldn't believe Mary's response. "You've been crying."

Mary absently lifted a hand to her cheek and drew it away. She felt her eyebrows go up in astonishment. "Oh," she said softly, not knowing what else to fill the quiet with.

"What's wrong?" asked Louise again.

Mary took a deep breath and let it out slowly. Louise was the closest thing she had to a friend here in the United States. And Keisha, the rape-crisis counselor she'd spoken to in Sudbury, seemed light-years away. But . . .

But no. She didn't want to talk about it; didn't want to give voice to her pain.

Or her guilt.

Still, she had to say something. "It's nothing," Mary said at last. "It's just . . ." She found a box of Wegman's tissues on her desk and wiped her cheeks. "It's just *men,*" she said.

Louise nodded sagely, as if Mary was talking about some—what would she call it? Some *affaire de coeur* that had gone wrong. Louise, Mary suspected, had had a lot of boyfriends over the years. "Men," agreed Louise, rolling her brown eyes. "You can't live with them, and you can't live without them."

Mary was about to nod agreement, but, well, she had heard that on Ponter's world what Louise had just said wasn't true. And, Christ, Mary wasn't some schoolgirl—not that Louise was, either. "They're responsible for so many of the world's problems," said Mary.

Louise nodded at this, too, and seemed to pick up the change of emphasis. "Well, it certainly isn't women behind most terrorist attacks."

Mary had to agree with Louise about that, but . . . "But it's not just men in foreign countries. It's men *here*—in the U.S., and in Canada."

Louise's brow knitted in concern. "What happened?" she asked.

And, finally, Mary answered, at least in part. "I got a phone call from someone at York University. She said there'd been a rape on the campus."

"Oh my God," said Louise. "Anybody you know?"

Mary shook her head, although in fact she realized that she didn't know the answer to that. *God,* she thought, what if it had been someone she knew—someone who had been one of her students?

"No," said Mary, as if her headshake had been insufficient to convey her meaning. "But it depressed me." She looked at

Louise—so young, so pretty—then dropped her gaze. "It's such a terrible crime."

Louise nodded, and it was that same worldly, sage nod she'd given earlier as if—Mary felt a constriction in her stomach—as if, perhaps, Louise really did know whereof Mary was speaking. But Mary couldn't explore that further without revealing her own history, and she wasn't ready to do that—at least not yet. "Men can be so awful," said Mary. It sounded ditzy, Bridget-Jonesish, but it was *true.*

God damn it to hell, it was true.

Chapter Fifteen

Ponter Boddit and Tukana Prat were made (or reaffirmed as—legal opinions varied) Canadian citizens at Canada's Parliament Buildings late that afternoon. The ceremony was performed by the Federal Minister for Citizenship and Immigration, with journalists from all over the world in attendance.

Ponter had done his best with the oath, which he had memorized under Hélène Gagné's tutelage; he only mispronounced a few words: "I affirm that I will buh faithful and bear true alluh-jance to Her Maj-us-tuh Quen Uh-lizabeth the Second, Quen of Canada, Her Heirs and Successors, and that I will faithful-luh observe the laws of Canada and fulfill my doo-tays as a Can-ad-aye-un citizen." Hélène Gagné was so pleased with Ponter's performance that she spontaneously applauded at the end of the speech, earning her a stern look from the minister.

Tukana had more of a struggle saying the words, but did manage to get them out, as well.

After the ceremony, there was a wine-and-cheese reception—at which Hélène noted Ponter and Tukana partook of neither. They didn't drink milk or eat any milk-derived food; nor did they seem to have any interest in things made from grains. Hélène had wisely fed them prior to the ceremony, lest they make short work of the trays of fruit and cold cuts, which were also present. Ponter seemed to particularly like Montreal smoked meat.

Each of the Neanderthals had been presented not just with a certificate of Canadian citizenship, but also an Ontario health plan card and a passport. Tomorrow, they would fly to the United States. But there was still one more official duty for them to perform in Canada first.

"Did you enjoy your dinner with the Canadian prime minister?" asked Selgan, sitting on his saddle-seat in his round office.

Ponter nodded. "Very much so. There were many interesting people there. And we ate great thick steaks of cattle from Alberta—another part of Canada, apparently. And vegetables, too, some of which I recognized, and some I did not."

"I should like to try this cattle myself," said Selgan.

"It can be very good," said Ponter, "although it seems to be almost the only mammal meat they eat—that, and a form of boar they have created through selective breeding."

"Ah," said Selgan. "Well, I should like to try that, too, someday." He paused. "So, let us see where we stand. You had safely returned to the other world, but circumstances had prevented you from seeing Mare yet. Still, you had met with the highest officials of the country you were in. You had eaten well, and you were feeling . . . what? Contentment?"

"Yes, I suppose you could say that. But . . ."

"But what?" asked Selgan.

"But the contentment did not last for long."

After the dinner at 24 Sussex Drive, Ponter had been driven to the Chateau Laurier hotel, and had retired to his massive suite of rooms. They were—*opulent* was the correct English word, he thought; far more ornately decorated than anything back in his world.

Tukana was off with Hélène Gagné, going over yet again

what would be an appropriate presentation to make tomorrow at the United Nations. Ponter didn't have to say anything there, but nonetheless he spent the evening reading up about that institution.

Actually, that wasn't quite true: neither he nor Hak could yet read English, but he was using a clamshell computer provided by the Canadian government, which had some sort of encyclopedia loaded onto it. The encyclopedia had a text-to-speech feature that read in an irritating mechanical tone—certainly Ponter's people could teach the Gliksins a thing or two about voice synthesis. Anyway, Hak listened to the English words spoken by the computer, and then translated them into the Neanderthal tongue for Ponter.

Early in the article on the United Nations, there was a reference to the organization's "Charter," apparently its founding document. Ponter was horrified by its opening:

> We the Peoples of the United Nations determined to save succeeding generations from the scourge of war, which twice in our lifetime has brought untold sorrow to mankind...

Two wars—within a single human lifetime! There had been wars in the history of Ponter's world, but the last one was almost twenty thousandmonths ago. Still, it had been devastating, and the sorrow was certainly not untold (which Hak translated as "not counted"). Rather, every youngster was taught the horrible truth, that fully 719 people had died in that war.

Such devastating loss of life! And yet these Gliksins had fought not one but two wars in as little as a thousand moons.

Still, who knew how old this United Nations was? Perhaps the "lifetime" in question had been long ago. Ponter asked Hak to listen to more of the article, and see if he could find a founding date. He did: one-nine-four-five.

The current year, as the Gliksins tallied them, was two-something, wasn't it? "Exactly how long ago was that?" asked Ponter.

Hak told him, and Ponter felt himself sagging against his chair. The lifetime in question—the lifetime in which not one but two wars had ravaged humankind—was *this* lifetime.

Ponter wanted to know more about Gliksin war. Hélène had opened the encyclopedia to the entry on the United Nations for him before she'd left with Tukana, but Ponter managed slowly to work out the completely nonintuitive interface. "Which one is their word for 'war?' " he asked.

Hak did an analysis of the text he'd heard and the words that had been displayed on the computer's screen. "It is the sixth character-grouping in from the right on the ninth line of text."

Ponter used his fingertip to help him find the spot on the flat screen. "That can't be right," he said. "That grouping only has three symbols in it." The Neanderthal word for "war" was *mapartaltapa;* Ponter had often wished since coming here that he knew more about linguistics—what a help it would have been!—but one principle he did understand is that you reserved short terms for common concepts.

"I believe I am correct," said Hak. "The word is pronounced 'war.' "

"But—oh."

Ponter looked down at the—*keyboard,* that was the term. He managed to find a match for the first symbol, *w,* but couldn't find any that looked like *a* or *r.* "If you select the word," said Hak, "I believe it can be cross-referenced."

Ponter struggled with the touch-sensitive area in front of the keyboard, moving the little pine tree on screen until its apex touched the word, and after some experimentation, he got the word highlighted. On the left side of the screen, a list of topics appeared, and—

Ponter felt his jaw drop, as Hak read out the names.

The Gulf War.
The Korean War.
The Spanish Civil War.
The Spanish-American War.
The Vietnam War.
The War Between the States.
The War of 1812.
The War of the Roses.

On and on.

More and more.

And . . .

And . . .

Ponter's heart was fluttering.

World War I.
World War II.

Ponter wanted to swear, but the only epithets he had at his command were the ones his species had come up with: references to the putrefaction of meat, to the elimination of bodily wastes. None of those seemed suitable just now. Until this moment, he hadn't understood the Gliksin style of imprecations that invoked a putative higher power, calling on a superior being to make sense of the follies of man. But that really was the sort of expression needed here. The entire world at war! Ponter was almost afraid to look at the articles, afraid to hear what the death tolls had been. Why, they must have run into the thousands . . .

He moved his finger on the touch-sensitive pad, and let the encyclopedia speak to Hak.

In World War I, ten million soldiers had died.

And in World War II, fifty-five million people—soldiers and civilians both—had died, from causes variously termed "combat," "starvation," "bombing raids," "epidemics," "massacres," and "radiation,"—although what that last could possibly have to do with war, Ponter had no idea.

Ponter felt physically sick. He got up from his chair, moved over to the hotel room's window, and looked out at the nighttime panorama of this city, this Ottawa. Hélène had told him the tall edifice he could see from here on Parliament Hill was called the Peace Tower.

He opened the window as much as it would allow—which was not a lot—and let some of the wonderfully cold exterior air come in. Despite the smell, it calmed his stomach a bit, but he still found himself shaking his head back and forth over and over again.

He thought about the question his beloved Adikor had asked him upon his return from his first visit to this world: *"Are they good people, Ponter?* Should *we be in contact with them?"*

And Ponter had said yes. The fact that there was any further contact with this race of—of *murderers,* of warriors—was his own doing. But he'd seen so little of their world the first time, and . . .

No. He'd seen *plenty.* He'd seen what they'd done to the environment, how they'd destroyed vast tracts of land, how they bred unchecked. He'd known what they were, even then, but . . .

Ponter took another restorative inspiration of the chill air.

He had wanted to see Mare again. And that desire had blinded him to what he'd known about the Gliksins. His nausea wasn't caused by the shock of what he'd just learned, he knew. Rather, it was caused by the realization that he'd deliberately suppressed his own best judgment.

He looked again at the Peace Tower, tall and brown with some sort of timepiece near its apex, right at the heart of the seat of government for this country he was in. Perhaps . . . perhaps the Gliksins had changed. They'd created this organization he would visit tomorrow, this United Nations, specifically, so its charter had said, to *save* succeeding generations from the scourge of war.

Ponter left the window open, moved over to his bed—he doubted he'd ever get used to these elevated, soft beds the Gliksins favored—and lay down on his back, arms behind his head, staring at the swirling plaster patterns on the ceiling.

Ponter and Tukana, accompanied by Hélène Gagné and two plainclothes RCMP officers who were serving as bodyguards, were taken by limousine to Ottawa International Airport. The two Neanderthals had both been exhilarated by their earlier flight from Sudbury to Ottawa: neither of them had ever seen the terrain of Northern Ontario—which was the same mixture of pines and lakes and shield rocks as in their version of Earth—from such a wonderful vantage point.

At first, Ponter had felt some inferiority in light of all these advanced Gliksin technologies—airplanes and even spaceships. But his research last night had made him realize why these humans had progressed so much in these areas; he'd gone back to exploring various articles in the encyclopedia.

It *was* a central concept for them, deserving of its short designation.

War had made—

Even the phrases they used to describe these breakthroughs were martial.

War had made the conquest of air, the conquest of space, possible.

They pulled up to the terminal, Hak noting the irony of this term's double meaning. Ponter had thought the building the miners used for changing clothes was huge, but this massive structure was the largest enclosed interior space he had ever seen. And it was packed with people, and their pheromones. Ponter felt woozy, and also rather embarrassed: many people were openly staring at him and Tukana.

They dealt with some paperwork formalities—Ponter didn't quite follow the details—and then were led to an odd oversize wicket. Hélène told him and Tukana to remove their medical belts and send them down a conveyor, and also to empty the storage pouches on their clothing, which they did. And then, at Hélène's gesture, Ponter walked through the wicket.

An alarm immediately went off, startling Ponter.

Suddenly a uniformed man was waving some sort of probe over Ponter's body. The probe shrieked when passing over Ponter's left forearm. "Roll up your sleeve," said the man.

Ponter had never heard that expression before, but he guessed its meaning. He undid the closures on his sleeve, and folded back the fabric, revealing the metal and plastic rectangle of his Companion.

The man stared for a time at this, and then, almost to himself, he said, "We can rebuild him. We have the technology."

"Pardon?" asked Ponter.

"Nothing," said the man. "You can go on ahead."

The flight to New York City was quite brief—not even half a daytenth. Hélène had warned Ponter both on this flight and yesterday's that he might experience some discomfort as the plane descended, since the air pressure would be changing quickly, but Ponter didn't feel a thing. Perhaps it was a peculiarly Gliksin affliction, caused by their tiny sinus cavities.

The plane, according to an announcement over the speakers, had to divert to the south and fly directly over the island known as Manhattan, to accommodate other air traffic. *Crowded skies,* thought Ponter. *How astonishing!* Still, Ponter was delighted. After having his fill of hearing about war last night, he'd turned to the encyclopedia's entry on New York City. There were, he discovered, many great human-made landmarks here, and it would be wonderful to get to see them from the air. He looked for, and found, the giant green woman with the dour expression, holding aloft a torch. But, try as he might, he couldn't spot the two towers that supposedly rose above the surrounding buildings, each an incredible hundred and ten stories tall.

When they were at last on the ground, Ponter asked Hélène about the missing—he found the word poetic—"skyscrapers."

Hélène looked very uncomfortable. "Ah," she said. "You mean the World Trade Center towers. Used to be two of the tallest buildings on the planet, but . . ." Her voice cracked slightly, which surprised Ponter. "I—I'm sorry to have to be the one to tell you this, but . . ." Another hesitation. "But they were destroyed by terrorists."

Ponter's Companion bleeped, but Tukana, who had clearly been doing research of her own, tipped her head toward Ponter. "Gliksin outlaws who use violence to try to force political or social change."

Ponter shook his head, once more astonished by the universe he'd come to. "How were the buildings destroyed?"

Hélène hesitated yet again before responding. "Two large airplanes with tanks full of fuel were hijacked and deliberately crashed into them."

Ponter could think of no reply. But he was glad he hadn't learned this until he was safely back on the ground.

Chapter Sixteen

When she had been eighteen, Mary's boyfriend Donny had gone to Los Angeles with his family for the summer. That had been before widespread e-mail or even cheap long-distance calling, but they'd kept in touch by letter. Don had sent long, densely packed ones at first, full of news and declarations of how much he missed her, how much he loved her.

But as the pleasant days of June gave way to the heat of July, and the sweltering humidity of August, the letters grew less frequent, and less densely packed. Mary remembered vividly the day one arrived with just Don's name at the end, standing there alone, not preceded by the word "Love."

They say absence makes the heart grow fonder. Perhaps it does in some cases. Perhaps, indeed, it had in the current case. It had been weeks since Mary had last seen Ponter Boddit, and she felt at least as much, if not more, affection for him than she had when he departed.

But there *was* a difference. After Ponter had left, Mary had gone back to being alone—not even a free woman, for she and Colm were only separated; divorce meant excommunication for both of them, and the process of pursuing an annulment had seemed hypocritical.

But Ponter had only been alone when he was here. Yes, he was a widower, although that wasn't the term he used for it, but when he'd gone back to his universe, he'd been surrounded by family: his man-mate Adikor Huld—Mary had committed the names to memory—and his two daughters, eighteen-year-old Jasmel Ket and eight-year-old Megameg Bek.

Mary was in an anteroom on the eighteenth floor of the Secretariat building at the UN, waiting for Ponter to get out of a meeting, so she could at last rendezvous with him. As she sat in a chair, too nervous to read, her stomach churned, and all sorts of thoughts went through her head. Would Ponter even recognize her? He must have seen plenty of late-thirties blondes here in New York; would all similarly colored Gliksins look alike to him? Besides, she'd cut her hair since Sudbury, and, if anything, was a pound or two heavier, God damn it.

And, after all, it had been *she* who had rejected him last time. Perhaps she was the last person Ponter wanted to see, now that he had returned to this Earth.

But no. No. He had understood that she was still dealing with the aftermath of the rape, that her inability to respond to his advance had nothing to do with him. Yes, surely, he had understood that.

And yet, there was—

Mary's heart jumped. The door was opening, and the muffled voices within suddenly became distinct. Mary leapt to her feet, her hands clasped nervously in front of her.

"—and I'll get you those figures," said an Asian diplomat, talking over his shoulder to a silver-haired female Neanderthal who must be Ambassador Tukana Prat.

Two more *H. sap* diplomats shouldered through the door, and then—

And then, there was Ponter Boddit, his dark blond hair parted precisely in the center, his arresting golden brown eyes obvious even at this distance. Mary lifted her eyebrows, but Ponter hadn't caught sight, or wind, of her just yet. He was speaking to one of the other diplomats, saying something about geological surveys, and—

And then his eyes did fall on Mary, and she smiled nervously, and he did a neat little sideways step, bypassing the people in front of him, and his face split into that foot-wide grin Mary knew so well, and he closed the distance between him and her, and swept her into his arms, hugging her close to his massive chest.

"Mare!" exclaimed Ponter, in his own voice, and then, with Hak translating, "How wonderful to see you!"

"Welcome back," said Mary, her cheek against his. "Welcome back!"

"What are you doing here in New York?" asked Ponter.

Mary could have said that she'd just come in hopes of collecting a DNA sample from Tukana; it was part of the truth, and it afforded an easy out, a face-saving explanation, but . . .

"I came to see you," she said simply.

Ponter squeezed her again, then relaxed his grip and stepped back, putting a hand on each of her shoulders, looking her in the face. "I am so glad," he said.

Mary became uncomfortably aware that the other people in the room were looking at her and Ponter, and, indeed, after a moment, Tukana cleared her throat, just as a Gliksin might.

Ponter turned his head and looked at the ambassador. "Oh," he said. "Forgive me. This is Mare Vaughan, the geneticist I told you about."

Mary stepped forward, extending her hand. "Hello, Madam Ambassador."

Tukana took Mary's hand and shook it with astonishing strength. Mary reflected that if she'd been sufficiently sneaky, she could have collected a few of Tukana's cells just in the process of shaking hands. "It is a pleasure to meet you," said the older Neanderthal. "I am Tukana Prat."

"Yes, I know," said Mary, smiling. "I've been reading about you in the papers."

"My feeling," said Tukana, a sly grin on her wide face, "is that perhaps you and Envoy Boddit would like some time alone together." Without waiting for an answer, she turned to one of the Gliksin diplomats. "Shall we go to your office and look over those population-dispersal figures?"

The diplomat nodded, and the rest of the party left the room, leaving Mary and Ponter alone.

"So," said Ponter, sweeping Mary into another hug. "How are you?"

Mary couldn't tell if it was her heart, or Ponter's, that was jackhammering. "Now that you're here," she said, "I'm fine."

The General Assembly hall of the United Nations consisted of a series of concentric semicircles facing a central stage. Ponter was baffled at the mix of faces he saw. In Canada, he'd noted a range of skin colors and facial types, and, so far, his experience of the United States had been similar. Here, in this massive chamber, he saw the same wide variety of coloration, which Lurt had told him almost certainly had resulted from prolonged periods of geographic isolation for each color group, assuming, as Mare had asserted, that they were indeed cross-fertile.

But here, all the representatives from each country were the same color—even Canada and the United States had only light-skinned representatives at this United Nations.

More: Ponter was used to seeing councils on his world consisting entirely of members of one gender, or councils with exactly equal numbers of males and females. But here there were perhaps ninety-five percent males, with only a smattering of females. Was it possible, wondered Ponter, that there was a hierarchy among the "races," as Mare had called them, with the light-skinned holding the ultimate power? Likewise, was it conceivable that Gliksin females were accorded lesser status, and only rarely allowed into the most senior circles?

Another thing that surprised Ponter was how *young* most of the diplomats were. Why, some were even younger than Ponter himself! Mare had once mentioned that she dyed her hair to hide its gray, a notion that was incredible to Ponter; to hide gray was to hide wisdom. Male Gliksins, he'd noticed, were less prone to coloring their hair—perhaps their wisdom was more often in question. But, still, there were few gray hairs in the group he was now seeing.

Ponter's concerns were allayed a bit when the top official, whose title was the puzzling "amanuensis-high-warrior," turned out to be a dark-skinned man of at least passable months. Hélène Gagné had whispered to Ponter that this man had recently won the Nobel Peace Prize, whatever that might be.

Ponter was seated with the Canadian delegation. Sadly, Mare had been denied a place on the main floor, although she was supposedly watching from a spectators' gallery high overhead. Above the podium, Ponter saw a giant version of the pale blue United Nations crest. Although intellectually Ponter had accepted the reality of where he was, there was still an emotional part of him that thought this strange world had nothing to do with *his* Earth. But the crest had at its center a polar-projection map of Earth, looking just like similar maps Ponter had seen in his own world. Surrounding it, though, were branches of some sort of plant. Ponter asked Hélène the significance of the branches; she said they were olive leaves, a sign of peace.

Peace Tower. Peace Prize. Leaves of Peace. For all their warmongering, it seemed peace was very much on the minds of Gliksins, and Ponter was reassured slightly to note that the word for peace contained no more syllables than did the word for war.

After a long opening statement by the amanuensis-high-warrior, it was at last Tukana's turn to speak. She got to her feet and walked to the podium while the assembled Gliksins did that thing they called "applauding." Tukana was carrying a small polished-wood box, which she placed on the podium.

The Secretary-General shook her hand and then vacated the stage.

"Hello, peoples of this Earth," said Tukana's implant, translating for her; it had taken some doing by Hélène to convey to the Companion the notion of "peoples," a plural form of a word that already was a plural. "I greet you on behalf of the High Gray Council of my world, and of that world's people."

Tukana continued, nodding in Ponter's direction: "The first time one of us came here, it was an unexpected accident. This time, it is deliberate and with great anticipation on the part of my people. We look forward to establishing ongoing peaceful relations with every one of the nations represented here . . ."

She went on in that vein for some time, saying little of substance. But the Gliksins, Ponter noted, were hanging on her every word, although some of those closest to him were discreetly examining Ponter, apparently fascinated by his appearance.

"And now," said Tukana, it apparently being time to get down to the marrow, "it is my pleasure to undertake the first-ever trade between our two peoples." She turned to the dark-skinned man, who was standing at the side of the stage. "If you would, please . . . ?"

The amanuensis-high-warrior returned to the stage, carrying a small wooden box of his own. Tukana opened her box, which had recently been sent over from the other side.

"In this box," said Tukana, "is an exact cast of the skull from our world of the anthropological specimen whose counterpart on this version of Earth is dubbed AL 288-1, an individual of what you call *Australopithecus afarensis* known here as Lucy"—Tukana had told her Companion to add the *ee* phoneme to the proper noun.

There was a murmur through the chamber. The significance had been explained to Ponter. On the two versions of Earth, originals of this particular adult female's skeleton had eroded out of the ground—in what the Gliksins called Hadar, Ethiopia, on this Earth, and the corresponding spot in northeast Kakarana on Ponter's version. But the weather patterns had not been identical. On this version, the one of New York and Toronto and Sudbury, the cranium of this fossil had been badly damaged by erosion before Donald Johanson found it in the year the Gliksins called 1974. But on Tukana and Ponter's version, the skeleton had been found before much erosion damage had occurred. It was a clever offering, Ponter knew, underscoring that all the same mineral and fossil deposits existed on both worlds, and that a swapping of identified locations would doubtless be mutually beneficial.

"I accept this with gratitude on behalf of all the peoples of this Earth," said the dark-skinned man. "And, in exchange, please accept this gift from us." He handed his box to Tukana. She opened it, and lifted out what appeared to be a rock encased in clear plastic. "This specimen of breccia was collected by James Irwin at Hadley Rille." He paused dramatically, obviously enjoying Tukana's lack of comprehension. "Hadley Rille," explained the amanuensis-high-warrior, "is on the moon."

Tukana's eyes went wide. Ponter was equally astounded. A piece of the moon! How could he have doubted that they were doing the right thing having relations with these humans!

Chapter Seventeen

Mary came running down the curving staircase to the United Nations lobby. Ponter and Tukana were leaving the General Assembly hall, surrounded by a quartet of uniformed police officers, obviously serving as bodyguards. Mary hurried toward the two Neanderthals, but one of the cops moved to block her way. "Sorry, ma'am," he said.

Mary shouted out Ponter's name, and Ponter looked up at her. "Mare!" he responded in his own voice, then, through his translator, "It is acceptable for her to pass, Officer. She is my friend."

The cop nodded and stood aside. Mary surged in, closing the distance between her and Ponter. "How do you think it went?" asked Ponter.

"Brilliantly," said Mary. "Whose idea was it to get a cast of your version of Lucy's skull?"

"One of the Inco geologists."

Mary shook her head in wonder. "A perfect choice."

Ambassador Prat turned to Mary. "We are about to leave this facility in order to eat. Will you please join us?"

Mary smiled. The older Neanderthal might not be the most practiced diplomat, but she certainly was gracious. "I'd love to," said Mary.

"Come then," said Tukana. "There is a—how do you phrase it?—a reservation for us at an eatery a short walk away."

Mary was glad to have a coat with her, although Ponter and Tukana seemed quite comfortable in their indoor clothes. They were both wearing the kind of pants Mary had seen Ponter wear before, which ended in pouches covering the feet. Ponter's were dark green, and Tukana's were maroon. And they both had on shirts that closed at the shoulders.

Mary took a second to look up at the United Nations tower, a great Kubrickian slab silhouetted against the sun. Besides Mary, the two Neanderthals were accompanied by two American diplomats, and two Canadian ones. The four cops surrounded the little group as it moved across the mall.

Tukana was talking with the diplomats. Ponter and Mary were trailing a little bit behind, chatting.

"How is your family?" asked Mary.

"They are well," said Ponter. "But you would be astonished to learn what happened in my absence. My man-mate, Adikor, was accused of murdering me."

"Really?" said Mary. "But why?"

"A long story, as you might say. Fortunately, though, I returned to my world in time to exonerate him."

"So he's okay now?"

"Yes, he is fine. I hope you can meet him at some point. He is—"

Three sounds, virtually simultaneous: Ponter going *"oof,"* one of the police officers shouting, and a loud crack, like a bolt of thunder.

As Ponter crumpled to the ground, Mary realized what had happened. She dropped to her knees next to him, probing his blood-soaked shirt for any sign of the entrance wound so she could stanch the flow of blood.

Thunder? thought Tukana. But no, that was impossible. The sky, although smelly, was clear and cloudless.

She turned and looked at Ponter, who—*astonishment!*—was prone on the pavement, blood pouring from him. That sound—a projectile weapon—a *gun,* that was the English term—had been fired, and—

And suddenly Tukana herself was pitching forward, slamming facefirst into the ground, her giant nose smashing against the pavement.

One of the Gliksin enforcers had jumped on Tukana's back, propelling her to the ground, using his body to shield hers. Noble, yes, but Tukana would have none of it. She reached back, grabbed the enforcer by the upper arm, and flipped him up and forward, so that he landed in front of her on his back, dazed. Tukana surged to her feet, and, despite the blood pouring from her nostrils, she had no trouble picking up the scent of the chemical explosion from the gun. She swung her head left and right, and—

There. A figure running away, and in his hand—

The stinking weapon.

Tukana took off after him, her massive legs pounding into the ground.

"Ponter has been shot in the right shoulder," said Hak through his external speaker to Mary. "His pulse is rapid, but weak. His blood pressure is falling, as is his body temperature."

"Shock," said Mary. Continuing to probe Ponter's shoulder, she found where the bullet had hit, her finger slipping into the wound up to the second knuckle. "Do you know if the bullet has left his body?"

One of the other cops was hovering over Mary; another was using a radio transceiver clipped to his chest to call for an ambulance. The third cop was hustling the American and Canadian diplomats back indoors.

"I am not sure," said Hak. "I did not detect its departure." A pause. "He is losing too much blood. There is a cauterizing laser scalpel in his medical kit. Open the third pouch on the right-hand side."

Mary extracted a device that looked like a fat green pen. "Is this it?"

"Yes. Rotate the scalpel's lower body until the symbol with two dots and a bar is lined up with the reference triangle."

Mary peered at the device, and did as Hak said. "How's that?" she said, holding the scalpel up to the Companion's lens.

"Correct," said Hak. "Now, follow my instructions precisely. Open Ponter's shirt."

"How?" said Mary.

"There are closures along the shoulder. They split apart when squeezed simultaneously from both sides."

Mary tried one, and it did indeed pop open. She continued until she had Ponter's entire left shoulder and arm exposed. The entrance wound was surrounded by terraces of bright red blood, filling the declivities of his musculature.

"The scalpel is activated by pressing on the blue square—do you see it?"

Mary nodded. "Yes."

"If you depress the square halfway, the laser will come on, but at low energy, so you can see where its beam is directed. Pressing in all the way will fire the laser at full strength, and it should sear shut the clipped artery."

"I understand," said Mary. She used her fingers to open the wound so that she could see within.

"Do you see the artery?" asked Hak.

There was so much blood. "No."

"Press the activation square halfway in."

A bright blue dot appeared in the middle of the gore.

"All right," said Hak. "The damage to the artery is eleven millimeters away from where you are pointing, on a line between your current position and Ponter's left nipple."

Mary repositioned the beam, marveling at the perspective Hak's sensing field gave him.

"A little farther," said Hak. "There! Stop. Now, use full power."

The dot flared in brightness, and Mary saw a whiff of smoke go up from the wound.

"Again!" said Hak.

She pressed the square in once more.

"And two millimeters farther along—no, the other way. There! Again!"

She fired the laser.

"Now move an equal distance farther along. Yes. Again!"

She pressed hard on the blue square, and more vaporized tissue assaulted Mary's nose.

"That should be enough," said Hak, "until he can be treated by a doctor."

Ponter's golden eyes fluttered open. "Hold on," Mary said, staring into them, and taking his hand. "Help is on its way." She took off her coat, and placed it over him.

Tukana Prat continued to run after the man. One of the Gliksin enforcers was shouting "Stop!" and it was only belatedly that Tukana realized the imperative was directed at her, not the escaping man. But none of the enforcers could run as fast as Tukana; if she gave up her pursuit, the man with the gun would get away.

Part of Tukana's mind was trying to analyze the situation. Guns, she was given to understand, could be deadly, but the element of surprise was gone now; it was unlikely the . . . *as-sailant*—that was the word—would turn and fire again. Indeed, he seemed intent solely on getting away, and, given that he was Gliksin, it probably didn't occur to him that as long as he held on to the recently fired gun, Tukana would have no trouble tracking him.

The street was crowded, but Tukana had little difficulty making her way through the throngs; indeed, these humans seemed quite interested in clearing out of the way of the charging Neanderthal as fast as possible.

The man she was chasing—and it was a man, a male Gliksin—seemed shorter than most of his breed. Tukana was devouring the distance between them rapidly; she could almost reach out and grab him.

The man must have heard the thunderous footfalls behind him. He chanced a look over his shoulder, and swung the arm holding his gun back. "He is aiming at us," said Tukana's Companion through her cochlear implants.

Tukana hadn't even thought about the blood in her nose; the airways were more than big enough to accommodate the huge intake that went with running. Indeed, she could feel the strength surging within her as her muscles became more, not less, oxygenated. She brought her legs down on the ground side by side, then pushed off, leaping forward, crossing the gap between her and the Gliksin. The man did fire, but the projectile went wide, although screams came from the crowd. Tukana fervently hoped they were only screams of terror, not that the bullet intended for her had hit someone else.

Tukana slammed into the man, knocking him forward onto the pavement, the two of them skidding ahead several paces. Tukana could hear the footfalls of the enforcers closing up the distance from the rear. The man beneath her tried to twist his spine around and get another shot off. Tukana seized the back of his strangely angular, narrow head in her massive hand, and—

It was her only choice. Surely, it was . . .

And smashed the man's head forward, into the artificial stone covering the ground, the skull shattering, the front of his head breaking open like a ripe melon.

Tukana could feel her heart pounding, and she took a moment just to breathe.

Suddenly, she became aware that three of the four enforcers had caught up with them, and were now deployed in front of her, guns out, each held in two hands, aimed at the downed man.

But, as Tukana rose to her feet, she saw the look of horror on one of the Gliksins' faces.

The enforcer in the middle doubled over and vomited.

And the third enforcer, wide-eyed, said, "Jesus Christ."

And Tukana looked down at the dead, dead, dead man who had shot Ponter.

And, as she stood there, the sound of sirens grew nearer.

Chapter Eighteen

"Crisis mode!" shouted Jock Krieger as he hustled his way down the halls of the Synergy Group building in Rochester. "Everybody down to the Conference Room!"

Louise Benoît stuck her head out of her lab's door. "What's up?" she said.

"Conference Room!" called Jock over his shoulder. "Now!"

It took no more than five minutes to get everyone assembled in what had been the palatial living room, back when people had actually lived in this mansion. "Okay, team," said Jock. "It's time to earn those big bucks."

"What's happening?" asked Lilly, from the imaging group.

"NP just got shot in New York," said Jock.

"Ponter shot?" said Louise, her eyes wide.

"That's right."

"Is he—"

"He's alive. That's all I know about his condition right now."

"What about the ambassador?" asked Lilly.

"She's fine," said Jock. "But she killed the man who shot Ponter."

"Oh my God," said Kevin, also from imaging.

"I think you all know my background," said Jock. "My field is game theory. Well, the stakes just got very, very high. *Some-*

thing is going to happen now, and we've got to figure out what, so we can advise the president, and—"

"The president . . ." said Louise, her brown eyes wide.

"That's right. Playtime is over. He needs to know what the Neanderthals are going to do in response to this, and then how we should respond to whatever they do. Okay, ladies and gentlemen—we need ideas. Start them coming!"

Tukana Prat looked down at the man she had killed. Hélène Gagné had caught up to her, and now had cupped Tukana's elbow. She helped the Neanderthal woman walk along, leading her away from the dead body.

"I did not mean to kill him," said Tukana, softly, dazed.

"I know," said Hélène, her tone soothing. "I know."

"He . . . he tried to kill Ponter. He tried to kill me."

"Everybody saw it," said Hélène. "It was self-defense."

"Yes, but . . ."

"You had no choice," said Hélène. "You had to stop him."

"To *stop* him, yes," said Tukana. "But to . . . to . . ."

Hélène swung Tukana around and gripped her upper arms. *"It was self-defense, do you hear me?* Don't even hint that it might have been something else."

"But . . ."

"Listen to me! This is going to be messy enough as it is."

"I . . . I have to speak to my superiors," said Tukana.

"So do I," said Hélène, "and—" Hélène's cell phone rang. She fished it out and flipped it open. *"Allô? Oui. Oui. Je ne sais pas. J'ai—un moment, s'il vous plaît."* She covered the mouthpiece, and spoke to Tukana. "The PMO."

"What?"

"The Prime Minister's Office." She switched back to the handset, and to French. *"Non. Non, mais . . . Oui—beaucoup de sang . . . Non, elle est sein et sauve. D'accord. Non, pas de problème. D'accord. Non, aujourd'hui. Oui, maintenant . . . Pearson, oui. D'accord, oui. Au revoir."* Hélène closed the phone and put it away. "I'm to take you back to Canada, as soon as the police here are finished questioning you."

"Questioning?"

"It's just a formality. Then we'll get you up to Sudbury, so that you can report back to your people." Hélène looked at the Neanderthal woman, blood smeared across her face. "What . . . what do you think your superiors will want to do?"

Tukana Prat looked back at the dead man, then over to where the ambulance attendants were bending over Ponter, who was lying on his back. "I have no idea," she said.

"All right," said Jock Krieger, pacing through the opulent living room of the mansion in Seabreeze, "there are only two positions they can take. First, that they, the Neanderthals, are the aggrieved party here. After all, with no provocation, one of our kind put a bullet in one of their kind. Second, that *we* are the aggrieved party. Sure, one of our guys took a shot at one of them, but their guy lived and our guy is dead."

Louise Benoît shook her head. "I don't like thinking of a terrorist, or an assassin, or whatever the hell he was, as one of 'our guys.'"

"Neither do I," said Jock. "But that's what it amounts to. The game is Gliksin versus Neanderthal; us versus them. And somebody has to make the next move."

"We could apologize," said Kevin Bilodeau, leaning back in the chair he'd taken. "Bend over backward telling them how sorry we are."

"I say we wait and see what they do," said Lilly.

"And what if what they do is slam the door?" said Jock,

wheeling to face her. "What if they pull the goddamned plug on their quantum computer?" He turned to Louise. "How close are you to replicating their technology?"

Louise made a *pffft!* sound. "Are you kidding? I've barely begun."

"We can't let them close the portal," said Kevin.

"What are you suggesting?" sneered one of the sociologists, a heavyset white man of fifty. "That we send over troops to prevent them from shutting down the portal?"

"Maybe we *should* do that," said Jock.

"You can't be serious!" said Louise.

"Have you got a better idea?" snapped Jock.

"They're not idiots, you know," said Louise. "I'm sure they've rigged some sort of fail-safe at their end to prevent us from doing precisely that."

"Maybe," said Jock. "Maybe not."

"It would be a diplomatic nightmare to seize the portal," said Rasmussen, a rough-hewn type whose field was geopolitics; he'd been trying to work out what core political units the Neanderthals might have, given that the geography of their world was the same as that of this one. "The Suez Crisis all over again."

"Damn it," said Krieger, kicking over a wastebasket. "God damn it." He shook his head. "The whole point of game theory is to work out the best realistic outcome for both sides in a conflict. But this isn't like nuclear brinksmanship—it's like schoolyard basketball. Unless we do something, the Neanderthals can take the ball and go home, putting an end to everything!"

Tukana Prat had flown Air Canada from JFK to Toronto's Pearson, and then from there via Air Ontario up to Sudbury, accompanied the whole way by Hélène Gagné. A car was waiting for them at the Sudbury Airport, and it whisked them to the Creighton Mine. The ambassador rode down the elevator, went along the SNO drift to the neutrino-observatory chamber, and headed back through the Derkers tube, across to the other side—to *her* side.

And now she was meeting in the Alibi Archive Pavilion with High Gray councilor Bedros, who, because the portal was in his region, was looking after all matters related to contact with the Gliksins.

The images Tukana's Companion implant—with its enhanced memory capacity—had recorded on the other side had now been uploaded to her alibi archive, and she and Bedros had watched the whole sorry mess unfold in the holo-bubble floating in front of them.

"There's really no question about what we should do," said Bedros. "As soon as he is well enough to leave the Gliksin hospital, we must recall Ponter Boddit. And then we should sever the link with the Gliksin world."

"I—I don't know if that's necessarily the correct response," said Tukana. "Ponter will be all right, apparently. It is a Gliksin who is dead."

"Only because he missed," said Bedros.

"Yes, but—"

"No buts, Ambassador. I'm going to recommend to the Council that we permanently shut the portal as soon as we can get Scholar Boddit back."

"Please," said Tukana. "There is an opportunity here that is too valuable to pass up."

"They have never had a purging of their gene pool," snapped Bedros. "The most abhorrent, dangerous traits still run rampant throughout their population."

"I understand that, but nonetheless . . ."

"And they carry weapons! Not for hunting, but for killing each other. And how many days did it take before such weapons were turned against members of our kind?" Bedros shook his head. "Ponter Boddit told us what happened to our kind on their world—remember, he learned that on his previous trip. They—the Gliksins—exterminated us. Now, think about that, Ambassador Prat. Think about it! Physically, the Gliksins are puny. Weakling stick figures! And yet they managed to wipe us out there, despite our greater strength and our bigger brains. How could they possibly have accomplished that?"

"I have no idea. Besides, Ponter only said that was *one* theory about what had happened to us in their world."

"They wiped us out through treachery," continued Bedros, as if Tukana hadn't spoken. "Through deceit. Through unimaginable violence. Swarms of them, armed with rocks and spears, must have poured into our valleys, overwhelming us with sheer numbers, until the blood of our kind soaked the ground and every last one of us was dead. *That's* their history. *That's* their way. It would be madness for us to leave a portal open between our two worlds."

"The portal is deep within the rocks, and can accommodate only one or two people traveling through it at a time. I really don't think we have to worry about—"

"I can hear our ancestors saying the same things, half a million months ago. 'Oh, look! Another kind of humanity! Well, I'm sure we have nothing to worry about. After all, the entrances to our valleys are narrow.' "

"We don't know for sure that that's what happened," said Tukana.

"Why take the risk?" asked Bedros. "Why risk it, for even one more day?"

Tukana Prat shut off the holo-bubble and paced slowly back and forth. "I learned something difficult in that other world," she said softly. "I learned that, by their standards, I am not much of a diplomat. I speak too succinctly and too plainly. And yes, I will plainly say that there are many unpleasant things about these people. You are right when you call them violent. And the damage they have done to their environment is beyond calculation. But they have *greatness* in them, too. Ponter is right when he says they will go to the stars."

"Good riddance to them," said Bedros.

"Don't say that. I saw works of art in their world that were astonishingly beautiful. They are *different* from us, and there are things by character and temperament that they can do that we cannot—wondrous things."

"But one of them tried to kill you!"

"One, yes. Out of six billion." Tukana was silent for a moment. "Do you know what the biggest difference between them and us is?"

Bedros looked like he was about to make a sarcastic remark, but thought better of it. "Tell me," he said.

"They believe there is a *purpose* to all this." Tukana spread her arms, encompassing everything around her. "They believe there is a *meaning* to life."

"Because they have deluded themselves into thinking the universe has a guiding intelligence."

"In part, yes. But it goes deeper than that. Even their *atheists*—the ones among them who don't believe in their God—search for meaning, for explanations. We exist—but they *live.* They *seek.*"

"We seek, too. We engage in science."

"But we do it out of practicality. We want a better tool, so we study until we can make one. But they preoccupy themselves with what they themselves call big questions: Why are we here? What is all this *for?*"

"Those are meaningless questions."

"Are they?"

"Of course they are!"

"Perhaps you're right," said Tukana Prat. "But perhaps not. Perhaps they are getting close to answering them, close to a new enlightenment."

"And then they'll stop trying to kill each other? Then they'll stop raping their environment?"

"I don't know. Maybe. There *is* goodness in them."

"There is *death* in them. The only way we will survive contact with them is if they kill themselves off before they manage to kill us."

Tukana closed her eyes. "I know you mean well, Councilor Bedros, and—"

"Don't patronize me."

"I'm not. I understand you have the best interests of our people at heart. But so do I. And my perspective is that of a diplomat."

"An *incompetent* diplomat," snapped Bedros. "Even the Gliksins think so!"

"I—"

"Or do you always kill the natives?"

"Look, *Councilor,* I am as upset about that as you are, but—"

"Enough!" shouted Bedros. "Enough! We never should have let Boddit push us into doing this in the first place. It's time for older and wiser heads to prevail."

Chapter Nineteen

Mary stepped quietly into Ponter's hospital room. The surgeons had had no trouble removing the bullet—postcranial Neanderthal anatomy was close to that of *Homo sapiens,* after all, and Hak had apparently conversed with them throughout the entire procedure. Ponter had lost enough blood that a transfusion would normally have been in order, but it had seemed best to avoid that until much more was known about Neanderthal hematology. A saline drip was hooked up to Ponter's arm, and Hak had frequent dialogues with the physicians about Ponter's condition.

Ponter had been unconscious most of the time since the surgery. Indeed, during it, he'd been given an injection to put him to sleep, using a chemical from his medical belt, as instructed by Hak.

Mary watched Ponter's broad chest rise and fall. She thought back to the first time she'd seen him, which had also been in a hospital room. Then, she'd looked at him with astonishment. She hadn't believed a modern Neanderthal was possible.

Now, though, she didn't look at him as a bizarre specimen, as a freak, as an impossibility. Now, she looked at him with love. And her heart was breaking.

Suddenly, Ponter's eyes opened. "Mare," he said, softly.

"I didn't mean to wake you," Mary said, crossing over to the bed.

"I was already awake," said Ponter. "Hak had been playing some music for me. And then I smelled you."

"How are you?" asked Mary, drawing a metal-framed chair up next to the bed.

Ponter pulled back his sheet. His hairy chest was naked, but a large pad of gauze, stained russet with dried blood, was held to his shoulder with white medical tape.

"I am to live," he said.

"I am so sorry this happened to you," said Mary.

"How is Tukana?" asked Ponter.

Mary raised her eyebrows, surprised that Ponter had not been informed. "She chased the man who shot you."

A wan smile touched Ponter's broad mouth. "I suspect he is in worse shape than she, then."

"I'll say," said Mary softly. "Ponter, she killed him."

Ponter said nothing for a moment. "We rarely take justice into our own hands."

"I listened to them arguing about that on TV while you were in surgery," Mary said. "Most are of the opinion that it was self-defense."

"How did she kill him?"

Mary shrugged a bit, acknowledging there was no nice way to say this. "She smashed his head into the pavement, and it . . . it burst open."

Ponter was quiet for a time. "Oh," he said at last. "What will happen to her?"

Mary frowned. She'd once read a courtroom drama that *The Globe and Mail* had raved about in which an extraterrestrial was put on trial in L.A., charged with murdering a human. But there was one key difference here . . .

"We exempt recognized foreign ambassadors from most

laws; it's called 'diplomatic immunity,' and Tukana has it, since she was appearing at the UN under the umbrella of being a Canadian diplomat."

"What do you mean?"

Mary frowned, looking for an example. "In 2001, Andrei Kneyazev, a Russian diplomat in Canada, got drunk and ran into two pedestrians with his car. He faced no charges in Canada because he was the representative of a recognized foreign government, even though one of the people he hit died. That's diplomatic immunity."

Ponter's deep-set eyes were wide.

"And, in any event, hundreds of people apparently saw this guy shoot you, and shoot at Tukana, before she . . . um, *reacted* . . . the way she did. As I say, it will probably be considered self-defense."

"Nonetheless," said Ponter, softly, "Tukana is a person of good character. It will weigh heavily on her mind." A beat. "Are you sure there is no danger now to her?" He tilted his head. "After what happened to Adikor when I disappeared, I guess I am a bit wary of legal systems."

"Ponter, she's already gone back home—to your world. She said she needed to speak to . . . what do you call it? The Gray Council."

"The *High* Gray Council," said Ponter, "if you are referring to the world government." A beat. "What about the dead man?"

Mary frowned. "His name was Cole—Rufus Cole. They're still trying to figure out who he was, and exactly what he had against you and Tukana."

"What are the options?"

Mary was momentarily confused. "Sorry?"

"The options," repeated Ponter. "The possible reasons he might have had for trying to kill us."

Mary lifted her shoulders slightly. "He could have been a

religious fanatic: someone opposed to your atheistic stance, or even to your very existence, since it contradicts the biblical account of creation."

Ponter's eyes went wide. "Killing me would not have erased the fact that I had existed."

"Granted. But, well—I'm just guessing here—Cole might have thought you an instrument of Satan—"

Mary cringed as she heard the bleep.

"The Devil. The Evil One. God's opponent."

Ponter was agog. "God has an opponent?"

"Yes—well, I mean, that's what the Bible says. But except for Fundamentalists—those who take every word of the Bible as literally true—most people don't really believe in Satan anymore."

"Why not?" asked Ponter.

"Well, I guess because it's a ridiculous belief. You know, only a fool could take the concept seriously."

Ponter opened his mouth to say something, apparently thought better of it, and closed his mouth again.

"Anyway," said Mary, speaking quickly; she really didn't want to get mired in this. "He might also have been an agent of a foreign government or terrorist group. Or . . ."

Ponter raised his eyebrow, inviting her to go on.

Mary shrugged again. "Or he might just have been crazy."

"You let crazy people possess weapons?" asked Ponter.

Mary's natural Canadian thought was that they were the only ones who wanted them, but she kept that to herself. "That's actually the best thing to hope for," she said. "If he was crazy, acting alone, then there's no special reason to worry about something like this happening again. But if he's part of some terrorist group . . ."

Ponter looked down—and, of course, his gaze fell on his

bandaged chest. "I had hoped that it would be safe for my daughters to visit this world."

"I would so much like to meet them," said Mary.

"What would have happened to this—this Rufus Cole . . ." Ponter frowned. "Imagine that! A Gliksin name I can say without difficulty, and it belonged to someone who wanted me dead! In any event, what would have happened to this Rufus Cole had he not been killed?"

"A trial," said Mary. "If he had been found guilty, he would probably have gone to jail."

Hak bleeped again.

"Umm, a secure institution, where criminals are kept separate from the general population."

"You say, 'if he had been found guilty.' He *did* shoot me."

"Yes, but . . . well, if he were crazy, that would be a defense. He might be found not guilty by reason of insanity."

Ponter lifted his eyebrow again. "Would it not make more sense to determine if someone is insane before you let them have the gun, rather than after they have used it?"

Mary nodded. "I couldn't agree with you more. But, nonetheless, there it is."

"What if . . . if I had been killed? Or Tukana had? What would have happened to this man then?"

"Here? In the States? He might have been executed."

The inevitable bleep.

"Put to death. Killed, as punishment for his crime, and as a deterrent to others who might contemplate the same thing."

Ponter moved his head left and right, his blond-brown hair making a whooshing sound against his pillow. "I would not have wanted that," he said. "No one deserves a premature death, not even one who would wish it on others."

"Come on, Ponter," said Mary, surprising herself with the

sharpness of her tone. "Can you really be that . . . that *Christ-like?* The bloody guy tried to kill you. Are you really worried about what would have happened to him?"

Ponter was quiet for a time. He didn't say, although Mary knew he could have, that someone had tried to kill him once before; during his first visit, he'd told Mary that his jaw had been shattered in his youth by a furious blow. Rather, he simply lifted his eyebrow and said, "It is moot, in any event. This Rufus Cole is no more."

But Mary wasn't ready to let it pass. "When you were hit, all those—all those *months* ago—the person who did it had not premeditated it, and he was immediately filled with regret; you told me so yourself. But Rufus Cole had clearly planned in advance to kill you. Surely that makes a difference."

Ponter shifted slightly on the hospital bed. "I will live," he said. "Beyond that, nothing after the fact could erase the scar I will bear until my dying day."

Mary shook her head, but she managed a good-humored tone. "Sometimes you're just *too* good to be true, Ponter."

"I have no response for that," said Ponter.

Mary smiled. "Which just proves my point."

"But I do have a question."

"Yes?"

"What will happen now?"

"I don't know," said Mary. "The doctor told me a diplomatic pouch was flown here for you from Sudbury. I guess that's it over there, on the table."

Ponter rolled his head. "Ah. Would you get it for me, please?"

Mary did so. Ponter opened the pouch and extracted a large thing like an envelope but of Neanderthal design, perfectly square. He opened that up—it unfolded like a flower blooming—and removed a tiny ruby-colored sphere from within it.

"What's that?" said Mary.

"A memory bead," replied Ponter. He touched his Companion, and Mary was surprised to see it pop open, revealing an interior compartment with a small cluster of additional control buds and a recessed hole about the diameter of a pencil. "It fits in here," he said, slipping it into place. "If you will . . ."

"I'll go," said Mary. "I know you need privacy."

"No, no. Do not leave. But please forgive me for a moment. Hak will play the recording into my cochlear implants."

Mary nodded, and she saw Ponter tip his head as was his habit when listening to Hak. A giant frown creased his face. After a few more moments, Ponter popped Hak open again and removed the bead.

"What did it say?" asked Mary.

"The High Gray Council wants me to return home at once."

Mary felt her heart sinking. "Oh . . ."

"I will not," said Ponter, simply.

"What? Why?"

"If I went back, they would close the portal between our worlds."

"Did they say that?"

"Not directly—but I know the Council. My people are aware that we are mortal, Mare—we know there is no afterlife. And so we do not take unnecessary risks. Continued contact with your people is something the Council would think is unnecessary, after what has happened. There were already many who were against reopening the portal, and this will provide new meat for them."

"Can you do that? Just decide to stay here?"

"I *will* do it. There may be consequences; I will bear them."

"Wow," said Mary, softly.

"As long as I am here, my people will keep the portal open. This will give those, like me, who believe contact should be maintained, time to argue that perspective. If the portal were closed, it would only be a small step to dismantling the quantum computer, and making sure there is no possibility of any further contact at all."

"Well, in that case, what do you want to do when you get out of the hospital?"

Ponter looked directly at Mary. "Spend more time with you."

Mary's heart fluttered again, but in a good way this time, and she smiled. "That would be terrific." And then a thought struck her. "Next week, I'm going to Washington, to present my Neanderthal-DNA studies at the Paleoanthropology Society meeting. Why don't you come along for that? You'd be the biggest hit they've had since Wolpoff and Tattersall squared off at the Kansas City meeting."

"This is a gathering of specialists in ancient forms of humanity?" asked Ponter.

"That's right," said Mary. "Most of the people who study such things from all over the world will be there. Believe me, they'd love to meet you."

Ponter frowned, and for a moment Mary was afraid that she had offended him. "How would I get there?"

"I'll take you," said Mary. "When do you get out of the hospital?"

"I believe they wish to keep me here for one more day."

"All right then," said Mary.

"Will there not be obstacles to us doing this?"

"Oh, yes," Mary said, smiling. "And I know just the man to make them disappear . . ."

Chapter Twenty

There was an irony, Ambassador Tukana Prat knew, in this particular man desiring privacy. And yet who could blame him for being a recluse? He was famous around the planet, honored wherever he went. And, indeed, soon the entire world would celebrate the thousandth month since his great invention. He would be expected to make hundreds of public appearances then—assuming, as one always had to when dealing with a person of his age, that he was still alive. He was a member of generation 138, one of fewer than a thousand individuals left in that group—and nobody from any earlier generation still lived.

Tukana had met 138s before, but not recently. It must have been fifty months since she'd last been in the company of one, and never before had she seen someone looking so old.

They say gray hair is a sign of wisdom—but the great man's hair was completely gone, at least from that famous, incredibly long skull. To be sure, he still had fine, almost transparent hair covering his arms. It was an odd sight: a man ancient and shriveled, with skin mottled gray and brown, but with piercing blue artificial eyes, eyes that consisted of polished metal balls and segmented irises, eyes that glowed from within. Of course, he could have gotten artificial eyes that matched his originals cosmetically, but this man, of all people, had no reason to hide implants. Indeed, Tukana knew that other implants governed the functioning of his heart and kidneys, that artificial bones had replaced major portions of his crumbling skeleton. Besides, she'd heard him quip once during a conversation with an Exhibitionist that when people were as old as he was, it was good for others to see that they had replacement eyes, because then they stopped assuming that you're too old to see anything.

Tukana entered the vast living room. The owner was old enough that the tree from which his home was made had reached a prodigious diameter, and he had hollowed out more and more of its interior as the months went by.

And how many months it'd been! A member of generation 138 would have seen over thirteen hundred moons by now—a staggering 108 years of life.

"Healthy day," said Tukana, taking a seat.

"At this point," said the surprisingly strong, deep voice, "I will take any day I can get, healthy or otherwise."

Tukana wasn't sure if the comment was meant humorously or ruefully, and so she just smiled and nodded. And then, after a moment, she said, "I can't tell you what an honor it is to meet you, sir."

"Try," said the old man.

Tukana was flustered. "Well, it's just that we owe you so much, and—"

But the man held up his hand. "I'm kidding, young lady." At this Tukana Prat did smile, for it had been ages since anyone had referred to her as "young lady." "In fact, you would honor me most if you *spared* me the honors. Believe me, I've heard them all before. In fact, in deference to how little time I have left, I would appreciate it if you wasted none of it. Please immediately tell me what you want."

Tukana found herself smiling again. As a diplomat, she'd met many important world leaders, but she'd never thought she would ever come face to face with the greatest inventor of them all, the renowned Lonwis Trob. Still, it was unnerving to look into his mechanical eyes, and so she found her gaze dropping to his left forearm, to the Companion implanted there. Of course, it wasn't the original Companion that Lonwis had invented all those many months ago. No, this was the latest model—and all its metal parts, Tukana was astonished to see, were made of gold.

"I don't know how much of this stuff about the parallel Earth you've been following, but—"

"Every bit of it," said Lonwis. "It's fascinating."

"Well then, you must know that I'm the ambassador selected by the High Gray Council—"

"Squabbling brats!" said Lonwis. "Fools, every one of them."

"Well, I can understand—"

"You know," said Lonwis, "I hear some of them dye their hair gray, just to make themselves look smart."

Lonwis seemed quite content to waste his own time, Tukana noted, but she supposed he'd earned that privilege. "In any event," she said, "they want to close the portal between our world and the Gliksin one."

"Why?"

"They're afraid of the Gliksins."

"You've met them; they haven't. I'd rather hear your opinion."

"Well, you must know that one of them tried to kill Envoy Boddit, and discharged a weapon at me, as well."

"Yes, so I heard. But you both survived."

"Yes."

"You know, my friend Goosa—"

Tukana couldn't help interrupting. "Goosa?" she repeated. Goosa *Kusk*?"

Lonwis nodded.

"Wow," said Tukana, softly.

"Anyway, I'm sure Goosa could figure out a way to protect against those projectile weapons the Gliksins use. The projectiles are propelled by a chemical explosion, as I understand it—which means although they're going fast, they're nowhere near as fast as light. So there'd be plenty of time for a laser to target and vaporize them. After all, my Companions are already scanning out to a radius of 2.5 armspans. Even if the projectile had reached the speed of sound, there would still be—" He paused for the barest instant, and Tukana wondered if he was doing the math himself, or listening to his Companion; she rather suspected it was the former. "—0.005 beats for the laser to target and fire. You'd need a spherical emitter—no time to swivel a mechanical part—probably mounted in a hat. A trivial problem." He looked at her. "So, was that what you needed? If so, I'll contact Goosa on your behalf, and get on with my day."

"Um, no," said Tukana. "I mean, yes, something like that would be fabulous. But that's not the reason I came here."

"Well then, get to it, young lady. What exactly do you want?"

Tukana swallowed. "It's not just a favor from you; we'll need a few of your esteemed friends, as well."

"To do what?"

Tukana told him, and was pleased to see the ancient man's face splitting into a grin.

Chapter Twenty-one

Louise Benoît had been right: Jock Krieger could pull just about any string imaginable. The idea of one of his Synergy researchers getting to spend more than a week picking the brain of a Neanderthal appealed to him greatly, and Mary found every possible obstacle to a trip with Ponter falling away. And Jock had concurred with Ponter that the longer he stayed in this world, the longer they would have in order to convince the Neanderthals not to shut down the portal.

Mary had decided on driving to Washington, D.C., with Ponter; it seemed simpler than hassling with airports and all the security. Plus, it would give her a chance to show Ponter some sights along the way.

Mary rented a silver Ford Windstar van with tinted windows, making it hard for people passing them to see who her passenger was. They drove first to Philadelphia, an unmarked escort vehicle discreetly following them. Mary and Ponter saw Independence Hall and the Liberty Bell, and had original Philly steak sandwiches at Pat's; despite the cheese, Ponter ate three of them—well, Mary was going to say "in one sitting," but it was standing room only at Pat's, and they ate outside. Mary felt a bit strange explaining U.S. history to Ponter, but she rather suspected she was doing a better job of it than an American would have at explaining Canadian history.

Ponter seemed almost completely recovered from his

trauma—he seemed not just strong as an ox, but to have an ox's constitution, too. That was appropriate, thought Mary, with a grin: they were, after all, visiting the home of the world's strongest constitution . . .

Ambassador Tukana Prat strode out onto the large semicircular stage at the front of the General Assembly hall. She was followed by one Neanderthal, then another, then another, and another still, more and more, until ten members of her race had lined up behind her. She stepped to the podium, and leaned into the microphone.

"Ladies and gentlemen of the United Nations," she said. "It is my pleasure to introduce you to our new delegation to your Earth. Despite the unfortunate circumstances of my last visit, we all come to you in peace and in friendship, with open arms. Not just me—not just a government functionary—but ten of our very best and brightest. They did not have to come here; each *chose* to make the trip. They are here because they believe in the ideal of free cultural exchange. We know you had assumed a—I believe your phrase is 'tit-for-tat'—approach: you give us something, we give you something in return. But this opening of contact between two worlds should not be the province of economists or businesspeople, and certainly not of warriors. No, such an interchange is the natural purview of idealists and dreamers, of those who have the most lofty of goals—those who have *humanitarian* goals." Tukana smiled out at the crowd. "This is already one of the longest speeches of my career, and so, without further ado, let me present our delegates."

She turned around and pointed to the first of the ten Neanderthals behind her, a man ancient beyond compare, with blue mechanical eyes glowing from beneath his browridge.

"This," said Tukana, "is Lonwis Trob, our greatest inventor.

He developed the Companion-implant and alibi-recording technologies that make our world safe day and night for all its inhabitants. The—what you would call 'patents,' the intellectual-property rights for these inventions—are his, and he comes to share them freely."

There was an astonished murmur through the crowd. Music began to play through the General Assembly's speakers, haunting music, stirring music, Neanderthal music.

"And this," said Tukana, indicating the next in line—in Neanderthal fashion, she was working from right to left—"is Borl Kadas, our leading geneticist." An elderly female, a 138, stepped forward. Tukana continued. "I have heard talk here about the patenting of the human genome. Well, Scholar Kadas led our equivalent of your Human Genome Project, some five decades ago. She comes here prepared to freely share that research, and all the benefits we have gathered from it."

Tukana noted the dropped jaws on many of the delegates.

"And this," she said, indicating a portly male, "is Dor Farrer, poet laureate of Bontar province, widely regarded as our greatest living writer. He carries with him computerized archives of all the great plays and poetry, fiction and nonfiction, iterative narratives, and imaginative transcripts created in the past by our people, and will aid in their translation into your many languages."

Farrer waved enthusiastically at the delegates. The music was becoming richer, additional instruments joining in.

"Next to him is Derba Jonk. She is our foremost specialist in the use of stem-cell technology to selectively clone body parts. We understand that you are just beginning research in that area; we have been doing it for four generations—four decades—and Scholar Jonk will be pleased to help your doctors leap ahead that far."

Many of the delegates made exclamations of astonishment.

"And next to her," said Tukana, "is Kobast Gant, our leading expert in artificial intelligence. Those of you who have spoken to Ponter Boddit or myself have already experienced Scholar Gant's handiwork—our intelligent Companions were programmed by him. Again, he comes to freely share his knowledge with your world."

Even the amanuensis-high-warrior was murmuring appreciatively now. Cube-drums had joined the musical arrangement, pounding like hearts swelling with pride.

"And next to Scholar Gant is Jalsk Lalplun, who holds the distinction of currently being the fastest human alive—in either universe I believe. We timed him yesterday: he can run one of your miles in three minutes, eleven seconds. Jalsk will share his approach to athletic training."

Jalsk's smile stretched from ear to ear. The music was gaining in tempo, in cadence.

"Next to Jalsk is Rabba Habrorn. She is one of our leading legal minds—the chief modern interpreter of our Code of Civilization. Many of you have wondered about our ability to have morals and ethics without recourse to a higher being. Adjudicator Habrorn will be pleased to answer all your questions in that area." A trio of ice-horns had joined the orchestra.

Habrorn tipped her head with great dignity. Despite Assembly-hall rules, several of the delegates had taken out cell phones and were making calls, presumably to their heads of state.

"Standing beside her," said Tukana, "is Drade Klimilk, head of our Philosophy Academy. Do not let his brown hair fool you; he is considered one of the wisest and most insightful thinkers in our world. Between him and Adjudicator Habrorn, you will learn all about our modes of thought."

Klimilk spoke, his voice deep and strong. "I am looking

forward to it." The symphony repeated an earlier movement, but with more volume, more gusto.

"Next to Scholar Klimilk is Krik Donalt, one of our greatest musical composers. It is her composition—called 'Two becoming One'—that you are hearing now."

Donalt bowed.

"And last—but, as you would say, not least—this is Dapbur Kajak, who some of your people are already familiar with. She invented the tunable-laser process that makes possible the decontamination of travelers between our two worlds. Scholar Kajak will share everything she knows about disinfecting humans, and about quantum-cascade laser physics."

The music swelled in a crescendo, cube-drums, ice-horns, percussion geodes, and more, all in perfect harmony.

Tukana continued. "All ten of them—scientists and engineers, philosophers and artists, athletes and scholars—come here to freely share with you everything they know about their individual fields of expertise." She looked out at the General Assembly. "Let us make this work, friends. Let us establish a relationship between our worlds that will benefit everyone, a relationship founded on peace. The past is *past;* our business now is the future. Let's make it as positive for all of us as possible."

It was, Tukana Prat thought, one of the Austrian delegates who first began slapping his hands together, but he was almost immediately joined by dozens, then hundreds, of others, and soon all the delegates were on their feet, making enthusiastic noises with their palms and mouths.

Incompetent? thought Tukana, beaming out at the crowd, thrilled with what she'd begun here today. *Incompetent, my hairy ass . . .*

Chapter Twenty-two

"We've only got one day here in Washington before the conference begins," said Mary, "and there's so much I want to show you. But I wanted to start with this. Nothing else says more about this country, and about what it means to be human—my kind of human."

Ponter looked at the strange vista in front of him, not understanding. There was a scar in the grass-covered landscape, a deep welt that ran for eighty paces then met, at an obtuse angle, another similar scar.

The scars were black and reflective—a . . . what was that word again? An *ox-uh-mor-on,* that was it; a contradiction in terms. Black, meaning it absorbed all light; reflective, meaning it bounced light back.

And yet that's precisely what it was, a black mirror, reflecting Ponter's face, and Mary's, too. Two kinds of humanity—not just female and male, but two separate species, two different iterations of the human theme. Her reflection showed what she called a *Homo sapiens* and he called a *Gliksin*: her strange upright forehead, minuscule nose, and—there was no word in Ponter's language for it—her *chin.*

And his reflection showed what she called a *Homo neanderthalensis* and he called a *Barast,* the word for "human" in his language: a Neanderthal's broad countenance, with a doubly arched browridge and a proper-sized nose extending across a third of his face.

"What is it?" asked Ponter, staring at the oblong blackness, at their reflections.

"It's a memorial," said Mary. She looked away from the black wall and waved her hand at objects in the distance. "This whole mall is filled with memorials. The pair of walls here point at two of the most important ones. That spire is the Washington Monument, a memorial to the first U.S. president. Over there, that's the Lincoln Memorial, commemorating the president who freed the slaves."

Ponter's translator bleeped.

Mary let out a sigh. Evidently there was still more complexity, more—what had she called it?—more dirty linen to be aired.

"We'll visit both those memorials later," said Mary. "But, as I said, I wanted to start here. This is the Vietnam Veterans Memorial."

"Vietnam is one of your nations, is it not?" said Ponter.

Mary nodded. "In southeast Asia—southeast Galasoy. Just north of the equator. An S-shaped bit of land"—she drew the letter with a finger in the air so that Ponter would understand—"on the Pacific seaboard."

"We call the same place Holtanatan. But on my version of Earth it is very hot, very humid, rainy, full of swamps, and overrun by insects. No one lives there."

Mary lifted her eyebrows. "Over eighty million people live there in this reality."

Ponter shook his head. The humans of this version of Earth were so . . . so *unrestrained.*

"And," continued Mary, "a war was fought there."

"Over what? Over swamps?"

Mary closed her eyes. "Over ideology. Remember I told you about the Cold War? This was part of that—but this part was hot."

"Hot?" Ponter shook his head. "You are not referring to temperature, are you?"

"No. *Hot.* As in a shooting war. As in people died."

Ponter frowned. "How many people?"

"In total, from all sides? No one really knows. Over a million of the local South Vietnamese. Somewhere between half a million and a million North Vietnamese. Plus . . ." She gestured at the wall.

"Yes?" said Ponter, still baffled by the reflecting blackness.

"Plus fifty-eight thousand, two hundred and nine Americans. These two walls commemorate them."

"Commemorate them how?"

"See the writing engraved in the black granite?"

Ponter nodded.

"Those are names—names of the confirmed dead, and of those missing in action who never came home." Mary paused. "The war ended in 1975."

"But this is the year you reckon as"—and Ponter named it.

Mary nodded.

Ponter looked down. "I do not think the missing are coming home." He moved closer to the wall. "How are the names arrayed?"

"Chronologically. By date of death."

Ponter looked at the names, all in what he'd learned were known as capital letters, a small mark—a bullet, isn't that what they called it, one of their many words that served double duty?—separating each name from the next.

Ponter couldn't read English characters; he was only beginning to grasp this strange notion of a phonetic alphabet. Mary moved in beside him, and, in a soft voice, read some of the names to him. "Mike A. Maksin. Bruce J. Moran. Bobbie Joe Mounts. Raymond D. McGlothin." She pointed at another line, apparently chosen at random. "Samuel F. Hollifield, Jr. Rufus Hood. James M. Inman. David L. Johnson. Arnoldo L. Carrillo."

And another line, farther down. "Donney L. Jackson. Bobby W. Jobe. Bobby Ray Jones. Halcott P. Jones, Jr."

"Fifty-eight thousand of them," said Ponter, his voice as soft as Mary's.

"Yes."

"But—but you said these are dead Americans?"

Mary nodded.

"What were they doing fighting a war half a world away?"

"They were helping the South Vietnamese. See, in 1954, Vietnam had been divided into two halves, North Vietnam and South Vietnam, as part of a peace agreement, each with its own kind of government. Two years later, in 1956, there were to be free elections throughout both halves, supervised by an international committee, to unify Vietnam under a single, popularly elected government. But when 1956 rolled around, the leader of South Vietnam refused to hold the scheduled elections."

"You taught me much about this country, the United States, when we visited Philadelphia," said Ponter. "I know how highly Americans value democracy. Let me guess: the United States sent troops to force South Vietnam to participate in the promised democratic election."

But Mary shook her head. "No, no, the United States supported the South's desire *not* to hold the election."

"But why? Was the government in the North corrupt?"

"No," said Mary. "No, it was reasonably honest and kind—at least up until when the promised election, which it wanted, was canceled. But there *was* a corrupt government—the one in the South."

Ponter shook his head, baffled. "But you said that the South was the one the Americans were supporting."

"That's right. See, the government in the South was corrupt, but capitalist; it shared the American economic system. The one in the north was Communist; it used the economic system of the Soviet Union and China. But the northern government was much more popular than the corrupt southern one. The United States feared that if free elections were held, the Communists would win and control all of Vietnam, which in turn, would lead to other countries in southeast Galasoy falling to Communist rule."

"And so American soldiers were sent there?"

"Yes."

"And died?"

"Many did, yes." Mary paused. "That's what I wanted you to understand: how important principles are to us. We will die to defend an ideology, die to support a cause." She pointed at the wall. "These people here, these fifty-eight thousand people, fought for what they believed in. They were told to go to war, told to save a weaker people from what was held to be the great Communist threat, and they did so. Most of them were young—eighteen, nineteen, twenty, twenty-one years old. For many, it was their first time away from home."

"And now they are dead."

Mary nodded. "But not forgotten. We remember them here." She pointed discreetly. Ponter's guards—now members of the FBI, arranged by Jock Krieger—were keeping people away from him, but the walls were long, so incredibly long, and farther down someone was leaning up against the black surface. "Scc that man there?" asked Mary. "He's using a pencil and a piece of paper to make a rubbing of the name of someone he knew. He's—well, he looks in his midfifties, no? He might have been in Vietnam himself. The name he's copying might be that of a buddy he lost over there."

Ponter and Mary watched silently as the man finished what he was doing. And then the man folded the piece of paper, placed it in his breast pocket, and began to speak.

Ponter shook his head slightly in confusion. He gestured at the Companion embedded in his own left forearm. "I thought you people did not have telecommunications implants."

"We don't," said Mary.

"But I do not see any external receiver, any—what do you call it?—any cell phone."

"That's right," said Mary, gently.

"Then who is he talking to?"

Mary lifted her shoulders slightly. "His lost comrade."

"But that person is dead."

"Yes."

"One cannot talk to the dead," said Ponter.

Mary gestured at the wall again, its obsidian surface pantomiming the sweep of her arm. "People think they can. They say they feel closest to them here."

"Is this where the remains of the dead are stored?"

"What? No, no, no."

"Then I—"

"It's the *names,*" said Mary, sounding somewhat exasperated. "The names. The names are here, and we connect with people through their names."

Ponter frowned. "I—forgive me, I do not mean to be stupid. Surely that cannot be right, though. We—my people—connect through faces. There are countless people whose faces I know but whose names I have never learned. And, well, I connect with you, and although I know your name, I cannot articulate it or even think it clearly. Mare—that is the best I can do."

"We think names are . . ." Mary lifted her shoulders, apparently acknowledging how ridiculous what she was saying must sound ". . . are *magical.*"

"But," said Ponter again, "you cannot communicate with the dead." He wasn't trying to be stubborn; really, he wasn't.

Mary closed her eyes for a moment, as if summoning inner strength—or, thought Ponter, as if communicating with someone somewhere else. "I know your people do not believe in an afterlife," said Mary, at last.

" 'Afterlife,' " said Ponter, serving up the word as though it were a choice gobbet of meat. "An oxymoron."

"Not to us," said Mary. And then, more emphatically, "Not to me." She looked around. At first Ponter thought it was simply an externalization of her thoughts; he presumed she was seeking some way to explain what she was feeling. But then her eyes lighted on something, and she started walking. Ponter followed her.

"Do you see these flowers?" said Mary.

He nodded. "Of course."

"They were left here, by one of the living, for one of the dead. Somebody whose name is on this panel." She pointed at the section of polished granite in front of her.

Mary bent low. The flowers—red roses—still had long stems, and were bundled together by string. A small card was attached to the bundle with a ribbon. " 'For Willie,' " said Mary, evidently reading from the card, " 'from his loving sister.' "

"Ah," said Ponter, having no better response at hand.

Mary walked farther. She came to a fawn-colored sheet of paper leaning against the wall, and picked it up. " 'Dear Carl,' " she read. She paused, and searched the panel in front of her. "This must be him," she said, reaching forward and lightly touching a name. "Carl Bowen." She continued to look at the incised name. "This one is for you, Carl," she said—apparently her own words, since she wasn't looking down at the sheet. She then lowered her eyes and read aloud, starting over at the beginning:

> Dear Carl—
>
> I know I should have come here earlier. I wanted to. Honest, I did. But I didn't know how you would take the news. I know I was your first love, and you were mine, and no summer has been as wonderful for me as that summer of '66. I thought of you every day you were gone, and when word came that you had died, I cried and cried, and I'm crying again now as I write these words.
>
> I don't want you to think I ever stopped mourning you, because I didn't. But I did go on with life. I married Bucky Samuels. Remember him? From Eastside? We've got two kids, both older now than you were when you died.
>
> You wouldn't recognize me, I don't think. My hair has got some gray in it, which I try to hide, and I lost all my freckles long ago, but I still think of you. I love Buck very much, but I love you, too . . . and I know someday, we'll see each other again.
>
> Love forever,
>
> Jane

" 'See each other again?' " repeated Ponter. "But he is dead."

Mary nodded. "She means, she'll see him when she dies, too."

Ponter frowned. Mary walked a few steps farther along. Another letter was leaning against the wall, this one laminated in clear plastic. She picked it up. " 'Dear Frankie,' " she began.

She scanned the wall in front of her. "Here he is," she said. "Franklin T. Mullens, III." She read the letter aloud:

Dear Frankie,

They say a parent shouldn't outlive a child, but who expects a child to be taken when he's only 19? I miss you every day, and so does your pa. You know him—he tries to be strong in front of me, but I hear him crying softly to this day when he thinks I'm asleep.

A mother's job is to look after her son, and I did the best I could. But now God Himself is looking after you, and I know you are safe in his loving arms.

We will be together again, my darling son.

Love,

Ma

Ponter didn't know what to say. The sentiments were so obviously sincere, but . . . but they were *irrational.* Couldn't Mary see that? Couldn't the people who wrote these letters see that?

Mary continued to read to him from letters and cards and plaques and scrolls that had been left leaning against the wall. Phrases stuck in Ponter's mind.

"We know God is taking care of you . . ."

"I long for that day when we will all be together again . . ."

"So much forgotten / So much unsaid / But I promise to tell you all / When we meet among the dead."

"Sleep now, beloved . . ."

"I look forward to when we are reunited . . ."

". . . on that wonderful day when the Lord will reunite us in Heaven . . ."

"Goodbye—God be with ye!—until we meet again . . ."

"Take care, bro. I'll visit you again next time I'm in D.C. . . ."

"Rest in peace, my friend, rest in peace . . ."

Mary had to pause several times to wipe away tears. Ponter felt sad, too, and his eyes were likewise moist, but not, he suspected, for the same reason. "It is always hard to have a loved one die," said Ponter.

Mary nodded slightly.

"But . . ." he continued, then fell silent.

"Yes?" Mary prodded.

"This memorial," said Ponter, sweeping his arm, taking in its two great walls. "What is its purpose?"

Mary's eyebrows climbed again. "To honor the dead."

"Not *all* the dead," said Ponter, softly. "These are only the Americans . . ."

"Well, yes," said Mary. "It's a monument to the sacrifice made by American soldiers, a way for the people of the United States to show that they appreciate them."

"Appreciated," said Ponter.

Mary looked confused.

"Is my translator malfunctioning?" asked Ponter. "You can appreciate—present tense—what still exists; you can only have appreciated—past tense—that which is no more."

Mary sighed, clearly not wishing to debate the point.

"But you have not answered my question," said Ponter, gently. "What is this memorial *for?*"

"I told you. To honor the dead."

"No, no," said Ponter. "That may be an incidental effect, I grant you. But surely the purpose of the designer—"

"Maya Ying Lin," said Mary.

"Pardon?"

"Maya Ying Lin. That's the name of the woman who designed this."

"Ah," said Ponter. "Well, surely her purpose—the purpose of anyone who designs a memorial—is to make sure people never forget."

"Yes?" said Mary, sounding irritated by whatever picayune distinction she felt Ponter was making.

"And the reason to not forget the past," said Ponter, "is so that the same mistakes can be avoided."

"Well, yes, of course," said Mary.

"So has this memorial served its purpose? Has the same mistake—the mistake that led to all these young people dying—been avoided since?"

Mary thought for a time, then shook her head. "I suppose not. Wars are still fought, and—"

"By America? By the people who built this monument?"

"Yes," said Mary.

"Why?"

"Economics. Ideology. And . . ."

"Yes?"

Mary lifted her shoulders. "Revenge. Getting even."

"When this country decides to go to war, where is the war declared?"

"Um, in the Congress. I'll show you the building later."

"Can this memorial be seen from there?"

"This one? No, I don't think so."

"They should do it right here," said Ponter, flatly. "Their leader—the president, no?—he should declare war right here, standing in front of these fifty-eight thousand, two hundred and nine names. Surely *that* should be the purpose of such a memorial: if a leader can stand and look at the names of all those who died a previous time a president declared war and still call for young people to go off and be killed in another war, then perhaps the war is worth fighting."

Mary tilted her head to one side but said nothing.

"After all, you said you fight to preserve your most fundamental values."

"That's the ideal, yes," said Mary.

"But this war—this war in Vietnam. You said it was to support a corrupt government, to prevent elections from being held."

"Well, yes, in a way."

"In Philadelphia you showed me where and how this country began. Is not the United States's most cherished belief that of democracy, of the will of the people being heard and done?"

Mary nodded.

"But then surely they should have fought a war to ensure that that ideal was upheld. To have gone to Vietnam to make sure the people there had a chance to vote would have been an American ideal. And if the Vietnam people . . ."

"Vietnamese."

"As you say. If they had chosen the Communist system by vote, then the American ideal of democracy would have been served. Surely you cannot hold democracy dear only when the vote goes the way you wish it would."

"Maybe you're right," said Mary. "A great many people thought the American involvement in Vietnam was wrong. They called it a profane war."

"Profane?"

"Umm, an insult to God."

Ponter rolled his eyebrow up his browridge. "From what I have seen, this God of yours must have a thick skin."

Mary tilted her head, conceding the point.

"You have told me," said Ponter, "that the majority of people in this country are Christians, like you, is that not so?"

"Yes."

"How big a majority?"

"Big," said Mary. "I was actually reading up on this when I moved down here. The U.S. has a population of about 270 million." Ponter had heard this figure before, so its vastness didn't startle him this time. "About a million are atheists—they don't believe in God at all. Another twenty-five million are nonreligious; that is, they don't adhere to any particular faith. All the other faith groups combined—Jews, Buddhists, Muslims, Hindus—add up to about 15 million. Everyone else—almost 240 million—say they are Christians."

"So this *is* a Christian country," said Ponter.

"Welllll, like my home country of Canada," said Mary, "the U.S. prides itself on its tolerance of a variety of beliefs."

Ponter waved a hand dismissively. "Two hundred and forty million out of two hundred and seventy million is almost ninety percent; it *is* a Christian country. And you and others have told me the core beliefs of Christians. What did Christ say about those who would attack you?"

"The Sermon on the Mount," said Mary. She closed her eyes, presumably to aid her remembering. " 'Ye have heard that it hath been said, An eye for an eye, and a tooth for a tooth: But I say unto you, That ye resist not evil: but whosoever shall smite thee on thy right cheek, turn to him the other also.' "

"So revenge has no place in the policies of a Christian nation," said Ponter. "And yet you say that is a reason it fights wars. Likewise, impeding the free choice of a foreign country should have had no place in the policies of a democratic nation, and yet it fought this war in Vietnam."

Mary said nothing.

"Do you not see?" said Ponter. "*That* is what this memorial, this Vietnam veterans wall, should serve as a reminder of: the pointlessness of death, the error—the *grave* error, if I may attempt my own play on words in your language—of declaring a war in contravention of your most dearly held principles."

Mary was still silent.

"That is the reason why future American wars should be declared here—*right here.* Only if the cause stands the test of supporting the most dearly held fundamental principles, then perhaps it is a war that *should* be fought." Ponter let his eyes run over the wall again, over the black reflection.

Mary said nothing.

"Still," said Ponter, "let me make a simpler proposition. Those letters you read—they are, I presume, typical?"

Mary nodded. "Ones like them are left here every day."

"But do you not see the problem? There is an underlying belief in those letters that the dead are not really dead. 'God is taking care of you.' 'We will all be together again.' 'I know you are watching over me.' 'Someday I will see you again.' "

"We've been down this road before," said Mary. "My kind of humanity—not just Christians, but most *Homo sapiens,* no matter what their particular religion—believe that the essence of a person does not end with the death of the body. The soul lives on."

"And that belief," said Ponter firmly, "is the problem. I have thought this since you first told me of it, but it is—what do you say?—it is driven home for me here, at this memorial, this wall of names."

"Yes?" said Mary.

"They are *dead.* They are eliminated. They no longer exist." He reached forward and touched a name he could not read. "The person who was named this." He touched another. "And the person who was named this." And he touched a third. "And the person who had this name. They are *no more.* Surely facing that is the real lesson of this wall. One cannot come here to speak with the dead, for the dead are *dead.* One cannot come here to beg forgiveness from the dead, for the dead are *dead.* One cannot come here to be touched by the dead, for the dead are *dead.* These names, these characters carved in stone—that is *all* that is left of them. Surely that is the message of this wall, the lesson to be learned. As long as your people keep thinking that this life is a prologue, that more is to come after it, that those wronged here will be rewarded in some *there* yet to come, you will continue to undervalue life, and you will continue to send young people off to die."

Mary took a deep breath and let it out slowly, apparently composing herself. She gestured with a movement of her head. Ponter turned to look. Another person—a gray-haired man—was placing a letter of his own in front of the wall. "Could you tell him?" asked Mary, speaking sharply. "Tell him that he's wasting his time? Or that woman, over there—the one on her knees, praying? Could you tell her? Disabuse her of her delusion? The belief that somewhere their loved ones still exist gives them comfort."

Ponter shook his head. "That belief is what *caused* this to happen. The only way to honor the dead is by ensuring that no more enter that state prematurely."

Mary sounded angry. "All right, then. Go tell them."

Ponter turned and looked at the Gliksins and their ebony reflections in the wall. His people almost never took human lives, and Mary's people did it on such large scales, with such frequency. Surely this belief in God and an afterlife had to be linked to their readiness to kill.

He took a step forward, but . . .

But, right now, these people did not look vicious, did not look bloodthirsty, did not look ready to kill. Right now, they looked sad, so incredibly sad.

Mary was still upset with him. "Go on," she said, gesturing

with a hand. "What's the holdup? Go tell them."

Ponter thought about how sad he himself had been when Klast had died. And yet . . .

And yet, these people—these strange, strange Gliksins—were taking some comfort from their beliefs. He stared at the individuals by the wall, kept away from him by armed agents. No, no, he would not tell these mourners that their loved ones were truly gone. After all, it wasn't these sad people who had sent them off to die.

Ponter turned toward Mary. "I understand the belief provides comfort, but . . ." He shook his head. "But how do you break out of the cycle? God making killing palatable, God providing comfort after the killing is done. How do you keep from repeating it over and over again?"

"I have no idea," said Mary.

"You must do *something,*" Ponter said.

"I do," said Mary. "I pray."

Ponter looked at her, looked back at the mourners, then turned once more to Mary, and he let his head hang, staring down at the ground in front of him, unable to face her or the thousands of names. "If I thought there was the slightest possibility it would work," he said softly, "I would join you."

Chapter Twenty-three

"Fascinating," said Jurard Selgan. "Fascinating."

"What?" Ponter's voice was tinged with irritation.

"Your behavior, while at the memorial wall commemorating those Gliksins who had died in southeast Galasoy."

"What about it?" said Ponter. His voice was sharp, like that of someone trying to talk while a scab was being picked off.

*"Well, this was not the first time your beliefs—*our *beliefs, as Barasts—had been in conflict with those of the Gliksins, was it?"*

"No, of course not."

"Indeed," said Selgan, "such conflicts must have come up on your first visit there, no?"

"I guess."

"Can you give me an example?" asked Selgan.

Ponter folded his arms in front of his chest. "All right," he said, in a smug, I'll-show-you tone. "I mentioned this to you right at the beginning: the Gliksins have this silly notion that the universe has only existed for a finite time. They've completely misconstrued the redshift evidence, thinking it indicates an expanding universe; they don't understand that mass varies over time. Further, they think the cosmic microwave background radiation is the lingering echo of what they call 'the big bang'—a vast explosion they believe started the universe."

"They seem to like things blowing up," said Selgan.

"They certainly do. But, of course, the uniformity of the background radiation is really caused by repeated absorption and emission of elec-

trons trapped in plasma-pinching magnetic-vortex filaments."

"I'm sure you're right," said Selgan, conceding that this wasn't his territory of expertise.

"I am right," replied Ponter. "But I didn't fight with them over that issue. During my first visit, Mare said to me, 'I don't think you're going to convince many people that the big bang didn't happen.' And I told her that was fine; I said: 'Feeling a need to convince others that you're right is something that comes from religion; I'm simply content to know that I am right, even if others don't know it.' "

"Ah," said Selgan. "And do you really feel that way?"

"Yes. To the Gliksins, knowledge is a battle! A territorial war! Why, to have their equivalent of the title 'Scholar' conferred upon you, you have to defend a thesis. That's the word they use: defend! But science isn't about defending one's position against all comers; it's about flexibility and open-mindedness and valuing the truth, no matter who finds it."

"I concur," said Selgan. He paused for a moment, then: "But you didn't spend much time looking for any evidence as to whether the Gliksins might have been right in their belief in an afterlife."

"That's not true. I gave Mary every opportunity to demonstrate the validity of that claim."

"Before this encounter at the memorial wall, you mean?"

"Yes. But she had nothing!"

"And so, as in the case of their finite cosmology, you let the matter go, content to know that you were right?"

"Yes. Well, I mean . . ."

Selgan raised his eyebrow. "Yes?"

"I mean, all right, sure, I argued with her about this belief in an afterlife. But that was different."

"Different from the cosmological question? Why?"

"Because so much more was at stake."

"Doesn't the cosmological question deal with the ultimate fate of the entire universe?"

"I mean, it wasn't just an abstract issue. It was—it is*—the heart of everything."*

"Why?"

"Because . . . because—gristle, I don't know why. It just seems terribly important. It's what lets them fight all those wars, after all."

"I understand. But I also understand that it is fundamental to their beliefs; it was something that surely you must have realized they weren't going to give up easily."

"I suppose."

"And yet, you continued to press the point."

"Well, yes."

"Why?"

Ponter shrugged.

"Would you like to hear my guess?" asked Selgan.

Ponter shrugged again.

"You were pushing this issue because you wanted to see if there was *some proof of this afterlife. Perhaps Mare, and the other Gliksins, had been holding out on you. Perhaps there was evidence that she would reveal if you kept pushing."*

"There cannot be evidence for that which does not exist," said Ponter.

"Granted," said Selgan. "But either you were trying to convince them that you were right—or you were trying to force them to convince you *that* they *were right."*

Ponter shook his head. "It was pointless," he said. "It is a ridiculous belief, this notion of souls."

"Souls?" said Selgan.

"The immaterial part of one's essence that they believe is immortal."

"Ah. And you say this is a ridiculous belief?"

"Of course."

"But surely they are entitled to hold it, no?"

"I guess."

"Just as they are entitled to their bizarre cosmological model, no?"

"I suppose."

"And yet, you couldn't let this question of an afterlife go, could you? Even once you'd left the memorial wall, you still tried to push this point, didn't you?"

Ponter looked away.

With the crisis over the closing of the portal at least temporarily averted—there was no way the Neanderthals would shut it down now with a dozen of their most valuable citizens on this side—Jock Krieger decided to return to the research he'd been doing earlier.

He left Seabreeze, driving his black BMW to the River Campus of the University of Rochester; the river in question was the Genesee. When he'd been setting up Synergy, a couple of phone calls from the right people was all it had taken to get his entire staff full priority access to the UR Library holdings. Jock parked his car in the Wilmot Lot, and headed into the brown brick Carlson Science & Engineering Library—named for Chester F. Carlson, the inventor of xerography. Journals, Jock knew, were on the first floor. He showed his university VIP ID to the librarian, a pudgy black woman with her hair in a red kerchief. He told her what he needed, and she waddled off into the back. Jock, never one to waste time, pulled out his PDA and scanned articles from that day's *New York Times* and *Washington Post.*

After about five minutes, the librarian returned, presenting Jock with the three back issues he'd requested—one of *Earth and Planetary Science Letters,* and two of *Nature*—which his Web-searching had shown contained follow-ups to the rapid-magnetic-reversal research by Coe, *et al.*

Jock found an unoccupied study carrel and sat down. The first thing he did was remove his HP CapShare from his briefcase—a battery-powered hand-held document scanner. He ran the device over the pages of the articles he was interested in, capturing them at 200 dpi, adequate for OCRing later. Jock smiled at the portrait of Chester Carlson mounted near where he was sitting—he'd have loved this little unit.

Jock then started reading the actual articles. What was most interesting about the original piece, the one in *Earth and Planetary Science Letters,* was that the authors freely acknowledged that the results they'd found were at odds with conventional wisdom, which held that magnetic collapses would take thousands of years to occur. That belief though, was apparently based not so much on established facts but rather just a general feeling that the Earth's magnetic field was a ponderous thing that couldn't rapidly stand on its head.

But Coe and Prévot had found evidence of extremely rapid collapses. Their studies were based on lava flows at Steens Mountain in southern Oregon, where a volcano had erupted fifty-six separate times during a magnetic-field reversal, providing time-lapse snapshots of the action. Although they couldn't determine the intervals between the eruptions, they did know how long the lava in each one must have taken to cool to the Curie Point, where the magnetization of the newly formed rocks would be locked in, matching the current orientation and strength of Earth's magnetic field. The study suggested the field had collapsed in as little as a few weeks, rather than over a period of millennia.

Jock read the follow-up article by Coe and company in *Nature,* as well as a critique of it by a man named Ronald T. Merrill, which seemed to amount to nothing more than what Merrill himself referred to as "the principle of least astonishment:" a dogmatic statement that it was simpler to believe that Coe and Prévot were flat-out wrong, rather than to have to accept such a remarkable finding, despite being unable to show any flaw in their work.

Jock Krieger leaned back in the study carrel's chair. It seemed what Ponter had told that Canadian-government geologist, Arnold Moore, was likely correct.

And that, Jock realized, meant there might be no time to waste.

Chapter Twenty-four

The Paleoanthropology Society met each year, alternately in conjunction with the Association of American Archeology and the American Association of Physical Anthropologists. This year, it happened to be the former, and the venue was the Crowne Plaza at Franklin Square.

The format was simple: a single track of programming, consisting of fifteen-minute presentations. There was only occasionally time for questions; John Yellen, the chair of the society, kept things on schedule with Phileas Fogg precision.

After the first day of papers, many of the paleoanthropologists adjourned to the hotel bar. "I'm sure people would love a chance to get to talk to you informally," said Mary to Ponter, as they stood in the corridor leading to the bar. "Shall we go in?"

Standing solemnly near them was an FBI agent, one of their shadows throughout this trip.

Ponter flared his nostrils. "There are people smoking in that room."

Mary nodded. "In a lot of jurisdictions, thank God, bars are the *only* place people can still smoke—and Ottawa and some other places have even outlawed it in bars."

Ponter frowned. "It is too bad this meeting could not be in Ottawa."

"I know. If you can't stand it, we don't have to go in."

Ponter considered. "I have had many little ideas for inventions while I have been here, mostly adapting Gliksin technology. But I suspect the one that would make the biggest contribution would be developing nasal filters so that my people will not be constantly assaulted by smells here."

Mary nodded. "I don't like the smell of tobacco smoke, either. Still . . ."

"We can go in," said Ponter.

Mary turned to the FBI agent. "Could you use a drink, Carlos?"

"I'm on duty, ma'am," he said crisply. "But whatever you and Envoy Boddit want to do is fine by me."

Mary led the way. The room was dark, with wood-paneled walls. A dozen or so scientists were sitting on stools at the bar, and three small groups were clustered around tables. A TV mounted high on one wall was showing a *Seinfeld* rerun. Mary recognized it at once: the one where Jerry turns out to be a raving anti-dentite. She was about to head farther into the room when she felt Ponter's hand on her shoulder. "Is that not the symbol of your people?" he said.

Ponter was pointing with his other hand, and Mary looked where he was indicating: an electric sign was mounted on the wall, advertising Molson Canadian. Ponter couldn't read the words, she knew, but he'd correctly identified the large red maple leaf. "Ah, yes," said Mary. "That's what Canada is most famous for down here. Beer. Fermented grain."

Ponter blinked. "You must be very proud."

Mary led the way across the room to one of the small groups sitting in bowl-shaped chairs around a circular table. "Carlos, do you mind?" said Mary, turning to the FBI man.

"I'll just be over there, ma'am," he said. "I've heard quite enough about fossils for one day." He moved to the bar, and sat on a stool, but facing them, rather than the bartender.

Mary turned to the table. "May we join you?"

The three seated people—two men and a woman—had been engaged in animated conversation, but they all looked up, and immediately recognized Ponter. "My God, yes," said one of the men. There was one vacant chair already at the table; he quickly grabbed another.

"To what do we owe the pleasure?" said the other man, as Mary and Ponter sat down.

Mary thought about telling part of the truth: no one was smoking at or near this table, and the cluster of chairs was situated in such a way that, even though others might wish to do so, there really wasn't room for anyone else to join their group—she didn't want Ponter to be overwhelmed. But she had no intention of telling the other part: that Norman Thierry, the pompous self-styled Neanderthal-DNA expert from UCLA, was sitting across the room. He'd be dying to get at Ponter, but wouldn't be able to do so.

Instead, Mary simply ignored the question and made introductions. "This is Henry Running Deer," she said, indicating a Native American man of about forty. "Henry's at Brown."

"*Was* at Brown," corrected Henry. "I've moved to the University of Chicago."

"Ah," said Mary. "And this"—she indicated the woman, who was white and perhaps thirty-five—"is Angela Bromley, from the American Museum of Natural History in New York."

Angela extended her right hand. "It's a real pleasure, Dr. Boddit."

"Ponter," said Ponter, who had come to understand that in this society one should not use another's first name until invited to do so.

Angela continued. "And this is my husband, Dieter."

"Hello," said Mary and Ponter simultaneously. And, "Are you an anthropologist, too?" asked Mary.

"No, no, no," said Dieter. "I'm in aluminum siding."

Ponter tipped his head. "You hide it well."

The others looked perplexed, but Mary laughed. "You'll get used to Ponter's sense of humor," she said.

Dieter got up. "Let me get you two something to drink. Mary—wine?"

"White wine, yes."

"And Ponter?"

Ponter frowned, clearly not knowing what to ask for. Mary leaned close to him. "Bars always have Coke," she said.

"Coke!" said Ponter, with delight. "Yes, please."

Dieter disappeared. Mary helped herself to some of the Bits & Bites sitting in a small wooden bowl on the round table.

"So," said Angela, to Ponter, "I hope you don't mind some questions. You've been turning our field upside down, you know."

"That was not my intention," said Ponter.

"Of course not," said Angela. "But everything we hear about your world challenges something we thought we knew."

"For instance?" asked Ponter.

"Well, it's said that your people don't practice agriculture."

"True," said Ponter.

"We'd always assumed that agriculture was a prerequisite of advanced civilization," said Angela, taking a sip of whatever mixed drink she was having.

"Why?" asked Ponter.

"Well," said Angela, "see, we thought that only through agriculture could you be guaranteed a secure food supply. That allows people to specialize in other jobs—teacher, engineer, government worker, and so on."

Ponter shook his head slowly back and forth, as if he were stunned by what he was hearing. "We have people on my world who choose to live according to the ancient ways. How long do you think it takes one of them to provide sustenance for itself"—Ponter's language had a gender-neutral third-person pronoun, Mary knew; this was Hak's attempt to render it—"and its dependents?"

Angela lifted her shoulders a little. "A lot, I presume."

"No," said Ponter, "it does not—not as long as you keep your number of dependents low. It takes about nine percent of one's time." He paused, either calculating for himself or listening to Hak provide a conversion. "About sixty of your hours a month."

"Sixty hours a *month,*" repeated Angela. "That's—my God—that's just fifteen hours a week."

"A week is a cluster of seven days?" asked Ponter, looking at Mary. She nodded. "Yes, then, that is right," Ponter said. "All the rest of one's time can be devoted to other activities. From the beginning, we have had much surplus time."

"Ponter's right," said Henry Running Deer. "Fifteen hours per week is the average workload today for hunter-gatherers on this Earth, too."

"Really?" said Angela, setting down her glass.

Henry nodded. "Agriculture was the first human activity for which rewards were directly proportional to effort. If you worked eighty hours a week plowing fields, your yield was twice as much as if you worked forty. Hunting and gathering isn't like that: if you hunt full-time, you'll kill off all the prey in your territory; it's actually counterproductive to work too hard as a hunter."

Dieter returned, placing glasses in front of Mary and Ponter, then sitting back down.

"But how do you get permanent settlement without agriculture?" asked Angela.

Henry frowned. "You've got it wrong. It's not agriculture

that gives rise to permanent habitation. It's hunting and gathering."

"But—no, no. I remember from school—"

"And how many Native Americans taught at your school?" asked Henry Running Deer in an icy tone.

"None, but—"

Henry looked at Ponter, then back at Mary. "Whites rarely understand this point, but it's absolutely true. Hunter-gatherers stay put. To live off the land requires knowing it intimately: which plants grow where, where the big animals come to drink, where the birds lay their eggs. It takes a lifetime to really know a territory. To move somewhere else is to throw out all that hard-won knowledge."

Mary lifted her eyebrows. "But farmers need to put down roots—umm, so to speak."

Henry didn't acknowledge the pun. "Actually, farmers are itinerant over a period of generations. Hunter-gatherers keep their family sizes small; after all, extra mouths to feed increase the work that an adult has to do. But farmers want big families: each child is another laborer to send out into the fields, and the more kids you have, the less work you have to do yourself."

Ponter was listening with interest; his translator bleeped softly now and again, but he seemed to be following along.

"I guess that makes sense," Angela said, but her voice sounded dubious.

"It does," said Henry. "But as the farmers' offspring grow up, they have to move on and start their own farms. Ask a farmer where his great-great-grandfather lived, and he'll name some place far away; ask a hunter-gatherer, and he'll say 'right here.' "

Mary thought about her own parents, living in Calgary; her grandparents in England and Ireland and Wales, and—God, she didn't have a clue where her great-grandparents had been from, let alone her great-great-grandparents.

"A territory isn't something you abandon lightly," continued Henry. "That's why hunter-gatherers value the elderly so much."

Mary still stung from Ponter thinking her foolish for dyeing her hair. "Tell me about that," she said.

Henry took a sip of his beer, then: "Farmers, they value the young, because farming is a business of brute strength. But hunting and gathering are based on knowledge. The more years you can remember back, the more you see the patterns, the more you know the territory."

"We *do* value our elders," said Ponter. "There is no substitute for wisdom."

Mary nodded. "We actually knew that about Neanderthals," she said, "based on the fossil record here. But I didn't understand why."

"I'm an *Australopithecus* specialist," said Angela. "What fossils are you referring to?"

"Well," said Mary, "the specimen known as *La-Chapelle-aux-Saints* had paralysis and arthritis, and a broken jaw, and most of his teeth were gone. He had obviously been looked after for years; there was no way he could have fended for himself. Indeed, someone probably had to pre-chew his food for him. But *La Chapelle* was forty when he died—ancient by the standards of a people who usually lived only into their twenties. What a storehouse of knowledge he must have had about his tribe's territory! Decades of experience! Same thing with *Shanidar I*, from Iraq. That poor fellow was also forty or so, and was in even worse shape than *La Chapelle;* blind in his left eye and missing his right arm."

Henry whistled a few notes. It took Mary a second, but she did recognize them: the theme from *The Six Million Dollar Man.*

She smiled and went on. "He, too, was looked after, not out of some sense of charity, but because a person that old was a fount of hunting knowledge."

"That may be," said Angela, sounding a bit defensive, "but, still, it was farmers who built cities, farmers who had technology. In Europe, in Egypt—places where people farmed—there've been cities for thousands of years."

Henry Running Deer looked at Ponter, as if appealing for support. Ponter just tipped his head, passing the floor back to the Native American. "You think Europeans had technology—metallurgy and all that—and we Natives didn't because of some inherent superiority?" asked Henry. "Is that what you think?"

"No, no," said poor Angela. "Of course not. But . . ."

"Europeans had that sort of technology purely by the luck of the draw. Collectible ores right on the surface; flints for making stone tools. You ever tried chipping granite, which is mostly what we've got here? It makes lousy arrowheads."

Mary hoped Angela would just let it go, but she didn't. "It wasn't just tools that the Europeans had. They also were clever enough to domesticate animals—beasts of burden to work for them. Native Americans never domesticated any of the animals here."

"They didn't domesticate them because they *couldn't,*" said Henry. "There are just fourteen large domesticable herbivores on this entire planet, and only one of those—the reindeer—is naturally found in North America, and it only in the far north. The five major domesticates are all Eurasian in origin: sheep, goats, cattle, horses, and pigs. The other nine are minor players, like camels—geographically isolated. You *can't* domesticate the North American megafauna—moose or bear or deer or bison or mountain lion. They simply aren't temperamentally suited to it. Oh, you can perhaps capture them in the wild, but you can't rear them, and they won't take riders no matter how hard you try to break them." Henry's voice grew cold as he went on. "It wasn't superior intelligence that led to Europeans having what they did. In fact, you could argue that we Natives here in North America showed *more* brains by surviving and thriving in the *absence* of metals and domesticable herbivores."

"But there were some Indians—I'm sorry, some Natives—who farmed," said Angela.

"Sure. But what did they farm? Corn, mostly—because that was what was here. And corn is very low in protein, compared to the cereal grains that all came from Eurasia."

Angela looked now at Ponter. "But—but Neanderthals: they originated in Europe, not North America."

Henry nodded. "And they had great stone tools: the Mousterian Industry."

"But they didn't domesticate animals, even though you said there were plenty in Europe that could have been. And they didn't farm."

"Hello!" said Henry. "Earth to Angela! *No one* domesticated animals when the Neanderthals lived on this Earth. And no one farmed then—not Ponter's ancestors, and not yours or mine. Farming began in the Fertile Crescent 10,500 years ago. That was long after the Neanderthals had died out—at least, in this timeline. Who knows what they would have done had they survived?"

"I do," said Ponter, simply.

Mary laughed.

"All right," said Henry. "Then tell us. Your people never developed agriculture, right?"

"That is right," said Ponter.

Henry nodded. "You're probably better off without farming, anyway. A lot of bad stuff goes along with agriculture."

"Like what?" said Mary, being careful, now that Henry had

apparently calmed down a bit, to have her voice convey curiosity rather than a challenge.

"Well," said Henry, "I already alluded to overpopulation. And the effect on the land is obvious: forests are chopped down to make farmland. Plus, of course, there are the diseases that come from domesticated animals."

Mary saw that Ponter was nodding. Reuben Montego had explained that to them back in Sudbury.

Dieter—who turned out to be pretty sharp for an aluminum-siding guy—nodded. "And there's more to it than just physical diseases; there are cultural diseases. Slavery, for instance: that's a direct product of agriculture's need for labor."

Mary looked at Ponter, feeling uncomfortable. That was the second reference to slavery Ponter had heard here in Washington. Mary knew she had some 'splaining to do . . .

"That's right," said Henry. "Most slaves were plantation workers. And even when you don't have literal slavery, agriculture gives rise to what amounts to the same thing: sharecropping, peonage, and so on. Not to mention the class-based society, feudalism, landowners, and all that; they're all directly a product of agriculture."

Angela shifted in her chair. "But even when it came to hunting, the archeological record showed our ancestors were much better at it than were the Neanderthals," she said.

Ponter had looked lost during the discussion of agriculture and feudalism. But he had clearly understood Angela's last statement. "In what way?" he asked.

"Well," said Angela, "we don't see any evidence of efficiency in your ancestors' approach to hunting."

Ponter frowned. "How do you mean?"

"Neanderthals only killed animals one at a time." As soon as the words were out, Angela clearly realized she'd made a mistake.

Ponter's eyebrow went up. "How did your ancestors hunt?"

Angela looked uncomfortable. "Well, um . . . what we used to do, was, well, we used to drive whole herds of animals off cliffs, killing hundreds at once."

Ponter's golden eyes were wide. "But—but that is so . . . so *profligate,*" he said. "Surely even your large populations could not make use of all that meat. And, besides, it seems cowardly to kill like that."

"I—I don't know that I'd put it that way," said Angela, reddening. "I mean, we think of it as foolhardy to put yourself at unnecessary risk, so—"

"You jump out of airplanes," said Ponter. "You dive off cliffs. You turn punching and hitting into an organized sport. I have seen this all on television."

"We don't *all* do those things," said Mary, gently.

"All right, then," said Ponter. "But in addition to hazardous sports, I have seen other behaviors that are common. He gestured toward the bar. "Smoking tobacco, drinking alcohol, both of which I am given to understand are dangerous, and"—he nodded at Henry—"both of which, incidentally, are products of agriculture. Surely those activities qualify as 'unnecessary risks.' How can you kill animals in such a cowardly fashion, but then take such risks as—oh, oh, wait. I see. I think I see."

"What?" said Mary.

"Yes, what?" asked Henry.

"Give me a moment," said Ponter, clearly pursuing an elusive thought. A few seconds later, he nodded, having captured what he was after. "You Gliksins drink alcohol, smoke, and engage in hazardous sports to demonstrate your *residual capacity.* You are saying to those around you, see, here, during flush times, I can run myself down substantially, and still function well, thereby proving to prospective mates that I am not currently operating at the peak of my abilities. Therefore, in lean times, I will obviously have the excess strength and endurance to still be a good provider."

"Really?" said Mary. "What a fascinating notion!"

"I understand it, because my kind does the same thing—but in other ways. When we hunt—"

Mary got it in a flash. "When hunting," she said, "you *don't* take the easy way out. You don't drive animals off cliffs, or throw spears at them from a safe distance—something my ancestors did, but yours did not, at least on this version of Earth. No, here your people engaged in close-quarters attacks on prey animals, fighting them one-on-one, and thrusting spears into them by hand. I guess it *is* the same thing as smoking and drinking: look, honey, I can bring down supper with my bare hands, so if things get tough, and I have to hunt in safer ways, you can be sure I'll still bring home the bacon."

"Exactly," said Ponter.

Mary nodded. "It makes sense." She gestured at a thin man sitting on the opposite side of the bar. "Erik Trinkaus, there, found that many Neanderthal fossils showed the same sort of upper-body injuries we find in modern rodeo riders, as if they'd been bucked by animals, presumably while in close combat with them."

"Oh, yes, indeed," said Ponter. "I have been thrown by a mammoth now and again, and—"

"You've what?" said Henry.

"Been thrown by a mammoth . . ."

"A *mammoth?"* repeated Angela, agog.

Mary grinned. "I can see we're going to be here a while. Let me get everyone another round . . ."

Chapter Twenty-five

"Excuse me, Ambassador Prat," said the young male aide, entering the lounge at the United Nations. "A diplomatic pouch has arrived for you from Sudbury."

Tukana Prat glanced at the ten esteemed Neanderthals who were variously sitting down, looking out the huge window, or lying on their backs on the floor. She sighed. "I've been expecting this," she said to them in their language, then, letting her Companion translate, she thanked the aide and took the leather pouch with the Canadian coat of arms tooled into it.

Inside was a memory bead. Tukana opened the faceplate on her Companion and inserted the bead. She told her Companion to play the message through its external speaker, so that everyone in the room could hear.

"Ambassador Tukana Prat," said Councilor Bedros's furious voice, "what you've done is inexcusable. I—*we*—the High Gray Council—insist that you and those you duped into traveling with you return at once. We're"—he paused, and Tukana thought she could hear him swallow, presumably trying to calm down—"we're very concerned about the safety of all of them. The contributions they make to our society are inestimable. You, and they, must return to Saldak immediately upon receipt of this message."

Lonwis Trob shook his ancient head. "Young whippersnapper."

"Well, there's no way they're going to close the portal with us on this side," said Derba Jonk, the stem-cell expert.

"That much is certain," said Dor Farrer, the poet, grinning.

Tukana nodded. "I want to thank you all again for agreeing to come with me here. I assume no one wants to heed Councilor Bedros's request?"

"Are you kidding?" said Lonwis Trob, his blue mechanical eyes turning to Tukana. "I haven't had so much fun in tenmonths."

Tukana smiled. "All right," she said. "Let's go over our schedules for tomorrow. Krik, you are to perform in the morning on a video program called *Good Morning America;* they're covering the expenses to have an ice-horn flown down overnight from the portal, and, yes, they understand that it has to be kept frozen. Jalsk, the U.S. track team for something called 'the Olympics' is coming to New York to meet you tomorrow; that will take place at the New York University athletics center. Dor, a Gliksin named Ralph Vicinanza, who is what they call a literary agent, wants to take you out for a midday meal. Adjudicator Harbron and Scholar Klimilk, you're lecturing at the Columbia Law School tomorrow afternoon. Borl, you and a UN official are to appear on something called *The Late Show with David Letterman,* which will be recorded in the afternoon. Lonwis, you and I are scheduled to speak tomorrow night at the Rose Center for Earth and Space. And, of course, there are a slew of meetings we have to attend here at the United Nations."

Kobast Gant, the AI expert, smiled. "I bet my old buddy Ponter Boddit is glad we're here. It must be taking some of the pressure off him; I know how he hates to be the center of attention."

Tukana nodded. "Yes, I'm sure he can use some rest, after what happened to him . . ."

Ponter, Mary, and the ever-present FBI man finally left the hotel bar and headed toward the bank of elevators. They were alone; no one else was waiting for a ride, and the night clerk at the front desk, dozens of meters away, was seated, quietly reading a copy of *USA Today* while munching on one of the free Granny Smith apples the hotel provided.

"It's past the end of my shift, ma'am," said Carlos. "Agent Burstein is on duty on your floor, and he'll keep an eye on you up there."

"Thank you, Carlos," said Mary.

He nodded, and spoke into a small communications device. "Foxy Lady and Beefcake are on their way up." Mary smiled. When told they were to be assigned code names by the FBI—which was *so* cool—she'd asked if she could choose them. Carlos turned his attention back to Mary and Ponter. "Good night, ma'am. Good night, sir." But of course he didn't leave the hotel; he just stepped a discreet distance away and waited until the elevator arrived.

Mary suddenly felt a bit flush, although she knew it was actually less warm here than it had been in the bar. And, no, it wasn't that she was nervous about the fact that she'd be alone with Ponter in the elevator. A strange man—yes, that would probably creep her out for the rest of her life. But Ponter? No. Never.

Still, Mary *did* feel warm. She found her eyes searching for anything other than Ponter's golden brown irises. She looked at the LEDs indicating what floors the five elevators were on; she looked at the framed notice above the call button advertising the hotel's Sunday brunch; she looked at the emergency notice for firefighters.

One of the elevators arrived, and its doors opened with

an interesting drumroll sound. Ponter made a gallant after-you gesture with his arm, and Mary entered the lift, waving goodbye to Carlos, who nodded solemnly. Ponter followed her in and looked at the control panel. He was fine at reading numerals—the Neanderthals might never have developed an alphabet, but they did have a decimal counting system, including a placeholder sign for zero. He reached over and tapped the square labeled 12, and smiled as it illuminated.

Mary wished her room wasn't also on the twelfth floor. She'd already had the conversation with Ponter about why there was no thirteenth floor. But if there *had* been a thirteenth floor, maybe she would have been on that one instead. It didn't matter; she wasn't superstitious—although, she reflected, Ponter would say she *was*. By his definition, everyone who believed in God was superstitious.

Still, if she'd been on another floor—*any* other floor—then their good night would be short and sweet. Just a jaunty wave and a "See you tomorrow" from whichever of them happened to get out first.

The boxy LED 8 above the doors lost a segment, becoming a 9.

But this way, thought Mary, *there would have to be more.*

She felt the elevator come to a stop, and the doors shuddered open. Waiting there was Agent Burstein. Mary nodded at him. She half hoped he would fall in beside Ponter and walk along the corridor with them, but he seemed content to stay by the elevator station.

And so, Ponter and Mary headed down the corridor, past the alcove with the ice machine, past room after room, until . . .

"Well," said Mary, heart pounding. She fished in her purse for her card key, "this one is mine."

She looked at Ponter. Ponter looked at her. He never got his key out early; it was always the last thing he thought of, coming from a world where few doors had locks, and those that did opened to signals from Companions.

Ponter said nothing. "So," she said, awkwardly, "I guess this is good night."

Ponter was still silent as he reached over and touched her hand, deftly extracting the card key. He pressed it into the lock and waited for the LED to flash. He then reached for the handle and opened the door, letting it swing wide.

Mary found herself looking over her shoulder, checking to see if the corridor was empty. Of course, there was the ever-present FBI man. She was hardly comfortable about that, but at least it wasn't one of the paleoanthropologists . . .

Ponter's hand now slid up Mary's arm, slowly, gently, and reached her shoulder. He then moved it oh so gently to the side of her face, sweeping her hair behind her ear.

And then, it finally happened.

His face came in toward hers, and his mouth touched her mouth, and Mary felt a wave of pleasure sweep over her body. His arms were around her now, and hers around him, and—

And Mary couldn't really say who was leading, but they danced sideways together, still embracing, through the door, and Ponter gently kicked it shut with his foot.

Suddenly, Ponter reached down and swept Mary up in his arms, carrying her, as if she were no heavier than a child, past the bathroom and over to the queen-sized bed, where he gently laid her down on top of the sheets.

Mary's heart was pounding even harder than before. She hadn't felt this way for twenty years, not since her very first time with Donny when his parents were away for the weekend.

Ponter hovered over her for a second, his eyebrow lifted questioningly, giving her a chance to stop things from going further. Mary smiled a little and reached up, slipping her arms around his massive neck, pulling him down toward her.

For a moment, Mary expected them to act out one of those scenes she'd seen so many times in movies but had never had the chance to play in real life, clothes magically melting off them as they rolled over and over on the sheets.

But that was not to be. Mary realized that Ponter really had no idea about undoing buttons, and was fumbling horribly, although she did enjoy the feeling of his knuckles bouncing against her breasts as he tried.

For her part, Mary had hoped to do a little better, having been instructed by Hak after the shooting in how to open the shoulder seals on a Neanderthal shirt. But the last time she'd done that, it had been broad daylight. Now, though, she and Ponter were mostly in the dark. Neither of them had turned on the room lights when they'd come in; the only illumination was what spilled in through the windows, whose heavy brown curtains weren't drawn.

They had rolled so that Mary was on top now, and she maneuvered until she was sitting up, straddling Ponter's chest. She reached for the top button on her blouse. It came free easily, and Mary looked down. She could see her little gold crucifix—the one she'd bought recently to replace the one she'd given Ponter on his first visit—sitting against the inverted triangle of white flesh the opening in her shirt exposed.

She undid a second button, and the shirt fell open wider, revealing parts of her plain white bra.

Mary looked down at Ponter, trying to read his expression, but he was looking at her chest, such as it was, and the overhang of his browridge made it impossible for her to see his eyes. Was he looking at her with pleasure, or with dismay? She had no idea how buxom Neanderthal women usually were, but judging by Ambassador Prat, they had a lot of body hair, and Mary's chest was hairless.

And then, in the half darkness, she heard Ponter speak, in his own voice, "You are beautiful."

Mary felt the concern, the inhibition, draining from her. She undid the remaining buttons and then reached behind her back and unclasped her bra. She let it slide off her breasts, and Ponter's hands moved up her stomach, reaching them, cupping them, weighing them in his hands. And then he pulled her down, shimmying her down his torso, and his wide mouth found her left breast, and Mary gasped, and he sucked its entirety into his mouth and teased and caressed it with his tongue.

And then his mouth shifted to her right breast, his tongue tracing a wet path across the flatness between the two of them, and he found her other nipple and drew it between his lips and sucked gently on it, and Mary felt electricity running up and down her spine.

Although Ponter was still fully clothed, Mary could feel his erection pressing against her thigh. She was suddenly desperate to see it; she'd seen him naked before, when they were quarantined together at Reuben's house, but never when he was aroused. She pushed herself up with her arms, her nipple slipping from between Ponter's lips, and shifted herself down his frame so that her hands were free to work upon his waist. But she was flummoxed about how to undo his pants; he'd shed his medical belt as soon as he arrived in the room, but his pants lacked a clasp—although the bulge of his penis was certainly obvious.

Ponter laughed, reached down, and did something to the garment, and suddenly it was loose about his waist. He arched his back and pulled it down over his hips, and—

And apparently Neanderthals didn't wear underwear.

Ponter was massive—thick and long. He was uncircumcised although his purpling glans was sticking well past the foreskin just now. Mary ran the flat of her hand slowly down the length of his penis, feeling it move with each beat of his heart.

She then shifted off of him, and helped pull his pants the rest of the way down. His feet were enclosed in pouches attached to the pant legs, belted tight in two places, but he quickly dealt with those. Now, he was naked from the waist down—and Mary was naked from the waist up. She slipped her legs off the bed, and stood up, quickly kicking off her shoes and unfastening her skirt, which she let drop to the floor. Ponter's eyes were locked on her body, and she saw them go wide. Mary looked down and laughed; she was wearing simple beige panties and in the dim light it looked as though she was completely smooth and featureless down there. She hooked her thumbs into the elastic waistband, and pulled the panties down, revealing—

She'd heard that it was fashionable these days for women to trim away much of their pubic hair; she'd once heard Howard Stern refer to what was left as a "landing strip." But Mary did nothing but neaten up the edges when she shaved her legs, and for the first time, she realized, Ponter was seeing thick body hair on a Gliksin female. He smiled, clearly delighted by the discovery, and rolled off the bed, standing as well. He touched the shoulders of his upper garment in a certain way, and they split open like Bruce Banner's shirt, falling apart, and dropping to the carpeted floor.

And now they were standing, with a meter between them, both completely naked, except for Ponter's Companion and the bandage on Ponter's shoulder, where he'd been shot. Ponter closed the distance between them, taking Mary again in his arms, and they tumbled sideways onto the bed.

Mary wanted him inside her—but not yet, not so soon. They had lots of time, and whatever tiredness had originally prompted Mary to call it a night had completely evaporated. But, still, how did Neanderthals make love? What, if anything was taboo, or considered disgusting? She decided to let Ponter lead, but he, too, was hesitating, presumably concerned by the same question, and finally Mary found herself doing something she'd never initiated before, working her tongue down Ponter's muscular, hairy torso, across the washboard contours of his stomach. After a moment's hesitation, giving Ponter a chance to stop her should he wish, she opened her mouth wide and slid it over his penis.

Ponter let out a contented sigh. Mary had performed fellatio before on Colm, but always halfheartedly, doing it because she knew he enjoyed it but deriving no pleasure from the process herself. This time, though, she devoured Ponter eagerly, passionately, enjoying the rhythmic bobbing of his massive organ and the salt taste of his skin. But she didn't want to finish him this way, and, if he were half as excited as she was, he would doubtless come soon if she continued. Mary let his penis exit her mouth in one long, slow, final slurp, and she looked up at him and smiled. He rolled her over and reciprocated, his tongue finding her clitoris at once and flicking against it. She gasped a little—only because she made a conscious effort not to gasp a lot. Ponter alternated between rapidly moving his tongue up and down and nibbling at her labia.

Mary was enjoying every second of it, but she didn't want to come this way, not her first time with him. She wanted him *inside* her. Ponter seemed to be thinking exactly the same thing, as he lifted his face from her and looked up, his beard glistening in the darkness with her moisture.

She'd expected him to simply shimmy up toward her, pushing his penis within as he did so, but he suddenly rolled her on her front. Mary gasped again, but this time just in surprise. She'd never had anal sex before and wasn't at all sure that she wanted to. But suddenly Ponter's hands were sliding over her bottom, reaching around front, and pulling her up so that she was squatting on all fours, and his long penis pushed into her vagina from behind. Mary found herself grunting as she took his girth, but she was also relieved that they hadn't moved into new sexual territory. His hands reached from behind, cupping her breasts as he pumped in and out of her. Mary and Colm had occasionally tried it doggy style, but Colm's penis hadn't been long enough to really please her when they did it like that. But Ponter—

Wonderful, wonderful Ponter!

In her fantasies of this moment—fantasies she'd tried to dismiss from her mind each time they'd occurred—she'd always pictured them doing it in the missionary position, his mouth smothering hers as he jackhammered into her, but—

But it was called the missionary position for a reason; it wasn't the favored sexual posture even everywhere on this Earth.

Ponter must have been wondering about the same thing. He spoke softly, and Hak translated just as softly. Still, the realization that Ponter's Companion was conscious of everything they were doing caused Mary's back to stiffen for a moment. She'd never done it with anyone watching before, and she'd successfully dissuaded Colm the two times he'd broached the topic of videotaping their lovemaking.

"Is this," Hak's voice had said, on Ponter's behalf, "how you do it?"

Mary tried to push the thought of Hak out of her mind, and said, "Actually, we tend to do it face to face."

"Ah," said Ponter, and Mary felt him pull out of her. She thought he was simply going to roll her onto her back, but he stood up next to the bed, and held a hand out to her. Perplexed, Mary reached up and took his hand, and he pulled her to her feet, his hard penis bumping against her soft belly. He then reached down with both massive hands, cupping each of her cheeks in one, and lifting her clear off the ground. Mary's legs naturally swung wide, encircling his waist, and he lowered her onto his penis, effortlessly lifting her up and down its length over and over again as he stood. Their lips moved together, and as they kissed, and as her heart pounded and his chest heaved, she came with a great shuddering sensation, moaning despite herself, and once she was done, Ponter increased the rate of his up/down oscillations even more, and Mary pulled away from him a bit, looking at his face, his gorgeous golden eyes locked on her, as his body racked in orgasm. And, at last, they tumbled sideways onto the bed, and he held her, and she held him.

Chapter Twenty-six

Mary and Ponter never had bothered to close the heavy drapes in the hotel room, and so when the sun came up, Mary found herself awake, and she could see that Ponter was awake, too. " 'Morning," she said, looking at him. But he had apparently been conscious for some time, and when he turned his head to face her, tears rolled out of the deep wells that contained his eyes.

"What's wrong?" asked Mary, gently wiping away the moisture with the back of her hand.

"Nothing," said Ponter.

Mary made a show of frowning. "Nothing my foot," she said. "What is it?"

"I am sorry," said Ponter. "Last night . . ."

Mary felt her heart sink. She'd thought it had been wonderful. Hadn't he shared that opinion? "What about it?"

"I am sorry," he said again. "It was the first time I had been with a woman since . . ."

Mary's eyebrows shot up, getting it. "Since Klast died," she finished softly.

Ponter nodded. "I miss her very much," he said.

Mary laid an arm across his chest, feeling it rise and fall with his every breath. "I'm sorry I never got to meet her," she said.

"Forgive me," said Ponter. "You are here; Klast is not. I should not be . . ."

"No, no, no," said Mary, softly. "It's all right. It's fine. I love . . ." She stopped herself short. "I love that you have such deep feelings."

She drew her arm tighter about his chest, pulling herself closer to him. She couldn't blame him for thinking of his late wife; after all, it hadn't been *that* long since she'd died, and—

And suddenly Mary thought of the one thing that *hadn't* come to mind since Ponter took her in his arms out in the corridor, the one faceless presence from her past that hadn't invaded their time together. But she found she could quickly dismiss that thought, and, with her arm on Ponter, and one of his, now, resting along her naked back, she fell asleep again, absolutely at peace.

"So you and this female Gliksin had intimate relations?" said Selgan, apparently trying to control his surprise.

Ponter nodded.

"But . . ."

"What?" demanded Ponter.

"But she . . . she is a Gliksin." Selgan paused, then lifted his shoulders. "She is of a different species."

"She is human," *said Ponter firmly.*

"But . . ."

"I will hear no buts!" said Ponter. "She is human. They are all *humans, these people of the other world."*

"If you say so. And yet—"

"You don't know them," said Ponter. "You haven't met even one of them. They are people. They are us."

"You sound defensive about this," said Selgan.

Ponter shook his head. "No. You have perhaps been right about other things, but not about this. I have no doubt in my mind. Mare Vaughan, Lou Benoît, Reuben Montego, Hélène Gagné, and all the others I met over there—they are human beings. You will come to know that; all of our people will come to know that."

"And yet you were crying."

"It was as I said to Mare. I was remembering Klast."

"You weren't feeling guilty?"

"About what?"

"Two were not One at this time."

Ponter frowned. "Well, I suppose that's true. I mean, I never thought about it. In the Gliksin world, males and females spend the entire month together, and . . ."

"And when in Bistob, do as the Bistobians do?"

Ponter shrugged. "Exactly."

"Do you think your man-mate would have shared your view of this?"

"Oh, Adikor wouldn't have minded. In fact, he'd have been thrilled. He's been wanting me to find a new woman, and well . . ."

"Well what?"

"Better a Gliksin when Two were supposed to be separate, than Daklar Bolbay at any time of the month. That would be his perspective, I'm sure."

Mary and Ponter finally emerged from the hotel room. They'd missed the first three papers being presented that morning, but that was all right; Mary had downloaded the PDF file containing the abstracts prior to their leaving New York, and knew that the morning sessions were devoted to *Homo erectus* and some attempts to resurrect *Homo ergaster* as a valid separate species. No DNA had ever been recovered from either of these ancient forms, so Mary wasn't particularly interested in them.

As they came down the corridor, one of the FBI men appeared. "Envoy Boddit," he said, "this just came for you via FedEx from Sudbury."

The man held out a diplomatic pouch. Ponter took the bag, opened it, and extracted a memory bead. He turned it over in his hand. "I should really listen to this."

Mary grinned. "Well, I certainly don't want to hear you being yelled at. I'm going to go and look at the poster displays."

Ponter smiled and went to his hotel room. The FBI man stood at attention in the corridor, and Mary proceeded to the elevator station.

The lift came. Mary headed down to the mezzanine where the Association of American Archeology poster displays were being set up. That conference didn't really start until tomorrow, and she and Ponter weren't going to stay for it, but several exhibitors had already put up their posters. Mary stood looking at a pair of panels about Hopi pottery.

After a while, though, she got worried about Ponter, and so she headed back up to the twelfth floor.

The FBI man was still there in the corridor. "Are you looking for Envoy Boddit, ma'am?" he said.

Mary nodded.

"He's in his own room," said the agent.

Mary went over to that room, and knocked on the door. After a moment, it opened. "Mare!" said Ponter.

"Hi," she replied. "Can I come in?"

"Yes, yes."

Ponter's suitcase—the strange trapezoidal one he'd brought from the other universe—was lying unfolded on the bed. "What are you doing?" asked Mary.

"Packing."

"They're making you go back? I thought you said you wouldn't do that." She frowned. Of course, now that there were a dozen Neanderthals in New York City, he really didn't have to stay any longer to force the portal to remain open, but, well, after last night . . .

"No," said Ponter. "No one is making me. The memory bead was from my daughter, Jasmel Ket."

"My God, is she okay?"

"Jasmel is fine. She has consented to be the woman-mate of Tryon, a young man she has been seeing."

Mary lifted her eyebrows. "You mean she's getting married?"

"It is comparable, yes," said Ponter. "I must return to my universe for the ceremony."

"When is it?"

"In five days."

"Wow," said Mary. "Things certainly move fast in your world."

"Actually, Jasmel has been dilatory. It will soon be time for Generation 149 to be conceived. Jasmel still has not selected a woman-mate, but that is not as time-sensitive an issue."

"Have you met this—this Tryon?"

"Yes, several times. He is a fine young man."

"Umm, Ponter, are you sure this isn't a trick? You know, to lure you back to the other side?"

"It is no trick. The message was really from Jasmel, and she would never lie to me."

"Well, we better get you back to Sudbury, then," said Mary.

"Thank you." Ponter was quiet for a moment, as if thinking, then: "Would you . . . would you like to accompany me to the bonding ceremony? It is customary for the children's parents to go, but . . ."

But Jasmel's mother Klast was dead. Mary found herself smiling. "I'd love to," she said. "But . . . do we have time to stay for the presentation of my paper? It's at two-thirty this afternoon. Not to use a military metaphor, but I'd really like to drop that bomb."

"Pardon?" said Ponter.

"It's going to be explosive."

"Ah," said Ponter, getting it. "Yes, of course, we can stay for that."

Mary's paper was indeed the hit of the conference—she was, after all, resolving one of the great ongoing debates of anthropology by declaring *Homo neanderthalensis* definitively a species in its own right. Normally, she would have had to have published an abstract in advance, which would have tipped her hand, but she'd been a last-minute addition to the programming, and her paper's title—"Neanderthal Nuclear DNA and a Resolution of Neanderthal Taxonomy Issues"—had been enough to ensure a packed meeting room.

And, of course, the room had erupted into great debates the moment she put up the overhead transparency of Ponter's karyotype. In the end, Mary was delighted that she and Ponter had to leave for Sudbury as soon as her fifteen minutes were up. Indeed, noting the length of the presentation slot, Ponter amazed her by saying, "That guy who painted soup cans would be proud of you."

Just before they left the hotel, Mary called Jock Krieger at the Synergy Group. Jock seemed delighted that Mary was enjoying her time with Ponter, and thrilled that she was going to get a chance to visit the Neanderthal world. Still, he did have one request. "I want you to do a simple experiment for me while you're there."

"Yes?" said Mary.

"Get a compass—a regular magnetic compass—and when

you arrive in the other world, orient yourself by some other method so that you're sure you're facing north. Use the North Star if it's at night, or the rising or setting sun to find east or west if it's day. Okay? Then check to see what direction the colored part of the compass needle points."

"It should point north," said Mary. "Shouldn't it?"

"That's what you get for missing staff meetings," said Jock. "The Neanderthals claim that their world has already undergone the pole reversal that's just beginning here. I want to find out if that's true."

"Why would they lie about something like that?"

"I'm sure they wouldn't. But they might be mistaken. Remember, they don't have satellites; most of our studies of Earth's magnetic field have been done from orbit."

"Okay," said Mary.

She paused, and Jock took it upon himself to wrap up the conversation. "All right then, Mary. Have a great trip."

She put down the phone. Just then, Ponter arrived at her room, to see if she was ready to leave.

"I've arranged to drop off the rental car in Rochester, which isn't too much out of our way" said Mary. "We can pick up my car there, and head on up to Sudbury, but . . ."

"Yes?"

"But, well, I'd like to stop over in Toronto on the way up to Sudbury," Mary said. "It's not really out of our way either, and, well, it's not like you can share the driving."

"That would be fine," said Ponter.

But Mary didn't let the matter drop. "I have a few . . . errands I need to run."

Ponter looked perplexed at her need to justify herself. "As your people would say, 'No problem.' "

Mary and Ponter arrived at York University. There really was no disguising who Ponter was. In winter, he could perhaps wear a toque pulled down over his browridge, and wraparound ski goggles, but he'd be just as conspicuous doing that this autumn day as he would be walking around with his face exposed. Besides—Mary shuddered—she didn't want to see Ponter in anything resembling a ski mask; she didn't ever want to confuse those two people in her mind.

They parked in a visitors' lot, and Mary and Ponter started walking across the campus. "I do not require security here?" asked Ponter.

"Handguns are banned in Canada," Mary said. "That's not to say there aren't some around, but . . ." She shrugged. "It's a different place than where we were. The last assassination in Canada was in 1970, and that had to do with Quebec separation. I honestly don't think you have any more to worry about than does any other celebrity in Canada. According to the *Star,* Julia Roberts and George Clooney are both in town making movies. Believe me, they'll be attracting more gawkers than either of us."

"Good," said Ponter. They passed the low edifice of York Lanes and continued on toward—

It was inevitable. Mary had known it from the start; the vicissitudes of visitors' parking. She and Ponter were about to pass the spot where the two concrete retaining walls intersected, the spot where . . .

Mary reached out, found Ponter's massive hand, and, splaying her own fingers wide, interlaced hers with his. She didn't say anything, didn't even glance at the wall, just walked, eyes straight ahead.

Ponter was looking around, though. Mary had never told him exactly where the rape occurred, but she could see him taking note of the enclosed space, of the shielding trees, of how far away the nearest lighting standard was. If he had figured it out, he didn't say anything, but Mary was grateful for the comforting pressure of his grip.

They headed on. The sun was playing hide-and-seek behind billowing white clouds. The campus was crowded with young people, one or two still in shorts, most in jeans, a few of the law students in jackets and ties.

"This is much bigger than Laurentian," said Ponter, swiveling his head left and right. Laurentian University, near where Ponter had first arrived in Sudbury, was where Mary had done her DNA studies to show that he really was a Neanderthal.

"Oh, yes indeed," she said. "And this is only one of the two—well, three—universities here in Toronto. If you want to see something truly huge, I'll show you U of T someday."

As Ponter looked around, people were looking at him. Indeed, at one point, a woman came up to Mary as though she were a long-lost friend, but Mary couldn't even remember the woman's name, and she'd passed by her hundreds of times before without either of them ever acknowledging the other's presence. But the woman, although limply shaking Mary's hand, was clearly using the opportunity to get a close look at the Neanderthal.

They finally got rid of her and continued on. "That's the building I work in," said Mary, pointing. "It's called the Farquharson Life Sciences Building."

Ponter looked around some more. "Of all the places I've been on your world, I think university campuses are the nicest. Open spaces! Lots of trees and grass."

Mary thought about it. "It *is* a good life," she said. "More civilized in a lot of ways than the real world." They reached Farquharson and headed up the stairs to the second floor. As she entered the corridor, Mary caught sight of someone she did know well at the other end. "Cornelius!" she called out.

The man turned around and looked. He squinted; apparently his eyesight wasn't as good as Mary's. But after a moment his face showed recognition. "Hello, Mary," he called, walking toward them.

"Don't look so concerned," Mary called back. "I'm only here for a visit."

"Does he not like you?" asked Ponter softly.

"No, it's not that," said Mary, chuckling. "He's the guy who's teaching my classes while I'm working for the Synergy Group."

As he came closer, Cornelius's eyes went wide when he realized who was accompanying Mary. But, to his credit, he recovered his composure quickly. "Doctor Boddit," he said, with a bow.

Mary thought about saying to Cornelius that, see, not all the bigwigs are called "Professor," but she decided against it; Cornelius was sensitive enough as it was.

"Hello," said Ponter.

"Ponter, this is Cornelius Ruskin." And, as she always did, Mary repeated the introduction with an exaggerated gap between the first and second names, so that Ponter could distinguish them. "He has a Ph.D.—our highest academic standing—in molecular biology."

"It is a pleasure to meet you, Professor Ruskin," said Ponter.

Mary didn't want to correct Ponter—he was trying so hard to get human niceties right; he certainly deserved an *A* for effort. But if Cornelius had noticed, he let it pass without sign, still clearly fascinated by Ponter's countenance. "Thank you," he said. "What brings you here?"

"Mare's car," said Ponter.

"We're on our way back to Sudbury," said Mary. "Ponter's daughter is getting married, and there's a ceremony he wants to attend."

"Congratulations," said Cornelius.

"Is Daria Klein around?" asked Mary. "Or Graham Smythe?"

"I haven't seen Graham all day," said Cornelius, "but Daria's in your old lab."

"What about Qaiser?"

"She might be in her office. I'm not sure."

"Okay," said Mary. "Well, I just want to pick up a few things. See you later."

"Take care," said Cornelius. "Goodbye, Dr. Boddit."

"Healthy day," said Ponter, and he followed Mary as she walked along. They came to an office, and Mary knocked.

"Who's there?" called a woman's voice.

Mary opened the door a bit.

"Mary!" exclaimed the woman, shocked.

"Hi, Qaiser," said Mary, grinning. She opened the door wider, revealing Ponter. Qaiser's brown eyes went wide.

"Professor Qaiser Remtulla," said Mary, "I'd like you to meet my friend, Ponter Boddit." She turned to Ponter. "Qaiser is the head of the genetics department here at York."

"Incredible," said Qaiser, taking Ponter's hand and shaking it. "Absolutely incredible."

Mary considered saying, "Yes, he is," but she kept the thought to herself. She chatted with Qaiser for a few minutes, catching up on all the departmental news, then, when Qaiser had to leave to teach a class, Mary and Ponter continued farther down the same corridor. They came to a door with a window in it, and Mary knocked, then walked in.

"Anybody home?" called Mary to the woman's back hunched over a worktable.

The young woman turned around. "Professor Vaughan!" she exclaimed with delight. "It's great to see you! And—my God! Is that—?"

"Daria Klein, I'd like you to meet Ponter Boddit."

"Wow," said Daria, and, as if that weren't quite enough, "Wow," she said again.

"Daria is working on her Ph.D. Her specialty is the same as mine—recovering ancient DNA."

Mary and Daria talked for a few minutes, and Ponter, always the scientist, looked around the lab, endlessly fascinated by Gliksin technology. Finally, Mary said, "Well, we've got to get going. I just wanted to pick up a couple of specimens I left here."

She walked across the room to the refrigerator used to store biological specimens, noting that a few new cartoons had been taped to it, joining the selection of Sidney Harris and Gary Larson panels she'd put up herself. She opened the metal door and felt the blast of cold air coming out.

There were maybe two dozen containers inside, of varying sizes. Some had laser-printed labels; others just had strips of masking tape that had been written on with Magic Marker. Mary couldn't see the specimens she was looking for; doubtless they'd been shuffled to the very back by others using the fridge in her absence. She started moving containers, taking out two big ones—"Siberian Mammoth Skin," "Inuit Placental Material"—and placing them on the counter, so that she could more easily see inside.

Mary felt her heart pounding.

She rummaged through the specimens again, just to make sure.

But there was no room for error.

The two containers she'd labeled "Vaughan 666," the two containers that held the physical evidence of her rape, were gone.

Chapter Twenty-seven

"Daria!" Mary shouted. Ponter loomed close to her, clearly wondering what was wrong. But Mary ignored him and shouted out Daria's name again.

The slim grad student dashed across the room. She said, "What's wrong?" in that defensive tone that implies, "What have I done now?"

Mary stepped away from the refrigerator so that Daria could see its interior, and she stabbed an accusatory finger toward it. "I had two specimen jars in here," said Mary. "What happened to them?"

Daria was shaking her head. "I didn't take anything. I haven't even been into that fridge since you left for Rochester."

"Are you sure?" said Mary, trying to control the panic in her voice. "Two specimen jars, both opaque, both labeled in red ink with the date August 2nd"—she would remember *that* date for the rest of her life—"and the words 'Vaughan 666.' "

"Oh, yeah," said Daria. "I saw those once—when I was working on Ramses. But I didn't touch them."

"Are you positive?"

"Yes, of course I am. What's wrong?"

Mary ignored the question. "Who has access to this fridge?" she demanded, although she already knew the answer.

"Me," said Daria, "Graham and all the other grad students,

the faculty, Professor Remtulla. And the janitorial staff, I suppose—anyone who has a key to this room."

The janitorial staff! Mary had seen a janitor working in the ground-floor corridor of this building, just before . . .

Just before she'd been attacked.

And—*God damn it, how could I be so stupid?*—you didn't need a bloody degree in genetics to recognize that something labeled with the name of the victim, the number of the beast, and marked with the date of the rape was what you were looking for.

"Is everything okay?" asked Daria. "Was it some of the passenger-pigeon material?"

But Mary yanked another container out of the fridge. "*That's* the fucking passenger pigeon!" she shouted, slamming the container down on the countertop.

Ponter's translator bleeped. "Mare . . ." he said, softly.

Mary took a deep breath and let it out slowly. Her whole body was shaking.

"Professor Vaughan," said Daria, "I swear I didn't—"

"I know," said Mary, forcing calmness back into her voice. "I know." She looked at Ponter, whose face was a study in concern, and Daria, whose expression was segueing to that from fear. "I'm sorry, Daria. It's just that—just that they were irreplaceable specimens." She shrugged a little, still furious at herself but trying not to show it. "I never should have left them here."

"What were they?" asked Daria, her curiosity getting the better of her.

"Nothing," said Mary, shaking her head and stalking across the room without looking to see if Ponter was following. "Nothing at all."

Ponter caught up with Mary in the corridor, and he touched her shoulder. "Mare . . ."

Mary stopped walking and closed her eyes for a second. "I *will* tell you," she said, "but not here."

"Then let us leave this place," said Ponter. And he and Mary headed down the stairs. On the way down, they passed a blue-shirted janitor coming up, taking the steps two at a time, and Mary thought her heart was going to rocket through the roof of her skull. But, no, no, it was Franco—she knew him well enough—and Franco was Italian. With brown eyes.

"Why, Professor Vaughan!" he said. "I thought you weren't going to be with us this year!"

"I'm not," said Mary, trying to sound normal. "Just dropping in for a visit."

"Well, have a good one," said Franco, as he passed them.

Mary exhaled and continued down. She exited the building, and Ponter followed her, and they headed for Mary's car, but this time Mary took a long detour to avoid the intersecting walls where she'd been attacked. At last they made it to the parking lot.

They got in the car. It was hotter than hell inside. Mary usually left the windows down a crack in the summer—and it was *still* summer, after all; fall didn't officially arrive until September 21—but she'd forgotten this time, her mind swirling with far too many other thoughts at returning to York.

Ponter immediately broke into a sweat; he hated the heat. Mary started the car. She pushed the button to lower the windows, and turned the air conditioner on full blast. It took a minute to begin to blow cool air.

With the car sitting there in the parking lot, engine running, Ponter said, simply, "So?"

Mary raised the windows, afraid that someone walking by might overhear. "You know I was raped," she said.

Ponter nodded, and touched her arm lightly.

"I didn't report the crime," Mary said.

"Without Companion implants and alibi archives," said Ponter, "I am sure there would have been little point. You told me most crimes go unsolved in this world."

"Yes, but . . ." Mary's voice broke, and she shut up for a time, trying to regain her composure. "But I didn't think about the consequences. Somebody else was raped here at York last week. Near Farquharson—that building we were just in."

Ponter's deep-set eyes went wide. "And you think it was done by the same man?"

"There's no way to know for sure, but . . ."

She didn't have to finish the thought; Ponter clearly understood. If she *had* reported the rape, perhaps the man might have been apprehended before he'd had a chance to do the same abominable thing to someone else.

"You could not have foreseen this turn of events," said Ponter.

"Of course I could have," snapped Mary.

"Do you know who the other victim was?"

"No. No, they keep that confidential. Why?"

"You need to release this pain—and the only way to do that is through forgiveness."

Mary's back immediately went stiff. "I could never face her, whoever she is," she said. "After what I allowed to happen to her . . ."

"It was not your fault," said Ponter.

"I was *going* to do the right thing," said Mary. "That's why I wanted to stop here, at York. I was going to turn over the physical evidence of my rape to the police."

"Is that what was in the missing containers?"

Mary nodded. The car was getting quite chilly now, but she

didn't touch the controls. She deserved to suffer.

After a time with no response from Mary, Ponter said, "If you cannot contact the other victim for forgiveness," he said, "then you must forgive yourself."

Mary thought about this for a moment, then, without a word, she put the car in reverse and backed out of the parking space. "Where are we going?" asked Ponter. "To your home?"

"Not exactly," said Mary, and she turned the car, heading out of the parking lot.

Mary entered the wooden booth, knelt on the padded railing in front of her, and crossed herself. The small window between her chamber and the priest's opened, and she could see Father Caldicott's strong profile silhouetted behind the crisscrossing wooden slats.

"Forgive me, Father," said Mary, "for I have sinned."

Caldicott had a slight Irish accent, even though he'd been in Canada for forty years. "How long has it been since your last confession, my child?"

"Since January. Eight months."

The priest's tone was neutral, nonjudgmental. "Tell me about your sin."

Mary opened her mouth, but no words came out. After a time, the priest prodded her. "Child?"

Mary took a deep breath, and let it slowly out. Then: "I . . . was raped."

Caldicott was quiet for a few moments, perhaps considering his own line of thought. "You say 'rape.' Were you attacked?"

"Yes, Father."

"And you gave no consent?"

"No, Father."

"Then, my child, you have not sinned."

Mary felt her chest tightening. "I know, Father. The rape was not my sin."

"Ah," said Caldicott, sounding as though he understood. "Did you—were you impregnated? Have you had an abortion, child?"

"No. No, I did not get pregnant."

Caldicott waited for Mary to go on, but, when she didn't, he tried again. "Was it because you were practicing artificial birth control? Perhaps, under the circumstances . . ."

Mary was indeed on the Pill, but she'd made her peace with that years ago. Still, she didn't want to actually lie to the priest, and so she chose her next words with great care. "That is not the sin I speak of," she said softly. She took another breath, gathered her strength. "My sin was that I did not report the rape."

Mary could hear the wood creaking as Caldicott shifted on his bench. "God knows about it," he said. "And God will punish the person who did this to you."

Mary closed her eyes. "The person has raped again. At least, I suspect it's the same person."

"Oh," said Caldicott.

Oh, thought Mary? *Oh?* If that's the best he can do . . .

But Caldicott continued. "Are you sorry you didn't report it?"

The question was probably inevitable; contrition was part of the quest for absolution. But Mary nonetheless found her voice cracking as she replied. "Yes."

"Why didn't you report it, child?"

Mary thought about that. She could say that she'd simply been too busy—which was almost true. The rape had occurred the night before she'd been whisked off to Sudbury. But she'd made her decision before she'd received the phone call from

Reuben Montego looking for a Neanderthal-DNA expert. "I was afraid," she said. "I'm . . . separated from my husband. I was afraid of what they'd do to me, what they'd say about me, about my morals, if this matter ever came to court."

"But now someone else has been hurt by your . . . by your *inaction,*" said Caldicott.

The priest's comment brought to mind a lecture she'd heard on AI a few months ago. The speaker, from the MIT Robotics Lab, had talked about Asimov's Laws of Robotics, the first of which was something like, "A robot may not injure a human being, or, through inaction, allow a human being to come to harm." It had occurred to Mary then that the world might be a better place if people lived by the same injunction.

And yet—

And yet, so many of the principles she used to guide her were exhortations *to* inaction. Most of the Ten Commandments were things you were *not* to do.

Mary's sin had been one of omission. Still, Caldicott would probably say that it was a venial sin, not a mortal one, but—

But something *had* died in Mary the day the crime was committed. And, she was sure, the same had happened to the animal's new victim, whoever it might have been.

"Yes," said Mary at last, her voice very small. "Someone else has been hurt because I didn't do anything."

She saw Caldicott's silhouette move. "I could prescribe some prayer or Bible reading as penance, but . . ." The priest trailed off, clearly inviting Mary to complete the thought.

And Mary nodded, finally giving voice to what she already had known. "But the only real solution is for me to go to the police and tell them everything I know."

"Can you find the strength in you to do that?" asked Caldicott.

"I was going to, Father. But the evidence I had of the rape—it's gone."

"Still, you may have information that can be of help. But, if you wish another penance . . ."

Mary closed her eyes again, and shook her head. "No. No, I will go to the police."

"In that case . . ." said Caldicott. "God, the Father of mercies, through the death and resurrection of His Son has reconciled the world to Himself and sent the Holy Spirit among us for the forgiveness of sins." Mary wiped her eyes, and Caldicott went on: "Through the ministry of the Church, may God give you pardon and peace, and I absolve you from your sins . . ."

Even though she was facing a most difficult task, Mary did feel a weight lifting from her.

". . . in the name of the Father . . ."

She'd go today. Right now.

". . . and of the Son . . ."

But she would not go alone.

". . . and of the Holy Spirit."

Mary crossed herself. "Amen," she said.

Chapter Twenty-eight

Ponter was sitting in a pew. As she approached, Mary was surprised to see that he had an open book in his lap and was flipping through the pages. "Ponter?" she said.

He looked up. "How did it go?" he asked.

"Fine."

"Do you feel better?"

"Somewhat. But there's still more I have to do."

"Whatever is required," said Ponter. "I will help in any way I can."

"Are you reading the Bible?" asked Mary, astonished, as she looked at the open book.

"Then I have guessed correctly!" said Ponter. "This *is* your religion's central text."

"Yes," said Mary. "But . . . but I thought you couldn't read English."

"I cannot. Nor can Hak, yet. But Hak is more than capable of recording the images on each page of this book, so that when he does acquire that capability, he can translate it for me."

"I can get you a talking Bible, you know—either one that uses an electronic device to speak the words, or tapes of an actor reading the words. There's a great set that James Earl Jones did . . ."

"I was unaware of such alternatives," said Ponter, simply.

"I didn't know you wanted to read the Bible. I, ah, didn't think it would be of any interest to you."

"It is important to you," said Ponter. "Therefore, it is important to me."

Mary smiled. "I am so lucky to have found you," she said.

Ponter tried to make a joke of it. "I am easy to spot in a crowd," he said.

Still smiling, Mary shook her head. "You are indeed." She looked up at the crucifix above the pulpit, and crossed herself once more. "But, come on, we should get going."

"Where to now?" asked Ponter.

Mary took a deep breath. "The police station."

" 'It's important to you,' " repeated Selgan. " 'Therefore, it's important to me.' "

Ponter looked at the personality sculptor. "That's what I said, yes."

"And was that truly your only motivation in consulting this book?"

"What do you mean?"

"I mean, was this not the book that contained the supposed historical accounts you mentioned earlier? Was this not the book that held their principal evidence for a life after death?"

"I honestly don't know," said Ponter. "It was quite a massive book—not overly thick, but the symbols in it were small, and the paper used was the thinnest I'd yet encountered. It will be quite some time before it is translated."

"And yet you were moved to examine it?"

"Well, there were many copies in the room I was waiting for Mare in. One in front of each position on the benches, it seemed."

"Have you consulted an audio version, as Mare suggested?"

Ponter shook his head.

"And so you still wonder about this supposed proof?"

"I am curious, yes."

"How curious?" asked Selgan. "How important is this issue to you?"

Ponter shrugged. "You accused me before of having a closed mind. But I don't. If there is truth in this outlandish claim, I want to know it."

"Why?"

"Just out of curiosity."

"Is that all?" asked Selgan.

"Of course," replied Ponter. "Of course."

The desk sergeant was looking Ponter up and down. "If any of you Neanderthals ever want a new job," he said, "we could use a hundred of you on the force." They were at 31 Division headquarters on Norfinch Drive, only a few blocks from York.

Ponter smiled awkwardly, and Mary laughed a little. The cop was indeed one of the strongest-looking *Homo sapiens* males Mary had seen in a long time, but there was no doubt who her money would be on in a fight.

"Now, ma'am, what can I do for you?"

"There was a rape last week at York University," said Mary. "It was reported in the campus newspaper, the *Excalibur,* and so I assume someone reported it here, as well."

"That'd be Detective Hobbes's department," said the cop. He shouted to somebody else. "Hey, Johnny, can you see if Hobbes is in?"

The other cop shouted back an acknowledgment, and a few moments later, a plainclothes officer—a white man with red hair, perhaps thirty—came forward. "Wassup?" he said. And then, realizing who Ponter was, "Holy cow!"

Ponter smiled wanly.

"The lady here would like to talk to you about the rape at York last week."

Hobbes gestured down the corridor. "This way," he said. Mary and Ponter followed him back to a small interrogation room, lit by fluorescent panels in the ceiling. "Hang on a sec; let me get the file." He returned a moment later with a manila file folder, which he placed on the desk in front of him. He sat down, and then his eyes went wide. "My God," he said to Ponter, "it wasn't you, was it? Christ, I'll have to get in touch with Ottawa . . ."

"No," said Mary sharply. "No, it was not Ponter."

"Do you know who it was?" asked Hobbes.

"No," said Mary, "but . . ."

"Yes?"

"But I was also raped at York. Near the same building—the life-sciences building."

"When?"

"Friday, August 2nd. About 9:30 or 9:35."

"At night?"

"Yes."

"Tell me about it."

Mary tried to bring all her scientific detachment to the task, but by the end of it she had tears running down her cheeks. This apparently wasn't abnormal for the interrogation room; a box of tissues was at hand, and Hobbes offered them to Mary.

She wiped her eyes and blew her nose. Hobbes made a few more notes on sheets inside the file folder. "All right," he said. "I'll let—"

Just then, there was a knock at the door. Hobbes got up and opened it. A uniformed cop was there, and he began to speak to Hobbes in hushed tones.

Suddenly, to Mary's astonishment, Ponter scooped up the

file folder from the desk, and flipped through the pages within it. Hobbes wheeled around, perhaps at a sign from the other cop. "Hey!" he shouted. "You're not allowed to look at that."

"My apologies," said Ponter. "Do not worry, though. I cannot read your language."

Ponter proffered the folder, and Hobbes grabbed it back.

"What likelihood is there that you will catch the criminal?" asked Ponter.

Hobbes was silent for a moment. "Honestly? I don't know. We've got two reported crimes now, two rapes in pretty much the same location within weeks of each other. We'll work with the campus police to keep a tighter eye on things. Who knows? We might get lucky."

Lucky, thought Mary. He meant yet another person might be attacked.

"Still . . ." continued Hobbes.

"Yes?"

"Well, if he's part of the York community, he has to know it's been written up in the campus paper."

"You do not anticipate success," said Ponter, simply.

"We will do what we can," said Hobbes.

Ponter nodded.

Ponter and Mary returned to her car. She'd left the windows down a bit this time, but it was still hot inside. She turned the key and activated the air conditioner.

"So?" she said.

"Yes?" said Ponter.

"You scanned the file. Anything interesting?"

"I cannot tell."

"Is there any way to show me what Hak saw?"

"Not here," said Ponter. "He is recording, of course, and

we have added storage capacity to him, so that everything he sees here will be saved. But until we can upload his recordings into my alibi archive in Saldak, there is no way for us to view them, although Hak can describe them."

Mary looked down at Ponter's forearm. "Well, Hak?" she said.

The Companion spoke through its external speaker. "There were eleven sheets of white paper in the folder. The ratio between the page height and width was 0.77 to 1. Six of the pages seemed to be preprinted forms, with spaces in which some text had been written in by hand. I am no expert on such things, but it seemed to be the same script Enforcer Hobbes was using to make his notes, although the ink was a different color."

"But you can't tell me what the forms said?" asked Mary.

"I *could* describe it to you. You read from left to right, correct?" Mary nodded. "The first word on the first page began with a symbol made by a vertical line topped by a horizontal line. The second symbol was a circle. The third—"

"How many total symbols are there in the report?"

"Fifty-two thousand, four hundred and twelve," said Hak.

Mary frowned. "Too many to work through a character at a time, even if I taught you the alphabet." She shrugged. "Well, I'll be curious to see what it says when we get to your world." She looked at the dashboard clock. "Anyway, it's a long trip to Sudbury. We'd better get cracking."

Chapter Twenty-nine

The last time Mary and Ponter had taken a ride down this metal-cage elevator, Mary had tried to make him understand that she *did* like him—indeed, that she liked him a lot—but that she hadn't been ready to start a relationship. She'd told Ponter about what had happened to her at York University, making him the only person to that point besides Keisha, the rape-crisis counselor, that Mary had told about it. Ponter's emotions had mirrored Mary's own: general confusion plus profound anger aimed at the rapist, whoever he might be. During that trip down, Mary had thought she was about to lose Ponter forever.

As they again made the long, long descent to the Creighton Mine's sixty-eight-hundred-foot level, Mary couldn't help recalling all of that, and she supposed the awkward silence from Ponter meant that he was remembering it, too.

There'd been some discussion about installing a new high-speed elevator directly down to the neutrino-observatory chamber, but the logistics were formidable. To sink a new shaft through two kilometers of gabbroic granite would be a major undertaking, and the Inco geologists weren't sure that the rock could take it.

There'd also been talk about replacing Inco's old open-cage elevator with a more luxurious, modern one—but that presupposed it would only be used for runs to and from the portal. In fact, the Creighton Mine was an active nickel-harvesting operation, and although Inco had been the soul of cooperation, they still had to move hundreds of miners up and down that shaft each day.

Indeed, unlike the last time, when Mary and Ponter had had the entire car to themselves, they were sharing this ride with six miners, heading down to the fifty-two-hundred-foot level. The group was evenly mixed between those who were politely looking at the muddy metal floor—there was no inside level indicator to watch studiously as one did in an office-building lift—and those who were staring quite openly at Ponter.

The elevator thundered down its rough-hewn shaft, passing the forty-six-hundred-foot level—painted signs outside revealed the location. Having been mined out, that level was now used as an arboretum to grow trees for reforestation projects around Sudbury.

The elevator then shuddered to a stop on the level the miners wanted, and the door rattled up, letting them disembark. Mary watched them depart: men she would have previously thought of as robust specimens, but who had looked positively feeble next to Ponter.

Ponter operated the bell that signaled the lift operator up on the surface, letting him know the miners were clear. The cab rumbled into motion again. It really was too noisy to talk, anyway—the conversation they'd had the last time had been mostly shouted, for all its delicate content.

Finally, the cab arrived at the sixty-eight-hundred-foot level. The temperature here was a constant, stifling forty-one degrees Celsius, and the air pressure was thirty percent above that on the surface.

At least here, the transportation situation had been improved. Instead of having to walk the twelve hundred meters horizontally to the SNO facility, a rather nifty all-terrain vehicle—a kind of dune buggy thing, with a sticker of the SNO logo on its front—was waiting for them. Two more such vehicles were stationed down here now, although the others must have been somewhere else.

Ponter gestured for Mary to take the driver's seat. Mary suppressed a grin; the big guy knew a lot of things, but how to drive wasn't one of them. He got in next to her. Mary took a minute to familiarize herself with the dashboard, and read the various warnings and instructions that had been affixed to it. It didn't really look any more difficult than a golf cart. She turned the key—it was attached to the dashboard with a chain, so that no one could accidentally walk off with it—and they set off down the tunnel, avoiding the railway tracks used for the ore cars. It normally took twenty minutes to walk to the SNO facility from the elevator station; the cart got them there in four.

Ironically, now that it was being used for travel to another world, the SNO facility wasn't being kept in clean-room conditions anymore. A visit to the shower stalls had been mandatory, and although they were still available for those who felt too grimy after the trip down from the surface, Ponter and Mary just walked right past them. And both doors were propped open to the vacuum chamber that used to suck dirt off of visitors to SNO. Ponter shouldered through, and Mary followed behind him.

They walked past all the Rube Goldberg plumbing contraptions that had once serviced the heavy-water tank, and made their way through the control room—which, as always now, had two armed Canadian Forces guards on hand.

"Hello, Envoy Boddit," said one of the guards, rising from the chair he'd been sitting in.

"Hello," said Ponter, speaking for himself; he had acquired

a couple of hundred words of English by now, which he could use—assuming he could pronounce them—without Hak's intervention.

"And you're Professor Vaughan, aren't you?" asked the soldier—doubtless, his rank was somehow indicated on his uniform, but Mary had no idea how to read it.

"That's right," Mary said.

"I've seen you on TV," said the soldier. "First time through for you, isn't it, ma'am?"

Mary nodded.

"Well, I'm sure you've been briefed on the procedure. I need to see your passport, and we have to take a DNA sample."

Mary did indeed have a passport. She'd first gotten one when she went to Germany to extract DNA from the Neanderthal type specimen at the *Rheinisches Landesmuseum,* and she'd renewed it since—why did Canadian passports last for only five years, instead of the ten that American passports did? She fished the passport out of her purse and presented it to the man. Ironically, she looked older in the photo than she did in life; it had been taken before she started dyeing her hair to cover the gray.

She then opened her mouth, and let the soldier run a Q-Tip along the inside of her right cheek—the guy's technique was a little rough, thought Mary; you didn't have to swipe that hard to get cells to slough off.

"All right, ma'am," said the soldier. "Have a safe trip."

Mary let Ponter lead the way out onto the metal deck that formed a roof over the ten-story-tall barrel-shaped cavern that used to house the Sudbury Neutrino Observatory. Instead of having to descend through a hatch just a meter on a side, as she'd done the last time she was here, a large opening had been carved into the decking, and an elevator had been installed—Ponter remarked that it was new since his latest arrival. The elevator had acrylic see-through walls; they'd been made especially for this site by Polycast, the company that had manufactured the acrylic panels of which the now-dismantled heavy-water containment sphere had been composed.

The elevator was the first of many modifications planned for this chamber. If the portal really did stay open for years, the chamber would be filled in with ten stories of facilities, including customs offices, hospital rooms, and even a few hotel suites. Currently, though, the elevator had only two stops: the chamber's rocky floor, and, three stories above that, the staging area that had been built up around the portal. Ponter and Mary got off at the staging area, a wide wooden platform with yet another couple of soldiers stationed on it. Along one side of the platform were the flags of the United Nations and the three countries that had jointly funded SNO: Canada, the United States, and Great Britain.

And, in front of her, was—

It indeed seemed to have acquired the popular name of "the portal," but because of the Derkers tube protruding through it, it looked more like a tunnel. Mary's heart was pounding; she could *see* through it—see the Neanderthal world, and—

My God, thought Mary. *My God.*

A brawny figure had passed by the far end of the tunnel, someone working on the other side.

Another Neanderthal.

Mary had seen much of Ponter and some of Tukana. Still, she had trouble really accepting that there were *millions* of other Neanderthals, but . . .

But there was another one, down the tunnel.

She took a deep breath, and, since Ponter was gallantly

indicating she should go first, Mary Vaughan, citizen of one Earth, started walking down the cylindrical bridge that led to another Earth.

A flat insert had been crafted for the bottom of the Derkers tube, making a smooth walkway. Mary could see the blue ring surrounding the tube, visible through its translucent white walls: the actual portal, the opening, the discontinuity.

She reached the threshold of that discontinuity, and stopped. Yes, Ponter had gone through in both directions now, and, yes, a number of *Homo sapiens* had preceded her in crossing over, but . . .

Mary broke into a sweat, and not just because of the subterranean heat.

Ponter's hand landed on her shoulder. For one horrible second, Mary thought he was going to push her through.

But of course he didn't. "Take your time," he whispered, in English. "Go when you are comfortable."

Mary nodded. She took a deep breath and stepped forward.

It felt like a ring of ants crawling over her body from front to back as she stepped across the threshold. She'd started with a slow step, but quickly hopped forward to put an end to the unsettling sensation.

And there she was—centimeters, and tens of thousands of years of divergence, from the world she knew.

She continued down to the end of the tunnel, Ponter's footfalls heavy behind her. And then she stepped out, into what she knew must be the quantum-computing chamber. Unlike the SNO cavity, which had been co-opted from its original purpose, Ponter's quantum computer was still fully operational; indeed, Mary was given to understand that without it, the portal would slam shut.

Four Neanderthals stood in front of her, all male. One was wearing a garish silver outfit; the others were wearing sleeveless shirts and the same strange pants with boots attached that Ponter had arrived in. All of them, like Ponter, had their light-colored hair parted precisely in the center; all were hugely muscled, with short limbs; all had undulating browridges; all had massive, potato-like noses.

Ponter's voice came from behind her, speaking in the Neanderthal language. Mary swung around in surprise. She heard Ponter whisper that language all the time, with Hak translating the words into English at a much-louder volume, but, till now, she'd never heard Ponter speak loudly and clearly in his native tongue. Whatever he'd said must have been a joke of some kind, as all four of the Neanderthals emitted deep, barking laughs.

Mary stepped away from the mouth of the tunnel, letting Ponter pass. And then—

She'd heard Ponter talk frequently about Adikor, of course, and had understood intellectually that Ponter had a male lover, but . . .

But, despite her liberal leanings, despite all her mental preparations, despite the gay men she knew back on her Earth, she felt her stomach clench as Ponter embraced the Neanderthal who must be Adikor. They hugged long and hard, and Ponter's broad face pressed against Adikor's hairy cheek.

Mary realized in an instant what she was feeling, but, God, it had been decades since she'd experienced that particular emotion, and it shamed her. She wasn't repulsed by the display of same-sex affection; not at all—hell, you couldn't flip channels on Toronto TV on a Friday night without running into some gay porn. No, she was . . .

It *was* shameful, and she knew she'd have to get over it fast if she was ever to have a long-term relationship with Ponter.

She was jealous.

Ponter let Adikor go, then he held up his left arm, facing

its inside toward Adikor. Adikor raised his arm in a matching gesture, and Mary saw symbols flash across the displays on each man's Companion implant; Ponter was presumably receiving his accumulated messages from Adikor, to whom they had been forwarded in his absence.

They lowered their arms at the same time, but Ponter only brought his halfway down, and he pivoted his forearm at the elbow to indicate Mary. *"Prisap tah Mare Vonnnn daballita sohl,"* he said, but, since he wasn't addressing her, Hak provided no translation.

Adikor stepped forward, smiling. He had a kind face, broader than Ponter's—indeed, as broad as a dinner plate. And his round deep-set eyes were an astonishing teal color. The overall effect was a Flintstones version of the Pillsbury Doughboy.

Ponter's voice dropped to a whisper, and Hak's voice provided a normal-volume translation. "Mare, this is my man-mate, Scholar Adikor Huld."

"Hollow," said Adikor. Mary was baffled for a moment, then realized that Adikor was trying to say "hello," but hadn't quite gotten the vowel sounds right. Still, she was impressed, and touched, that he'd tried to learn some English.

"Hello," said Mary. "I've heard a lot about you."

Adikor tipped his head, presumably listening to a translation through his own Companion's cochlear implants, and then, in a startlingly normal response, he smiled, and, in his accented English, said, "All good, I hope."

Mary couldn't help but laugh. "Oh, yes," she said.

"And this," said Hak's voice, speaking for Ponter, "is an Exhibitionist."

Mary was taken aback. Ponter was referring to the guy dressed all in silver. She wasn't quite sure what she'd do if this strange Neanderthal whipped it out in front of her. "Umm, pleased to meet you," she said.

The stranger didn't have the trick down of whispering his own words while his Companion translated loudly. Mary had to struggle to separate the Neanderthal noise from the English. "I have learned," she picked out, "that in your world, I might be called a reporter. I go to interesting places, and let people tune into what my Companion is broadcasting."

"All Exhibitionists wear silver," said Ponter, "and nobody else does. If you see someone dressed this way, be warned that many thousands of people are watching you."

"Ah-hah!" said Mary. "An Exhibitionist. Yes, I remember you telling me about them now."

Ponter introduced the two other Neanderthals, as well. One was an enforcer, apparently something akin to a cop, and the other was a portly Neanderthal roboticist named Dern.

For half a second, the feminist in Mary was outraged that no women were present in the quantum-computing facility, but of course there would be no women anywhere around here; the mine, she knew, was located beyond Saldak Rim.

Ponter led Mary through the grid of cylinders clamped to the floor, up a short flight of stairs, through a door, and out into the control room. Mary was chilled; the Neanderthals didn't like heat, and it would naturally have been just as hot this far below the surface here as it had been in Mary's world. They clearly air-conditioned the rest of the facility; indeed, Mary looked down and was embarrassed to see her nipples pushing out against her top. "How do you keep it cool down here?" she asked.

"Superconductivity heat pumps," said Ponter. "They work like an established scientific fact."

Mary looked around the control room. She was surprised

at how *strange* the consoles looked. She hadn't ever thought about the fact that human industrial designers had arbitrarily decided what instrumentation should look like, that their "high-tech" designs were only one possible way to go. Instead of the burnished metal and black and gray colors of so much human equipment, these consoles were mostly a coral pink, had no sharp corners, and seemed to have little control doodads that pulled out rather than pushed in. There were no LEDs, no dials, and no toggle switches. Instead, indicators seemed to be reflective, rather than illuminated, and text displays were in dark blue symbols on a soft gray background; she would have thought them preprinted labels, but the strings of characters being shown kept changing.

Ponter moved her quickly through the small room, and they came to the decontamination facility. Before she knew what was happening, Ponter had undone the shoulder clasps on his shirt and pulled it off. A second later, he was removing his pants. He stuffed his clothes into a cylindrical hamper and walked into the chamber, which had a circular floor. Ponter stood still and the floor slowly turned, presenting first his broad back—and all that was below it—and then his broad chest—and all that was below *that*—to her. She could see laser emitters on one side of the chamber, and pinpoints of laser light hitting the opposite side, passing through Ponter's body as if it were not even there, but, so she understood, zapping foreign biomolecules as they did so.

It took several minutes, and several rotations, for the process to be completed. Mary tried to keep her eyes from dropping down. Ponter was utterly unselfconscious. The previous times she'd seen him naked had been in dim light, but here—

Here he was illuminated with all the intensity of a hardcore porno film. His body was mostly covered with fine blond hair, his abdominal muscles were firm, his pectorals almost made him look buxom, and . . .

And she looked away; she knew she shouldn't be staring.

Finally, Ponter was done. He stepped out of the chamber, and gestured for Mary to take her turn.

And suddenly Mary's heart jumped. She'd been briefed about the decontamination procedure, but . . .

But it had never occurred to her that Ponter would be watching her as she went through it. Of course, she could simply tell him that that made her uncomfortable, but . . .

Mary took a deep breath. When in Rome . . .

She undid her blouse, and put it in the same hamper Ponter had used. She removed her black shoes, and, after a confirming nod from Ponter, put those in the hamper as well. She then removed her pants, and—

And there she was, in cream-colored bra and white panties.

If the lasers could zap bacteria and viruses right through her skin, they should be able to do that through her underwear, too, but . . .

But her underwear, and all her clothes, her purse, and her luggage, were to be sonically cleaned and exposed to high-intensity ultraviolet. The lasers were good at getting microbes; they weren't nearly powerful enough to get the much larger mites and ticks that could be lurking in the folds of fabric. Everything, Ponter said, would be delivered to them later, after a thorough cleaning.

Mary reached up and unclasped her bra. She remembered back in college when she could pass the pencil test, but those days were long behind her. Her breasts flopped down. Mary instinctively crossed her arms over her chest, but she had to lower them to take off her panties. She wasn't quite sure whether it was more ladylike to face forward or backward as she peeled them off; either way displayed a lot of flesh in unflattering geometry. At last, she turned around, and quickly pulled them down, straightening up as fast as she could.

Ponter was still looking on, smiling encouragingly. If the harsher light here made her any less attractive to him than the dim light in the hotel room, he gave no sign.

Mary put her panties into the hamper and stepped into the chamber, which began its humiliating rotation. Yes, she had looked at Ponter, but her gaze had been admiring—he was, after all, very well muscled, and, not to put too fine a point on it, quite nicely hung, too.

But she was a woman on a collision course with forty, with twenty pounds of fat she didn't need, with pubic hair that made abundantly plain the fact that she dyed the hair on her head. How in God's name could Ponter possibly be admiring all that soft whiteness he was seeing?

Mary closed her eyes and waited for the procedure to finish. She didn't feel a thing; whatever the lasers were doing to her innards was completely painless.

At last, it was over. Mary stepped through to the other side of the chamber, and Ponter led her to another room where they could dress. He indicated a wall full of cubic cubbyholes, each containing clothes. "Try the upper-right," said Ponter. "They are arranged in ascending order of size; that one should be the smallest."

The smallest, thought Mary, and she cheered up a little. In this world, it seemed she'd get to shop in the petite section.

Mary got dressed as quickly as she could, and Ponter led her to the elevator station. Once again, Mary was taken aback by the immediately obvious differences between Gliksin and Barast technology. The elevator cab was circular, with a couple of pedals on the floor to operate it. Ponter stomped on one of them, and the car started going up. How handy that would be when one's arms were full! Mary had once accidentally dumped all her groceries, including a carton of eggs, onto the floor of the elevator at her condo.

There were four vertical rods equally spaced around the interior. At first Mary thought they were structural columns, but they weren't. Shortly after they'd started the long ride up—presumably two kilometers, just like on her Earth—Ponter started shimmying his back against one of the poles. It was a back-scratching device, and seemed a good way to make use of the time.

Mary wondered aloud about the idea of a circular cab, though. Wouldn't it tend to rotate within its shaft?

Ponter nodded his massive head. "That is the idea," Hak said, translating for him. "The lifting mechanism is in the shaft walls, rather than overhead as in your elevators. The channels that guide the elevator are not perfectly vertical. Rather, they spiral around very gently. In this particular shaft, the elevator starts off facing east at the bottom, but will be facing west by the time we reach the top."

During the trip up, Mary also had a chance to notice the lighting being used. "My God," she said, looking up, "is that luciferin?"

A glass tube ran around the upper edge of the cylinder, filled with a liquid that was glowing with greenish blue light.

Hak bleeped.

"Luciferin," repeated Mary. "It's the substance that fireflies use to make their tails glow."

"Ah," said Ponter. "Yes, this is a similar catalytic reaction. It is our principal source of indoor illumination."

Mary nodded to herself. Of course the Neanderthals, adapted for a cold environment, wouldn't like incandescent bulbs that give off more heat than light. The luciferin/luciferase reaction was almost completely efficient, producing light with hardly any heat.

The elevator continued its ascent, the blue-green illumination making Ponter's pale skin look oddly silverish and his golden brown irises seem almost yellow. There were ventilation holes in the roof and floor of the cab, creating a bit of a breeze, and Mary hugged herself against the chill.

"Sorry," said Ponter, noting her actions.

"That's okay," said Mary. "I know you like it cold."

"It is not that," said Ponter. "Pheromones build up in a closed space like this, and the ride up is a long one. The vents make sure passengers are not overly influenced by each other's scents."

Mary shook her head in wonder. She hadn't even made it out of the mine yet, and she was already overwhelmed by the differences—and she'd known she was heading to another world! Her heart again went out to Ponter, who had originally arrived on her Earth with no warning, but had somehow managed to keep his sanity.

At last the elevator reached the top, and the door opened. Even that, though, happened in an unfamiliar way, with the door, which had appeared seamless, folding out of the way like an accordion.

They were in a square chamber perhaps five meters on a side. Its walls were lime green, and the ceiling was low. Ponter went over to a shelf and brought back a small flat box that seemed to be made of something like blue cardboard. He opened the box and removed a shiny construct of metal and plastic.

"The High Gray Council realizes it has no choice but to let people from your world visit ours," Ponter said, "but Adikor said they have imposed one condition. You must wear this." He held up the object, and Mary could see that it was a metal band, with a face on it very much like Hak's.

"Companions are normally implants," said Ponter. "But we understand that subjecting a casual visitor to surgery is too much to ask. However, this band is unremovable, except in this facility; that is, the computer within knows its location and will only allow the clasp to reopen here."

Mary nodded. "I understand." She held out her right arm.

"It is usual," said Ponter, "for the Companion to go on the left arm, unless the bearer is left-handed."

Mary retracted one arm, and extended the other. Ponter busied himself with attaching the Companion. "I've been meaning to ask you about that," said Mary. "Are most Neanderthals right-handed?"

"About ninety percent are, yes."

"That's what we thought from the fossil record."

Ponter's eyebrow rolled up. "How could you possibly determine handedness from fossils? I do not believe we have any idea what the distribution of hand preferences was among ancient Gliksins on this world."

Mary smiled, pleased at the ingenuity of her species. "It came from fossil teeth."

"What have teeth got to do with handedness?"

"A study was done of eighty teeth from twenty individual Neanderthals. See, we figured with those great jaws of yours, you probably used your teeth as clamps, to hold hides in place while you defleshed them. Well, hides are abrasive, and they grind down the front of the teeth, leaving little nicks. In eighteen of the individuals, the nicks angled toward the right—which is what you'd expect if a scraper was being used on the hide with the right hand, pulling the hide in that direction."

Ponter made what Mary had learned was the Neanderthal "impressed" face, which consisted of a sucking in of the lips, and a bunching toward the center of the eyebrow. "Excellent reasoning," said Ponter. "In fact, to this day, we hold flensing parties, where hides are cleaned in that manner; of course, there are other, mechanized techniques, but such parties are a social ritual."

Ponter paused for a moment, then: "Speaking of hides . . ." He walked to the opposite side of the room, the wall of which was lined with fur coats, hanging, it appeared, from shoulder clamps attached to a horizontal bar. "Please select one," he said. "Again, those at the right are the smallest."

Mary pointed at one, and Ponter did something she didn't catch that caused one of the coats to be released from the clamps. She wasn't quite sure how to put it on—it seemed to open at the side, rather than the shoulders, but Ponter helped her into it. There was a part of Mary that thought about objecting; she never wore natural fur back home, but this was, of course, a different place.

It certainly wasn't a luxurious pelt, like mink or sable; it was coarse, and an uneven reddish brown. "What kind of fur is it?" said Mary, as Ponter did up the clasps that sealed her within the jacket.

"Mammoth," he said.

Mary's eyes went wide. It might not be as nice as mink, but a mammoth coat would be worth infinitely more on her world.

Ponter didn't bother with a jacket for himself. He started walking toward the door. This one was more normal, attached to a single vertical tube that let it swing just as though it were on hinges. Ponter opened it, and—

And there they were, on the surface.

And suddenly all the strangeness evaporated.

This *was* Earth—the Earth she knew. The sun, low in the western sky, looked exactly as she was used to seeing it. The sky was blue. The trees were pines and birches and other varieties she recognized.

"It's cold," she said. Indeed, it felt about four degrees cooler than the Sudbury surface they'd left behind.

Ponter smiled. "It *is* lovely," he said.

Suddenly, a sound caught Mary's attention, and for one brief moment she thought perhaps a mammoth was bearing down on them to avenge its kin. But no, that wasn't it. It was an air-cushion vehicle of some sort, cubic in shape but with rounded corners, flying across the rocky ground toward them. The sound Mary had heard seemed to be a combination of fans blowing downward that let it hover a small distance above the surface, and a large fan, like one of those on the boats used in the Everglades, blowing to the rear.

"Ah," said Ponter, "the travel cube I called for." Mary assumed he'd done it with Hak's aid, and without the words translated into English. The strange vehicle settled down in front of them, and Mary could see that it had a Neanderthal driver, a hulking male who looked twenty years older than Ponter.

The cube's clear side swung open, and the driver spoke to Ponter. Again, the words weren't translated for Mary's benefit, but she imagined they were the Neanderthal equivalent of "Where to, Mac?"

Ponter gestured for Mary to precede him into the car. "Now," he said, "let me show you my world."

Chapter Thirty

"This is your house?" asked Mary.

Ponter nodded. They had spent a couple of hours touring some public buildings, but it was now well into the evening.

Mary was astonished. Ponter's home wasn't made of brick or stone. Rather, it was made mostly of wood. Of course, Mary had seen many wooden houses before—although the building code actually banned them in many parts of Ontario—but she'd never seen one like *this*. Ponter's home seemed to have been *grown*. It was as if a very thick, but very short, tree trunk had expanded to fill every part of a giant mold shaped into room-sized cubes and cylinders, and then the mold had been removed, leaving behind the tree, the interior of which had subsequently somehow been partially hollowed out without actually killing it. The house's surface was still covered with dark brown bark, and the tree itself was apparently still alive, although the leaves on the branches extending up from its central, shaped body had started to change color for the autumn.

Some carpentry had clearly been performed, though. Windows were perfectly square, presumably cut through the wood. Also, a deck extending on one side of the house had been built from planks.

"It's . . ." Adjectives were warring for supremacy in Mary's mind—*bizarre, wonderful, odd, fascinating*—but the one that won out was, ". . . beautiful."

Ponter nodded. One of Mary's people would have said "thank you" in response to a compliment like that, but Mary had learned that the Neanderthals didn't routinely acknowledge praise for things they weren't personally responsible for. Early on, she'd remarked that one of Ponter's shoulder-closing shirts was quite attractive, and he had looked at her perplexed, as if wondering why anyone would choose to wear something that *wasn't* attractive.

Mary gestured to a large black square on the ground next to the house; it measured perhaps twenty meters on a side. "What's that? A landing pad?"

"Only incidentally. It is really a solar collector. It converts sunlight into electricity."

Mary smiled. "I guess you have to shovel snow off it in winter," she said.

But Ponter shook his head. "No. The hover-bus that takes us to work lands there and uses its jets to blast the snow clear as it does so."

Her hatred of shoveling snow had been one of the reasons Mary opted for an apartment after she and Colm split up. She rather suspected that in her world, the TTC would balk at sending a bus with a plow on its front around to everyone's home after each snowfall.

"Come on," said Ponter, walking toward the house. "Let us go in."

The door to Ponter's house swung in. The interior walls were polished wood—the actual substance of the tree around them. Mary had seen hundreds of wood-paneled rooms before, but never one where the grain made one continuous pattern right around the room. If she hadn't seen the house first from the outside, she would have been absolutely baffled about how it had been accomplished. Little niches had been carved into the walls at various points, and they contained small sculptures and bric-a-brac.

At first Mary thought the floor was carpeted with green fabric, but she quickly realized it was actually moss. She seemed to be in what corresponded to a living room. There were a couple of freestanding oddly shaped chairs, and there were two couches protruding from the walls. There was no framed art, but the entire roof had been painted in a complex mural, and—

And suddenly Mary's blood ran cold.

There was a wolf inside the house.

Mary froze, her heart pounding.

The wolf began its charge, rushing toward Ponter.

"Look out!" shouted Mary.

Ponter turned and fell backward onto one of the couches.

The wolf was upon him, its jaws opening wide, and—

And Ponter laughed as the wolf licked his face.

Ponter was repeating a handful of words over and over in his own language, but Hak wasn't translating them. Still, Ponter's tone was one of affectionate amusement.

After a moment, he pushed the wolf off him and rose to his feet. The creature turned toward Mary.

"Mare," said Ponter, "this is my dog, Pabo."

"Dog!" exclaimed Mary. The animal was completely lupine, as far as she could tell: savage, ravenous, predatory.

Pabo crouched down next to Ponter, and, lifting her muzzle high, let out a long, loud howl.

"Pabo!" Ponter said, his tone remonstrative. And his next word must have been the Neanderthal for "Behave!" He smiled apologetically at Mary. "She has never seen a Gliksin before."

Ponter led Pabo over to Mary. Mary felt her back go stiff, and she tried not to tremble, as the toothy animal, which must have weighed at least a hundred pounds, sniffed her up and down.

Ponter spoke to the dog for a few moments, his words untranslated, in the same lilting tone people from Mary's world used when talking to their pets.

At that moment, Adikor entered through an archway, coming from another room. "Hello, Mare," he said. "Did you enjoy your tour?"

"Very much so."

Ponter moved over to Adikor and drew him into a hug. Mary looked away for a moment, but, when she looked back, they were standing side by side, holding hands.

Mary again felt pangs of jealousy, but—

No, no. Surely that was unseemly. Surely Ponter and Adikor were just behaving as they always did, plain in their affection for each other.

And yet—

And yet, had it been Adikor who had initiated the hug? Or Ponter? She honestly couldn't tell. And the clasping of hands had occurred while she wasn't looking; she couldn't say who had reached out for whom. Maybe Adikor was staking out his territory, making a show for Mary's sake of his relationship with Ponter.

Pabo, apparently now satisfied that Mary wasn't some sort of monster, padded away and jumped up on one of the couches growing—quite literally—out of the wall.

"Would you like to see the rest of the house?" asked Ponter.

"Sure," said Mary.

She was led into an area—not really a separate room—that must have been the kitchen. A sheet of glass covered the mossy floor. Mary didn't recognize any of the appliances, but she assumed the small cube might be something akin to a microwave oven, and the large unit, consisting of two identical blue cubes, one atop the other, might be a refrigerator of some sort. She gave voice to these guesses, and Adikor laughed.

"Actually, that is a laser cooker," he said, pointing at the small unit. "It uses the same rotating of frequencies we employ in the sterilizer you went through, but this time so it can cook the meat evenly inside and out. And we do not use refrigeration to store food much anymore, although we used to. That is a vacuum box."

"Ah," said Mary. She turned, and was taken aback. One wall was filled with four perfectly square, flat monitor screens, each showing a completely different view of the Neanderthal world. She'd been concerned from the beginning about the Orwellian aspects of Neanderthal society, but hadn't expected Ponter to be involved in monitoring his neighbors.

"That's the Voyeur," said Adikor, coming over to join them. "It's how we monitor the Exhibitionists." He stepped over to the quartet of monitors and made an adjustment. Suddenly the four separate squares merged into one large one, with a magnified view of the Exhibitionist who had been in the lower-right. "That one is my favorite," said Adikor. "Hawst is always up to something interesting." He took in the view for a second. "Ah, he is at a *daybatol* game."

"Come *on,*" said Ponter, motioning for them both to follow. His tone suggested that once Adikor started watching a *daybatol* match, it was hard to get him away from the Voyeur.

Mary followed him, as did Adikor. The next room was clearly their bedroom/bathroom. It had a large window looking out over a brook, and a recessed square pit filled with square cushions, forming a large sleeping surface. On top were a few disk-shaped pillows. At the side of the room was a circular pit, again recessed into the ground. "Is that the bath?" asked Mary.

Ponter nodded. "You are welcome to use it, if you wish."

Mary shook her head. "Maybe later." Her gaze fell back on the bed, pictures of a naked Ponter and Adikor entwined in sexual acts forming in her mind.

"And that is it," said Ponter. "That is our home."

"Come," said Adikor. "Let us go back into the living room."

They did so, Ponter leading the way. Adikor shooed Pabo off one of the couches and lay down on his back upon it. Ponter indicated that Mary could take the other couch. Perhaps being recumbent was the normal leisure posture for Neanderthals; certainly it would be the best way to look at ceiling murals.

Mary did indeed take the other couch, thinking that Ponter would sit next to her. But instead he moved over to where Adikor was lying down and gave him an affectionate rap on the top of his head. Adikor sat up for a moment. Mary expected him to swing his feet around, sitting properly on the couch, but as soon as Ponter had sat down at the end of the couch, Adikor lowered himself, placing his head in Ponter's lap.

Mary felt a knotting in her stomach. Still, Ponter had probably never entertained a female he was romantically involved with in his house before.

"So," said Ponter, "what do you think of our world so far?"

Mary took the opportunity to look away from Ponter and Adikor, as if she needed to visualize all that she'd seen already in her mind's eye. "It's . . ." She shrugged. "Different." And then, realizing that might sound offensive, she quickly added, "But nice. Very nice." She paused. "Clean."

Her own comment made Mary laugh a bit on the inside. *Clean.* That's what Americans always said when they visited Toronto. *What a clean city you have!*

But Toronto was a pigsty compared to what Mary had seen of Saldak. She'd always thought it economically impossible for a large population of humans to not have a devastating effect on the environment, but . . .

But it wasn't a *large* population that did such things. Rather, it was a constantly growing population. With their discrete generations, it seemed that the Neanderthals had enjoyed zero population growth for centuries.

"We like it," said the recumbent Adikor, apparently trying to move the conversation along. "Which, of course, is why it is the way it is."

Ponter stroked Adikor's hair. "Their world has its charms, too."

"I understand your cities are much bigger," said Adikor.

"Oh, yes," said Mary. "Many have millions of people; Toronto, where I'm from, has almost three million."

Adikor shook his head, rotating it back and forth in Ponter's lap. "Astonishing," he said.

"We will take you into the Center after dinner," said Ponter. "Things are more compacted there; buildings are only a few tens of paces apart."

"Is that where the bonding ceremony will be held?" asked Mary.

"No, that will occur halfway between Center and Rim."

A thought suddenly occurred to Mary. "I—I didn't bring anything fancy to wear."

Ponter laughed. "Do not worry. No one will be able to tell which Gliksin clothes are normal and which are for special occasions. They *all* look strange to us." Ponter then tipped his head down, looking at Adikor's face. "Speaking of which, you have a meeting tomorrow with Fluxatan Consortium, do you not? What are you going to wear for that?" Rather than cut Mary off from the conversation, Hak continued to translate.

"I do not know," Adikor said.

"What about the green jerkin?" said Ponter. "I like the way it shows off your biceps, and—"

Suddenly, Mary could take no more. She shot to her feet and made a beeline for the front door. "I'm sorry," she said, trying to catch her breath, trying to calm down. "I am so sorry."

And she stepped outside into the dark.

Chapter Thirty-one

Ponter followed Mary out, closing the door behind him. Mary was shivering. Ponter didn't seem the least disturbed by the evening air, but he was clearly aware of Mary's reaction to it. He moved closer to her, as if to encircle her in his massive arms, but Mary shrugged her shoulders violently, rejecting his touch, and turned away from him, looking out at the countryside.

"What is wrong?" asked Ponter.

Mary took a deep breath and let it out slowly. "Nothing," she said. She knew she sounded petulant, and she hated herself for it. What *was* wrong? She'd *known* Ponter had a male lover, but—

But it was one thing to be aware of it as an abstract fact; it was another to see it in the flesh.

Mary was astonished at herself. She'd felt more jealous just now than she had been when she'd first seen Colm with his new girlfriend after he and Mary had split up.

"Nothing," said Mary again.

Ponter spoke in his own tongue in a voice that sounded both confused and sad. Hak's translation had a more neutral tone. "I am sorry if I offended you . . . somehow."

Mary looked up at the dark sky. "It's not that I'm offended," she said. "It's just that . . ." She paused. "This is going to take some getting used to."

"I know our world is different from yours. Was my home too dim for you? Too cool?"

"It's not that," said Mary, and she slowly turned around "It's . . . Adikor."

Ponter's eyebrow rolled up his browridge. "Do you not like him?"

Mary shook her head. "No, no. It isn't that. He seems nice enough." She sighed again. "The problem isn't with Adikor. It's *you* and Adikor. It's seeing the two of you together."

"He is my man-mate," said Ponter, simply.

"In my world, people have only one mate. I don't care whether it's someone of the opposite sex, or someone of the same sex." She was about to add, "Really, I don't"—but was afraid she would be protesting too much. "But for us to be—well, whatever it is that you and I are—while you are involved with someone else is . . ." She trailed off, then lifted her shoulders. ". . . is difficult. And to have to watch the two of you being affectionate . . ."

"Ah," said Ponter, and then, as if the first utterance hadn't been sufficient, "Ah," he said again. He was quiet for a time. "I do not know what to tell you. I love Adikor, and he loves me."

Mary wanted to ask him what his feelings were for her—but this wasn't the time: she'd probably repelled him with her narrow-mindedness.

"Besides," said Ponter, "within a family, there is no ill feeling. Surely you would not feel hurt if I were showing affection to my brother or my daughters or my parents."

Mary considered that in silence, and, after a few moments, Ponter went on. "Perhaps it is trite, but we have a saying: love is like intestines—there is always plenty to go around."

Mary had to laugh, despite herself. But it was an uncomfortable honking laugh that caused tears to escape from her eyes. "But you haven't touched me since we came here."

Ponter's eyes went wide. "Two are not One."

Mary was quiet for a long time. "I—Gliksin women . . . and Gliksin men, too—we need affection all the time, not just four days a month."

Ponter took a deep breath and let it out slowly. "Normally . . ."

He trailed off, and the word hung between them. Mary felt her pulse increasing. Normally, a person here would have two mates, one male and one female. A Neanderthal woman didn't lack for affection—but for most of the month it came from her woman-mate. "I know," said Mary, closing her eyes. "I know."

"Perhaps this was a mistake," said Ponter, as much, it seemed, to himself as to Mary, although Hak dutifully translated his words. "Perhaps I should not have brought you here."

"No," said Mary. "No, I wanted to come, and I'm glad to be here." She looked at him, staring into his golden eyes. "How long is it until Two next become One?" she asked.

"Three days," said Ponter. "But . . ." he paused, and Mary blinked. "But," he continued, "I suppose it cannot hurt anything for me to show affection to you before then."

He opened his massive arms, and, after a moment, Mary stepped into them.

Mary, of course, could not stay with Ponter, for Ponter lived out in the Rim, which was the exclusive province of males. Adikor suggested the perfect solution: having Mary stay with his woman-mate, Lurt Fradlo. After all, she was a chemist, as Neanderthals defined the term—one who worked with molecules. And Mary, by that definition, was a specialized sort of chemist, focusing on deoxyribonucleic acid.

Lurt had agreed at once—and what scientist of either world

wouldn't leap at the chance to host one from the other? And so, Ponter had Hak summon a travel cube, and Mary headed into the Center.

The driver happened to be a female—or maybe Hak had requested that; after all, the artificial intelligence knew everything about Mary's rape that Ponter did. Mary's removable Companion had had Hak's database transferred into it, and Mary made use of that fact now, conversing with the driver during the trip out.

"Why are your cars shaped like cubes?" Mary asked. "It doesn't seem very aerodynamic."

"What shape should they be?" asked the driver, who had a voice almost as low as Ponter's and as resonant as Michel Bell's when singing "Ol' Man River."

"Well, on my world they are rounded, and—" she thought briefly of *Monty Python*—"they're thin at one end, thick in the middle, and thin again at the other end."

The driver had short hair that was the darkest Mary had yet seen on a Neanderthal, meaning it was the color of milk chocolate. She shook her head. "Then how do you stack them?"

"*Stack* them?" repeated Mary.

"Yes. You know, when they are not being used. We stack them one on top of the other, and fit the stacks together side by side. It cuts down on the amount of space that has to be set aside to accommodate them."

Mary thought of all the land her world wasted on parking lots. "But—but how do you get at your own car when you need it, if it's at the bottom of the stack?"

"My own car?" echoed the driver.

"Yes. You know, the one that belongs to you."

"The cars all belong to the city," said the driver. "Why would I want to own one?"

"Well, I don't know . . ."

"I mean, they are costly to manufacture, at least here."

Mary thought about her monthly car payments. "They are in my world, too."

She looked out at the countryside. Off in the distance, another travel cube was flying along, going in the opposite direction. Mary wondered what Henry Ford would have thought if someone had told him that, within a century of releasing the Model T, half the surface area in cities would be devoted to accommodating the movement or storage of cars, that accidents with them would be the leading cause of death of men under the age of twenty-five, that they would put more pollution into the air than all the factories and furnaces in the world combined.

"Then why own a car?" asked the female Neanderthal.

Mary shrugged a little. "We like to own things."

"So do we," she said. "But you cannot use a car ten tenths a day."

"Don't you worry about the guy who used the car before you having, well, left it a mess?"

The driver operated the control sticks she was holding, turning the cube so that it would avoid a group of trees ahead. And then she simply silently held up her left arm, as if that explained it all.

And, thought Mary, she guessed it did. No one would leave behind garbage, or damage a public vehicle, if they knew that a complete visual record of what they'd done was being automatically transmitted to the alibi archives. No one could steal a car, or use a car to commit a crime. And the Companion implants probably kept track of everything you'd brought with you into the car; there would be little possibility of accidentally leaving your hat behind and having to track down the same car you'd used before.

It had grown very dark. Mary was astonished to realize that

the car was no longer passing through barren countryside, but was now in the thick of Saldak Center. There were almost no artificial lights; Mary saw that the driver wasn't looking out the transparent front of the travel cube, but rather was driving by consulting a square infrared monitor set into the panel in front of her.

The car settled to the ground, and one side folded away, opening the interior to the chilly night air. "Here you are," said the driver. "It's that house, there." She pointed at an oddly shaped structure dimly visible a dozen meters away.

Mary thanked the driver and got out. She had planned to make a beeline for the house, finding it rather disconcerting to be out in the open at night on this strange world, but she stopped dead in her tracks and looked up.

The stars overhead were glorious, the Milky Way clearly visible. What had Ponter called it that night back in Sudbury? "The Night River," that was it.

And there, there was the Big Dipper; the Head of the Mammoth. Mary drew an imaginary line from the pointer stars, and quickly located Polaris, which meant that she was facing due north. She fished into her purse for the compass she'd brought with her at Jock Krieger's request, but it was too dark to make out its face. So, after taking in her fill of the gorgeous heavens, Mary walked over to Lurt's house and asked her Companion to let the occupant know that she'd arrived.

A moment later, the door opened, and there was another female Neanderthal. "Healthy day," said the woman, or, at least, that's how Mary's unit translated the sounds she made.

"Hello," said Mary. "Uh, just a sec . . ." There was plenty of light spilling out through the open door. Mary glanced down at the compass needle, and felt her eyebrows lifting in astonishment. The colored end of the needle—metallic blue, as opposed to the naked silver of the other end—was pointing toward Polaris, just as it would have on Mary's side of the portal. Despite what Jock had said, it seemed this version of Earth hadn't yet undergone a magnetic-field reversal.

Mary spent a pleasant night at Lurt's home, meeting Adikor's young son Dab, and the rest of Lurt's family. The only truly awkward moment came when she needed to use the bathroom. Lurt showed her the chamber, but Mary was absolutely flummoxed by the unit in front of her. After staring dumbly at it for most of a minute, she reemerged from the chamber, and called Lurt over.

"I'm sorry," Mary said, "but . . . well, it's nothing like a toilet in my world. I don't have any idea how to . . ."

Lurt laughed. "I am sorry!" she said. "Here. You place your feet in these stirrups, and you grab these overhead rings like this . . ."

Mary realized she'd have to completely remove her pants to make it work, but there was a hook on the wall that seemed designed to hold them. It actually was quite comfortable, although she yelped in surprise when a moist spongelike thing came in of its own accord to clean her when she was done.

Mary did notice that there was no reading matter in the bathroom. Her own, back home in Toronto, had the latest copies of *The Atlantic Monthly, Canadian Geographic, Utne Reader, Country Music,* and *World of Crosswords* on the toilet tank. But, even with great plumbing, she supposed that Neanderthals, because of their acute senses of smell, would never dally in the bathroom.

Mary slept that night on a pile of cushions arranged on the floor. At first, she found it uncomfortable: she was used to a more uniformly flat surface, but Lurt showed her how to arrange the pillows just so, providing neck and back support, separating her knees, and so on. Despite all the strangeness, Mary fell rapidly to sleep, absolutely exhausted.

The next morning, Mary went with Lurt to her workplace, which, unlike most of the buildings in the Center, was made entirely of stone—to contain fire or explosion should some experiment go wrong, Lurt explained.

It seemed that Lurt worked with six other female chemists, and Mary was already falling into the habit of classifying them into generations, although instead of calling them 146s, 145s, 144s, 143s, and 142s, as Ponter did, referring to the number of decades since the dawn of the modern era, Mary thought of them as women who were pushing thirty, forty, fifty, sixty, and seventy years old, respectively. And although Neanderthal women didn't age quite the same way as *Homo sapiens* females did—something about the way the browridge pulled on the skin of the forehead seemed to prevent pronounced wrinkling there—Mary had no trouble telling who belonged to which group. Indeed, with generations born in discrete bunches at ten-year intervals, the idea of trying to be coy about one's age doubtless never even occurred to a female Neanderthal.

Still, it didn't take long for Mary to stop thinking of the people at Lurt's lab as Neanderthals and to start thinking of them as just women. Yes, their appearance was startling—women who looked like linebackers, women with hairy faces—but their mien was decidedly . . . well, not *feminine,* Mary thought; that word came loaded with too many expectations. But certainly *female:* pleasant, cooperative, chatty, collegial instead of competitive, and, all in all, just a whole heck of a lot of fun to be around.

Of course, Mary was of a generation—hopefully, the last such in her world—in which far fewer women worked in the sciences than men. She'd never been in a department where women were the majority—although it was getting close to that at York—let alone held all the positions. Perhaps in such circumstances, the working environment would be like this on her Earth, too. Mary had grown up in Ontario, which, for historical reasons, had two separate government-funded school boards, one "public"—in the American, not the British, sense—and the other Catholic. Since religious education was only allowed in religious institutions, many Catholic parents had sent their children to the Catholic schools, but Mary's parents—mostly at her father's insistence—had opted for the public system. Still, there'd been some talk when she was fourteen about sending her to a Catholic girls' school. Mary had been struggling back then in math; her father and mother had been told she might do better in an environment without boys. But ultimately her parents had decided to keep her in the public system, since, as her father said, she'd have to deal with men after high school, and so she might as well get used to it. And so Mary's high-school years were spent at East York Collegiate Institute, instead of nearby St. Teresa's. And although Mary had eventually overcome her mathematical difficulties, despite the co-ed learning, she did sometimes wonder about the benefits of all-girl schools. Certainly, some of the best science students she'd taught at York had come up through such institutions.

And, indeed, maybe there really was something to be said for extending that notion right into adult life, into the workplace, letting women labor—funny how that word had a double meaning for females, Mary thought—in an environment free of men and their egos.

Although Neanderthal timekeeping quite sensibly divided the day into ten equal parts, starting at the point that was dawn on the vernal equinox, Mary still relied on her Swatch, rather than the cryptic display on her Companion band—after all, although she'd traveled to another universe, she *was* still in the same time zone.

Mary was quite used to the rhythm of morning and afternoon coffee breaks, and an hour off for lunch, but the Neanderthal metabolism didn't let them go that long without eating. There were two long breaks in the workday, one at about 11:00 A.M., and the other at about 3:00 P.M., and at both of them, great quantities of food were consumed, including raw meat—the same laser technique that killed infections inside people made uncooked meat quite safe to eat, and Neanderthal jaws were more than up to the task. But Mary's stomach wasn't; she sat with Lurt and her colleagues while they ate, but tried to keep from looking at their food.

She could have excused herself during the meal breaks, but this was Lurt's time off, and Mary wanted to talk with her. She was fascinated by what the Neanderthals knew about genetics—and Lurt seemed quite willing to freely share it all.

Indeed, Mary learned so much in her short time with Lurt, she was beginning to think just about anything was possible—especially if there were no men around.

Chapter Thirty-two

Mary had been to a dozen or so weddings over the years—several Catholic, one Jewish, one traditional Chinese, and a few civil services. So she thought she knew in vague terms what to expect at Jasmel's bonding ceremony.

She was wrong.

Of course, she knew that the ceremony could not take place in a hall of worship—the Neanderthals had no such thing. Still, she'd expected some sort of official venue. Instead, the event took place out in the countryside.

Ponter was already there when a travel cube dropped off Mary; they were the first to arrive, and, since no one was around, they indulged in a long hug.

"Ah," said Ponter, after they'd separated, "here they come." It was bright out here. Mary had discovered she'd forgotten her sunglasses back on the other side, and she had to squint to make out the approaching party. It consisted of three women—one in her late thirties, Mary thought, another who was a teenager, and a child of eight. Ponter looked at Mary, then at the approaching women, and back again. Mary tried to read the expression on his face; had he been one of her own kind, she might have thought it was profound discomfort, as if he'd realized that he'd unexpectedly landed in an awkward situation.

The three females were walking, and they were coming

from the east—from the direction of the Center. The oldest and youngest were carrying nothing, but the middle one had a large pack strapped to her back. As they got nearer, the little girl shouted out, "Daddy!" and ran toward Ponter, who scooped her up in a hug.

The other two were walking more slowly, the older female keeping pace beside the younger one, who seemed to be trudging along, weighed down by the pack.

Ponter had now released the eight-year-old, and, holding one of the child's hands, turned and faced Mary. "Mare, this is my daughter, Mega Bek. Mega, this is my friend, Mare."

Mega had clearly had eyes only for her father to this point. She looked Mary up and down. "Wow," she said at last. "You are a Gliksin, right?"

Mary smiled. "Yes, I am," she said, letting her strapped-on Companion translate her words into the Neanderthal tongue.

"Would you come to my school?" asked Mega. "I would like to show you to the other kids!"

Mary was a bit startled; she'd never thought of herself as a show-and-tell exhibit. "Umm, if I have the time," she said.

The other two had now drawn near. "This is my other daughter, Jasmel Ket," said Ponter, indicating the eighteen-year-old.

"Hello," said Mary. She looked at the girl, but had no idea whether she was considered attractive by Neanderthal standards. Still, she did have her father's arresting golden eyes. "I'm—" she decided not to embarrass the girl by putting forth a name she wouldn't be able to pronounce. "I'm Mare Vaughan."

"Hello, Scholar Vaughan," said Jasmel, who must have heard of her before; otherwise, she'd have had no idea how to parse Mary's name. And, indeed, Jasmel's next comment confirmed that. "You gave my father that bit of metal," she said.

Mary was lost for a moment, but then realization dawned. The crucifix. "Yes," said Mary.

"I saw you once before," said Jasmel, "on a monitor when we were rescuing my father, but . . ." She shook her head in wonder. "Even so, I still did not really believe it."

"Well," said Mary, "here I am." She paused. "I hope you don't mind me coming to your bonding ceremony."

Whether she really did or not, Jasmel had her father's courtesy. "No, of course not. I am delighted you are here."

Ponter spoke up quickly, perhaps, thought Mary, detecting that his daughter was secretly displeased, and wanting to move along before the topic came into the open. "And this is—*was*—my daughter's guardian." He looked at the thirty-eight-year-old. "I, ah, hadn't expected you," he said.

The Neanderthal woman's eyebrow moved up her browridge. "Apparently not," she said, glancing at Mary.

"Ah," said Ponter, "yes, well, this is Mare Vaughan—the woman I told you about from the other side. Mare, this is Daklar Bolbay."

"My God," said Mary, and her Companion bleeped, unable to translate the phrase.

"Yes?" said Daklar, prodding Mary to try again.

"I—ah, I mean, pleased to meet you. I've heard a lot about you."

"And I you," said Daklar evenly.

Mary forced a smile and looked away.

"Daklar," explained Ponter, "was the woman-mate of my woman-mate, Klast, and so she had served as Jasmel's guardian. He turned pointedly to Daklar. "Until Jasmel reached the age of majority when she reached 225 months in the spring, that is."

Mary tried to follow the undercurrents. It seemed that Ponter was saying that since Daklar had no official role in Jasmel's life anymore, she shouldn't be here. Well, Mary could certainly understand Ponter's discomfort. Daklar, after all, had tried to have Adikor castrated.

But whatever awkwardness Ponter felt was interrupted by the arrival of still more people: a male and a female Neanderthal, each looking to be approaching fifty.

"These are Tryon's parents," said Ponter. "Bal Durban," he continued, indicating the male, "and Yabla Pol. Bal, Yabla, this is my friend Mare Vaughan."

Bal had a booming voice. "No need to introduce her," he said. "I've been watching you on my Voyeur."

Mary tried to suppress a shudder. She'd caught sight of the occasional silver outfit, but she'd had no idea that she had been the object of the Exhibitionists' attention.

"Look at you!" said Yabla. "All skin and bones! Do they have enough food in your world?"

In her whole life, no one had ever referred to Mary as "skin and bones." She rather liked the sound of it. "Yes," she said, blushing a bit.

"Well, tonight we feast," said Yabla. "One meal cannot undo tenmonths of neglect, but we will make a good start!"

Mary smiled politely.

Bal turned to his woman-mate. "What is keeping that boy of yours?" he said.

"Who knows?" said Yabla, her tone one of gentle teasing. "He clearly got his time sense from you."

"Here he comes," shouted Jasmel, still wearing her heavy pack.

Mary looked in the direction the girl was pointing. A figure was emerging in the distance, trudging toward them, something large slung across his shoulders. It looked like it would be several minutes before he closed the distance, though. Mary leaned over to Ponter. "What's your daughter's intended's name again?"

Ponter frowned for a moment, evidently listening to Hak trying to make sense out of the question. "Oh," he said at last. "Tryon Rugal."

"I don't understand your names," said Mary. "I mean, 'Vaughan' is my family name: both my parents, both my brothers, and my sister all share it." She shielded her eyes with a hand as she looked out at the approaching boy again.

Ponter was looking that way, too, but his browridge was all the shielding he needed. "The last name, the one that is used by the outside world, is chosen by the father; the first name, the one that is used by those one knows well, is chosen by the mother. You see the sense of it? Fathers live at the periphery; mothers in the center. My father chose 'Boddit' for me, which means 'wonderfully handsome' and my mother chose 'Ponter,' which means 'magnificently intelligent.' "

"You're kidding," said Mary.

Ponter cracked his giant grin. "Yes, I am. Sorry; I just wanted something as impressive as your own 'mother of God.' Seriously, 'Ponter' means 'full moon,' and 'Boddit' is the name of a city in Evsoy, known for its great painters."

"Ah," said Mary. "Then—my God!"

"Well," said Ponter, still in a kidding mood, "he certainly is not mine."

"No, look!" She pointed at Tryon.

"Yes?" said Ponter.

"He's carrying a deer carcass!"

"You noticed that?" Ponter smiled. "It is his hunting offering to Jasmel. And in her pack, she has her gathering offering for him."

Indeed, Jasmel was finally unslinging her pack. Perhaps,

thought Mary, it was traditional to wait until the man had seen that the woman had brought the goods herself. As Tryon came closer, Ponter moved toward him and helped him get the deer off his shoulders.

Mary's stomach turned. The deer's hide was bloody, a half dozen wounds piercing its torso. And, as Tryon bent over, she saw that his own back was slick with deer blood.

"Does someone have to officiate over the ceremony?" asked Mary.

Ponter looked confused. "No."

"We have a judge or a representative of the church do it," said Mary.

"Jasmel and Tryon's pledges to each other will automatically be recorded at the alibi archives," said Ponter.

Mary nodded. Of course.

Now that Tryon was free of the deer, he ran toward his dear. Jasmel accepted him with open arms, and they hugged tightly, and licked each other's faces, rather passionately. Mary found herself looking away.

"Come on," said Tryon's father, Bal. "It will take tenths to roast that deer. We should get on with it."

The two let go of each other. Mary saw that Jasmel's hands were now stained red from running them up Tryon's back. It disgusted Mary, but Jasmel just laughed when she noticed it.

And, without further preamble, the ceremony was apparently under way. "All right," said Jasmel. "Here we go." She turned to Tryon. "I promise to hold you in my heart twenty-nine days a month, and to hold you in my arms whenever Two become One."

Mary looked at Ponter. The muscles of his wide jaw were bunching; he was clearly moved.

"I promise," continued Jasmel, "that your health and your happiness will be as important to me as my own."

Daklar was clearly moved, too. After all, as Mary understood it, she and Jasmel had lived together all of Jasmel's life.

Jasmel spoke again: "If, at any time, you tire of me, I promise to release you without acrimony, and with the best interests of our children as my highest priority."

Mary was impressed by that. How much simpler her own life would have been if she and Colm had made a similar pledge. She looked again at Ponter, and—

Jesus!

Daklar had moved to stand next to him, and—Mary could scarcely believe it—the two of them were holding hands!

It was apparently Tryon's turn to speak now. "I promise," he said, "to hold you in my heart twenty-nine days a month, and to hold you in my arms whenever Two become One."

Two becoming One, thought Mary. Surely that had already happened once here in the time between Ponter's first returning home and his reappearance on Mary's Earth. She'd assumed he'd spent that time alone, but . . .

"I promise," said Tryon, "that your happiness and well-being will be as important to me as my own."

"If you ever tire of me," he continued, "I promise to release you without pain, and with the best interests of our children as my highest priority."

Ordinarily, Mary would be delighted to hear such absolute parity in the marital pledges—Colm had once opined that it was too bad Catholic services didn't include "and obey." But that thought was entirely subordinate to her shock to find that Ponter and Daklar were affectionate toward each other—and after what she'd done to Adikor!

Little Mega startled Mary by clapping her hands together once. "They are bonded!" she squealed. For half a second,

Mary thought the girl was referring to Ponter and Daklar, but, no, no, that was ridiculous.

Bal slapped his own hands against his stomach. "Now that we have finished with that," he said, "let us get to work preparing the feast!"

Chapter Thirty-three

"What are you?" asked Selgan, shaking his head in wonder. "A moron?"

"Daklar wasn't supposed to be there!" said Ponter. "A bonding ceremony involves only parents and the two children being bonded. There's no role for the same-sex mates of the parents."

"But Daklar was tabant *of your daughters."*

"Not of Jasmel," said Ponter. "Jasmel had reached the age of majority; she no longer had a legal guardian."

"But you had brought Mare along," said Selgan.

"Yes. I make no apology for that: it was my right to bring someone in Klast's place." Ponter frowned. "Daklar should not have been there."

Selgan scratched his scalp where it was exposed by his wide part. "You people in the physical sciences," he said, shaking his head again. "You expect humans to behave predictably, to follow immutable laws. But they don't."

Ponter snorted. "Tell me about it."

To Mary's horror, everyone was supposed to participate in flensing the deer. Bal and Yabla, as parents of the—the "groom"; Mary couldn't help using the term—had brought sharp metal knives, and Bal slit the deer from throat to tail. Mary hadn't been prepared for the sight of so much blood, and she excused herself, walking a short distance away.

It was cold here, in the Neanderthal world, and it was getting colder. The sun was close to setting.

Mary had her back to the group, but after a few moments, she heard footfalls on the first autumn leaves behind her. She assumed it was Ponter, come to offer some comfort . . . and an explanation. But Mary's heart jumped when she heard Daklar's deep voice.

"You seem uncomfortable with the skinning of the deer," she said.

"I've never done anything like that before," Mary replied, turning around. She could see that Yabla and little Mega were now off gathering wood for a fire.

"That is all right. We have an extra pair of hands here anyway."

At first Mary thought Daklar was making a reference to her own presence, which had clearly surprised Ponter. And then, Mary thought, perhaps Daklar was taking a dig at her. "Ponter invited me," Mary said, not liking the defensive tone in her voice.

"So I see," said Daklar.

Mary, knowing she would regret doing so but unable to stop herself, pushed the issue. "I don't see how you can be here all sweetness and light after what you did to Adikor."

Daklar was quiet for a time, and Mary was unable to read her expression. "I see," the Neanderthal woman said at last, "that our Ponter has been telling you things."

Mary didn't like the phrasing "our Ponter," but said nothing in reply. After a moment, Daklar continued: "What precisely did he tell you?"

"That while Ponter was in my world, you had Adikor charged with his murder—Adikor! Whom Ponter loves!"

Daklar lifted her eyebrow. "Did he tell what the principal piece of evidence against Adikor was?"

Mary knew that Daklar was a gatherer, not a hunter, but Mary felt as though she were being maneuvered into a trap. She shook her head through an arc of only a few degrees. "There was no evidence," said Mary, "because there was no crime."

"Not that time, no. But before." Daklar paused, and her tone sounded a little haughty, a little condescending. "I'm sure Ponter hasn't told you about his damaged jaw."

But Mary wanted to assert her intimacy with the man. "He told me *all* about it. I've even seen X rays of it."

"Well, then, you should understand. Adikor had tried once before to kill Ponter, so—"

Suddenly Daklar broke off, and her eyes went wide as she apparently read some sign in Mary's face. "You did not know it was Adikor, did you? Ponter had not taken you that far into his confidence, had he?"

Mary felt her heart pounding rapidly. She didn't trust herself to make a reply.

"Well," said Daklar, "then I *do* have new information for you. Yes, it was Adikor Huld who punched Ponter in the face. I submitted as evidence images from Ponter's alibi archive showing the attack."

Mary and Colm had had their problems—no question—but he had never hit her. Although she knew it was all too common, she couldn't imagine staying with a physically abusive spouse, but . . .

But it had been just once, and—

No. No, had Ponter been female, Mary never would have forgiven Adikor for hitting him even once, just as . . .

She hated to think about it, hated whenever it came to mind.

Just as she had never forgiven her father for having once hit her mother, decades ago.

But Ponter *was* a man, was physically the equal of Adikor, and—

And yet, nothing—*nothing*—excused such behavior. To hit someone you were supposed to love!

Mary had no reply for Daklar, and, after sufficient time had elapsed that this was obvious, the Neanderthal woman went on. "So you see, my charge against Adikor was *not* unfounded. Yes, I regret it now, but . . ."

She trailed off. To this point, Daklar had shown no unwillingness to give voice to any thought, and so Mary wondered what it was that she was leaving unsaid. And then it hit her. "But you were blinded by the thought of losing Ponter."

Daklar neither nodded nor shook her head, but Mary knew she had hit upon it. "Well, then," Mary said. She had no idea what, if anything, Ponter had said to Daklar about his relationship with Mary during the first time he'd come to Mary's world, and . . .

. . . and surely he'd had no opportunity to speak to Daklar of the relationship that had deepened since, but . . .

But Daklar was a woman. She might weigh over two hundred pounds, and she might be able to bench-press twice that amount, and she might have soft fur on her cheeks.

But she *was* a woman, a female of genus *Homo,* and she could doubtless read things as clearly as Mary could. If Daklar hadn't known about Ponter's interest in Mary before today, she surely did now. Not just because of the blindingly obvious—that Ponter had brought Mary to fill the role of his dead woman-mate at his daughter's bonding—but in how Ponter looked at Mary, how he stood close to her. His posture, his body language, surely spoke as eloquently to Daklar as they did to Mary.

"Well, then, indeed," said Daklar, echoing Mary's words.

Mary looked back at the wedding party. Ponter was working

on the deer corpse with Jasmel and Tryon and Bal, but he kept glancing in this direction. Had he been a Gliksin, perhaps Mary would have been unable to read his expression at such a distance, but Ponter's features, and his emotions, were writ large across his broad face. He was clearly nervous about the conversation Mary and Daklar were having—and well he should be, thought Mary.

She turned her attention back to the female Neanderthal standing before her, arms crossed in front of her broad, but not particularly busty, chest. Mary had noticed that none of the Neanderthal women she'd met were, well, *stacked,* the way Louise Benoît was. She supposed that with males and females living mostly separate lives, secondary sexual characteristics wouldn't be as important.

"He is of my kind," said Daklar, simply.

And, indeed he was, thought Mary, *but* . . .

But.

She refused to meet Daklar's eyes, and, without another word, Mary Vaughan, woman, Canadian, *Homo sapiens,* walked back to join the group stripping the reddish brown hide from the carcass of the animal that one of them had killed apparently with nothing more than thrusts from his spear.

Mary had to admit the meal was excellent. The meat was juicy and flavorful, and the vegetables were tasty. It reminded her a bit of a trip she'd made two years ago to New Zealand for a conference; everyone had gone out for a Maori *hangi* feast.

But soon enough it was over, and, to Mary's astonishment, Tryon left with his father. Mary leaned close to Ponter. "Why are Tryon and Jasmel separating?" she asked.

Ponter looked surprised. "It is still two days until Two next become One."

Mary remembered the misgivings she'd had walking down the aisle with Colm, all those years ago. If she'd been given days for second thoughts, she might have backed out; after all, she could have gotten a real Roman Catholic annulment—not one of the fake ones she'd someday have to get—if the marriage hadn't been consummated.

But . . .

Two days!

"So . . ." said Mary, slowly, and then, gaining her courage: "So you won't want to go back to my world until after that's over, right?"

"It is a very important time for . . ." He trailed off, and Mary wondered if he had intended to finish his sentence with "my family," or with "us"—for his kind. It did, after all, make all the difference in the worlds . . .

Mary took a deep breath. "Do you want me to go home before then?"

Ponter took a deep breath of his own, and—

"Daddy, Daddy!" Little Megameg ran up to her father.

He bent down to be at her eye height. "Yes, sweetie?"

"Jasmel is going to take me home now."

Ponter hugged his daughter. "I will miss you," he said.

"I love you, Daddy."

"I love you, too, Megameg."

She put her little hands on her little hips.

"Sorry," said Ponter, raising a hand. "I love you, too, Mega."

The girl smiled. "When Two become One, can we go on another picnic with Daklar?"

Mary felt her heart jump.

Ponter looked up at Mary, then quickly lowered his head enough that his browridge concealed his eyes from her. "We will see about that," he said.

Jasmel and Daklar came close. Ponter straightened up and

turned to his elder daughter. "I am sure you and Tryon will be very happy."

Again, Mary was somewhat taken aback by the phraseology. In her world, the word "together" would have been tacked on to that sentiment, but Jasmel and Tryon, although now bonded, were going to spend most of their lives apart. Indeed, Jasmel would presumably have another bonding ceremony in her future, when she chose her woman-mate.

Mary shook her head. Maybe she *should* just go back home.

"Come on," said Daklar, stepping forward and speaking to Mary, "we can share a travel cube back into the Center. I assume you are staying at Lurt's again?"

Mary looked for a moment at Ponter, but even the bride wasn't getting to sleep with the groom tonight. "Yes," she said.

"All right," said Daklar. "Let us go." She closed the distance between herself and Ponter, and after a moment of hesitation, Ponter drew her into a farewell hug. Mary looked away.

Mary and Daklar said little to each other during the trip back. Indeed, after some awkward silence, Daklar engaged the driver in conversation. Mary looked out at the landscape. There was virtually no old-growth forest left in her Ontario, but there was plenty here.

At last, she was deposited back at Lurt's home. Lurt's woman-mate, and Lurt herself, wanted to hear all about the bonding ceremony, and Mary tried to oblige. Young Dab seemed awfully well behaved, sitting silently in a corner—but Lurt eventually explained that he was engrossed in a story being read to him by his Companion.

Mary knew she needed advice, but—damn!—these family relationships were so complex. Lurt Fradlo was Adikor Huld's woman-mate, and Adikor Huld was Ponter Boddit's man-mate.

But, if Mary understood things correctly, there was no special relationship between Lurt and Ponter, just as . . .

Just as there was supposed to be no special relationship between Ponter, whose woman-mate had been Klast Harbin, and Daklar Bolbay, who had been Klast's woman-mate.

And yet clearly there *was* a special relationship between them. Ponter had made no mention of it to Mary during his first visit to her Earth, although he'd spoken often of what he felt he'd lost by being transported from his home world, apparently with no way ever to return. He'd talked repeatedly of Klast, whom he had already lost, and of Jasmel and Megameg and Adikor. But never Daklar—at least, not as someone he was missing.

Could the relationship between them be that new?

But, if it were, would Ponter have left his world for an extended time?

No, wait. Wait. It wasn't really that extended a time; it was less than three weeks—three weeks that fell between two successive occurrences of Two becoming One. He couldn't have seen Daklar during that period even if he had stayed home.

Mary shook her head. She needed not just advice—she needed answers.

And Lurt seemed the only person who could possibly provide them in the short time left between today and when Two next became One. But she'd have to get Lurt alone—and there would be no chance of that until the morning, at Lurt's lab.

Ponter was lying on one of the couches extending from the wooden walls of his house, staring up at the painting on the ceiling. Pabo was stretched out on the mossy floor next to Ponter, sleeping.

The front door opened, and Adikor entered. Pabo roused

and hurried over to meet him. "That's a girl," said Adikor, reaching down to scratch the dog's head.

"Hey, Adikor," said Ponter, not getting up.

"Hey, Ponter. How was the bonding ceremony?"

"Let me put it this way," said Ponter. "What's the worst thing that could have happened?"

Adikor frowned. "Tryon speared himself in the foot?"

"No, no. Tryon was fine; the actual ceremony was fine."

"Then what?"

"Daklar Bolbay was there."

"Gristle," said Adikor, mounting a saddle-seat. "That must have been awkward."

"You know," said Ponter, "they say it's only males who are territorial, but . . ."

"So what happened?"

"I don't even know. It's not like Mare and Daklar had an argument or anything, but . . ."

"But they both know about the other."

Ponter's voice sounded defensive, even to him. "I wasn't keeping anything from either of them. You know that Daklar's interest took me by surprise, and, well, I didn't know then that I'd ever see Mare again. But now . . ."

"Two become One the day after tomorrow. You won't be spending any time with Jasmel, I can guarantee that. I remember the first Two becoming One after my bonding to Lurt; we hardly came up for air."

"I know," said Ponter. "And although Mega will be around for some of it . . ."

"You'll still have to determine who you're going to spend your time with—and at whose home you are going to sleep."

"This is ridiculous," said Ponter. "I've no commitment to Daklar."

"You have no commitment to Mare, either."

"I know. But I cannot let her be abandoned during Two becoming One." Ponter paused, hoping Adikor would not take offense at his next words. "Believe me, I know how lonely that can be."

"Maybe she should go back to her world before then," said Adikor.

"I don't think she would like that."

"Who do you want to be with?"

"Mare. But . . ."

"Yes?"

"But she has her world, and I have mine. The obstacles are formidable."

"If I may be so bold, old boy, where do I fit in?"

Ponter sat up on the couch. "What do you mean? You're my man-mate. I would never let that change."

"Oh?"

"Of course not. I love you."

"And I love you. But you told me about Gliksin ways. Mare isn't looking for a man-mate that she might see for a few days out of each month, and I doubt she wants to find a woman-mate at all."

"Well, yes, the customs of her people are different, but . . ."

"It's like mammoths and mastodons," said Adikor. "Sure, they look a lot alike, but try mixing a male mammoth with a female mastodon, and watch out!"

"I know," said Ponter. "I know."

"I don't see how you can make it work."

"I know, but . . ."

"May I say something?" It was Hak's voice.

Ponter looked down at his left forearm. "Sure."

"You know I usually stay out of these things," said the Companion. "But there is a factor you are not considering."

"Oh?"

Hak switched to Ponter's cochlear implants. "You may wish me to say this in private."

"Nonsense," said Ponter. "I have no secrets from Adikor."

"Very well," said Hak, switching back to the external speaker. "Scholar Vaughan is recovering from a traumatic experience. Her emotions and behavior of late may be atypical."

Adikor tipped his head. "What traumatic experience? I mean, I know that eating a meal Ponter has helped prepare can be pretty devastating, but . . ."

"Mare was raped," said Ponter. "Back in her own world. Just before I came there."

"Oh," said Adikor, immediately sobering. "What did they do to the guy who raped her?"

"Nothing. He got away."

"How could he possibly—"

Ponter raised his left arm. "No Companions. No justice."

"Marrowless bone," said Adikor. "What a world they must live in."

Chapter Thirty-four

The next day, Mary walked down the corridor of the laboratory building, stepping aside to make room for one of the spindly robots that darted about the corners of Neanderthal society. She wondered for a moment about the economics of this world. They had AI, and they had robots. But they also had what amounted to cab drivers; clearly not all jobs that *could* be automated had been automated.

Mary continued on, until she came to the room Lurt was working in. "Were you planning to take a break anytime soon?" asked Mary, knowing how much she herself hated to be interrupted when work was going well.

Lurt glanced at the display on her Companion, presumably noting the time. "Sure," she said.

"Good," said Mary. "Can we go for a walk? I need to talk."

Mary and Lurt stepped out into the daylight. Lurt adopted the posture Mary had seen frequently now amongst Neanderthals, slightly tipping her head forward so that her browridge provided maximal shading for her eyes. Mary held one hand above her own flat brow, trying to achieve the same effect. Although she had weightier matters on her mind, having forgotten her FosterGrants back on the other side was getting to be a nuisance. "Do your people have sunglasses?" asked Mary.

"If they need them. We have them for our daughters, too."

Mary smiled. "No, no, no." She pointed up. "Sunglasses. Glasses that are tinted to block out some of the sunlight."

"Ah," said Lurt. "Yes, such things are available, although we call them"—she had spoken continuously, but there was a pause in the translation, as Mary's Companion considered how to interpret what Lurt had said—"snow-glare shields."

Mary understood immediately. Browridges were all well and good for shielding against light from above, and although the broad face and wide nose probably helped shield the deep-set eyes from light reflected off the ground, there would still be times when tinted glasses would be useful.

"Is it possible I could get a pair?"

"You need two of them?" asked Lurt.

"Um, no. We, ah, we refer to glasses in the plural—you know, because there are two lenses."

Lurt shook her head, but it was in a good-humored way. "You might as well refer to a pair of 'pants,' then," she said. "After all, they have two legs."

Mary decided not to pursue that. "In any event, is it possible to get a 'snow-glare shield' for me?"

"Certainly. There is a lens grinder just over there."

But Mary hesitated. "I don't have any money—any way to pay for them. I mean, for *it.*"

Lurt gestured at Mary's forearm, and, after a moment Mary realized that she was indicating the strapped-on Companion. Mary presented her forearm to Lurt's inspection. She pulled a couple of the tiny control buds on it, and watched as symbols danced across its display.

"As I thought," said Lurt. "This Companion is tied to Ponter's account. You may acquire anything you wish, and he will be billed for it."

"Really? Wow."

"Come, the lens grinder's shop is over here."

Lurt crossed a wide strip of tall grass, and Mary followed. She felt a certain guilt spending Ponter's money, given what she wanted to talk to Lurt about, but she was getting a headache, and she didn't want to have so sensitive a conversation within earshot of Lurt's coworkers. No, more than that: Mary was becoming savvy in the ways of Neanderthals. She knew that when they were indoors or when the wind was still, a Neanderthal could tell much about what the person she was with was thinking or feeling simply by inhaling his or her pheromones. Mary felt disadvantaged, and naked, under such circumstances. But there was a good breeze today, and while she and Lurt walked, Lurt would have to take Mary's words at face value.

They entered the building Lurt had indicated. It was a large facility, made out of three shaped trees close enough together that their branches intertwined into a single canopy overhead.

Mary was surprised by what she saw. She'd expected some alternate-world LensCrafters, devoted to eyewear, but so much of the eyewear business was driven by mercurial fashion in frames, and the Neanderthals, with their conserving natures, didn't go in for fads. Also, with a smaller population, infinite specialization of work apparently wasn't possible. This lens grinder made all manner of optics. Her shop was filled with what were clearly telescopes, microscopes, cameras, projectors, magnifying glasses, flashlights, and more. Mary tried to take it all in, sure that Lilly, Kevin, and Frank would barrage her with questions about it when she returned to the Synergy Group.

An elderly Neanderthal woman emerged. Mary tested herself, trying to identify the female's generation. She looked to be getting on to seventy, so that would make her—let's see—a 142. The woman's eyes went wide at the sight of Mary, but she quickly recovered. "Healthy day," she said.

"Healthy day," responded Lurt. "This is my friend Mare."

"Yes, indeed," said the 142. "From the other universe! My favorite Exhibitionist has been catching glimpses of you ever since you arrived."

Mary shuddered.

"Mare needs a snow-glare shield," said Lurt.

The woman nodded and disappeared into the back of her shop for a moment. When she returned, she was holding a pair of dark lenses—dark blue, they seemed to be, not the green or amber Mary was used to—attached to a wide band that looked liked the elastic out of a pair of Fruit of the Looms. "Try this on," she said.

Mary took the offered lenses, but wasn't sure exactly how to wear them. Lurt laughed. "Like this," she said, taking the contraption from Mary and stretching the elastic until she was able to get it easily over Mary's head. "Normally, the band would fit in here," said Lurt, running her finger along the furrow between her own prominent browridge and forehead. "That would keep them from slipping down."

And, indeed, the band did seem to want to slip down. The lens maker clearly realized this. "Let me get you one for a child," she said, disappearing into the back.

Mary tried not to be embarrassed. Gliksins had tall heads; Neanderthals had long ones. The woman returned with another pair, one with a less generous elastic band. These seemed to fit snugly.

"You can flip the lenses up or down, as needed," said the woman, demonstrating for Mary.

"Thank you. Umm, how do I . . . ?"

"Pay for it?" provided Lurt, smiling. "Just walk out of the shop; your account will be billed."

That was one way to deal with shoplifters, thought Mary. "Thank you," she said, and she and Lurt headed outdoors again. With the lenses down, Mary found it much more comfortable, although the blue cast to everything made her feel even colder than she already did. As she and Lurt walked along, Mary broached the topic she wanted to talk about.

"I don't know what the protocols are here," said Mary. "I'm not a politician or a diplomat or anything like that. And I certainly don't want to offend you or put you in an awkward spot, but . . ."

They were walking down another wide strip of grass, this one decorated at intervals with carved life-size statues of presumably great Neanderthals, all female. "Yes?" prodded Lurt.

"Well, I'm wondering about Ponter's relationship with Daklar Bolbay."

"Daklar was woman-mate to Ponter's woman-mate. Our technical term for that interaction is *tulagark.* Ponter is Daklar's *tulagarkap,* and Daklar is Ponter's *tulagarlob.*"

"Is that normally a . . . a close relationship?"

"It can be, but it does not have to be. Ponter is my own *tulagarkap,* after all—the same-sex mate of my opposite-sex mate, Adikor. Ponter and I do happen to be quite close. But it just as often is a merely cordial relationship, and occasionally one of some hostility."

"Ponter and Daklar seem to be . . . close."

Lurt made a cold laugh. "Daklar brought charges against my Adikor in Ponter's absence. There can be no affection between Ponter and Daklar now."

"So I would have thought," said Mary. "But there *is.*"

"You are misreading the signs."

"Daklar herself told me."

Lurt stopped walking, perhaps startled, perhaps to try to catch a whiff of Mary's pheromones. "Oh," she said at last.

"Indeed. And, well . . ."

"Yes?"

Mary paused, and then motioned for them to begin walking again. The sun moved behind a cloud. "You have not seen Adikor since Two last became One, is that right?"

Lurt nodded.

"Have you spoken to him?"

"Briefly. On a matter concerning Dab."

"But not about . . . about Ponter and . . . and me?"

"No," said Lurt.

"Are you . . . are you obliged to share everything with Adikor? I don't mean possessions; I mean knowledge. Gossip."

"No, of course not. We have a saying: 'What happens when Two are separate is best kept separate.' "

Mary smiled. "All right, then. I really don't want this to get back to Ponter, but . . . well, I, um, I like him."

"He has an agreeable disposition," said Lurt.

Mary suppressed a grin. Ponter himself had told her he wasn't good-looking by the standards of his own people, not that Mary cared or could even tell. But Lurt's words reminded her of what was usually said about homely people in her own world.

"I mean," said Mary, "I like him a lot." God, she felt fourteen years old again.

"Yes?" said Lurt.

"But he likes Daklar. They spent part—maybe all—of the last Two becoming One together."

"Really?" said Lurt. "Astonishing." She stepped aside, making room for a couple of younger women, holding hands, to pass by them. "Of course, the last Two becoming One occurred prior to reestablishing contact with your world. Did you and Ponter have sex when he was there the first time?"

Mary was flustered. "No."

"And have you had sex since? Two have not been One

since, but I understand Ponter spent considerable time in your world over the last couple of tendays."

Mary knew from Ponter that discussions about sexual matters weren't taboo in his world. Still, she felt her cheeks warming. "Yes."

"How was it?" asked Lurt.

Mary thought for a second, and then, having no idea how the translator might render the word, but not having a better one at hand, she said simply, "Hot."

"Do you love him?"

"I—I don't know. I think so."

"He has no woman-mate; I am sure you know that."

Mary nodded. "Yes."

"I do not know how long this portal between our two worlds will stay open," said Lurt. "It might be permanent; it might close tomorrow—even with so many of our greatest on the other side, the portal itself might be unstable. But even if it were permanent, do you propose somehow to make a life with Ponter?"

"I don't know. I don't know if that is even a possibility."

"Do you have children?"

"Me?" said Mary. "No."

"And you have no man-mate?"

Mary took a deep breath, and examined a stack of three travel cubes they were passing. "Wellllll," she said, "it's complex. I was married—bonded—to a man named Colm O'Casey. My religion"—a *bleep*—"my belief system does not allow an easy dissolution of such bonds. Colm and I haven't lived together for years, but technically we are still bonded."

" 'Lived together?' " repeated Lurt, astonished.

"In my world," said Mary, "a man lives with his woman-mate."

"What about his man-mate?"

"He doesn't have one. There are only two people in the relationship."

"Incredible," said Lurt. "I love Adikor dearly, but I certainly would not want to live with him."

"It's the way of my people," said Mary.

"But not of mine," said Lurt. "If you were to pursue this relationship with Ponter, where would the two of you live? His world, or yours? He has children here, you know, and a man-mate, and work he enjoys."

"I know," said Mary, her heart aching. "I know."

"Have you talked to Ponter about any of this?"

"I was going to, but . . . but then I found out about Daklar."

"It would be very difficult to make it work," said Lurt. "Surely you must understand that."

Mary exhaled noisily. "I do." She paused. "But Ponter isn't like the other men I know." A silly comparison occurred to Mary: Jane Porter and Tarzan of the Apes. Jane had fallen head over heels for Tarzan, who truly had been unlike any man she'd ever met. And Tarzan, feral, raised by simians after the death of his parents, Lord and Lady Greystoke, was unique, truly one of a kind. But Ponter had said there were a hundred and eighty-five million people in his world, and perhaps all those men were like Ponter, and so unlike the rough, rude, mean, petty men of Mary's world.

But after a moment, Lurt nodded. "Yes, Ponter is not like other men that I know, either. He is amazingly intelligent, and truly kind. And . . ."

"Yes?" said Mary, eagerly.

But it was a while before Lurt went on. "There was an event, in Ponter's past. He was . . . injured . . ."

Mary touched Lurt's massive forearm gently. "I know about

what happened with Ponter and Adikor; I know about Ponter's jaw."

Mary saw Lurt's continuous eyebrow roll up her browridge before Mary turned her attention back to the path in front of them. "Ponter told you this?" asked Lurt.

"About the injury, yes—I'd seen it in his X rays. Not who did it. I learned that from Daklar."

Lurt spoke a word that wasn't translated, then: "Well, you know that Ponter forgave Adikor, totally and completely. It is something few people could have done." She paused again. "And, I suppose, given his admirable history in such matters, it is little surprise that he has apparently forgiven Daklar, too."

"So," said Mary, "what should I do?"

"I have been given to understand that your people believe in some sort of existence after this one," said Lurt.

Mary started at the apparent *non sequitur.* "Um, yes."

"We do not, as I am sure Ponter must have told you. Perhaps if we believed there was more to life than just this existence, we might have a different philosophy, but let me tell you what tends to be our guiding principle."

"Please," said Mary.

"We live our lives so as to minimize deathbed regrets. You are a 145, no?"

"I'm thirty-nine . . . years old, that is."

"Yes. Well, then you are perhaps halfway through your life. Ask yourself if in . . . in another thirty-nine years, to phrase it as you would, when your life is ending, will you regret not having tried to make a relationship with Ponter work?"

"Yes, I believe so."

"Listen carefully to my question, friend Mare. I am not asking you if you would regret not pursuing this relationship if it were to succeed. I am asking you if you would regret not pursuing it *even if it fails.*"

Mary narrowed her eyes, although they were comfortable behind the blue lenses. "I'm not sure what you mean."

"My contribution is chemistry," said Lurt. "Now. But it was not my first choice. I wanted to write stories, to create fiction."

"Really?"

"Yes. But I failed at it. There was no audience for my tales, no positive response to my work. And so I had to make a different contribution; I had an aptitude for mathematics and science, and so I became a chemist. But I do not regret having tried and failed at writing fiction. Of course, I would have preferred to succeed, but on my deathbed I knew I would be more sad if I had never tried, had never tested to see if I might succeed at it, than I would be had I tried and failed. So I did try—and I did fail. But I am happy for the knowledge that I made the attempt." Lurt paused. "Obviously, you will be happiest if your relationship with Ponter works out. But will you be happier on your deathbed, friend Mare, to know that you tried and failed to have a long-term relationship with Ponter than that you never tried at all?"

Mary considered this. They walked on in silence for several minutes. Finally, Mary said, "I need to try," she said. "I would hate myself if I didn't at least try."

"Then," said Lurt, "your path is clear."

Chapter Thirty-five

It was still one more day until Two became One, but Ponter and Mary had rendezvoused at the Alibi Archive Pavilion. Ponter had led her into the south wing, and they were now standing in front of a wall full of little compartments, each containing a reconstituted granite cube about the size of a volleyball. Mary had learned to read Neanderthal numerals. The particular cube Ponter was holding his Companion up to was number 16,321. It was identified in no other way, but, like all the other cubes, it had a blue light glowing in the center of one side.

Mary shook her head in wonder. "Your whole life is recorded in there?" she asked.

"Yes," said Ponter.

"Everything?"

"Well, everything except my work down in the quantum-computing facility—the signals from my Companion couldn't penetrate the thousand armspans of rock overhead. Oh, and my entire first trip to your world is missing, too."

"But not the second trip?"

"No, that was uploaded starting as soon as the alibi archives reacquired Hak's signal—when we emerged from the mine. An entire record of that trip is stored here."

Mary wasn't quite sure how she felt about that. She certainly wasn't the stereotype of the good Catholic girl, but there was now one hell of a porno film in there . . .

"Amazing," said Mary. Lilly, Kevin, and Frank back at the Synergy Group would kill to be standing right here. She looked again at the reconstituted granite block. "Can you edit the stored memories?"

"Why would you want to do that?" asked Ponter. But then he looked away. "Sorry. Stupid question."

Mary shook her head. Despite what they'd come to research, Mary hadn't been contemplating the rape. "Actually," she said, "I was just thinking about my first marriage."

Suddenly she felt her cheeks go flush. She'd never before referred to it as her *first* marriage. "Anyway," she said, "let's get on with it."

Ponter nodded and led them to the front desk, where he spoke to an elderly woman. "I'd like to access my own archive, please."

"Ident?" said the woman. Ponter waved his forearm over a scanning plate on the desktop. The woman looked at a square monitor screen. "Ponter Boddit?" she said. "I thought you were dead."

"Funny," said Ponter. "Funny woman."

The female grinned. "Come with me." She led the way back to Ponter's alibi cube. Ponter held Hak up to the blue light. "I, Ponter Boddit, wish to access my own alibi archive for reasons of personal curiosity. Timestamp."

The light turned yellow.

The elderly woman then held up her Companion. "I, Mabla Dabdalb, Keeper of Alibis, hereby certify that Ponter Boddit's identity has been confirmed in my presence. Timestamp." The light turned red, and a tone sounded.

"All set," said Dabdalb. "You can use room seven."

"Thank you," said Ponter. "Healthy day."

"And to you," said the woman as she scurried back to her desk.

Ponter led the way to the viewing room, and Mary followed. For the first time, she really understood what Ponter must have felt like in her world. She could feel every eye in this vast place trained on her, gawking. She tried not to look flustered.

Ponter entered the room, which had a small yellow wall-mounted console and two of those saddle-shaped chairs the Neanderthals liked, presumably because of their wide hips. He moved over to the control panel and started pulling out the buds that operated the unit. Mary peered over his shoulder. "How come you don't use buttons?" asked Mary.

"Buttons?" repeated Ponter.

"You know, those mechanical switches that you press in."

"Oh. We do in some applications. But not many. If someone trips and falls, they can accidentally press buttons with their hand. Control buds must be pulled out; we consider them safer."

Mary had a brief thought of a *Star Trek* episode in which Spock, of all people, accidentally pushed some buttons while hauling himself to his feet, alerting the Romulans to the *Enterprise*'s presence. "Makes sense," she said.

Ponter continued to pull out buds. "All right," he said at last. "Here it is."

To Mary's astonishment, a large transparent sphere appeared in the middle of the room, floating freely. It split into smaller and smaller spheres, each tinted a slightly different color. The subdividing continued until Mary realized she was seeing a three-dimensional image of the interrogation room at the police station back in Toronto. There was Detective Hobbes, with his back to them, speaking to somebody. And there was Mary herself, looking chunkier than she liked, and Ponter. Ponter's hand snaked out, grabbing the file folder

Hobbes had left on the table and quickly leafing through it. The images of the pages within went by too fast for Mary to see, but Ponter returned to the beginning, then played everything back slowly. To Mary's astonishment, there was no motion blur at all; she could easily read the pages as they flipped by, although she had to cock her head at an odd angle to do so.

"Well?" said Ponter.

"Just a sec . . ." said Mary, looking for anything she didn't already know. "No, nothing there. Can you advance to the next page, please? There! Hold it. Okay, let's see . . ."

Suddenly Mary felt a churning in her gut. "Oh my God," she said. "Oh my God."

"What is it?" asked Ponter.

Mary staggered backward. She bumped up against a saddle-seat, and used it to support herself. "The other victim," said Mary . . .

"Yes? Yes?"

"It was Qaiser Remtulla."

"Who?"

"My boss. My friend. The head of the genetics department at York."

"I am sorry," said Ponter.

Mary closed her eyes. "So am I," she said. "If I'd only . . ."

"Mare," said Ponter, placing a hand on her arm, "the past is done. There is nothing you can do about it. But there may be something you can do about the future."

She looked up but said nothing.

"Read the rest of the report. There may be useful information."

Mary took a moment to compose herself, then returned to the hologram and read on, despite the stinging in her eyes, until—

"Yes!" she exclaimed. "Yes, yes!"

"What is it?"

"The Toronto Police," Mary said. "They have physical evidence from the attack on Qaiser. A complete rape kit." She paused. "Maybe they *will* catch the bastard after all."

But Ponter frowned. "Enforcer Hobbes seemed doubtful."

"I know, but . . ." Mary sighed. "No, you're probably right." She was quiet for a time. "I don't know how I'll ever manage to face Qaiser again."

Mary hadn't intended to bring up the issue of going home—really she hadn't. But if she were to see Qaiser again, she'd have to go back, and so now there it was, out in the air, floating between them.

"She will forgive you," said Ponter. "Forgiveness is a Christian virtue."

"Qaiser's not Christian; she's Muslim." Mary frowned, embarrassed by her own ignorance. Did Muslims hold forgiveness in high regard, too? But, no, no. That didn't matter. If the situation were reversed, could Mary really have forgiven Qaiser?

"What are we going to do?" said Mary.

"About the rapist? Whatever we can, whenever we can."

"No, no. Not about the rapist. About tomorrow. About Two becoming One."

"Ah," said Ponter. "Yes."

"Jasmel will be spending all her time with Tryon, won't she?"

Ponter grinned. "Oh, yes, indeed."

"And you just saw Megameg."

"I can never see her enough—but I take your point."

"And that leaves . . ."

Ponter sighed. "That leaves Daklar."

"What are you going to do?"

Ponter considered. "I have already violated tradition by coming into the Center a day early. I suppose it will not compound matters significantly if I go see Daklar now."

Mary's heart jumped. "Alone?"

"Yes," said Ponter. "Alone."

Ponter stood outside the door to Daklar's office, trying to summon his courage. He felt like he was back in the Gliksin world; every female he'd passed on the way here had stared at him as though he didn't belong.

And, indeed, he did not—not here, not until tomorrow. But this couldn't wait. Still, despite having turned it over in his mind repeatedly on the long walk in from the Alibi Archive Pavilion, he had no idea how to begin. Perhaps—

Suddenly, the door to Daklar's office folded aside. "Ponter!" she exclaimed. "I thought I smelled you!"

She opened her arms, preparing to receive him, and he stepped into the hug. But she must have felt the stiffness in his back. "What is it?" she said. "What's wrong?"

"May I come in?" asked Ponter.

"Yes, of course." She retreated into her office—semicircular, half the hollowed-out core of a massive tree—and Ponter followed, closing the door behind him.

"I will not be here, on this world, for Two becoming One."

Daklar's eyes went wide. "Have you been called back to the other Earth? Is something wrong there?"

Ponter knew the things wrong there were beyond enumerating, but he shook his head. "No."

"Then, Ponter, your daughters will want to see you."

"Jasmel won't want to see anyone but Tryon."

"And Mega?"

Ponter nodded. "She will be saddened, yes."

"And—me?"

Ponter closed his eyes for a moment.

"I am sorry, Daklar. I am very sorry."

"It's *her,* isn't it?" said Daklar. "That Gliksin woman."

"Her name is"—and Ponter fervently wished he could defend her properly, wished he could pronounce her name correctly "—is Mare."

But Daklar seized upon the issue. "Listen to yourself! You can't even say her real name! Ponter, it can *never* work between the two of you. You're from different worlds—she's not even one of us!"

Ponter lifted his shoulders. "I know, but . . ."

Daklar let out a massive sigh. "But you're going to try. Gristle, Ponter, you men never cease to amaze me. You'll stick it in *anything.*"

Ponter flashed back 229 months, back to when he'd been at the Science Academy with Adikor, back when they'd had that stupid fight, back when he'd provoked Adikor so much that he'd launched his fist toward Ponter's face. He'd long ago forgiven Adikor, but now, finally he *understood,* understood being so enraged that violence seemed the only alternative.

He turned around and stormed out of the building, looking for something to destroy.

Chapter Thirty-six

Mary and Ponter returned to the quantum-computing facility. Waiting for them there was a distinguished-looking 143 male, whom Ponter immediately recognized. "Goosa Kusk," he said, his voice full of wonder. "It is an honor to meet you."

"Thank you," said Goosa. "I heard about that nasty business in the other world—you getting shot with some sort of projectile weapon, and all that."

Ponter nodded.

"Well, Lonwis Trob contacted me and suggested an idea for preventing such a thing from happening again. His suggestion was interesting, but I have decided to go another way with it." He picked up a long, flat metal object from a table. "This is a force-field generator," he said. "It detects any incoming projectile as soon as it enters your Companion's sensor field, and, within nanoseconds, throws up an electrostrong force barrier. The barrier is only about three handspans wide, and only lasts for about a quarter of a beat—anything longer would take too much power. But it is completely inelastic, and completely impenetrable. Whatever strikes it will bounce right off. If someone shoots you with one of those metal projectiles, the barrier will deflect it. It will also deflect spears, knife thrusts, fast punches, and so on. Anything moving slower than a preset rate does not trigger the barrier, so it will not interfere with people touching you or you touching them. But it will mean that if another

Gliksin wants to try to kill you, it is going to have to come up with a better method."

"Wow," said Mary. "That's amazing."

Goosa shrugged. "It is science." He turned back to Ponter. "Here, it straps onto your forearm on the opposite side of the Companion, see?" Ponter held out his left arm, and Goosa attached the device. "And this fiber-optic lead connects to your Companion's expansion jack—like so."

Mary looked at it in wonder. "It's like a personal air bag," she said. Then, noting Goosa's expression, "I don't mean that it works the same way—air bags are safety restraints that inflate almost instantly in high-speed automobile collisions. But it's sort of the same principle—a fast-deploying safety shield." She shook her head. "You could make a fortune selling these on my Earth."

But Goosa shook his head. "For my people, these devices treat the underlying problem: your people shooting us with guns. For your people, they would merely be a palliative. The real solution is not to protect against guns, but to get rid of them."

Mary smiled. "I'd love to see you debate Charlton Heston."

"This is wonderful," said Ponter. "You are sure it works?" He saw Goosa's expression. "No, of course it does. Sorry I asked."

"I have already shipped eleven of these through to our contingent still on the other side," Goosa said. He paused. "One often wishes another a safe journey. That is ensured now. So, instead, I will merely wish you a pleasant trip."

Mary and Ponter headed down the tunnel, crossing the threshold between universes. On the other side, Lieutenant Donaldson, the same Canadian Forces officer Ponter had met previously, greeted them. "Welcome back, Envoy Boddit. Welcome home, Professor Vaughan."

"Thank you," said Ponter.

"We weren't quite sure when, or if, you'd be coming back across," Donaldson said. "You'll have to give us a little time to arrange for bodyguards. What's your destination? Toronto? Rochester? The UN?"

Ponter looked at Mary. "We have not decided," he said.

"Well, we'll have to work out an itinerary—make sure you have proper protection at all times. There's a liaison from CSIS at Sudbury police headquarters now, and—"

"No," said Ponter simply.

"I—I beg your pardon?" said Donaldson.

Ponter reached into one of the spare pouches on his medical belt and removed his Canadian passport. "Does this not allow me free access to this country?" he said.

"Well, yes, but—"

"Am I not a Canadian citizen?"

"Yes, you are, sir. I saw the ceremony on TV."

"And are not citizens free to come and go as they please, without armed escort?"

"Well, normally, but this—"

"This is *normal,*" said Ponter. "This is normal from now on: people from my world passing into your world, and people from your world passing into mine."

"All this is for your protection, Envoy Boddit."

"I understand that. But I require no protection. I am carrying a shield device that will prevent me from being injured again. So: I am at no risk, and I am not a criminal. I am a free citizen, and I wish to move about unfettered and unaccompanied."

"I—um, I'll have to contact my superior," said Donaldson.

"Let us not waste time on intermediaries," said Ponter. "I dined recently with your prime minister, and he said if I ever needed anything, I should call him. Let us get him on the phone."

Mary and Ponter rode up the mining elevator and got in Mary's car, which had been parked at the SNO surface building since she'd gone over to the other side. It was early enough in the day that they were able to drive back to Toronto, and, although at first Mary thought they were nonetheless being followed, soon enough they were the only car on the road. "Astonishing," said Mary. "I never thought they'd let you go on your own."

Ponter smiled. "What sort of romantic trip would this be if we were accompanied everywhere we went?"

The rest of the drive back to Toronto was uneventful. They went to Mary's condo on Observatory Lane in Richmond Hill, showered together, changed—Ponter had brought along his trapezoidal case, full of his clothes—then drove off to the 31 Division police station. Mary needed to deal with that bit of unfinished business first, saying she wouldn't be able to relax until she'd done so. She brought her scrapbook with her.

To get to the police station, they actually drove through the York campus, and then into what even Ponter could tell was a rough neighborhood. "I noticed this on our first trip here," said Ponter. "Things seem in disrepair in this area."

"Driftwood," said Mary, as if that explained everything. "It's a very poor part of the city."

They continued on, passing a number of dilapidated apartment buildings and a small strip mall with iron bars across all the shop windows, and at last parked in the tiny lot next to the police station.

"Hello, Professor Vaughan," said Detective Hobbes, after he'd been summoned to the front desk. "Hello, Envoy Boddit. I didn't expect to see you two again."

"Can we talk in private?" said Mary.

Hobbes nodded and led them back to the same interrogation room they'd been in before.

"You know who I am?" Mary asked. "Outside of this case, I mean?"

Hobbes nodded. "You're Mary Vaughan. You've been in the press a lot lately."

"Do you know why?"

Hobbes jerked a thumb at Ponter. "Because you've been accompanying him."

Mary waved a hand dismissively. "Yes, yes, yes. But do you know *why* I was called in to see Ponter in the first place?"

Hobbes shook his head.

Mary lifted her scrapbook and placed it on the table in front of Hobbes. "Have a look at this."

Hobbes opened the pressed-cardboard cover. The first page had a clipping from the *Toronto Star* taped to it: "Canadian Scientist Receives Japanese Award." He turned the page. There was a piece from *Maclean's:* "Breaking the Ice: Ancient DNA Recovered in Yukon." And the facing page had a little item from the *New York Times:* "Scientist Extracts DNA from Neanderthal Fossil."

He turned the page again. A press release from York was tipped in: "York Professor Makes Prehistory: Vaughan Recovers DNA from Ancient Man." Facing that was a sheet torn out of *Discover:* "Degraded DNA Yields Secrets."

Hobbes looked up. "Yes?" he said, perplexed.

"I am . . . Well, some would say that I'm . . ."

Ponter interjected. "Professor Vaughan is a geneticist, and this world's leading expert on recovering degraded DNA."

"And?"

"And," said Mary, speaking more forcefully now that the topic wasn't her, "we know you have a full rape kit from the attack on Qaiser Remtulla."

Hobbes looked up sharply. "I can't confirm or deny that," he said.

"Of course it's true," said Mary, feeling guilty even as she said it. "Is there any way we could know that unless Qaiser had told me herself? She's my friend, and my colleague, for God's sake."

"Be that as it may," said Hobbes.

"I'd like to examine the rape kit," Mary said.

Hobbes looked stunned by the suggestion. "We have our own experts."

"Yes, yes. But, well—"

"None of them can possibly be as qualified as Professor Vaughan," said Ponter.

"Perhaps so, but—"

"Have you done any work on the rape kit?" asked Mary.

Hobbes took a deep breath, biding time. Finally, he said, "If there is a rape kit, we wouldn't do much of anything with it until we had a subject to match the DNA against."

"DNA degrades quickly over time," said Mary, "especially if it's not stored in absolutely ideal conditions. If you wait, it may be impossible to get a DNA fingerprint."

Hobbes's tone was level. "We know how to refrigerate specimens, and we've had considerable success in the past."

"I'm aware of that, but—"

"Ma'am," said Hobbes, gently. "I understand this case is important to you. *Every* case is important to its victims."

Mary tried to keep from sounding annoyed. "But if you'd just let me take the rape kit to my lab at York, I'm sure I can recover much more DNA from it than you'll be able to."

"I can't do that, ma'am. I'm sorry."

"Why not?"

"Well, for one thing, York isn't cleared for doing forensic work, and—"

"Laurentian," said Mary, at once. "Send the kit up to Laurentian University, and I'll do the work there." The labs at Laurentian, the university where she'd first studied Ponter's DNA, did contract forensics work for the RCMP and the Ontario Provincial Police.

Hobbes raised his eyebrows. "Well, now," he said, "Laurentian's a different story, but . . ."

"Whatever paperwork it takes," said Mary.

"Perhaps," said Hobbes, but he sounded very dubious. "It would be highly irregular, though . . ."

"Please," said Mary. She couldn't stand the thought of something happening to the only remaining physical proof. "Please."

Hobbes spread his arms. "Let me see what I can do, but, honestly, I wouldn't hold out much hope. We've got very strict rules about the chain of custody for evidence."

"But you'll try?"

"Yes, all right, I'll try."

"Thank you," said Mary. "Thank you."

Ponter spoke up, surprising Mary. "Can she at least *see* the rape kit here?"

Hobbes looked as astonished as Mary felt. "Why?" asked the detective.

"She should be able to tell at a glance if it is in adequate condition for her technique to work." He looked at Mary. "Is that not right, Mare?"

Mary wasn't sure what Ponter was up to, but she trusted him completely. "Umm, yes. Yes, that's right." She turned to the detective and flashed her most charming smile. "It'd just take a second. Might as well find out up front if there's any point to this. Don't want to put you through all that red tape if the specimens have already degraded."

Hobbes frowned and looked into the middle distance for a time, thinking. "All right," he said at last. "Let me get it."

He left the room, and returned a few minutes later holding a cardboard container about the size of a shoe box. He removed its lid, and showed the box's contents to Mary. Ponter stood up and looked over her shoulder. Inside were some glass specimen slides and three Ziploc bags, each labeled with various information. One appeared to contain a pair of panties. Another, a small pubic comb with a few hairs caught in it. The third had a few vials, presumably containing vaginal swabbings.

"It's been in the fridge the whole time," said Hobbes, defensively. "We do know what we're—"

Suddenly Ponter's right arm shot out. He grabbed the bag with the panties, ripped it open, and brought it to his nose, inhaling deeply.

Mary was mortified. "Ponter, stop!"

Hobbes exploded. "Give that back!" He tried to grab the bag from Ponter, but Ponter easily fended him off, and took another massive inhalation.

"Jesus, what are you?" shouted Hobbes. "Some kind of pervert?"

Ponter pulled the bag away from his nose and, without a word, offered it to Hobbes, who snatched it from his hand. "Get the hell out of here," Hobbes snapped. Two more cops had appeared at the entrance to the interrogation room, presumably coming in response to the shouts.

"My apologies," said Ponter.

"Just get the hell out!" said Hobbes, and then, to Mary: "We'll look after our own evidence, lady. Now beat it!"

Chapter Thirty-seven

Mary stormed out of the police station, seething. But she didn't say a word until she and Ponter were back in her car, sitting in the parking lot.

Mary turned to him. "What the hell was that?" she demanded.

"I am sorry," said Ponter.

"I'll never get to analyze those specimens now," said Mary. "Christ, I'm sure the only reason he didn't charge you was because he'd have to report his own stupidity in letting you get near the evidence."

"Again, I apologize," said Ponter.

"What in God's name were you thinking?"

Ponter was silent.

"Well? Well?"

"I know," he said simply, "who committed Qaiser's rape, and presumably yours as well."

Mary, absolutely stunned, sagged back against the driver's seat. "Who?"

"Your co-worker—I cannot say his full name properly. It is something like 'Cor-nuh-luh-us.'"

"Cornelius? Cornelius Ruskin? No, that's crazy."

"Why? Does anything in his physical appearance contradict your recollections of that night?"

Mary was still huffing and puffing from shouting. But all

the anger was gone from her voice, replaced with astonishment. "Well, no. I mean, sure, Cornelius has blue eyes—but lots of people do. And Cornelius doesn't smoke."

"Yes, he does," said Ponter.

"I've never seen him."

"The odor was on him when we met."

"He might have been in one of the campus pubs and picked it up there."

"No. It was on his breath, although he'd apparently tried to mask it with some chemical."

Mary frowned. She knew a few secret smokers. "I didn't smell anything."

Ponter said nothing.

"Besides," said Mary, "Cornelius wouldn't hurt me or Qaiser. I mean, we were co-workers, and—"

Mary fell silent. Ponter finally prodded her. "Yes?"

"Well, *I* thought of us as co-workers. But he—he was just a sessional instructor. He had a Ph.D.—from Oxford, for God's sake. But all he could get was sessional teaching assignments—not a full-time appointment, and certainly not tenure. But Qaiser and I . . ."

"Yes?" Ponter said again.

"Well, I'm a woman, but Qaiser really won the lottery when it came to tenure-track appointments in the sciences. She's a woman *and* a visible minority. They say rape isn't a sexual crime; it's a crime of violence, of power. And Cornelius clearly felt he had none."

"He also had access to the specimens refrigerator," said Ponter, "and, as a geneticist himself, he surely suspected what a female geneticist might do under such circumstances. He would know to look for, and destroy, any evidence."

"My God," thought Mary. "But—no. No. It's all circumstantial."

"It *was* all circumstantial," said Ponter, "until I got to examine the physical evidence of Qaiser's rape—safely stored at the police station, where Ruskin could not get at it. I smelled him when we first met in the corridor outside your lab, and his smell, his scent, is on those specimens."

"Are you sure?" asked Mary. "Are you absolutely sure?"

"I never forget a smell," said Ponter.

"My God," said Mary. "What should we do?"

"We could tell Enforcer Hobbes."

"Yes, but—"

"What?"

"Well, this isn't your world," said Mary. "You can't just demand that someone produce an alibi. There's nothing in what you've said that would enable the police to require a DNA specimen from Ruskin." He was no longer "Cornelius."

"But I could testify about his scent . . ."

Mary shook her head. "There's no precedent for accepting such claims, even as a lead. And even if Hobbes bought your assertion, he couldn't even call Ruskin in for questioning based on it."

"This world . . ." said Ponter, shaking his head in disgust.

"You are absolutely certain?" said Mary. "There isn't a shadow of a doubt in your mind?"

"A shadow of—? Ah, I understand. Yes, I am absolutely certain."

"Not just beyond a reasonable doubt?" asked Mary. "But beyond all doubt?"

"I have no doubt whatsoever."

"None?"

"I know your noses are small, but my capability is not remarkable. All members of my species, and many other species, can do it."

Mary thought about this. Dogs certainly could distinguish

people by scent. There really was no reason to think Ponter was mistaken. "What can we do?" she asked.

Ponter was quiet for a long time. Finally, softly, he said, "You told me the reason you did not report the rape was because you feared your treatment at the hands of your judicial system."

"So?" snapped Mary.

"I do not mean to aggravate," said Ponter. "I just wanted to make sure I understood you correctly. What would happen to you or to your friend Qaiser if there were a public investigation?"

"Well, even if the DNA evidence were admissible—and it might not be—Ruskin's attorney would try to prove that Qaiser and I had consented."

"You should not have to go through that," said Ponter. "No one should."

"But if we don't do something, Ruskin will strike again."

"No," said Ponter. "He will not."

"Ponter, there's nothing you can do."

"Please drive me to the university."

"Ponter, no. No, I won't."

"If you will not, I will walk there."

"You don't even know where it is."

"Hak does."

"Ponter, this is crazy. You can't just kill him!"

Ponter touched his shoulder, over the bullet wound. "People in this world kill other people all the time."

"No, Ponter. I won't let you."

"I must prevent him from raping again," said Ponter.

"But—"

"And although you may be able to stop me today, or tomorrow, you will not be able to intercede forever. At some point, I will be able to elude you, return to the campus, and eliminate this problem." He fixed his golden eyes on her. "The only question is whether that will happen before he rapes again. Do you really wish to delay me?"

Mary closed her eyes for a moment and listened as hard as she ever had in her life for God's voice, listened to see whether He was going to intervene. But there was nothing.

"I can't let you do this, Ponter. I can't let you kill somebody in cold blood. Not even him."

"He must be stopped."

"Promise me," said Mary. "Promise me you won't."

"Why do you care so much? He does not deserve to live."

Mary took a deep breath and let it out slowly. "Ponter, I know you think I'm being silly when I talk about an afterlife. But if you kill him, your soul will be punished. And if I let you kill him, my soul will be punished, too. Ruskin already gave me a taste of hell. I don't want to spend eternity there."

Ponter frowned. "I want to do this *for* you."

"Not this. Not killing."

"All right," said Ponter at last. "All right. I will not kill him."

"Do you promise? Do you swear?"

"I promise," said Ponter. And then, after a moment, "Gristle."

Mary nodded; that was the only kind of swearing Ponter knew how to do. But then she shook her head. "There's a possibility you're not considering," she said at last.

"And that is?" said Ponter.

"That Qaiser and Cornelius had *consensual* sex *before* she was raped by someone else. It would hardly be the first time a man and a woman who worked together had been getting it on in the office."

"I would not know," said Ponter.

"Trust me. It happens all the time. And wouldn't that leave his smell on—well, on her panties, and so forth?"

Bleep.

"Panties," said Mary. "The, um, inner garments. What you saw in the specimen bag."

"Yes. What you suggest is possible."

"We have to be certain," said Mary. "We have to be absolutely sure."

"You could ask Qaiser," Ponter said.

"She won't tell me."

"Why not? I thought you were friends."

"We are. But Qaiser is married—bonded—to another man. And, trust me: *that* happens all the time, too."

"Ah," said Ponter. "Well . . ."

"I'm not sure that there's anything we can do," said Mary.

"There is much we can do, but you have made me promise not to."

"That's right. But . . ."

"We should let him know that he has been found out," said Ponter. "That his movements are under surveillance."

"I couldn't face him."

"No, of course not. But we could leave a note for him."

"I'm not sure what good that would do," said Mary.

Ponter held up his left hand. "It is the whole philosophy behind the Companion implants. If you know you are being observed, or that your actions are being recorded, then you modify your behavior. It has worked well in my world."

Mary took a deep breath, then let it out slowly. "I suppose . . . I suppose it couldn't hurt. What are you thinking of? Just an anonymous note?"

"Yes," said Ponter.

"You mean, let him know that he's being watched constantly from now on? That there's no way he can get away with it again?" Mary considered this. "I suppose he'd have to be an idiot to rape again after he knows someone is on to him."

"Indeed," said Ponter.

"I guess a note could be slipped into his box at York."

"No," said Ponter. "It should not be left at York. He took steps to destroy evidence there already, after all. I presume he thought you would not return for an entire year, and so he could safely dispose of the specimens you had retained without anyone being able to work out exactly when they had disappeared. No, this note should be left at his dwelling."

"His dwelling? You mean his home?"

"Yes," said Ponter.

"I get it," said Mary. "Nothing's more threatening than someone knowing where you live."

Ponter made a perplexed face, but said, "Do you know where his home is."

"Not far from here," said Mary. "He doesn't have a car—he lives by himself, and can't really afford one. I've given him lifts home a few times during snowstorms. It's an apartment just off Jane Street—but no, wait. I know what *building* he lives in, but I have no idea what his apartment number is."

"His is a multifamily dwelling, like yours?"

"Yes. Well, not nearly as nice as mine."

"Will there not be a directory near the entrance identifying which unit houses which person?"

"We don't do that anymore. We have code numbers and buzzboards—the whole idea is to prevent people from doing what we're talking about: finding out exactly where someone lives."

Ponter shook his head, astonished. "The lengths you Gliksins go to to avoid having to have Companion implants . . ."

"Come on," said Mary. "Let's drive by his building on the way back to my place. I'll know it to see it, and at least we can get the street number."

"Fine," said Ponter.

Mary found herself tensing up as they drove along Finch,

and turned onto the street that contained Ruskin's apartment building. It wasn't that she was afraid of running into him, she realized—although that would certainly freak her out. It was simply thinking about a possible, eventual rape trial. *Do you know where the man you're accusing lives, Ms. Vaughan? Have you ever been to his home? Really? And yet you say this was nonconsensual?*

Driftwood, the area around Jane Street and Finch Avenue West, was not somewhere a sane person wanted to be for long. It was one of Toronto's—hell, of North America's—most crime-ridden neighborhoods. Its proximity to York was an embarrassment to the university, and probably, despite years of lobbying, the reason that the Spadina subway line had never been extended to the campus.

But Driftwood had one advantage: rents were cheap. And for someone trying to make ends meet on a sessional instructor's piecework fees, someone who couldn't afford a car, it was the only place within walking distance of the university that was affordable.

Ruskin's apartment building was a white brick tower with rusting balconies filled with junk, and a third of the windows covered by taped-up newspaper or aluminum foil. The building looked to be about fifteen or sixteen stories tall, and—

"Wait!" said Mary.

"What?"

"He lives on the top floor! I remember now: he used to call it his 'penthouse in the slums.' " She paused. "Of course, we still don't know what unit number, but he's lived here for at least two years. I'm sure his letter carrier knows him—we academics tend to get a lot of journals and things like that in the mail."

"Yes?" said Ponter, clearly not understanding.

"Well, if we mail a letter to 'Cornelius Ruskin, Ph.D.' at this address, and simply say 'Top Floor' as part of the address, I'm sure it'll get to him."

"Ah," said Ponter. "Good. Then our business here is finished."

Chapter Thirty-eight

Personality sculptor Selgan regarded Ponter for a time. "You have a flair for the ironic, I see."

"What do you mean?"

" 'Our business here is finished.' You told me you committed a crime on the Gliksin world—it is easy enough to guess what it is."

"Is it? I rather doubt you've figured it out."

Selgan shrugged slightly. "Possibly not. But I have figured out one thing that perhaps has *eluded you."*

Ponter sounded irritated. "And what is that?"

"Mare suspected you were going to do something to Ruskin."

"No, no, she is completely innocent."

"Is she? A woman of her intelligence—and yet she accepted your flimsy excuse for her to show you where Ruskin dwelled?"

"We had every intention of sending a warning letter! Just as we had discussed. Mare is pure, without sin—that is what her name means! She is named for the mother of her God incarnate, a woman who was conceived immaculately, devoid of original sin. I learned this during my first trip to her world. She would never—"

Selgan held up a hand. "Calm down, Ponter. I didn't mean to give offense. Please, continue with your narrative . . ."

"Ponter?" said Hak, through Ponter's cochlear implants.

Ponter moved his head in a tiny nod of acknowledgment.

"Judging by her breathing patterns, Mare is sleeping deeply. You won't disturb her if you go now."

Ponter gently got out of Mary's bed. The glowing red digits on the night-table clock said 1:14. He walked out of the room, down the small corridor to Mary's living room. As always, he put on his medical belt, and he checked in one of the pouches to make sure that he had the spare card key Mary had given him; he knew he'd need that to get back into her apartment building.

Ponter then opened Mary's front door, entered the corridor, headed to the elevator, and rode down to the ground floor—he'd learned that sometimes humans wrote the number one as "1" and sometimes as "L"; it was the latter style that was used on the elevator's control panel.

Ponter walked through the large lobby, then headed out the set of double doors, exiting into the night.

But how unlike the night of his world it was! There was illumination everywhere: from windows, from electric lights hoisted high on vertical poles, from vehicles going by on the road. It would probably have been easier if it were really dark. Although from a distance he knew he didn't look *that* different from a Gliksin—at least, from a Gliksin weightlifter—he would have much preferred to make this journey in total darkness.

"All right, Hak," Ponter said softly. "Which way?"

"To your left," Hak replied, still using the cochlear implants. "Mare usually takes a road designed exclusively for motor vehicles, rather than pedestrians, when coming home from York."

"The Four-oh-Seven," said Ponter. "That's what she calls it."

"In any event, we will have to find another, safer route that parallels it."

Ponter started jogging along. It was about five thousand armspans from here to his destination—it shouldn't take more than a daytenth to get there, if he maintained a decent speed.

The night was cool—wonderfully so. And, indeed, although he'd seen many deciduous leaves that had already changed color back in his world, here they all seemed green—yes, green; even in the middle of the night, there was more than enough illumination to discern colors easily.

Ponter had never thought of killing anyone before in his life, but . . .

But no one had ever so grievously injured someone he cared so much about before, and . . .

And, even if someone had, in a *civilized* world that person would have been easily captured and dealt with by the government.

But here! Here, on this mad, mirror Earth . . .

He *had* to do more than just send an anonymous paper letter. He had to make sure that Ruskin knew not just that he'd been discovered, but *who* it was that had discovered him. He had to be made to understand that there would be no possibility of him ever getting away with such a crime again. Only then, Ponter felt sure, could Mare begin to find the peace that had been eluding her. And only then would he know whether there was any truth to Hak's earlier suggestion that Mare's current behavior toward him was atypical for her kind.

Ponter was heading down a street lined with two-story residences, many with trees on their anterior lots of grass. As he continued running along, he saw another person—a Gliksin male, with white skin and hardly any head hair—walking toward him. Ponter jogged across the street, so that he wouldn't pass close to this person, and he continued on, heading west.

"Turn left here," said Hak. "There doesn't seem to be a way out at the end of this block of residences."

Ponter did so and continued his easy run along the perpendicular street. He went only one block, then Hak had him turn right again, resuming his westward course toward York.

A small cat crossed the street in front of Ponter, its tail sticking up in the air. Ponter was amazed that these humans had chosen to domesticate cats, which were useless for hunting and wouldn't even fetch a stick. *But,* he thought, *to each his own* . . . He continued to jog along, his flat feet slapping against the stony road surface.

A short distance later, Ponter saw a large, black dog, padding toward him. Now, dogs as pets he understood! He'd noted that the Gliksins had many different kinds of dogs—apparently created through selective breeding. Some did seem ill suited for hunting, but he assumed their appearance was pleasing to their owners.

Then again, Ponter had heard paleoanthropologists talking at the meeting in Washington about his own appearance. Apparently his features were what were called "classic Neanderthaloid"—and an extreme form, at that. These scholars were surprised that Ponter's people hadn't seen a reduction in browridge prominence and nose size, and even the beginning of that preposterous projection from the front of the mandible.

But since the moment true consciousness had flowered in his people and the universe had therefore split, some half-million months ago, it had been deliberate selection of mates that had led to the retention, and, indeed, the amplification, of the features his people found so beautiful.

"Getting tired yet?" asked Hak.

"No."

"Good. You're about halfway there."

Suddenly Ponter was startled by a loud bark. Another dog—large, brown—was coming toward him, and it did not look happy. Ponter knew he couldn't outrun the quadruped, so he stopped and turned. "There, there," he said, in his own language, hoping the dog would understand the soothing tone if not the words. "There's a good doggy."

The brown beast continued toward Ponter, still barking. A light had gone on in a window on a nearby dwelling's second floor.

"That's a nice doggy," said Ponter, but he could feel himself tensing—which he knew was a dumb thing to be doing. Just like a Barast, a dog could smell fear on another . . .

Why the dog was barreling toward him, Ponter couldn't say. He presumed it didn't attack everyone who came down this street, but just as he could tell a Gliksin from a Barast by scent, so presumably could this beast—and although it had surely never encountered one of Ponter's people before, it knew when something foreign had come onto its turf.

Ponter was getting ready to try to seize the dog by the neck when the animal crouched and leapt toward him, and—

A flash of light in the semidarkness—

A sound like wet leather hitting ice—

And the dog yelping in pain.

It had leapt at Ponter with enough force to trigger the shield Goosa Kusk had given him. The dog, startled, dazed, and—as Ponter could smell—bleeding from its muzzle, turned tail and ran away as fast as it had approached. Ponter took a deep, calming breath, then resumed his jog.

"All right," said Hak, after a time. "Here's where we have to cross over that roadway, the Four-oh-Seven. Head left, and make your way over that bridge, there. Be careful you aren't hit by a car."

Ponter did as Hak had asked, and soon he was on the other side of the highway, jogging south. Way, way off in the distance, he could see the blinking lights atop the CN Tower, down at Toronto's lakeshore. Mare had told him how magnificent the view from it was, but so far, he'd yet to see the structure except from a great distance.

Ponter crossed another wide road, which had cars zipping along, even at this time of night, every few beats. Within a short time, he found himself on the York University campus, and Hak directed him through it, past buildings and parking lots and through open spaces, to the far side.

And, after several hundred armspans of additional jogging, Ponter found himself standing on a small dirty street, near the building that Ruskin lived in. Ponter bent over and placed his hands on his knees, panting to catch his breath. *I guess I* am *getting old* . . . he thought. A nice wind was blowing directly into his face, cooling him off.

Mare might have awoken by now, and noticed his absence, but she had been, in his brief experience of sharing a bed with her, a very sound sleeper, and it was still most of two daytenths until the sun would come up. He'd be home before then, although not *long* before, and—

"Reach," hissed a voice from behind Ponter's back, and he felt something hard stick into his kidney. And suddenly Ponter realized the flaw in Goosa Kusk's shield design. Oh, sure, it could deflect a bullet fired from some distance away, but it wouldn't do anything about one discharged into a person from a gun in direct contact with that person.

Still, this *was* Canada—and Mare had said there were few handguns here. But the thought that what was sticking into his kidney was only a knife didn't really comfort Ponter.

Ponter didn't know what to do. At the moment, in the dim light, from behind, whoever was accosting him presumably didn't know that Ponter was a Neanderthal. But if he spoke, even softly, in his own tongue so that Hak could translate, that fact would certainly be given away, and—

"What do you want?" said Hak, in English, taking the initiative.

"Your wallet," said the voice—male, and sounding, Ponter was disheartened to hear, not the least bit nervous.

"I do not have a wallet," said Hak.

"Too bad for you," said the Gliksin. "Either I get money—or I get blood."

Ponter had no doubt he could beat just about any unarmed Gliksin in hand-to-hand combat, but this one clearly had a weapon. Indeed, at that moment, Hak must have realized that Ponter couldn't see what the weapon was. "He is holding a steel knife," he said into Ponter's cochlear implants, "with a serrated blade about 1.2 handspans long, and a handle whose thermal signature suggests that it is polished hardwood."

Ponter thought about turning rapidly around, hoping that the sight of his Barast face would be enough to startle the Gliksin, but the last thing he wanted was a witness to his having come to Ruskin's home.

"He keeps shifting from his left foot to his right," said Hak through the cochlear implants. "Do you hear it?"

Ponter nodded ever so slightly.

"He's leaning on the left . . . now on the right . . . the left. Have you got the rhythm?"

Another slight nod.

"What's it going to be?" hissed the Gliksin.

"All right," said Hak, to Ponter. "When I say 'now,' bring your right elbow back and up with all your strength. You should hit the man's solar plexus, and, at the very least he will stagger backward, meaning that your shield should protect you from any incoming knife thrust." Hak switched to his external speaker. "I really do not have any money"—and, as he said that, Ponter realized Hak had made a mistake, for the "ee" sounds in "really" and "money" were provided by recordings of a Gliksin voice that didn't match Hak's own.

"What the—?" said the Gliksin, clearly puzzled by the sound. "Turn around, you piece of—"

"Now!" said Hak into Ponter's inner ears.

Ponter jerked his elbow back with all his might, and he could feel it connecting with the Gliksin's stomach. The Gliksin made an *ooof!* sound as air was forced from his lungs, and Ponter wheeled around to face him.

"Jesus!" said the Gliksin, catching sight of Ponter's browridged, hairy face. The Gliksin lunged forward, fast enough that Ponter's shield came up with a flash of light, blocking the knife blade. Ponter shot his own right arm out, and seized the Gliksin by his scrawny neck. The person looked to be about half Ponter's age. For a brief moment, Ponter thought about closing his fist, crushing the young man's larynx, but no, he couldn't do that.

"Drop the knife," said Ponter. The Gliksin looked down. Ponter did the same, and saw that the knife's blade was bent from its impact with the shield. Ponter tightened his fingers a bit. The Gliksin's grip opened as Ponter's own closed, and the knife fell to the roadway with a clattering sound.

"Now get out of here," said Ponter, and Hak translated. "Get out of here, and speak to no one of this."

Ponter let go of the Gliksin, who immediately started gasping for breath. Ponter raised his arm. *"Go!"* he said. The Gliksin nodded and scuttled off, one hand clutching his belly where Ponter's elbow had hit it.

Ponter wasted no time. He headed up the cracked-concrete walk leading to the apartment building's entrance.

Chapter Thirty-nine

Ponter waited silently in the building's entryway, one glass door behind him, another in front. It had taken several hundred beats, but finally someone was approaching, crossing over from the elevators that Ponter could see inside to the inner glass door. He turned his back, hiding his face, and waited. The approaching Gliksin left the lobby, and Ponter easily caught the glass door before it swung shut. He quickly crossed the tiled floor—about the only place he ever saw squares in Gliksin architecture was in floor tiles—and pushed the button to call an elevator. The one that had just delivered the Gliksin was still there, and Ponter went inside.

The floor buttons were arranged in two columns, and the top two had the symbol pairs "15" and "16." Ponter selected the one on the right.

The elevator—the smallest, dirtiest one he'd ever been in on this world, even dirtier than the mining elevator in Sudbury—rumbled into motion. Ponter watched the indicator above the dented steel door, waiting for it to match the symbol pair he had selected, which, at last, it did. He got out of the elevator and entered the hallway, whose simple beige carpeting was worn through in some places and stained in most others. The walls were lined with thin sheets of paper decorated with green-and-blue swirls; some of the sheets had partially peeled away from the wall.

Ponter could see four doorways on each side of the hall to his left, and four more on each side to his right: a total of sixteen apartments. He moved to the closest doorway, brought his nose to the seam opposite the hinges, sniffing up and down rapidly, trying to isolate the smells that were emanating from within from the general mildewy stink of the hallway's carpeting.

Not this one. He moved to the next door, and sniffed up and down the seam again. Here he did recognize a smell—the same acrid burning he'd experienced wafting up from Reuben Montego's basement sometimes when Reuben and Lou Benoît had been down there.

He continued to the third door. There was a cat inside, but, at present, no humans.

In the next apartment, he could smell urine. Why these Gliksins did not always flush their toilets he would never understand; once the technology had been explained to him, Ponter had never failed to do so. He also smelled the scents of four or five people. But Mare had said that Ruskin lived alone.

Ponter had reached the end of the corridor. He switched to the opposite side and inhaled deeply at the first door there. Cow had recently been cooked within, and some pungent vegetable matter. But there was no human scent he recognized.

He tried the next door. Tobacco smoke, and the pheromones of one—no, two—women.

Ponter moved along to the next door—but it turned out to be different from the others, lacking a suite number or any lock. Upon opening it, he found a little room with a much smaller door that hinged down, revealing some sort of chute. He moved on to the next apartment, waving a splayed hand in front of his face, trying to clear the stench that had come up from the chute. He took a deep breath, and—

More tobacco smoke, and—

And a man's scent . . . a thin man, one who did not perspire too much.

Ponter sniffed again, running his nose up and down the length of the door's seam. It might be . . .

Yes, it was. He was sure of it.

Ruskin.

Ponter was a physicist, not an engineer. But he'd been paying attention in this world, and so had Hak. They conferred for a few moments, standing in the corridor outside Ruskin's apartment, Ponter whispering, and Hak speaking through the cochlear implants.

"The door is doubtless locked," said Ponter. Such things were rarely seen in his world; doors were usually only secured to protect children from hazards.

"The simplest solution," said Hak, "is if he opens the door of his own accord."

Ponter nodded. "But will he? I believe that"—he pointed—"is a lens, allowing him to see who is outside."

"Despite his despicable qualities, Ruskin is a scientist. If a being from another world showed up at your door in Saldak Rim, would you refuse to open it?"

"It's worth a try." Ponter rapped his knuckles on the door, as he'd seen Mare do upon occasion.

Hak had been listening carefully. "The door is hollow," he said. "If he does not let you in, you should have no trouble breaking it down."

Ponter rapped again. "Perhaps he is a heavy sleeper."

"No," said Hak. "I hear him approaching."

There was a change in the quality of the light behind the door's viewing lens: presumably Ruskin looking through to see who was knocking at this time of night.

Finally, Ponter heard the sound of a metal locking mechanism working, and the door opened slightly, revealing Ruskin's pinched face. A small gold-colored chain at shoulder height seemed to be securing the door against opening farther. "Doc—Doctor Boddit?" he said, clearly astonished.

Ponter had planned to spin a story of how he needed Ruskin's help, in hopes of gaining easy access to the apartment, but he found himself unable to speak in civilized tones to this . . . this *primate.* He shot his right hand up, palm out, connecting with the door. The chain snapped, the door burst open, and Ruskin tumbled backward.

Ponter quickly entered and closed the door behind him.

"What the—!" shouted Ruskin, scrambling back to his feet. Ponter noted that Ruskin was dressed in normal day clothes, despite the late hour—and that made him think he'd only just returned home, possibly from yet another attack on a woman.

Ponter started moving closer. "You raped Qaiser Remtulla. You raped Mare Vaughan."

"What are you *talking* about?"

Ponter kept his volume low. "I can kill you with my bare hands."

"Are you crazy?" shouted Ruskin, backing away.

"No," said Ponter, stepping forward. "I am not crazy. It is this world of yours that is crazy."

Ruskin's eyes were darting left and right in the messy room, clearly looking for an escape route . . . or a weapon. Behind him was an opening in the wall—a pass-through, isn't that what Mare called the one in her apartment?—into what looked like it might be a food-preparation area.

"You will face me," said Ponter. "You will face justice."

"Look," said Ruskin, "I know you're new to this world, but we have laws. You can't just—"

"You are a multiple rapist."

"What are you *on*?"

"I can prove it," Ponter said, still moving closer.

Suddenly Ruskin spun around and arched his body, reaching through the pass-through. He turned back around, holding a heavy frying pan—Ponter had seen such things before when he was quarantined at Reuben Montego's house. Ruskin held the pan up in front of him, gripping its handle with both hands. "Don't come any closer," he said.

Ponter continued his advance undeterred. When he was only a pace from Ruskin, Ruskin swung. Ponter brought up his left arm to shield his face. Air resistance must have slowed the pan enough that the shield didn't kick in, and so Hak took much of the impact. Ponter's right hand shot forward and seized Ruskin's larynx.

"Drop that object," said Ponter, "or I will crush your throat."

Ruskin tried to speak, but Ponter constricted his fingers. The Gliksin managed to get one more good blow with the pan to Ponter's shoulder—fortunately, not the one with the bullet wound. Ponter lifted Ruskin off the ground by the neck. "Drop that object!" Ponter growled.

Ruskin's face had turned purple, and his eyes—his blue eyes—were bugging out. He finally dropped the pan, which hit the hardwood floor with a loud clang. Ponter spun Ruskin around and slammed him against the wall adjacent to the pass-through. The wall material caved in somewhat under the impact, and a large crack appeared. "Did you see the media coverage of Ambassador Prat killing our attacker?"

Ruskin was still gasping for air.

"Did you?" demanded Ponter.

Finally, Ruskin nodded.

"Ambassador Prat is a 144. I am a 145; I am ten years younger than her. Although my wisdom does not yet equal what she possesses, my strength exceeds hers. If you provoke me further, I will cave in your skull."

"What—" Ruskin's voice sounded incredibly raw. "What do you want?"

"First," said Ponter, "I want the truth. I want you to admit your crimes."

"I know that thing on your arm is a recorder, for Christ's sake."

"Admit the crimes."

"I never—"

"The Toronto Enforcers have samples of your DNA from Qaiser Remtulla's rape."

Ruskin choked out the words. "If they knew it was my DNA, they'd be here, not you."

"If you persist in denial, I will kill you."

Ruskin managed to shake his head slightly, despite Ponter's crushing grip. "A coerced confession is no confession at all."

Hak bleeped, but Ponter guessed the meaning of *coerced.* "All right, then convince me that you are innocent."

"I don't have to convince you of squat."

"You were passed over for advancement, and for job security, because of your skin tone and gender," said Ponter.

Ruskin said nothing.

"You hated the fact that others—that females—were being advanced ahead of you."

Ruskin was struggling, trying to get away from Ponter, but Ponter had no trouble holding him.

"You wished to hurt them," Ponter said. "To humiliate them."

"Keep fishing, caveman."

"You were denied that which you wanted, and so you took that which should only be given."

"It wasn't like that . . ."

"Tell me," hissed Ponter, bending one of Ruskin's arms backward. "Tell me what it *was* like."

"I deserved tenure," said Ruskin. "But they kept screwing me over. Those bitches kept screwing me over, and—"

"And what?"

"And so I showed them what a man could do."

"You are a *disgrace* to manhood," said Ponter. "How many did you rape? *How many?*"

"Just . . ."

"More than Mare and Qaiser?"

Silence.

Ponter pulled Ruskin away from the wall, then slammed him into it again. The crack grew longer. *"Were there any others?"*

"No. Just . . ."

He bent Ruskin's arm farther. "Just who? Just who?" The beast yowled with pain. "Just who?" repeated Ponter.

Ruskin grunted, and then, through clenched teeth: "Just Vaughan. And that Paki bitch . . ."

"What?" said Ponter, baffled, as Hak bleeped. He twisted the arm again.

"Remtulla. I raped Remtulla."

Ponter relaxed his grip somewhat. "It stops now, do you understand? You will never do this again. I will be watching. Others will be watching. Never again."

Ruskin grunted inarticulately.

"Never again," said Ponter. "Make that pledge."

"Ne-ver . . . again," said Ruskin, his teeth still clenched.

"And you will never speak of my visit here, to anyone. To do so would bring your society's punishment for your crimes. Do you understand? *Do you?"*

Ruskin managed a nod.

"All right," said Ponter, briefly loosening his grip. But then he slammed Ruskin against the wall again, this time a piece of its material falling free. "No, no, it is not all right," Ponter continued, his own teeth clenched. "It is not enough. It is not justice." He threw his weight against Ruskin once more, his groin slamming against the Gliksin's backside. "You will find out what it is like to be a woman."

Ruskin's whole body tensed. "No, man. Christ, no—not that—"

"It is only justice," said Ponter, reaching down into his medical belt, and pulling out a compressed-gas injector.

The device hissed against the side of Ruskin's neck. "What the hell is that?" he shouted. "You can't just . . ."

Ponter felt Ruskin collapse. He lowered him to the floor.

"Hak," said Ponter. "Are you all right?"

"That was quite an impact earlier," said the Companion, "but, yes, I am undamaged."

"Sorry about that." Ponter looked down at Ruskin, lying on his back in a heap on the floor. He grabbed the man's legs, stretching them out.

Ponter then reached for Ruskin's waist. It took some time, but finally he figured out how the belt worked. Once the belt was unbuckled, Ponter found the snap and the zipper that closed the pant. He undid them both.

"You should remove his footwear first," said Hak.

Ponter nodded. "Right. I keep forgetting they are separate." He worked his way down to Ruskin's feet, and, after some experimentation, got the laces undone and the shoes removed. Ponter winced at the odor that came up from the feet. He moved back, walking on his knees, up to Ruskin's waist, where he pulled down the Gliksin's pant, removing it from the body. He then pulled down the underwear, shimmying it down the almost-hairless legs, and finally getting it over the feet.

At last, Ponter looked at Ruskin's genitalia. "Something is wrong . . ." said Ponter. "He is disfigured somehow." He moved his arm, to give Hak's lens an unobstructed view.

"Astonishing," said the Companion. "He has no preputial hood."

"What?" said Ponter.

"No foreskin."

"Are all Gliksin males like that, I wonder?" said Ponter.

"It would make them unique among primates," replied Hak.

"Well," said Ponter, "it doesn't affect what I'm going to do . . ."

Cornelius Ruskin came to sometime the next day; he could tell it was morning by the light streaming in through his apartment's windows. His head was pounding, his throat was aching, his elbow was aflame, his backside hurt, and it felt as though he'd been kicked in the nuts. He tried to raise his head from the floor, but a wave of nausea overcame him, so he let his head back down onto the hardwood. He tried again a moment later, and this time did manage to raise himself up on one elbow. His shirt and pants were on, and so were his socks and shoes. But the shoelaces were untied.

God damn it, Ruskin thought. *God damn it.* He'd heard the Neanderthals were gay. Christ, though, he hadn't been ready for *that.* He rolled onto his side and placed a hand over the seat of his pants, praying that they wouldn't be bloody. Vomit crawled up his aching throat, and he fought it back down with a swallow that was excruciating.

"Justice," Boddit had said. Justice would have been getting a decent job, instead of being passed over by a bunch of underqualified women and minorities . . .

Ruskin's head was pounding so much he thought Ponter

must still be there, smashing the frying pan into his skull over and over again. Ruskin closed his eyes, trying to gather his strength. There were so many aches, so much pain, he couldn't focus on anything.

Goddamned ape-man's idea of poetic justice! Just because he'd put it in Vaughan and Remtulla, showing them who was really boss, Boddit had apparently figured it would be fair play to sodomize him.

And it was doubtless a warning, too: a warning to keep his mouth shut, a warning of what was in store for him if he ever accused Ponter of anything, of what would happen to him in prison if he ever did get sent up for rape . . .

Ruskin took a massive breath and moved a hand to his throat. He could feel indentations in it, left by the ape-man's fingers. Christ, it was probably bruised something awful.

Finally, Ruskin's head stopped swirling enough for him to try to haul himself to his feet. He used the lip on the pass-through to steady himself, and stood there, waiting for the flashes of light to die away in his eyes. Rather than bend over to tie the shoelaces, he kicked his shoes off.

He waited another full minute, until his head stopped pounding enough that he thought he wouldn't keel over if he let go of his support. Then he limped his way down the short corridor to the apartment's single, dingy bathroom, painted in a sickly green chosen by some previous tenant. He entered and closed the door behind him, revealing a full-length mirror, cracked at one corner where it had been screwed into the door. He undid his belt and lowered his pants, and then turned his back to the mirror, and, steeling himself for what he might see, lowered his underwear.

He'd been worried that the same sort of fingerprint indentations would be in his ass cheeks, but there was nothing, except a large bruise on one side—which, he realized, must have come from when Ponter first knocked him across the room when he broke through the chained door.

Ruskin grabbed one of the cheeks himself, pulling it aside so he could have a look at his sphincter. He had no idea what to expect—blood, maybe?—but there was nothing unusual.

He couldn't imagine such an attack would leave no mark, but it seemed that had been the case. Indeed, as far as he could tell, nothing at all had been done to his rear end.

Perplexed, he shuffled over to the toilet, his pants and briefs down around his ankles. He faced the porcelain fixture and reached for his penis, got hold of it, took aim, and—

No!

No, no, no!

Jesus H. Christ, no!

Ruskin felt around, bent over, straightened back up, then staggered back to the mirror for a better look.

God, God, God . . .

He could see himself, see his blue eyes round in absolute horror, see his jaw hanging down, and—

He loomed into the mirror, trying to get a good view of his scrotum. There was a vertical line running along it that looked like—

Could it be?

—like it had been *seared* shut.

He felt around again, probing the loose, wrinkled sack, hoping that somehow he'd been mistaken the first time.

But he wasn't.

For the love of God, he wasn't.

Ruskin staggered back against the sink and let out a long, piercing howl.

His testicles were gone.

Chapter Forty

Jurard Selgan was quiet for several moments. Of course, what Ponter had told him was absolutely confidential. Discussions between a patient and his or her personality sculptor were timecoded. Selgan would never dream of revealing what any patient had told him, and no one could unlock either his or his patients' alibi archives for the time spent in therapy sessions. Still, what Ponter had done. . . .

"We don't take the law into our own hands," Selgan said.

Ponter nodded. "As I said at the outset, I'm not proud of what I did."

Selgan's tone was soft. "You also said you would do it again, if given the chance."

"What he was doing was wrong,*" said Ponter. "Much more wrong than what I did to him." He spread his arms, as if searching for a way to justify his behavior. "He had hurt women, and he was going to go on hurting women. But I put a stop to that. Not just because he now knew I could identify him by his smell, but for the same reason we've always sterilized violent males in that particular way. We aren't just preventing their genes from being passed on, after all. By eliminating their testicles, we cause their testosterone levels to fall dramatically, making their aggression abate."*

"And you felt if you did not act, no one would?" said Selgan.

"Exactly! He would have gotten away with it! Mare Vaughan thought she had the upper hand originally, that the rapist didn't know what he was dealing with, attacking a geneticist. But she was wrong.

He knew precisely *what he was dealing with. He knew how to make sure that he would never be convicted of his crimes."*

"Just as," said Selgan, softly, "you knew that you would never be convicted of your crime in castrating him."

Ponter said nothing.

"Does Mare know? Have you told her?"

Ponter shook his head.

"Why not?"

"Why not?" repeated Ponter, astonished by the question. "Why not? I'd committed a crime—a grievous assault. I did not want her to become involved in that; I did not want her to have any culpability."

"Is that all?"

Ponter was silent, and examined the all-encircling wooden wall, with its polished grain.

"Was it?" prodded Selgan.

"Of course, I did not want her to think less of me," said Ponter.

"She might have thought more *of you," said Selgan. "After all, you did this for her, to protect her, and others like her."*

But Ponter shook his head. "No. No, she would have been angry with me, disappointed in me."

"Why?"

"She is a Christian," he said. "The philosopher whose teachings she follows held that forgiveness was the greatest of all virtues."

Selgan rolled his gray eyebrow up his browridge. "Some things are very difficult to forgive."

"Don't you think I know that?" *snapped Ponter.*

"I did not mean what you did; I mean what he—this Gliksin male—had done to Mare."

Ponter took a deep breath, trying to calm himself.

"Is—is this Ruskin the only Gliksin you castrated?"

Ponter's gaze jerked back onto Selgan. "Of course!"

"Ah," said Selgan. "It's just that . . ."

"What?"

Selgan ignored the question for the moment. "Have you told anyone else what you did?"

"No."

"Not even Adikor?"

"Not even Adikor."

"But surely you can trust him?" said Selgan.

"Yes, but . . ."

"Do you see?" said Selgan, after Ponter had trailed off. "In our world, we don't just sterilize the perpetrators of a violent crime, do we?"

"Well, no. We . . ."

"Yes?" said Selgan.

"We sterilize the criminal and *everyone who shares at least fifty percent of his or her genetic material."*

"And that would be?"

"Siblings. Parents."

"Yes. And?"

"And—well, and identical twins. That's why we say at least *fifty percent; identical twins have one hundred percent of their DNA in common."*

"Yes, yes, but you're forgetting another group."

"Brothers. Sisters. The criminal's mother. The criminal's father."

"And . . ."

"I don't know what you're . . ." Ponter fell silent. "Oh," he said, softly. He looked at Selgan again, then dropped his gaze. "Offspring. Children."

"And you have children, don't you?"

"My two daughters, Jasmel Ket and Mega Bek."

"And so if anyone were to learn of your crime, and somehow they let it slip out, or the court ordered access to their alibi archives, not just you would be punished. Your daughters would be sterilized, too."

Ponter closed his eyes.

"Isn't that right?" said Selgan.

Ponter's voice was very soft. "Yes."

"I asked you earlier if you'd sterilized anyone else in the other world, and you yelled at me."

Ponter said nothing.

"Do you know why you yelled?"

A long, shuddering sigh escaped from Ponter's mouth. "I only *sterilized the actual perpetrator, not his relatives. You know, I'd never given much thought to the . . . the* righteousness *of sterilizing innocents just to improve the gene pool. But . . . but Hak and I* have *been working through this Gliksin Bible. In the very first story, all the offspring of the original two humans were cursed because those original humans committed a crime. And that seemed so wrong, so unfair."*

"And as much as you wanted the Gliksin gene pool to be purged of Ruskin's evil, you couldn't bring yourself to track down his close relatives," said Selgan. "For if you did, you'd be admitting that your *close relatives—your two daughters—deserved to be punished for the crime* you *had committed."*

"They are innocent,*" said Ponter. "No matter how wrong what I did was, they do not deserve to suffer for it."*

"And yet they will if you come forward and admit your crime."

Ponter nodded.

"And so what do you intend to do?"

Ponter lifted his massive shoulders. "Carry this secret with me until I die."

"And then?"

"I—I beg your pardon?"

"After you are dead, then what?"

"Then . . . then nothing.*"*

"Are you sure of that?"

"Of course. I mean, yes, I have been studying this Bible, and I know Mare is sane and intelligent and not delusional, but . . ."

"You have no doubt that she is wrong? No doubt that there is nothing after death?"

"Well. . . ."

"Yes?"

"No. Forget it."

Selgan frowned, deciding it wasn't yet quite time to press this point. "Have you wondered about why *Mare is attracted to you?"*

Ponter looked away.

"I heard what you said earlier about them also being humans. But, still, you are less like her than any other human she had ever met to that point."

"Physically, perhaps," said Ponter. "But mentally, emotionally, we have much in common."

"Still," said Selgan, "since Mare had been hurt by a male of her own species, she might—"

"Don't you think that's already occurred to me?" snapped Ponter.

"Speak it aloud, Ponter. Get it out in the open."

Ponter snorted. "She might be attracted to me because in her eyes I am not *human—not one of those who hurt her."*

Selgan was quiet for a few beats. "It's a thought worth reflecting on."

"It doesn't matter," said Ponter. "It doesn't matter one bit. I love *her. And she loves me. Nothing besides those two facts is important."*

"Very well," said Selgan. "Very well." He paused again, and let his tone sound absent, as if an odd thought had just occurred to him, rather than that he'd been waiting for the right moment to present this. "And, say, have you given any thought as to why you are attracted to her?"

Ponter rolled his eyes. "Personality sculptors!" he said. "You're about to tell me that she reminds me of Klast in some way. But you couldn't be more wrong. She doesn't look anything like Klast. Her personality is completely different. Mare and Klast have nothing *in common."*

"I'm sure you're right," said Selgan, gesturing with his hand as if to dismiss the notion. "I mean, how could they? They aren't even members of the same species . . ."

"That's right," said Ponter, folding his arms across his chest.

"And they come from completely different belief systems."

"Exactly."

Selgan shook his head. "Such a bizarre notion, isn't it? This idea of a life after death . . ."

Ponter said nothing.

"Do you ever contemplate it? Ever wonder if, just maybe . . ." Selgan trailed off and waited patiently for Ponter to fill the void.

"Well," said Ponter at last, "it is *an appealing concept. Ever since Mare first told me of it, I've been thinking about it." Ponter raised his hands. "I mean, sure, sure, I know that there is no afterlife—at least not for me. But . . ."*

"But she lives in an alternative physical plane," supplied Selgan. "Another universe. A universe where things might *be different."*

Ponter's head moved vertically in the slightest of nods.

"And she isn't even Barast, is she? She belongs to another species. Just because we *don't have these—what do they call them? These immortal souls? Just because* we *don't have immortal souls, doesn't mean that they don't, does it?"*

"Do you have a point?" snapped Ponter.

"Always," said Selgan. "You lost your own woman-mate twenty-odd months ago." He paused, and made his voice as soft as he could. "Mare is not the only one recovering from a trauma."

Ponter lifted his eyebrow. "Granted. But I hardly see how Klast's death would propel me into the arms of a woman from another world."

There was silence for an extended time. Finally, Hak, who had been quiet all through the therapy to this point, addressed Selgan through his external speaker. "Do you want me to tell him?"

"I'll do it," said Selgan. "Ponter, please take this gently, but . . . well, you have told me of Gliksin beliefs."

"What about them?" said Ponter, an edge still in his voice.

"They believe the dead are not really dead. They believe that the consciousness of the individual lives on after the body."

"So?"

"So maybe you're looking to insulate yourself from the same kind of pain that you suffered when Klast died. If your woman-mate believed in this . . . this immortality of the mind, or if you thought, however irrationally, that she might actually have *such immortality, then . . ." Selgan trailed off, inviting Ponter to finish the thought for him.*

Ponter sighed, then did so. "Then if the unthinkable were to happen, and I were to lose my woman-mate again, I might not be so devastated, since she might not really be totally gone."

Selgan lifted his eyebrow and both shoulders slightly. "Exactly."

Ponter rose to his feet. "Thank you for your time, Scholar Selgan. Healthy day."

"I'm not sure we're finished yet," said Selgan. "Where are you going?"

"To do something I should have done long ago," said Ponter, marching out of the circular room.

Louise Benoît came into Jock Krieger's office at the Synergy Group. Jock didn't have any geologists on staff, but Louise was a physicist, and she'd spent all that time working down at the bottom of the Creighton Mine, so he'd assigned this task to her.

"Okay," she said. "I've worked it out, I think." She spread two large charts on the worktable in Jock's office. Jock got up from behind his desk and joined Louise at the table.

"This one," she said, pointing a red-painted fingernail at the chart on the left, "is a standard paleomagnetic chronology made by our people."

Jock nodded.

"And this one"—she indicated the other chart, which was filled with strange symbols—"is the comparable chart we got from the Neanderthals."

Even though Mary Vaughan had found no evidence that the Neanderthal magnetic field really had reversed, Jock had used his clout to make the swapping of paleomagnetic information a top priority. If the Neanderthals were wrong about the magnetic field collapsing rapidly, well, then Jock would know he was worrying for nothing. But he wanted to be sure.

"Okay," said Louise. "As you can see, we've mapped a lot more geomagnetic reversals than they have—over 300 in the last 175 million years. That's because there's a more complete record in sea-floor rocks than there is in meteorite finds."

"Score one for our side," said Jock, dryly.

"So," continued Louise, "what I've done is pair up the reversals that *do* match—that is, the ones that both they and we have evidence for. As you can see, although their record has many holes in it, there's a one-to-one correspondence almost all the way to the present."

Jock looked at the sheets, Louise's finger guiding his eyes. "Okay."

"Well," said Louise, "that makes perfect sense, of course. You know my theory: that there was only one long-term universe until consciousness dawned forty thousand years ago."

Jock nodded. Although quantum-mechanical events caused countless brief splittings of the universe, and probably had since the beginning of time, those splittings made no macroscopic difference, and so the resulting universes had always collapsed back together after a nanosecond or two.

But the acts of conscious beings caused splits that could not be healed, and so, when the Great Leap Forward took place forty thousand years ago—when consciousness emerged—the first ever permanent split occurred. In one universe, *Homo sapiens* acquired that initial consciousness; in the other, *Homo neanderthalensis* did—and they had been diverging ever since.

"But wait a minute," said Jock, peering at the Neanderthal chart. "If that one there is the last recorded magnetic reversal that we know about—"

"It is," said Louise. "They've got it listed as about ten million months ago, which is 780,000 years ago."

"Okay," said Jock. "But if that's the most recent one on our chart, what's this one here?" He pointed to what was apparently another, more-recent reversal indicated on the Neanderthal chart. "Is that the one they said began twenty-five years ago?"

"No," said Louise. She had too much of the academic in her for Jock's taste. She was clearly leading him to make his own discovery, but she obviously already knew the answer herself. He wished she'd just tell him.

"Then when was that one?"

"Half a million months ago," said Louise.

Jock made no effort to hide his irritation. "Which is?"

Louise's full lips spread into a grin. "Forty thousand years ago."

"Forty thou—! But that's when . . ."

"Exactly," said Louise, pleased with her pupil. "That's when the Great Leap Forward occurred, when consciousness emerged, when the universe split apart for good."

"But . . . but how is it that *they* know about a magnetic reversal then and we don't?"

"Remember what I said the first time we were talking about this? After the magnetic field dies away, it's a fifty-fifty chance as to what polarity the new field will come up with. Half the time, it'll be normal, and—"

"And half the time it will be reversed! So this event must

have happened *after* the universes split—and since the universes were no longer in lockstep, it happened that the polarity came up reversed in the Neanderthal world—"

Louise nodded. "Leaving a record in meteorites."

"But in our world, it came up with the same polarity it had had before the collapse—leaving no record."

"Oui."

"Fascinating," said Jock. "But wait—wait! They had a reversal forty thousand years ago, right? But Mary says that when she took a compass reading in the Neanderthal world, it now has the same polarity as our world does, so . . ."

Louise nodded encouragingly; he was on the right track.

". . . so," continued Jock, "there *was* a recent, rapid field collapse in the Neanderthal world, and this time, when the field came up again, just six years ago, it had flipped its polarity once more, back to matching what it is on this Earth."

"Exactly."

"All right then," said Jock. "Well, that's what I wanted to know."

"But there's more to it than that," said Louise. "Much more."

"Spit it out, girl!"

"Okay, okay. It's like this. Earth—the one and only Earth that existed at that time—experienced a magnetic-field collapse forty thousand years ago. While the magnetic field was down, consciousness emerged—and I can't think that that's a coincidence."

"You mean the collapsing of the magnetic field had something to do with why we developed art?"

"And culture. And language. And symbolic logic. And religion. Yes."

"But how?"

"I don't know," said Louise. "But remember, anatomically

modern *Homo sapiens* have existed since one hundred thousand years ago, but they didn't get consciousness until forty thousand years ago. We had the same physical brains for sixty thousand years without ever making art or exhibiting any of the other signs of true sentience. Then—*click!*—something happened, and we were conscious."

"Yes," said Jock.

"You know some birds use magnetite in their brains to tell direction?"

Jock nodded.

"Well, we—*Homo sapiens*—have magnetite in our brains, too. No one knows why, since we obviously aren't using it as a built-in compass. But when the magnetic field collapsed forty thousand years ago, I think something happened to the magnetite that caused the—the 'booting up,' shall we say, of consciousness."

"So what's going to happen when the magnetic field collapses again?"

"Well, on the Neanderthal world, nothing happened during their most recent collapse," said Louise. "But . . ."

"But?"

"But they don't use fossil fuels. They don't have billions of cars. They don't use chlorofluorocarbons for air-conditioning."

"Yes? So?"

"So their atmosphere—and their ozone layer—is completely intact. Ours isn't."

"What's that got to do with magnetic reversals?"

"Earth has two methods for shielding its surface from solar and interstellar radiation: the atmosphere, and the magnetic field. If one goes down, the other covers for it . . ."

Jock's eyes went wide. "But one of ours is *already* down."

"Exactly. Our ozone layer is depleted; our atmosphere is chemically altered. When the magnetic field collapses again—

and it looks like it's starting to do that right now—there's not going to be any backup shielding in place."

"What's going to happen?"

"*Je ne sais pas,*" said Louise. "We'll have to do a lot more modeling before we're sure. But . . ."

"Again with the buts! What? What?"

"Well, consciousness booted up during a field collapse—and this is going to be the mother of all field collapses, as far as its effects are concerned. This time, consciousness might . . . well, not to stretch the metaphor too much, but this time consciousness might *crash.*"

Epilogue

Ponter thanked the travel-cube operator, and disembarked. He could feel the eyes of females on him, feel their disapproving stares. But even though it was only another day until Two next became One, this couldn't wait.

After most of a month back on her version of Earth, Ponter and Mary had returned to the Neanderthal world three days earlier. He'd said the timing would allow him to see both Adikor and his children on the same trip, which was certainly true. But, since Mary had to go back to staying with Lurt until Two became One, it also let him see a personality sculptor, in hopes of ridding himself of the insomnia and bad dreams that had been plaguing him.

But now Ponter was approaching Lurt's lab—guided by Hak; Ponter himself had never been there before. Entering the all-stone building, he asked the first woman he saw to direct him to where Mare Vaughan was working. The astonished woman—a 146—pointed, and Ponter marched down the corridor. He walked into the room that had been indicated, and saw Mary and Lurt huddled over a worktable.

This is it, thought Ponter. He inhaled deeply, and—

"Ponter!" said Mary, looking up. She was delighted to see him, but—

But, no. This was *his* world—and it wasn't the right time. She tried to keep her tone calm. "What's wrong?"

Ponter looked at Lurt. "I need to speak to Mare alone," he said.

Lurt's eyebrow went up. She squeezed Mary's forearm, then left the room, closing the door behind her.

"What is it?" asked Mary. She could feel her heart pounding. "Are you okay? Has something happened to Jasmel or—"

"No. Everyone is fine."

Still nervous, Mary tried to make light of things. "You shouldn't be here, you know. Two aren't One right now."

But Ponter had an edge in his tone. "To . . . to *hell* with that," he said.

"Ponter, what is it?"

Ponter took a deep breath, then said some words to her in his language. For the first time ever, the words were not immediately translated, and Mary saw Ponter tilt his head in the way that meant he was listening to Hak over his cochlear implants.

Ponter spoke again, sharply, and Mary heard the Neanderthal word *"ka,"* which she knew meant "yes." Perhaps Hak had said, "Are you sure you really want to say that?" If he had, Ponter must have told him that yes, he did, and perhaps had admonished the Companion for interfering. There was silence for a couple of seconds, then Ponter opened his mouth again, but apparently that was enough of a cue for Hak to finally issue the English equivalent of Ponter's earlier utterance. "I love you," said the machine-synthesized voice.

How Mary had longed to hear those words! "I love you, too," she said. "I love you so much."

"We should build a life together, you and I," said Ponter. "If—if you will have me, that is."

"Yes, yes, of course!" said Mary. But then her spirits began to sag. "But . . . but it would be complex, making such a relationship work. I mean, you have a life here, and I have a life *there.* You have Adikor and Jasmel and Megameg, and I have . . ." She paused. She'd been about to say "no one," but if only that were true. She *did* have a husband, estranged to be sure, but still her lawfully wedded spouse. And, sweet Jesus, she thought, if God disapproved of divorce, what would he make of a relationship across species lines?

"I want to try," said Ponter. "I want to try to make this work."

Mary smiled. "Me too." But then she felt her smile fade. "Still, there's so much to consider. Where would we live? What about Adikor? What about—"

"I know it will be difficult, but . . ."

"Yes?" said Mary.

Ponter closed the distance between himself and Mary, and he looked into her eyes. "But your people have traveled to the moon, and mine have opened a portal to another universe. Things that are difficult *can* be done."

"There will be sacrifices," said Mary. "For both of us."

"Perhaps," said Ponter. "Perhaps not. Perhaps we can extract the marrow but still keep the bone for toolmaking."

Mary frowned for a moment, then got it. " 'Have our cake and eat it, too.' That's how my people would phrase it. But I guess you're right: our people aren't that dissimilar. Wanting it all, why, that's just . . ." Mary trailed off, unable to find an appropriate word.

But Ponter knew it. Ponter knew exactly what it was. "That is just human," he said, taking Mary in his arms.

About the Author

Robert J. Sawyer is one of only seven writers in history to win all three of the world's top awards for best science fiction novel of the year: the Hugo (which he won for *Hominids*), the Nebula (which he won for *The Terminal Experiment*), and the John W. Campbell Memorial Award (which he won for *Mindscan*). The ABC TV series *FlashForward* is based on his novel of the same name.

In total, Rob has won forty-three national and international awards for his fiction, including ten Canadian Science Fiction and Fantasy Awards ("Auroras"), as well as *Analog* magazine's Analytical Laboratory Award, *Science Fiction Chronicle* magazine's Reader Award, and the Crime Writers of Canada's Arthur Ellis Award, all for best short story of the year, as well as the Collectors Award for Most Collectible Author of the Year, as selected by the clientele of Barry R. Levin Science Fiction & Fantasy Literature, the world's leading SF rare-book dealer.

Rob has won the world's largest cash prize for SF writing, Spain's 6,000-euro Premio UPC de Ciencia Ficción, an unprecedented three times. He's also won a trio of Japanese Seiun Awards for best foreign novel of the year, as well as China's Galaxy Award for "Most Popular Foreign Science Fiction Writer." In addition, he's received an honorary doctorate from Laurentian University and the Alumni Award of Distinction from Ryerson University.

About the Author

Rob's books are top-ten national mainstream bestsellers in Canada and have hit number one on the bestsellers' list published by *Locus,* the American trade journal of the SF field. *Quill & Quire,* the Canadian publishing trade journal, included him as one of only three authors on its list of "The CanLit 30: The Most Influential, Innovative, and Just Plain Powerful People in Canadian Publishing."

Rob lives in Mississauga, Ontario, Canada, with his wife, poet Carolyn Clink. His website and blog are at sfwriter.com, and on Twitter and Facebook he's RobertJSawyer.